Praise for

The Virgin's Daughters

"Takes the reader on a poignant journey into the hearts and minds of three dynamic Elizabethan women, including the queen herself. Intimate characterization and beautifully rendered settings and customs make us realize that the tumultuous Tudor times are both unique and yet not so very different from our own. A compelling, unforgettable historical novel."

—Karen Harper, author of *The Queen's Governess*

"Two well-crafted love stories set against the backdrop of the court of Elizabeth the First create high drama and at the same time paint an unforgettable portrait of the last Tudor monarch."

—Kate Emerson, author of *Secrets of the Tudor Court: The Pleasure Palace*

"A suspenseful tale of royal power and the grip of an iron queen on the destiny of her ladies-in-waiting. Vivid characters and compelling dialogue illuminate the Elizabethan court where danger lurks in the shadows, love can be treason, and every step could be the last. You'll find yourself looking over your shoulder in this engrossing read."

—Sandra Worth, author of *The King's Daughter*

"Westin has brought the Elizabethan court vividly to life. Her heroines walk a delicious knife-edge between love and disaster. I couldn't put it down." —Anne Gracie, author of *His Captive Lady*

"Westin knows her history, and the inner workings of her characters' minds as well. She presents Elizabeth I through the eyes of two of her ladies-in-waiting. Rich, colorful details of court life, captivating characters with suppressed sexuality, scandal and intrigue thrust the reader into the era in this top-notch novel."

—*Romantic Times* (4½ Stars)

continued . . .

"Fantastic story. Here is a unique approach to showing us more of Queen Elizabeth. I loved the way the author weaves two stories into this look at the queen—both distinctly separate, yet still connected. . . . Utterly fascinating and a must for everyone to read."

—Romance Reviews Today

"This is a Tudor novel not to be missed. . . . Well told and well researched, this book gripped me from its earliest pages and wouldn't let go until I'd read all the way through the readers guide at the end. I became caught up in the lives of these two relatively unknown ladies of Elizabeth's court, and the way Westin ties both tales together is unique and riveting. What might have been merely two love stories truly became history brought to life. Highly recommended."

—*The Historical Novels Review*

OTHER NOVELS BY JEANE WESTIN

The Virgin's Daughters

HIS LAST LETTER

❧

ELIZABETH I AND THE EARL OF LEICESTER

JEANE WESTIN

 New American Library

New American Library
Published by New American Library, a division of
Penguin Group (USA) Inc., 375 Hudson Street,
New York, New York 10014, USA
Penguin Group (Canada), 90 Eglinton Avenue East, Suite 700, Toronto,
Ontario M4P 2Y3, Canada (a division of Pearson Penguin Canada Inc.)
Penguin Books Ltd., 80 Strand, London WC2R 0RL, England
Penguin Ireland, 25 St. Stephen's Green, Dublin 2,
Ireland (a division of Penguin Books Ltd.)
Penguin Group (Australia), 250 Camberwell Road, Camberwell, Victoria 3124,
Australia (a division of Pearson Australia Group Pty. Ltd.)
Penguin Books India Pvt. Ltd., 11 Community Centre, Panchsheel Park,
New Delhi - 110 017, India
Penguin Group (NZ), 67 Apollo Drive, Rosedale, North Shore 0632,
New Zealand (a division of Pearson New Zealand Ltd.)
Penguin Books (South Africa) (Pty.) Ltd., 24 Sturdee Avenue,
Rosebank, Johannesburg 2196, South Africa

Penguin Books Ltd., Registered Offices:
80 Strand, London WC2R 0RL, England

First published by New American Library,
a division of Penguin Group (USA) Inc.

First Printing, August 2010
10   9   8   7   6   5   4   3   2   1

Copyright © Jeane Westin, 2010
Readers Guide copyright © Penguin Group (USA) Inc., 2010
All rights reserved

Letter facsimile on page 361 courtesy of the National Archives of the UK, REF. SP12/215.

REGISTERED TRADEMARK—MARCA REGISTRADA

LIBRARY OF CONGRESS CATALOGING-IN-PUBLICATION DATA:

Westin, Jeane Eddy.
    His last letter: Elizabeth I and the Earl of Leicester/Jeane Westin.
        p. cm.
    ISBN 978-0-451-23012-6
    1. Elizabeth I, Queen of England, 1533–1603—Fiction.   2. Leicester, Robert Dudley,
Earl of, 1532?–1588—Fiction.   3. Great Britain—History—Elizabeth, 1558–1603—
Fiction.   I. Title.
    PS3573.E89H57 2010
    813'.54—dc22   2010010431

Set in Garamond
Designed by Spring Hoteling

Printed in the United States of America

To my dear extended family:
Norm, Pam and Skye

AUTHOR'S FOREWORD

His Last Letter is set during 1585–88, the last three years of Queen Elizabeth's and Robert, the Earl of Leicester's life together, the time period I did not cover in my first book about Elizabeth's court, *The Virgin's Daughters*.

I soon found that their emotional responses and reactions to these eventful years were grounded in what had happened to them in all the years they had spent together in peril and in love, both of them fighting for dominance over each other and their own feelings. This realization dictated the structure of *His Last Letter*. The following chapter guide may help clarify as you read the time and place in which each scene takes place.

CHAPTER GUIDE

❧

CHAPTER GUIDE

HIS LAST LETTER

PROLOGUE

"He made the wynds and waters rise
To scatter all myne enemies."

—*From a victory song by Queen Elizabeth after England's
defeat of Spain's Armada*

Elizabeth

September 1588
Whitehall Palace, Westminster

*B*right explosions of fireworks arched over the Thames from Baynard's Castle near the Strand to Billingsgate downriver, sending flashes of light through the tall open windows of Whitehall's presence chamber. The shouts of Londoners could be heard as they wildly celebrated with gunpowder mixed with strong English ale. Their virgin queen Elizabeth's glorious victory over Spain's invincible armada had come in answer to her prayers.

Trumpets and drums announced the queen's approach from her privy chambers.

Lord Treasurer William Cecil and the queen's philosopher,

Dr. John Dee, in court from his home in Mortlake, moved through the crowd of courtiers toward the chamber doors. Cecil produced a rare smile from his sober face. "I have seen Her Majesty in moments of triumph before, but none to match the glory of this victory, the jewel of her reign."

Dee nodded, his mouth scarcely visible within his full white beard that came to a point at his waist. "My lord, the victory was foretold in her stars . . . and in my lord the Earl of Leicester's. It was inevitable."

"Good Doctor, although God commands the winds, perhaps Lord Howard and her majesty's sea dogs, Hawkins, Drake and Frobisher, with their new naval guns and fast ships, aided the Almighty," Cecil said in his slightly amused way, which showed a little of his disdain for Dee and all necromancers. Still, his gaze never left the chamber doors.

Dee, in defense of his art, refused to yield. "I would have to cast the captains' natal charts to determine what was written in their stars."

Before one could give further offense to the other, the huge double doors of the presence chamber opened and red-and-black-liveried yeoman guards entered, their tall pikes rigidly upright.

Trumpeters and drummers marched in and stepped to the side, followed by a retinue of lords, ladies and gentlemen pensioners, and at last by the queen. Elizabeth paused for a moment just inside the chamber, dazzling in the torchlight from her jeweled scarlet slippers, past ropes of pearls looped about her white brocade gown, heavily embroidered with silver thread, to the great ruby-and-diamond crown glittering on her head. Her thoughts blazed through her eyes and were read by every courtier who knew her well: *I will remember this day as the best of my life;*

my great triumph when Spain was no longer master of sea and land!

She straightened her already near-rigid back, her corset allowing no real respite, nor did she want it. Although she loved her flowing gowns and dazzling jewels, her flower scents and the line of lovely ladies-in-waiting behind her, she never forgot that she was a queen before she was a woman.

Elizabeth stopped near Cecil, who bowed, since he had her permission to stay on his feet and save his old knees. "My Lord Treasurer, today England takes its rightful place in the world."

"Your Grace, it is a day your realm will remember and celebrate down the ages."

"My lord," the queen announced in full voice, as much for her gathered court as for Cecil, "Philip of Spain claimed all shipping lanes from east to west." She tossed her head and laughed. "Now he knows that the seas are no longer a Spanish pond!"

Rough shouts and approving laughter spread throughout the chamber as Elizabeth moved on down the double line of uncovered and kneeling courtiers, who shouted, "Huzzah! Huzzah!" At the foot of her canopied throne, she saw Sir Walter Raleigh waiting. He was not on his knees. The handsome rogue took unusual liberties even for a man who thought himself a favorite of his sovereign . . . and who had from his elegant boots to his perfect face every bit the look of a favorite. *Robin never makes such a mistake; he observes all court protocol, bless him.*

Raleigh, not to have his achievements forgotten for a moment, took his pipe and lit it, drawing every lady's gaze. It was said that he was growing rich on the tobacco he had brought back from the New World. Perhaps she should consider a tax.

"Sir Walter, we have seen many men turn gold into smoke, but you have managed to turn smoke into gold."

The jibe was greeted by polite laughter, enough to reward the queen and yet not offend a rising courtier. She watched him brave it all with ease. He needed a small reprisal. "Are you then so much a hero after your voyage to Virginia that you need not be on your knees to your sovereign?"

"Majesty, forgive me," said Sir Walter Raleigh, choking on his weed a little before falling to his knees as Elizabeth mounted the dais to sit on her canopied throne. "Each burst of victorious light from the city brings added beauty to your perfect face and I am dazzled."

She laughed at his very pretty excess, admiring his quick recovery from her rebuke. Planned or not, she believed him. What courtier was not a little in love with Elizabeth Tudor? Still, she knew she could not play this game of courtly love with her usual zest. Not on this day. Today she was in love with her country. England was her husband, the people her children, and she had given them their greatest victory since Agincourt.

Sir Walter, sensing her heart's distance, stepped down and bowed low so that she could see the perfect dark waves in his hair and how at the bottom of his tanned sailor's neck his hair curled up—probably pomaded to do so—in the arrogant way of a handsome young man who was determined to heat every woman he saw. And almost certainly succeeding with most. *And perhaps, at times, with me.*

Elizabeth could not help but erupt into gleeful laughter at her own private entertaining thoughts, since she had seen many handsome young men determined to catch her eye and favor—perhaps a grant of land or a better title—though she gave the ever-watchful court another reason for her obvious delight. A loud burst of gunpowder and flash of light brought her to her feet, her fist raised in victory imitating the Greek goddess of war,

Pallas Athena. She regretted not wearing the breastplate and gorget she had worn at Tilbury last month.

The court cheered. "Down with all Spanish papists! Up with our good Queen Elizabeth!"

Raleigh raised his voice and it rang through the large chamber above all others. "Majesty, it seems your loyal English people would sink Philip's armada . . . a second time!" He bowed with a flourish of his hand, no longer callused from the sea, but soft as any courtier's.

"Nay, Sir Walter, we think that King Philip's fleet, his 'Great Enterprise of England,' is already well sunk, or soon will be in the storms off the Irish coast. He must be content to creep about inside his Escorial palace and hide from us. We did more than singe his beard in the channel. We left him hairless as a babe!"

The court erupted into laughter and Elizabeth knew that her every word would soon be repeated in the streets of London and shouted back at her when she rode down Cheapside on her way to St. Paul's for the service of thanksgiving. Even more, one foreign ambassador or another, seeking to curry Philip's favor, would report every word to him, probably sending the Spanish king to his knees again to beg God to strike Elizabeth down. But God was listening to her and not to Philip. She shook with silent laughter.

Raleigh bowed again, undefeated as always. "Madam," he said, his hand over his heart, "my only regret is that my lord Leicester could not be here to witness this celebration. He left court two weeks ago to take the waters at Cornbury. I long for news of his recovery. A man of his years cannot be too careful."

The chamber hushed.

Two weeks only? It seems longer. But how dare Raleigh? Elizabeth was tempted to slap his perfect face for giving Robin his sly backhand, but such a cocksure court rival needed different handling. She would have him take care of his words, but not beaten down. Still, there was bitter reproof in her face that she did not bother to remove. He must learn that Elizabeth was the only person in the realm who could challenge Robert, Earl of Leicester, not a lowborn sailor from Devonshire . . . no matter how a queen might favor his too-handsome face, well-turned calf and artful love poetry.

She waved Sir Walter away, giving him the back of her hand in curt dismissal. "Your love and care for the earl are well-known to us, Sir Walter."

Immediately, she signed for the musicians in the gallery above to begin playing to cover her own dismay. "Let us have one of my father's galliards. 'Time to Pass with Goodly Sport,' if you remember it." She and Robin had danced it for Henry when they were yet youngsters in the palace school. Whirling about with Robin at Greenwich Palace in front of her father's throne was like yesterday in her mind and always would be.

How could she have reveled for an hour, even for a minute, while Robin was sick these many weeks with his old fever? He had suffered a recurrence in the swampy land around Tilbury in July and August, while waiting to lead her faithful troops against the Spanish armies if they landed at the mouth of the Thames. Everyone had thought they would wait to make an assault on London and try to capture England's queen alive. They had planned to take her to Pope Sixtus to be tried for heresy. Ha! God had other plans for His anointed Elizabeth. He had sent a great storm to douse the heretic's fire that Rome would have lit for her.

The queen tapped her foot to the galliard. How she had danced it with her sweet Robin, who now even in his middle years was still the most manly, most well-favored man, never to age in her eyes and heart. The world may have seen them change, but they had never changed to each other. She was sure of that. Robin was the one man in her world of whom she could be in no doubt. Always.

Cecil stepped forward again, unusually merry. Would he be smiling if he knew what she planned? What she hugged to herself? She wanted to see his face when she announced that she would name Robin Lord Lieutenant of England and grant him the title of duke, ranking him above every other peer; indeed, he would rank next to her as sovereign. In spirit, he would be her heir.

Cecil bowed. "Majesty, it does my heart good to see you so triumphant."

"My thanks, Spirit," she said, using the nickname she had given him on her first day as queen. She turned her gaze from him. If he thought to read what she was thinking, he would be confounded.

She had told no one of her plans, especially not Cecil, who would most certainly disapprove, perhaps threaten to resign again. Such power for Robin would gall her Lord Treasurer, all her council and the rest of the country's peers. Sir Walter would be most unhappy, having expected a peerage for himself. She would give him a manor in his native Devon with enough sheep and wool to ease his pain.

"Play another galliard, master lutenist," she called to the gallery. "We command that there be no gloom here this day. Let us be lively and dance so that King Philip will hear we held revels as the last of his defeated, starving sailors and soldiers struggled toward home, their ships broken by good English shot and God's gales, heaven and earth against him."

Drums, pipes and guitars accompanied the sound of the

court's laughter, as she saw Dr. John Dee weave his slow way among the dancing couples and bow, his long beard tucked neatly into the belt of his doctor's robe. *Why do old men grow huge beards as if to proclaim a manhood that has long since fled?*

"What news of Lord Leicester to explain the melancholy I see behind Your Majesty's joy?" he asked, keeping his voice confidential.

"Do you look in my face as into your scrying glass, good Doctor?" she answered softly. "There is no news, though I have sent to know."

"No news explains melancholy, Majesty," he said, his breath blowing the long hairs of his mustache that drooped over his lips. "And yet Sir Walter is here for your merriment."

The queen frowned. "Good Dr. Dee, you are a man of travel and learning. You talk to spirits and angels and yet you cannot see to Rycote and tell me when the Earl of Leicester will return."

"Your Grace, only God sees all. I see only the little he allows me to see in my magical glass."

His face was somber, but Elizabeth's voice nearly shook with anger. "Jesu, good Doctor, tell me what is the little that you *do* see."

She had her answer in the next moment, though it was an answer that came not from Dr. Dee, or from an angel in heaven, but from hell.

A gentleman pensioner walked toward her holding up a dusty lad, his thin legs unsteady, nearly staggering from fatigue.

A message from Robin at last. Elizabeth sighed with relief, eagerly motioning the boy forward. "Young Tracey," she called aloud down the length of the hall, "what news from my lord of Leicester?"

Cecil took the lad's arm and led him to the throne, where the boy dropped to his knees in both exhaustion and courtesy, breathing hard.

"What news of my lord Leicester's health, lad?" The words crowded past a full throat, her heart beginning to beat faster.

"Majesty, I am sent to tell you that—"

He took a shuddering breath and, Jesu help her, she yelled at the used-up boy. "Tell us what!"

"The Earl of Leicester is dead, Majesty, these two days gone."

She opened her mouth to shout down his lie, but at that moment came a great boom of cannon from the Tower and what the queen howled was neither heard nor understood by anyone in the presence chamber, least by herself. It was a cry of denial from the deepest well of her heart.

Cecil hastened forward and offered his arm. "Majesty, please you, come at once out of this crowd into a private place."

She said something, but it was lost in a swift-moving red pain that filled her and became a sound . . . a name. . . . *Robin . . . my long love. How could I have forgotten you for a moment, even in my greatest triumph,* our *greatest triumph?*

"Majesty, you should come away to your chambers. I would not have the court see you thus. A queen does not—"

"Does not!" she shrieked at her faithful advisor of thirty years and more. "Does not feel agony, does not . . ." She lost the words spilling from her heart, if she had ever had words instead of shrieks of disbelief. It could not be. Not Robin. He had promised never to leave her.

Cecil took her arm and spoke on determinedly: "A queen does not allow her subjects to see her shaken so."

She had no more strength to dispute him; she could scarcely lift her legs, though she stumbled into the hall from the presence chamber, her gown weighted with heavy embroidery and pearls suddenly pressing her down, her arms almost too weak to hold on to Cecil's arm so that, with the aid of his cane, he must hold them both upright. Her body was empty as death.

"And yet," she croaked, "my people know I am a woman born with a woman's heart."

"You are a queen first, Majesty. That is what you have always been from the cradle and must remain until . . ."

"I die. Oh, God above, let me go to Robin." It was a howl that rang through the hall, bringing her yeoman guards to greater attention, their pikes trembling, for what they did not know.

"Majesty," Cecil said as they reached the privy chamber doors, "you must go on. Lord Leicester would hav—"

She turned to rage at him. "What do you know of what Robin wanted? He wanted life . . . life with me, beside me. I could not give him more than a little . . . what I could, but never enough. . . ." Now she shook and sagged once more toward the floor.

"Majesty," Cecil urged, his tone reminding her of herself just enough to keep her from a faint.

Once inside the anterooms, Cecil beat on the doors to the royal apartment, loudly calling for her ladies-of-the-bedchamber.

The doors opened on the large privy bedchamber and she could see the flashing victory explosions from London City through her mullioned windows and the fire in her fireplace that burned day and night in this damp old palace beside the Thames. She saw the arras tapestries that covered her walls and the intricate Flemish lace on her bed bolsters. She feared madness. *I can see only things. I have no sense of myself. I can't think. I can no more believe.*

She croaked a question as her ladies helped her to her bed and bent to her. "Did you know, my lord Cecil?" she cried.

"No, Majesty. Not for a certainty. I have this for you from young Tracey."

He held a letter in front of her eyes so that she could read. It was Robin's handwriting, shaky, scrawled in his illness with fading strength.

His last letter.

CHAPTER 1

❦

"Come Kiss Me Now"

———— ❦ ————

EARL OF LEICESTER

Three years earlier
August 1585
Nonsuch Palace

*A*s he paced the queen's outer chambers, Robert, the Earl of Leicester's heart pounded in his ears with the hollow echo of surging surf. He turned at the long, narrow room's end, avoiding Henry VIII's enormous commanding portrait that Elizabeth carried everywhere, from castle to castle and on her summer progresses, in its own special cart, his hope trying to overcome doubt about how Elizabeth would receive him. He had been gone from court, lying with his wife, time enough for his enemies to whisper in Elizabeth's ears, time enough for her imaginings to swamp her feelings. Had they changed from the love he had always known, the love she had always shown him?

He remembered King Philip's envoy, the Duke de Feria, saying within weeks of the queen's ascension: "She gives orders and has her way as absolutely as her father did." And so she had with him. Would she reject or welcome him today? She had forgiven him many times, as he had forgiven her. They had hurt with words as cleverly cruel children in a battle for dominance until both had been made miserable. Then tears and wretchedness had forced them to forgive and fall into each other's arms. He had been gone from her for less than a fortnight, but who had plied her ears with lies or unpalatable truth in those days?

Only this woman could reduce a peer of England and a man of his natural confidence to such pitiful self-questioning. Even so, he hid amusement and a bit of jealousy for the queen's tall, fine-looking gentleman usher in a gilt breastplate, noting that the man met all of Elizabeth's requirements in the men she wanted to serve near her, requirements that perhaps he no longer met in full. He brushed aside that possibility. Despite all else, even his marriage to Elizabeth's hated cousin Lettice, they had always been together in their hearts since childhood. That would never change, he was certain . . . almost, though who could be completely certain with the mercurial Elizabeth Tudor?

Bowing low, the usher opened the huge doors to the queen's privy chamber. "Good day, my lord," he murmured before announcing the earl. "I pray God give comfort to you and your countess for your loss."

At that reminder, Robert didn't trust his voice, but nodded his thanks and walked through the outer room accompanied from the hall by the sweet, clear voices of Elizabeth's boy choristers singing William Byrd's "John, Come Kiss Me Now." Had she ordered that tune by her favorite composer as a sign to him? Had she finally forgiven him for marrying Lettice? No, he doubted she ever would quite forgive him for what she saw as a betrayal. But could a woman . . . could this woman . . . be forgiving enough to keep some part of their long love?

Who could ever be certain? She was like some willful spirit, changing her mind on the turn of a phrase, especially changeable if he were not near her and his enemies filled her ears with doubts.

Did all of Elizabeth's affection die because a proud man could not live on his knees before her throne and not as a husband sitting beside her? Did she still not understand that a man of his spirit must be a man in every way? His heart continued to pound against his black velvet doublet, lifting his device of bear and double ragged staff with each beat, though doubt was still at battle with the greeting he hoped to receive. He had dressed carefully in the new longer breeches and he wore the Garter of that Order on his left thigh with the gold dirk and rapier that were important to the ceremonial dress. She had so honored him and he would not allow her to forget it.

The queen motioned him forward toward the throne and he strode all the way through the room hung with black wall cloth of stars and moon. He bowed three times as he went even though they were alone. No ladies-of-the-bedchamber or yeoman guards stood ready to serve . . . to gossip about what they overheard through the palace and to foreign ambassadors who were always thirsty for secrets and willing to pay for news of what favor Her Majesty showed the Earl of Leicester. He walked the last open space swiftly and arrived at the dais where she sat one step above him. Always that one step separated them. He knelt and bowed his head, her true man still. He wanted her to know that would never change. She *must* know that.

"My good Earl of Leicester," the queen said in her presence

chamber voice, only a shade huskier, giving him her hand to kiss after removing her glove . . . a signal honor. He took her hand, finding her skin smooth and warm, but not as warm as his lips, which burned a kiss into her flesh. He held her hand overlong and at last she pulled away from his grasp, stood and motioned for him to rise.

She stepped from her throne and she was as she had always been, tall and straight, her beautiful hands with their long, white fingers held gracefully before her. Her striking eyes, blue shot through with dark flashes, surrounded by the white lead and alum Mask of Youth that she had made the fashion covering her face and neck. Yet she was always to him as he had ever known her from their childhood: her fair face, the pale eyebrows and lashes giving her a startled look that drew every gaze to her, wondering what would come next. He stretched both hands to her. *My own Bess.*

"Rob," she breathed, and he knew what that soft whisper had once invited. When she was a young queen and at last free to follow her heart, he would have taken her into his arms and kissed her sweet and yielding lips, her throat, her fluttering eyelids . . . her breasts. At court masques, he would have lifted her high over his head to prove that his ability at lavolte was with him always. She would have kicked her feet in protest and commanded, sounding like her father, King Henry VIII, to be set upon the floor, but with desire caught in her throat and her body yielding to his hands.

He would have lowered her slowly down the length of himself as he had done so long ago at many masques, in full view of the shocked court, when they were young and unable to keep their heat from showing, daring a scandal, caring little for what was said everywhere.

This time the moment passed swiftly, for they were no longer young and he was not free as, in truth, she had never been, married to her realm as she had forever declared, each assertion a wound to his heart and his manhood.

"Rob," she said again in her low voice.

At the sound of his name he knelt at once, showing her his neck in obedience. "Bess, my love." For his boldness, she could call her guards or order him to the Tower, which was what she had wanted to do when she'd discovered his marriage to her hated cousin Lettice. She was the queen of England and he had betrayed her love, committed treason in her mind.

But instead of calling for her guards, the queen sat down on the step to her throne.

He sat next to her, but without touching her voluminous white gown heavy with seed pearls, her oversleeves showing rubies and diamonds embroidered with the serpent sign of wisdom.

"Marriage to that She-Wolf has tamed you," she said, leaning away from him at remembrance of his wife, her eyes clouding, whether at a loving memory like his own or anger, he did not want to know. "Nor did it get you the heir you wanted." Her voice was a bit proud and vengeful, and he thought cruel, as she could be. "An empty bargain, I think, my lord."

He stared above her head with still-unspent heartache.

"Oh!" Her hand was again warm on his. "Rob . . . forgive me. At times, when I am a woman and forgetful of my crown and even my honor . . ."

"You are jealous?" he asked, though he hoped his smile took away any sting from an accusation that women did not like to hear.

"Nonsense . . ." Her voice trailed away, and then, coming as close to an apology as she ever came, she whispered, "I truly grieve for you and your little son."

He heard a catch in her voice and almost believed her. Yes, he did believe her. Her temper had always been quick, and she had been unable to restrain it at times because she looked for so much from him . . . *too much from any man.* Yet her face told him what he wanted to know and his chest ached with the knowledge: She still needed him beside her. Needed *him*! Not one of her old favorites like Kit Hatton, Tom Heneage, or her new favorite, Raleigh, but her Robin, always.

Still, he dared not confess that her grief for the loss of his son was welcome, since Lettice seemed to feel so little for their little lost boy, Robert, his Noble Imp, dead at age four of a strange and sudden fever. All of Lettice's love had been transferred to her older boy, the Earl of Essex, who carried the Devereux name of her first marriage. Now she would insist that he be named heir to the Earl of Leicester, too, and she would have her way as she did in all but one thing: She wanted to be received at court again, but would never be as long as he could stop it. When he was with Elizabeth, he was all her man and no husband to Lettice . . . and he would keep it that way. Oh, on some public occasions he would plead with the queen to accept his wife, but only to keep the appearance of a loving husband and save Bess from gossip.

The queen's hand tightened on his and, Jesu help him, his grief came pouring out. "All my hopes, Bess—" He gulped down an unmanly sob, which he could not allow her to hear. "All swept away in a few short hours. How my little Imp suffered . . . the best doctors and all my pleading prayers could not save him." He turned his face from hers, fearing tears might start.

"Rob, are you ill?" The old, deep concern was in her voice. He shook his head.

"You look spent and weary. I will have my apothecary make up my own special herbal potion for you. Take it twice a day."

She moved closer and cradled his head against her breast. "Sweet Robin . . ."

The endearing name of their youth had come easily to her lips. He raised his head reluctantly from her only softness and looked full into her face. Did she love him still, as they had loved then? His breath quickened: as they had loved for one night at Rycote?

Her eyes narrowed as she returned his gaze. What did she see? The lines radiating like a web from his eyes?

"Have you been eating too well?" she said, probably remembering the youthful waist he no longer had. "Taking too much meat and sweet puddings . . . and not taking exercise as you promised me?" She laughed and repeated an old joke between them: "Remember you must eat only the wing of a wren for dinner and the little leg for supper."

He had to smile and thought he and Bess were like a long-married husband and wife where finally all former faults become dear. He knew that he and Lettice would never be so; her faults were beyond loving, though he had to bear some blame for them. What beautiful woman could bear to be unloved, to have been wanted only because she looked like the woman her husband really loved? It had made Lettice scheming and cold. Yet how could he rightly censure her?

He tightened his hold on the hand Bess kept in his. Did she comfort him as a grieving father, or as the man she still loved? Did she see him as he had once been, or as a man with silver in his hair and beard? He could not ask and risk a distressing answer.

They sat that way at the foot of her throne chair for a quiet time and the pressure in his chest was relieved. "I'm at ease here with you, Bess. Your potion is at work before I swallow it."

She laughed, a true laugh, one that he'd often heard in days past as she'd ridden breakneck upon her favorite hunter beside him on the chase. As always, due to the same stars they'd been born under on the same day of the same year, she had read his worry and silently reassured him with a memory.

Those minutes passed too swiftly, and she was queen again, putting the woman aside as she could do, as he had never learned to do with his manhood. "Lord Robert, you know that we are happy for your return, having great need of your service in this matter of Spain bringing the Inquisition to the Hollanders across the channel. Their parliament, the States-General, has offered me their crown again and has put their begging ambassadors in my presence chamber every day."

"Majesty, you have denied them your rule many times for at least a decade."

"And will continue to deny them," she said sharply before standing and walking away, then back again. Pacing had always helped her to think. But he felt the loss of her warm hand and was happy when she came back to him, though not as near. He stood to face her, for she was obviously troubled.

It was an old worry.

"Since Spain claims the Hollanders' northern provinces as their own, if we accept the Dutch throne, as you must know, my lord, that act would give Philip his perfect excuse to send his Spanish legions to invade England."

He missed the loss of his loving Bess, but royal duties had reclaimed her as they always did. He could best show his love by helping her think through the political problems that troubled her. "Majesty, King Philip needs no *perfect* excuse, nor any excuse." He allowed her a moment to think on what they both knew was true, although she always tried to push such difficult truth away and think there must be a way to negotiate even with

Philip. "Spain has not conquered the northern provinces yet, Majesty. These people are Protestant and look to a Protestant queen for help. They will fight popery until their last breath."

Elizabeth frowned, making an irritated *pup, pup* sound with her lips. "Or until our last gold mark, my lord! They always plead for English treasure and troops. They would bankrupt my purse."

He knelt. "My queen, I beg you to help them." He knew her face flared pink under its mask.

Angrily, she shouted, "We know you have long sought our men and money for their good."

He tried not to allow her frustration to hurt him, having felt it many times. "Majesty, I have always loyally counseled what I thought good for you and England."

"Yes, yes, we know." She admitted the truth of his protest, though she did not like it when other truth differed from her own.

She began to pace again. "My lord, we have given the matter much thought and we have listened to our good councilors. Cecil, Lord Burghley, and especially Walsingham repeat your warnings. Our own people along with most of the Commons in Parliament urge us to give aid to the Dutch Protestants." She raised a hand in frustration, then let it fall. "Very well. If you all join together against me and would have us send an army, then you will be our lieutenant general, for we cannot trust any as we trust you . . . yet we need you here by our side."

The last words were tender and he thought she might embrace him again. Was he to her as she was to him, ever the same as when they'd first loved in youth, despite the years since then and the troubles they'd endured?

CHAPTER 2

❧

WHEN THEY WERE YOUNG

❧

ELIZABETH

Early June 1550
Richmond Castle

*P*rincess Elizabeth ignored Lord Robert Dudley, young son of the Earl of Warwick, who bowed to her as she walked with her nurse and ladies. He gave her their private signal to meet later, but she turned away most pointedly, knowing her eyes were as dark as two thunderclouds and meaning them to be. Yet she heard the faint crackle of paper in the oversleeve of her gown, a poem she had begun for Robin that now he would never see.

Jesu in chains! What did he want from her . . . a wedding gift? The news was everywhere spoken in the castle. He was to marry Amy Robsart in a week, a country gentleman's pretty daughter with property. Did he think to keep such news secret in a royal palace? Not for the space of an hour.

He hurried after her. Did he want to explain? There was

never an explanation for betrayal. You were either a betrayer or you weren't. She would not listen. Yet as she walked on, her head held high, she could not stop herself from urging her maids to hurry inside while lingering in the end gallery beside a window alcove.

He approached her and bowed, but she turned away. Not this time. No! She would not be cozened by his proud, handsome face and blazing black eyes or his knightly carriage. Indeed, she would erase her memory of everything they had been and she had hoped would be. *Short of marriage, that is.*

"Bess," he pleaded. "Please."

"Please? No, Robin, you do not please me and never will again." She pulled at her arm, but he held her until she pulled harder.

He let her go, his face now suddenly pale, and she softened as much as she could allow.

"Bess . . . what can I do?" he begged. "I am a younger son. I have little but what the king or my father grants me. Amy Robsart comes with property and is heiress to much more. And I am to have Hemsby Manor for my own. Our fathers have signed the contract. What choice—"

"And she is pretty, I hear," Elizabeth said, the words spit from between her lips. She was exhausted from the deepest disappointment she had ever known, deeper than her father's dislike, deeper than Lord Admiral Thomas Seymour's implying that he had compromised her, which had cost him his head and almost cost her the same had she not kept her wits when questioned. And she had known many other betrayals by men. Her father had killed her mother. There was no greater betrayal. But nothing else. She swore it! No one had taken her virginity. She would avow it on her deathbed.

She sat down quickly on a window seat in the darkened alcove, the sun behind clouds. "Speak not of choice to me, Robin." Her lips trembled beyond control, though she reached deep to gather more. "You are seventeen years old, as I am, and are a legal man grown. You have more choice than I, daughter of a king, who has none. The council will promise me to some foreign prince, or sweep me off to a German duchy, or anyone who will take a royal bastard and daughter of a witch and a great whore, the 'little whore,' as all Europe knows me to be." She pressed her lips tight and regained her poise. She had been practicing that for her life long.

"Never to see you again?" he asked, choking on the words. He wove his hand through her red-blond hair, brushed by her ladies until it shone without the need for sun or torchlight. "Never to touch this again." He brought a glorious tress to his lips. "I could not bear that, Bess."

She had to pull back. She could not stand the touch she had always loved. "Robin, you are cruel to make me love you still. Make me hate you, if you care for me, or as your duty to a royal princess. I care not how. Just do it. . . . Help me."

"You ask the impossible, sweetheart. And you are not a bastard or a whore. Not so known to me, although . . . perhaps a witch . . . for you have bewitched me." He grinned to take the sting out of that word, a word that could bring a woman to the stake for burning, a name her mother, Anne Boleyn, had been called, was still called. "You know that you have always been my beloved princess, and someday you will be my queen."

She jerked away from him and looked about fearfully. "Never call me so! Don't you know that I have Catholic enemies in this court behind every pillar, followers of my sister, Mary, the next of my father's children to inherit the throne? They will do anything to deny another Protestant the crown."

"But your brother will have children. . . ."

Elizabeth stared at him. Never had she heard such wishful thinking, though she already knew passion was full of it.

"I know, Bess," he whispered. "Edward is sickly. It is whispered everywhere. . . ."

"Do not say so to me. I am my brother's loyal subject. I daily pray with my chaplain for his good health."

The sun edged behind a late-spring cloud and the alcove turned almost midnight after the torch on the nearest column went out. "Bess, dearest," he whispered, and she felt her body move toward him, creeping into his warm arms.

"Sweetheart, if it were possible . . ."

His breath brushed her cheek and she thought, *I cannot live without him.* But this was impossible to say.

"Robin, it is not likely that we can be together and I truly know it as you do, though I like it little. My nurse, Kat Ashley, says all young men and women want what is not promising for them and that I must let wiser heads guide me." She watched his face. "Do you believe that, Robin?"

"My father says the same," he answered, his wide shoulders rising with an effort at his old swagger.

"Your father, Warwick, may be high in my brother's favor, but someday I will decide which wiser head pleases me most."

He grinned at her because she sounded like herself again. "You will, Bess, you *will*. I swear that I will pray for that day."

Elizabeth had to ask the question most in her heart. "Robin, do you love her, this Amy Robsart?"

He hesitated and she knew that he liked her well enough. Faithless man!

"There is a good settlement."

His caution wasn't appreciated. Elizabeth pulled away from

him, violently, and slapped his face. "That is commerce, not love!"

His hand went to his cheek and she hoped he was stung by her fury, but he took her shoulders and drew her close, breathing near her ear, overheating her.

"If you don't know whom I love by now, you will—"

"Tell me, Robin. Give me the memory of the sound of it." *Give me that!*

He breathed in deeply, looking a little dizzy, though he kept his body firm. Or, she wondered, was it firm without his command? "I love you, Elizabeth Tudor, my darling Bess, now and forever."

"Again," she commanded, tossing her head back, knowing she looked every inch a queen.

He repeated his words and added, "I have loved you since we were children and you knew your Latin verbs better than I in the Greenwich Palace schoolroom."

"Since I outrode you that day in the Windsor Great Park deer hunt!" she proclaimed, always loving to best him.

"Since that day, before, after and still until the day I die. We were fated to love from our natal day. Dr. Dee tells me our stars foretold it. There is no help for love that is destined by heaven."

Elizabeth sat up as straight as a pikeman and shook herself. "Yes, but I must bear my fate alone. I *will* bear it. Watch me!" Her face was filled with pride and she knew it.

"Lord God forgive me, Bess."

"He may, but I never shall."

"You cannot mean those words, Bess."

And when he put his cheek to hers, she retrieved her anger. "No, I cannot mean those words, although I will come to mean them with the help of Jesu and all the saints."

Though pledged to Amy, Robin kissed her until they were so close that she knew even the full appearing sun could not send its rays between them.

A stern voice accomplished what the sun could not.

"Princess, you forget your royal self! I'm happy to find you before someone else carries this tale to the king, your brother." Sturdy Kat Ashley stood not a man's length from them, speaking in her soft, cajoling Devon accent: "Come now, my sweet princess, before someone less eager for your good name sees you in Lord Robert's betrothed arms."

Robin stood and kissed Elizabeth's hand. She believed it a final caress. He bowed to Kat, who would never betray them.

Elizabeth thrust a piece of paper into his hand and walked away from him, too proud to allow herself to send a last, yearning look back to him. She would not fall into her bed weeping, to be ill for days while doctors bled her until she could not rise. This was her life. Eventually, everyone she loved left her.

CHAPTER 3

❧

"Protect Her or I Am Not Your Son"

———————— ❧ ————————

Earl of Leicester

June 1550
Robin's Wedding

*R*obert Dudley, his chest tight, only his large codpiece keeping him safe from male jibes and women's laughter, stopped behind a pillar to read Bess's note:

> *No means I find to rid him from my breast,*
>
> *Till by the end of things it be supprest.*

He placed it inside his doublet next to his heart, swearing that he would allow nothing to harm her. Never.

He returned through the presence chamber to the king's apartment to find him ailing again. Two of Robert's brothers, Guildford and Ambrose Dudley, waited upon His Majesty.

"Read to me, my lord Robert," the king said, and pointed to

his Book of Common Prayer always by his chair. Archbishop Thomas Cranmer was revising the book, but the young king was overseeing it himself. Edward was far more solemn than his years, a miniature in appearance of his father, Henry VIII, and now, unfortunately, of his sickly mother, Jane Seymour, who had not survived her only son's birth.

Robert picked up the book, glad to read the new English translation and not the old Latin. He pronounced the morning prayer, needing God's solace himself.

When he started on the order of service, Edward soon dozed and Robert rose and looked out the window as gardeners below snipped at the spring growth in the knot garden and cleaned the fountains.

The king's voice followed a tap on his shoulder. Dudley turned and knelt at once.

"Robert, my doctors have prescribed country air and I have decided to attend your wedding."

"Majesty, my family and I are honored beyond—"

"Yes, yes. And my sister, the Princess Elizabeth, will be in my train."

Robert's head remained low. A fool could have read what was in his face, and Edward, though not quite thirteen years old, was no fool.

The murmurs of conversation in the room ceased. "Yes, Robert, it will quiet any foul gossip that my court is so fond of . . . for I will not abide my pious sister to be defamed."

Dudley swallowed to steady his words. "Most gracious Majesty. I am ever your good and obedient servant." What talk could there be? He and Bess had been as cautious as a bear facing a pack of dogs at a baiting.

The next morning, as he rode away from Richmond with his

father and brothers, his mother in a curtained litter, he looked back, but Bess did not stand at her window. Kat would be keeping her at her embroidery with her ladies, or, if he knew his Bess, she would be at her lessons, losing herself in her Latin and Greek books, where she had always hidden her young sorrows. He well knew that he could find no comfort in any ancient language—it would take another woman's arms—but he did not doubt that Bess would find her solace in Plutarch. From her childhood she had escaped all her many troubles in deep study.

He spurred his horse to pull close to his father, the Earl of Warwick. "My lord father, I am most grateful for the property you have settled on me and my soon-to-be wife."

The duke nodded, his mind obviously full of his young sovereign's business.

"Father, there is one more gift I would beg of you, and if you give it, I will return the manor and property you have settled on me."

The duke turned to him. "What is this nonsense? What more could you wish?"

"The life of the Princess Elizabeth. I think it is at risk."

The Earl of Warwick frowned and spurred his horse on down the cart road. Robert kicked his own mount into a canter. "Don't meddle in state business, my son."

Robert lowered his voice, aware that to even speak of the king's death was treason. "If the king dies young, I know you fear that the public will rise up to demand a Protestant queen."

"I will see that England gets the queen it needs and it won't be Catholic Mary."

"Will it be Elizabeth?"

"Elizabeth was declared illegitimate by the king, her father, and by Parliament."

"But her father also put her in his will of succession. If you persuade the king to name another, she is in danger from the new queen . . . or from you."

His father's reply was harsh. "You go very far into realms you do not know."

Robert's answer was not timid. "Protect her, my lord father. If she dies, I am not your son." He meant his voice to be angry and determined.

His father raised a hand and Robert steeled himself for a blow. When the hand fell back to the reins, Robert was heartened. "I beg of you, Father. If you save her, I will be faithful to you in all else you ask of me forever."

The duke looked at him with some sympathy. "The king is already dissatisfied with the Duke of Suffolk and his Seymour family. They are sure to o'erreach, Robert. Then our family will rise higher than we ever hoped. How would you like to be son to the Duke of Northumberland?" He lowered his voice until he could just be heard. "Do you love Elizabeth so much that you would defy me, our family's prospects and your own?" He spurred ahead without hearing Robert's answer. He knew his stubborn son.

Robert Dudley's June wedding day dawned warm, and with a perfect, cool Norfolk breeze and the scents of opening lavender and roses in the air. Amy, with her dark hair loose about her back, the sign of a maid, was very pretty in a green satin gown newly finished by her seamstress. She stepped daintily through the lush new grass to his side. He bowed to the king, searching for Bess until he found her chatting gaily amongst her ladies, her face turned away from him.

He took Amy's hand and smiled into her upturned, trusting eyes, Bess's poem in its place next to his beating heart.

CHAPTER 4

❧

See All and Speak Nothing

Earl of Leicester

Summer 1585
Nonsuch Palace

*M*ore than thirty years had passed since he and Elizabeth had parted at his marriage to Amy. Their lives had changed completely in many ways. Bess had ascended to the throne on her sister Mary's death, but she had never forgotten Robert Dudley. She had raised him with her to become the most powerful lord in England.

One thing had not changed: She ruled alone, never willing for him to rule beside her as her husband, although he had clung to that dream for two decades until all hope flared and died in their last summer together at Kenilworth, the palace and garden of pleasures he had made for her.

The afternoon of his return to the court after the death of his Imp, the Earl of Leicester attended the queen's council, sitting in his usual place at the queen's right hand, the nearest he would ever come to her now, though it had not always been so.

He watched the Lord Treasurer, William Cecil, now Lord Burghley, seated down the table facing the queen. Was Cecil friend or foe today? Robert was certain that sober-faced Cecil was wary of war, often saying: "War is soon kindled, but peace very hardly procured."

In that Elizabeth and Cecil usually agreed. Would both finally realize this day that the Netherlands, if controlled completely by Spain with a large army across the narrow English Channel, would be a dire threat? Thanks be to God, at last Bess seemed to fully understand the Spanish menace and be willing to act, unless she had changed her mind again.

Robert's gaze shifted to Sir Christopher Hatton on the other side of the long council table. Although he tried to reject the thought, it was obvious to him that Hatton was the kind of faithful, unmarried man that Elizabeth had always found attractive. He was tall, graceful, fair as a Dane, with an immaculate curled beard and intelligent, adoring speech. Bess was not a woman to ignore such qualities.

Hatton had been infatuated with her for years—whether as queen or woman, Robert could not guess. Most likely both. Had Bess seen this? Of course she had. She loved every moment of romantic attention. The whole world could court her and it wouldn't make up for a father who'd kept her from him, largely ignored her when she was there and beheaded her mother and her cousin. Even Elizabeth's shortsightedness and refusal to wear her gold-rimmed spectacles did not keep her from seeing a fine-looking man forever at her feet, and Kit was still handsome and slender. Did Elizabeth see that her Robin's middle was thicker and his hair sparser? Was she comparing the two of them?

Robert breathed in deeply, keeping his back very straight. Hatton stayed near the throne like Thomas Heneage, an even earlier favorite, still cheerfully hoping to receive a favorite's rewards, although Bess's eyes had lately turned to the adventurer Walter Raleigh. He had returned from the New World after naming it Virginia in honor of his virgin queen. He had added to the queen's entertainment with a smoking plant and a rare bulb called a potato. Yet none of them could bring the queen victory in the Low Countries as could the Earl of Leicester. Although he believed that Bess loved him and that he was her paramount love, he wanted her to want him alone, and that she could never do. He wanted from her what he could never accomplish himself, though men were not meant for solitary love, as everyone knew . . . except, perhaps, Elizabeth.

"Majesty," Cecil intoned in his council voice, lifting the first document from the pile in front of him, "about the matter of troops for the Netherlands."

"My Lord Treasurer, we will discuss that another day," the queen replied impatiently.

Cecil cleared his throat and Robert could see he hardly knew how to proceed from that royal pronouncement. "As you wish, madam. Shall we move on to discuss the Earl of Leicester's appointment as—"

"Another day for all like matters, my lord."

Robert did not blink or frown in consternation. Elizabeth's chronic inability to commit to war was not unexpected. Still, she was closer to a decision than she had ever been and he dared to raise a question: "Majesty, have you forgotten that the Duke of

Parma's troops are killing Protestant Dutch women and children every day?" Someone had to ask, and he was the only one who could question the queen without sending her into a rage, or, if enraging her, survive it.

"We forget nothing, my lord, as you should know!"

Robert slumped, then straightened himself again. Bess lost no opportunity to remind him of Lettice. For a moment, he thought the queen would rage, but she drew in a deep breath and spoke with only normal irritation. "Yes, yes, my lord Leicester, we know King Philip's lack of tolerance for his Protestant subjects." She frowned and slapped her hand angrily upon the table, scattering her papers. "We ask you, sirs, why can't the king of Spain allow his Protestant subjects to go to the devil in their own way?"

No one dared laugh, but Robert knew all of them thought that the queen herself did not allow her Catholic subjects to go to the devil except by her hand. Still, no one pointed out the inconsistency. Queens were never humored by a joke at their expense. In her own way, Elizabeth had given warning that the discussion was at an end until she was ready for it to begin once more.

Robert hardly followed the rest of the business, keeping his disappointment from showing, swallowing it as he always had except in private, when he felt he owed her honesty, though she often did not want it even then. He was quite able to give his opinion when it was sought, and he knew she would come to him for his truth after she had considered further. As the council ended, he stood.

Elizabeth put a hand on his arm. "Remain for a time, my lord Leicester."

"As it please you, Majesty." Perhaps the queen played one game for her council and one for him.

Hatton lingered near the door.

"When I have need, Sir Christopher, I will send for you," the queen said with her back to him.

Robert smiled to himself. She could give in one minute and take away in the next, always controlling the men around her by fomenting uncertainty. When they were alone in the council chamber, Robert spoke first. "With your leave, madam, I would be off to my manor of Wanstead immediately. It is a good ride, but with a change of horses, I can arrive home before full dark." He had given her notice that he would not be intimidated by her changeableness, or hang about Nonsuch like a love-struck boy.

She was angry, but for once held her tongue. "Nay, Rob, I would have you here beside me at court. I cannot do without you in these grave times. I am not against the Hollander venture, but I must think on it longer. . . . *Video et taceo.*"

Robert bowed to the inevitable. The queen's motto, "I see all and speak nothing," was as well chosen as any motto could be. He had almost made his old mistake of confusing what Elizabeth said with what she would do. Convincing her to act, to risk Spain's anger and retribution, would take time. He would suffer through many such changes as the queen grasped at every chance to avoid war, thinking her superior wiles sufficient to avoid it.

"Come, Rob, no more gloom," she said, taking his arm as they returned to her privy chamber. Her ladies, trailing behind and seeing the intimacy, revived the old scandals in their minds, though they would never dare utter them in her hearing. "Let us talk no more of the Netherlands venture today, but visit as dear friends, met again."

"As you will it, Your Grace." He had not really wanted to leave court, to return to his wife, Lettice, and to Wanstead, where the ghostly cries of his Imp still rang in every room. He had asked Bess's permission to return home to discover whether Raleigh, her new favorite, had replaced him completely. Her answer had told him all he wanted to know. His place in her heart was yet secure. Raleigh had not taken it, as Christopher Hatton and Thomas Heneage before him had not. Bess still needed him at her side as she always had, and now that he was here with her, he found it impossible to leave. He was her prisoner for life, as much as he had been a prisoner under a death sentence in the Tower during her sister Bloody Mary's reign.

He drew in a deep breath at the awful memory. He and his father and brothers had tried valiantly to keep Mary, Henry VIII's oldest daughter, from succeeding after King Edward's youthful death at not quite sixteen years. His father, advanced to Duke of Northumberland, had placed his only unmarried son, Guildford Dudley, and his Protestant wife, Jane Grey, on the throne, and it was his family's duty and ambition to keep them there. Catholic Mary Tudor could not rule. But they were seen by many Englishmen as usurpers and had not been able to stop a popular uprising in Mary's favor. The entire Dudley family, save only his mother, had been condemned.

Elizabeth took his arm as they approached the royal apartments. "Come, Rob, we will have our supper and then walk together in my walled garden in the eventide." She laughed softly. "Far better than marching along the leads at the Tower. Remember?"

"There is no forgetting between us, Bess. It was in the Tower that I knew the years would change nothing between us."

CHAPTER 5

❧

"Is Lady Jane's Scaffold Removed?"

❧

Elizabeth

Late Winter 1554
Tower of London

*T*he clang of armored feet and the clink of chain mail sounded on the stone stairs to her cell in the Bell Tower and Elizabeth's body became rigid. This was a sound she feared to hear night or day. Were they coming for her as they had come for her mother, Anne Boleyn, eighteen years earlier; as they had come for Lady Jane Grey just days ago? Would she be as brave before the ax as her mother and her beautiful, virtuous cousin? She tensed herself not to tremble before the Tower guards.

"My lady Elizabeth." A yeoman guard opened her cell door and stepped inside while more guards crowded behind him. Her ladies looked up from their embroidery, but Elizabeth could not. She was determined to hide her terror at every guard's appearance.

Then she could not stop her words. "Is Lady Jane's scaffold removed?"

"My lady, I am not allowed to say."

Her gaze darted to his hands, looking for the vellum order signed by her sister, Queen Mary, a death warrant to take the traitorous prisoner Elizabeth to the block on Tower Green, the same green where her father, Henry VIII, had sent her mother. *Every royal family has its troubles.* She clamped her teeth together to suppress an almost hysterical desire to giggle. She had been so often near death, gallows humor was all the jest she could allow herself. But let no other defame a Tudor!

She dreaded another questioning in the dungeon below with Mary's Catholic bishops and her council, circling, threatening, reminding her of her mother's fate amidst the screams of tortured prisoners, probably Protestant heretics. It had taken all of her will, her father's courage . . . and yes, her mother's . . . to act as princess royal and heir to the throne. She had not been broken, nor admitted to any slight knowledge of the recent Protestant uprising led by Sir Thomas Wyatt. They would not use her own words to damn her. Could she help it if Mary's Protestant subjects rebelled against their queen's harsh conversion measures, wishing to set Elizabeth on the throne? She'd refused to admit to the knowledge or commission of any traitorous acts, her blood running cold in her veins as screams from the rack's victims reached her. Her questioners intended to frighten her, but her back remained straight and she kept all fear from her face until they were well and truly reminded of whom they questioned, and withdrew.

Elizabeth kept her gaze on weaving her needle in and out of the thick material as though determined to catch the last slanting ray of late sun. They would not see her terror or her strange humor. When fully composed, she lifted her face to reply. "I remind you, sir, that I am the daughter of a king and therefore a princess. I refuse to answer to the title of Lady Elizabeth."

The yeoman sighed, having heard this response many times, and continued with his message. "The Lord Lieutenant of the Tower requests my lady's presence at supper this day at five of the clock."

"How good of the Lord Lieutenant. I shall wear my best shackles." Elizabeth dropped her gaze again to her embroidery before she said more that could be reported as insolence and not true contrition.

"My lady, his other guests are Lords Ambrose and Robert Dudley."

She half stood at that, but with a creak of wood and a clang of iron hasps the yeoman withdrew. Her heart raced as the name leaped from her heart and imprinted on her brain. *Robert Dudley. Robin! After all these years apart, we meet here, you condemned and me waiting for a traitor's death, if the queen's council dares put the heir to the throne on trial for treason or behead her without a trial. But Robin was tried and walked through London with the ax man before him, showing all the people that he was condemned to the block. Jesu Christo, this supper could be our last chance to meet outside of heaven.* She laid a hand on her breasts to calm their heaving. Her tongue licked at her dry lips, where his kiss was the last she had known, perhaps the last she would ever know.

S'blood, enough of gloom!

"Quickly now, Kat," she said, throwing aside her embroidery hoop, "my yellow gown, my red satin slippers and my best embroidered stomacher. And my hair must be brushed." She paused at Kat's raised eyebrow. "The Lord Lieutenant must know I honor his invitation."

"Wearing your 'best shackles' will hardly prove honor to him," Kat, her nurse since childhood, said, reproving her as only she could. By the alarm in her face, Kat Ashley urged caution, but Elizabeth threw off her plain gown and the Spanish hood her sister, the queen, had demanded she wear.

Kat came with a hairbrush, and Elizabeth calmed with the gently repeated strokes, loving the way her soft hair lay about her shoulders like a glowing cloak. "Tonight, I will wear no Spanish hood," she announced. She would probably be reported by those set to keep watch over her every heretical and willful action, but she would wear her hair loose, as Robin had loved it.

She had been born knowing that boldness erased fear, while cowardice invited it and earned her only more ill treatment. No matter how she shook with dread in private, she would never show fear before her questioners or her guards. In men's minds fear was a certain mark of guilt.

Four guards came for her as the bell in her tower rang out. One led the way, with another on either side and the last at her back, almost stepping on her gown. "Good yeomen," she said in a mocking voice, "am I, a young maid, so fearsome a foe that you must bring an army to protect yourselves?" She laughed lightly to take away any sting, but she had made them feel ridiculous, which was her intention.

The tall guard marching to her left spoke scarcely above a whisper. "Princess, I am John Carpenter, a good Protestant, who does an unpleasant duty for our anointed queen. When you are queen, as I pray God you will be in His good time, I will serve you as faithfully."

"When that day comes, John Carpenter, I will not forget you," she said in her softest voice.

"God preserve Your Grace," he answered, his lips moving as if he had begun his evening prayers.

Elizabeth walked through the garden in front of the Lord Lieutenant's quarters. She tried not to notice the drift of gray ash an untimely easterly wind had carried from the Smithfield burnings. Protestants were being sent to hell as fast as they could be tried and condemned by Mary's ecclesiastical court under the devilish Bishop Gardiner. Instead, she smiled on the early blooming snowdrops and crocus and, under a bare tree, yellow-centered aconites with their silver-trimmed leaves. She breathed in fresh air sweeping up the Thames from the channel, so deeply her chest hurt, and she realized how shallow her breathing had been in her crowded cell with its damp, moldy air. She was reminded with her every breath that she was locked away . . . and that her sister might want her to disappear into the Tower's deep dungeons like the little Plantagenet princes in Richard III's time. Elizabeth winced because her situation was so much the same; she was in the power of a ruler who feared and hated her claim to the throne. Half sister or no, Mary did hate her, was never willing to forgive the child for what her mother, Anne Boleyn, had done: taken the king away from Mary's mother, Queen Catherine of Aragon, and exiling her to a lonely death.

Breathing deeply, Elizabeth caught the scent of a wood fire and roasting venison from the Lord Lieutenant's dwelling. But it was the sound of marching boots and the sight of Ambrose and Robert Dudley being escorted from the Beauchamp Tower into the garden in flaring torchlight that stopped her.

Robin. There was nothing left of the handsome boy she had loved so furiously and met so secretly to feel his arms about her and his lustful young lips on hers. That youth with a prince's jeweled doublet and peacock-feathered cap she had last seen, or refused to see in some misery, at his wedding. Now, here came a man grown, taller than his older brother, his shoulders filled out to a man's width, his legs beneath finely knit mauve hose carved with muscle, his Gypsy eyes and dark features compelling her not to turn away from him. There must have been something more than recognition in her face, though she had tried to keep it hidden, because he smiled at her and winked like some preening courtier before his mirror until she turned aside and marched into the Lord Lieutenant's cottage.

"My lady, welcome," the Tower commander said with a deep bow, deep enough for a royal princess whether or not she could own her true rank. His wife curtsied with as much honor and welcomed her kindly. The Lord Lieutenant escorted her to a trestle table with benches. He seated her in his own high-backed chair at the head of the table.

"Please be seated, all," he said. "My lord Robert, I have good news for you. Your lady wife will be visiting you tomorrow. The queen has decided to allow it."

Robert bowed. "Good news, indeed, my Lord Lieutenant. Surely that means the queen has decided to pardon me."

The Lord Lieutenant did not comment. "You and Lord Ambrose may sit near the Lady Elizabeth, if it please her."

Elizabeth smiled, but said nothing, lest she bite the words in two. Amy Robsart to walk in and out of Robin's cell as if she owned it . . . and him. She thought to let Robin wonder at her mood, although she had given him ample indication with her now-unsmiling face, yet she doubted she could keep from her gaze some of what she felt at seeing him again. "My Lord Lieutenant, I thank you and your good wife for this greeting." She nodded to Robin formally and smiled at Ambrose. "My lord Ambrose, you are well?"

"As well as may be, my lady."

"Princess," Robin acknowledged, boldly looking into her eyes with just enough amusement playing on his mouth to anger her further. Did he presume to know her still?

She turned her face away, showing nothing, or hoping to. Yet she thought that to a man like Robin, her efforts would only make him more daring . . . she hoped—and then brought herself away from hoping that there was anything of the old Robin left. Too much had happened to chill them both. "My Lord Lieutenant Bridges," she said, smiling, "the scent of your good roast venison reached me in my poor cell."

His lady, bustling and buxom, hovered near Elizabeth and motioned for a servant to fill her wine cup. Elizabeth raised her hand. "Very weak wine, I thank you, mistress."

Robert motioned to the servant, pointing to his cup. "A man's stomach demands a strong wine. Spanish, if you will."

He did not look at Elizabeth, but she felt his foot slide over and nudge her slipper under the table while he looked the opposite way. Elizabeth knew he was trying to best her as he had always done. God's death, the man took liberties. She kicked him and had the pleasure of seeing him hold tight to his surprise. Then, of a sudden, she lost all the pleasure of revenge for his marriage. The ax hung above his head as well as hers. What did Amy Robsart matter now? She could soon be a widow. But she would have been his wife. What would Elizabeth be? A woman with only memories of a young, fumbling love, a few stolen kisses, brief touches, a poem she had not had time to finish.

She touched his knee and he reached casually for her hand

as his muttered words came to her above the clatter of pewter plates and knives.

"Don't," she whispered.

"Nothing has changed with me."

"You waste your charms, Lord Robert, for the ax hangs now over my head."

"Do not fear, Bess. Master Bridges received an unsigned death warrant from Bishop Gardiner at Westminster Palace, but would not execute it without the queen's signature lest he lose his own head. When he went to the palace, the queen denied the warrant."

"The councilors." The words grated between her teeth. "They want me dead or they would not go so far."

"True, but your sister, the queen, could not bring herself to sign when Bridges showed the order to her. Bess, you are destined to live and rule. It is written in your stars and your stars are my stars. I will live to serve you yet."

"How will you serve me, my lord?"

"Well, sweetheart, very well."

She drew back, not wanting to draw her host's attention by further intimacy, or they were sure to be reported. "There are some doubters that the stars foretell us anything, Lord Robert," she said gaily, as if arguing over astrology.

"I am not such a one and neither are you, Princess," he said, with a half smile, though his eyes were misty in the candlelight as his gaze searched her face.

Elizabeth knew he must be as terrified as she. For over a year now Robin had been imprisoned. He had watched as his brother Guildford and his father, made Duke of Northumberland by King Edward, were taken in chains to the block on Queen Mary's orders. He had seen his father's execution from his cell window and his brother's body and head brought from Tower Hill in a cart.

He lowered his voice again, looking down at his plate. "The queen *must* let you go, Bess. Just last week, Sir Thomas Wyatt recanted his confession, swearing on the scaffold that you had no knowledge of his rebellion. Everyone knows that a man does not swear to a lie before he meets his God."

"But the scaffold remains."

"Rest easy, Bess. I overheard Bridges give the order for it to come down on the morrow."

Elizabeth looked at him, fighting to keep her relief from showing. Was he so naive that he believed her to be completely innocent of Wyatt's rebellion? True, she had not read or answered Wyatt's letters to her revealing his plans to gather troops in Kent and the west of England to march on London and bring down Queen Mary and her Spanish husband, Philip. Elizabeth could swear to that in good conscience, having left them to be found unopened, although she knew their content. The letters had been intercepted by the queen's ministers, read and sent on as a trap for her they were waiting to spring. They had brought her from her Hatfield home ailing with her nervous dropsical illness and in a litter to interrogate her in Whitehall and then in the Tower dungeon, thinking to frighten her in those stony depths into damning admissions of treason. She was frightened, true enough—near out of her wits, if it be known—but she had steadfastly denied all knowledge of treasonous plots. Her interrogators tried in every clever way to gain an admission from her, promising leniency, promising forgiveness, promising a return to her beloved Hatfield. She had known better than to believe them.

A look of surprise and then fear rose in Robin's face as he

realized something of what she was hiding. Speaking his words behind his cup, he said, "Have great care, Bess. Great care."

Elizabeth raised her cup to her host. "My Lord Lieutenant and host, I thank you for this kindness." She raised her cup higher. "I pray God grant a long and healthy life to my sister, Queen Mary . . . and many sons." All the men rose and echoed her toast.

As she left to return to her cell, the Lord Lieutenant sank to his knees, recognizing her royalty. Elizabeth nodded, her heart thrilling to the possibility that her bonds might be loosening. "Thank you again . . . for everything."

"Would that I might do more to preserve your comfort," he said in a humble tone.

Elizabeth took a deep breath. "I wish for more fresh air, good sir. My cell is close, ill-smelling and crowded."

He hesitated, his brow wrinkling in thought. "I am not supposed to give you any freedom."

She shrugged and turned to the door. "I want no other comfort."

"But," he said, hurrying after her, "you may walk on the leads between Bell and Beauchamp towers before dusk every day . . . with a guard."

She nodded her thanks, or rather his remembrance that someday she might be his queen and best to not forget. Having gained one concession, she pushed for more. "A guard is hardly fit company for the princess royal, sir. It would be more pleasant if Lord Robert could join me. A man's conversation is such a wondrous change from the prattling of my women." She raised her eyes. He was a man, after all, and susceptible to flattery of his sex.

"Oh, no, Your Grace," he said, a nervous twitch under his

eye. "I would exceed my authority by too much. There would be suspicion that you two were plotting . . ."

"What, my Lord Lieutenant! Raising an army of two? Planning, with witchcraft, to fly over the battlements and swim away down the Thames?" She walked away in apparent disgust, muttering: "The queen does not choose her servants for their good sense."

He came hurrying after her. "Princess, do not despair. There is strong rumor that your sister may send you from this place to the country and keep you less confined."

"Thank you, Lord Lieutenant."

"Please remember, Princess, that I will always keep your interest close."

The next night she was led out as a sliver of moon rose in the east to glimmer on the Thames flowing swiftly past at high tide. She wore her best gown and all the jewels imprisoned with her. From Beauchamp Tower she saw Robin emerge, a guard behind him.

His guard commanded: "No talking together allowed, my lord."

Robin walked toward her and bowed.

She mocked: "And how is your good wife, my lord?"

"You come to me like starlight, thick with jewels." His whisper was husky to almost breaking.

He turned at the end of the lead, a walkway on the Tower curtain wall, and made his way back to her, bowing more elaborately at every passing, until even the guards were laughing. While they were distracted, Robin slipped her a note and disappeared inside Beauchamp.

"The breeze from the river is chilling," Elizabeth announced, and was immediately taken back to her cell.

Not knowing which of her Spanish ladies might be spying on her, unable to resist performing a valuable service for the reigning queen or her council, Elizabeth waited to unfold the scrap of vellum until she was in her alcove bed just before she pinched out the candle. *Semper Eadem*, it read. *Always the same*, Robin had written. It had double meaning, being Anne Boleyn's motto and now, apparently, Robin's promise to her. And hers to him, she thought, kissing the paper. . . . Always, always the same.

Ro-bin. Ro-bin. His name is like the beat of my own heart. Elizabeth turned her face into her bolster. *When I am queen, we will never be parted. I will ever command it.*

She pressed the note against her breast, where it warmed her through the chill, dark night in her cell.

CHAPTER 6

❧

THE OTHER

---❧---

EARL OF LEICESTER

October 1585

Nonsuch Palace

*J*ohn, she will not let me go!" His body servant could not help him, but his need for understanding overwhelmed good sense.

Two months had passed since Robert, Earl of Leicester, rode into Nonsuch to rejoin the council and help plan to meet the Holland crisis. Most nights he slept fitfully, once again finding himself immersed in court ritual, his life directed again by Elizabeth's will and whim, sometimes sure of her intention to name him head of her army and at other times as unsure of her intention as ever. As unsure, perhaps, as she was about going to war.

Last night, he had found little rest in his bed and now rose to a gray sky promising blustery rain. He stretched his aching joints while his body servant, John Tamworth, dressed him, carefully brushing his dark velvet doublet, having great care for the precious gold metal threads woven into the bear-and-double-ragged-staff insignia he wore on his sleeve and the heavy jeweled embroidery everywhere.

Staring out his tall oriel window overlooking the four-story central gate of Nonsuch, he gazed beyond the great curtain wall to the fields and thick woods beyond, its leaves falling thick in gold and red—the color of Elizabeth's hair?—to carpet the landscape. He smiled at the thought of Bess commanding the trees of her realm, but he believed it possible, nonetheless.

He grasped the window ledge to steady himself. The queen and Raleigh came riding across the fields and into the central courtyard, their high spirits and the clouds of frosty breath from their winded horses visible through the thick glass panes of his window.

God's bones! Raleigh dared ride so close, his knee touched Bess's tan buskin in the stirrup. And she did not appear to rebuke him! Instead, her face was alight, dewy fresh and young as she had ever been, her long veil flowing from her hat over her hunter's hindquarters. For every man who saw her, including himself, she was Gloriana!

Once, he would have been with her on their best hunters, racing through the deer park hot on the hunt, but not this day. She would have called at dawn for her Eyes, as she had long ago named him, because he seemed to see what she needed. But not this day. Today, she had ridden out laughing with Raleigh, whom she called Water because he had sailed to the New World, adding new and distant lands to her realm. Robert smiled. He had gotten a certain revenge when he'd given her a jewel from which hung an onyx water bucket. The symbolism had not escaped her. Although she had not laughed in Raleigh's presence, Robert suspected she had roared in the privacy of her privy chamber.

Had she really chosen Raleigh as her favorite, or had she rejected Robin, her lifelong love, having heard a vicious report about him from some lying ill-wisher?

"My lord," Tamworth said beside him, looking out the same window, "I cannot set your doublet to rights if you jolt about so." In a thoughtful voice, he added: "I know you are troubled about this current scandal."

"Troubled and heartsore." He shrugged. "But there have always been such terrible rumors. They whispered that I once poisoned the Earl of Essex, my wife's first husband, and the Lady Douglass's husband, Baron Sheffield."

Tamworth kept brushing. "My lord, no man with a beautiful wife can die in England but what you are suspected."

Robert had to smile. "Surely not."

"Aye, my lord, laugh at them."

"I will do more than laugh. I will call them out for the lying cowards they are." He frowned. "But I worry that Her Majesty . . . Bess . . ."

"She would never believe such a thing of you, my lord. I have seen her many moods, but never doubting your nobility and love for her without great pain."

"My good Tamworth. You know her as well as you know me."

"No, my lord, I would never think such, but I know that the queen would never believe such slanders of you. The lowborn must always devise lies about their betters to prove their own faults are little. Alehouse tittle-tattles have no greater lord to talk about than the Earl of Leicester."

"You take liberty to advise me?" He hadn't realized until this moment, though he should have, that knowing so much made Tamworth think himself higher than a servant . . . a confidant.

He shrugged. And why not? No man was a mystery to his body servant.

"I take liberty only for you, my lord, as I have done these many years since I came to you as a young man. I would say nothing but what will do you good"—he laid his brush aside—"and I say again the queen will never believe such ill of you."

"But this latest slander!" Robert said, his voice breaking. "That I poisoned my own son because I didn't count him perfect . . . it's monstrous!"

"Aye, my lord, it is that, and will soon be replaced by another slur."

"How could any man think I could kill my own son and heir, least say the words publicly?" Robert asked, unable to accept such a villainy. The lie squeezed his heart until he could scarcely breathe and he felt guilt, not for himself, but for what he did think, an idea he tried to push away, though it would not stay in the dark corner where he pushed it.

Could Lettice have done such a deed? The boy had died so suddenly, without cause and with some signs of poison, although the doctors had assured him they thought it was a tertian fever, which had similar symptoms of coughing, sweat and stomach pains. Still, each time he reassured himself, suspicion lurked just beyond. Could his countess, Lettice, want so much for her older son, the Earl of Essex, to inherit his estates and title that she would kill her youngest boy, their only child in marriage, his one legitimate heir?

He tried to rid himself of such a thought, thinking instead of the delight Lettice had shown for this last child of her womb, the times he had seen them romping together on the lawns of Wanstead, their shouts of laughter difficult to separate. Yet the gloom outside his window and inside his heart did not help. If a bright sun had shone and Raleigh not been with Bess, he might have dismissed from his mind such evil thoughts about his wife, though they would return later. Why? Was it so easy for his heart to believe ill of her because he had suspected her of sending poisoned physicks to her first husband in Ireland?

Jesu help him! He had been glad of the earl's death of stomach complaints at the time, ignoring the rumors because he needed to. Lettice had come back to court after that summer with Bess at Kenilworth and again he was nearly crazed when she came to his bed every night costumed and perfumed as Elizabeth. When he closed his eyes, it was almost as if the long years of waiting for Bess to be in his bed again were over. It was almost as if he had won.

"My lord, refresh yourself," Tamworth said with a final swipe of the soft brush. He handed Robert a ready cup of ale and a silver plate of fine manchet bread centered with a meat pudding, still warm from the royal kitchens.

"The queen will expect her old Robin," his servant whispered confidentially as only he could, knowing much of what had passed between the queen and his master when they were younger, and now forever faithful and silent about what he knew.

The earl broke off a piece of bread and dipped it in the pudding. He took a bite and returned the rest to the plate, having no appetite. Today, he was determined to discover whether Bess's feelings for him were as they had ever been. He could never allow Raleigh, or any man, to take his place with her.

He left his loyal Tamworth behind and approached the presence chamber. Clerks with ink-stained fingers and porters with heavy chests were entering and exiting every door along the halls. The court was moving on to Greenwich Palace, Nonsuch being in great need of sweetening. This late-summer heat had made the queen's small palace too full of courtiers even more unlivable. Bad odors had always offended Elizabeth's delicate nose. Before he reached the presence chamber, he heard trumpets and drums ahead and saw the queen and her train of ladies and lords making their way past kneeling courtiers.

Robert pulled down hard on his doublet to hide his thickening waist and to safely express some frustration at the queen's inaction. For weeks now, he had put aside everything, all his grief and hurtful suspicions, for the greater needs of England. Still, she had been unable to make up her mind about naming him to head her army for the Netherlands, one day signing orders for troops and supplies, setting plans in motion, the next day recalling everything. Twice, he had left Nonsuch to gather troops, only to be overtaken on the road with her message commanding his return. Robert knew Bess's apprehension. She was always in hopes that inaction would allow time for a problem to resolve itself. And she had been right often enough to reinforce her natural inclination. But this time the Hollanders' situation had only grown worse, the Spanish army storming more towns, raping, looting, putting the burghers to the sword and, worse, to the stake as heretics.

"Come, my good Lord Leicester," the queen called, in full voice from her morning gallop with Raleigh and still pink faced from exercise, putting a glow to her mask. "We need you by our side." She waved at him a large sprig of thyme she carried as a pomander and then returned it to her nose.

He bowed and moved to her side. "Majesty," he said softly in a voice that held all that he couldn't say to her aloud, "I am gladdened that you would still have need of your old Eyes."

She pinched his arm, her playful signal that she was happy to greet him. "Rob, why the gloomy face?" She tapped his chest with the thyme. "Are you angry that I did not ride out with you?"

He stiffened. "I would never criticize my queen for riding with any man she pleases."

She laughed and slipped her hand into his. "Then you have changed, my lord."

"I am older and wiser."

She tightened her hold on him, though she continued to nod to those bowing to her along the way. "I think I liked my young, very unwise Robin much better."

It seemed a good time to broach the open question that hung between them. "Bess, I have been waiting weeks for you to decide on the Netherlands matter and appoint me as your—"

Pup! Pup! She made her usual sounds of annoyance. "And you *will* wait, my lord of Leicester. You have truly changed, and much for the worse, if you do not like the company of your queen."

"Bess, you know that is not true, never true," he reassured her, as she needed him to do. And as *he* needed to do.

"I must have time to think of what sending an army to the northern Holland provinces would cost. There are heavy calls on my treasury to build more ships at Deptford. King Philip is gathering a huge fleet in Spanish ports to come against me. His Great Enterprise of England, he calls it. His ambassador reproached me—reproached *me*, a queen—for what a few pirates have taken from him. Philip blames me when, as all know . . ."

All did know at that. Elizabeth sent her sea dogs out to capture Spanish treasure, although she swore she did not.

Her voice was amused as it always was when she spoke of the Spanish king, once her brother-in-law and later a suitor for her hand. She had kept him dangling for several years.

Robert tried to control his anger as she avoided the issue at hand, and he gained control with sarcasm. "Of course, let us wait, Your Majesty. So a few town walls are overthrown and a few Protestant burghers, who look to the channel for us in vain, are becoming smoke for their religion—"

Behind her white Mask of Youth, he knew her face now reddened with anger. "Enough, my lord Leicester! Do not think because we raised you from the dust that we cannot return you there!"

She pulled her arm violently from his at the door to the presence chamber and he watched her stalk between rows of bowing petitioners and members of her court. They looked from her angry face to his wounded one and, having heard the hateful words, as she had intended, they were pleased at the queen's all too apparent fury. Few of them would not welcome an earl's downfall and the redistribution of his estates, where they might hope to catch some falling crumbs of wealth. Many tried to think of a way to sympathize with the queen's travails and see that it reached her ears. After a lifetime at Tudor courts, Robert knew exactly what was going through their ever-busy little minds, ready to grasp at all opportunity.

William Cecil moved up to stand by Robert, resting his gouty leg against his walking stick. "Good morrow, my lord," he said as Robert matched his stride to Cecil's halting steps. "I trust you do well."

"Well enough, Cecil," Leicester grumbled.

"Do not despair. The queen is slowly coming to see that she must keep the Hollanders from being overrun by Spain, or have England surrounded by a papist Europe that longs to come against us."

"I am happy to hear it, my Lord Treasurer, though I long to

hear it from Her Majesty's lips," Robert said. "I pray it's not too late to save the Hollanders." After they'd been early antagonists because of Cecil's fear that Elizabeth would marry her Eyes, their long years of working together on the council had made them into cordial enemies and—in late years, after all hope of their marriage had passed—collaborators for the queen's good. Although there was one slight difference remaining: Cecil did what was for England's good, and Robert what was good for Elizabeth. Sometimes, as now with the Dutch question, the two coincided.

"And, my lord," Cecil added, moving slowly away toward his place near the throne, "do not be disturbed by the ugly gossip about court."

"My lord, if I know names, I will call out the blackguards."

"Have a care, my lord Leicester; you know the queen's mind about dueling."

"I'll risk the Tower to protect the honor of my name."

Cecil was now out of hearing, but Dr. Dee heard him and moved near him until his philosopher's black gown with its huge hanging sleeves, covered in stars and signs of the heavens, touched Leicester's boots. "My lord," the doctor said, "remember that you and the queen were born under the same sign of the Virgin, which is ruled by the planet Mercury."

Robert looked grim. "The same god Mercury who had wings on his feet."

"Just so, my lord."

Robert had to suppress a raucous laugh. "Doctor, I think Her Majesty's wings might have been clipped."

"Remember the Virgin's sign also puts great study and detail into her understanding before she acts on her duty."

"But I am not so, and we were born under the same stars, as you say."

"Aye, my lord, but the male is urged on by his natural essence of manly combat. His wings are not clipped."

Robert smiled, somewhat rueful. "Except by a virgin queen."

"We will look into my scrying glass, my lord, and call a spirit to tell us what your future holds."

"I will have naught to do with sorcery."

"No sorcery, my lord."

Robert's tight mouth relaxed. "Then I thank you, Doctor."

"Come to me in the third hour after twelve of the clock." Dee moved away, his once-grand velvet gown a little frayed from sweeping the floor behind him.

The presence chamber was full of petitioners and foreign ambassadors seeking recognition for the gifts they presented. Today's pearls, emeralds and tiny skeletons of curious horse-headed sea creatures were notably ordinary, since the queen scarcely gave them a second look.

Raleigh approached with a string of pearls of modest size, but lustrous. He did not mount to the throne, and instead handed his gift to one of the queen's ladies. "Majesty, fain would I climb, but that I fear to fall."

He thinks to get an invitation before the court, Robert thought.

Elizabeth looked at Raleigh, amused. "If thy heart fail thee, sir, do not climb at all."

The court laughed and Raleigh bowed to hide his consternation.

Satisfied, Robert motioned a servant to him and then stepped forward and knelt before the canopied throne with Elizabeth's motto, *video et taceo*, written behind in gilt letters. He offered a rare unicorn's horn on a purple-and-gold-tasseled velvet pillow and raised his eyes to the queen. "Majesty, it is said that the horn of the unicorn protects against poisoning. While I am away from you in Holland, it will shield you from ill. If you take a small amount ground into milk or oil before eating any food, or drinking any wine, its magical properties will surely protect you from evildoers and thereby comfort my heart as I lead your army." There, that should halt any evil whisperers, who always thought he sought the throne, a dream he had forsaken to keep Bess's love.

Robert could see that the queen was pleased that he had a thought for her life, but was less pleased he took his appointment as lieutenant general of her army for granted. "Your life is precious to all England," he added, his eyes on her face, seeing her as he always saw her, young and beautiful and ready for his kiss, never to change, God willing.

"My lord, we thank you for having such care for us. We have made no decision about the Dutch Protestants, but when we do, we are more certain than ever that we would make a right choice in you." She motioned for him to stand, which he did gladly to spare his knees from the unyielding marble floor.

Robert refused to allow his heart to beat faster, or his hopes to rise, to even think that she had finally decided to name him head of her army. He had not been on the battlefield since he was a young man. He must prove to Bess, and perhaps to himself, that the Earl of Leicester could lead an army to victory as well as a Devon country knight could sail an ocean to Virginia.

The queen motioned to Sir Francis Walsingham, her spymaster, and he stepped forward from the crowd of councilors. "Your Grace, my lords and gentlemen," he began, "we have received sad news that Antwerp has fallen to the Duke of Parma's Spanish army. The situation in Holland is now dire."

So the trouble had not fixed itself, as Bess had hoped and probably prayed. Above the murmurings of the court, Robert raised his voice. "I beg Your Majesty, there is time for no more delay, or the northern provinces of the Dutch will be past any remedy an English army can bring."

"Surely God will be moved to help them," the queen said, but she no longer seemed convinced by her own words. Everyone in the presence chamber looked to Elizabeth for her resolution, and with a great sigh she raised her hand to stop Robert from proceeding. "I see that there is no other assistance for this. We must be drawn into their fight, but it will be on my terms, my lord. Come to me in my privy chamber later, my lord of Leicester."

"When, Majesty?"

Her white shoulders rose and fell, anxiety plain on her face. "We will send for you."

Is this yet another delay? He feared so when hours passed and her call did not come; indeed, the queen was said to be distracted by a gaggle of country dancers.

In the third hour after noon, he went to Dr. Dee's library and chambers. "I must know what the future holds, Doctor, or else I shall go mad waiting."

Dee smiled. "Her Majesty keeps you here because she thrives with you beside her and fails when you are gone from her."

Robert hoped that was true, but he also knew that Bess desired to keep him from his wife. Which was more true?

"Come with me," Dee said, and led the way into his library, said to hold the rarest books in the world, including a copy of Guillaume Postel's *De Originibus*, which revealed through the medium of an Ethiopian priest the language God had taught to Adam in the Garden of Eden. Dee had been trying to decipher it for years, but so far had failed.

The doctor sent his servants from the room after one poured two cups of wine.

When the doors had closed, Dee locked them. "What I am about to show you, my lord, is often misunderstood. Ignorant people think I call upon devils."

Robert did not speak, but he was uncomfortable. Taking part in magical séances was against the church's teaching. There were departures from scripture that even an earl should not make, and this was one. Still, his need to see his future was the greater need.

"Sit here, my lord," Dee said after they finished their wine, patting the back of a chair set square in front of a viewing glass the size of a large open book. It rested on a stand placed upon a small table made of various light and dark woods and much carved. The doctor lit a candle in front of the glass. One by one, Dee snuffed out every other light in the room, but the room continued as bright as before. It seemed that a hundred candles were reflected in Dee's scrying glass, each candle growing smaller until the last was but a dot of light with nothing but darkness beyond.

"What now, Doctor?"

Dee bent over Leicester's shoulder and called: "Uriel, I have need of you."

Robert half rose. "Are you calling your spirit familiar?"

"Quiet yourself, my lord. In order to see and hear, you must look into the light without wavering."

"I see nothing."

"My lord, I will call again upon the angel Uriel, who will deliver your message." He took a deep breath. "Uriel!"

Again, Robert almost stood in alarm until he felt Dee's hand hard on his shoulder.

"Do not be uneasy," Dee said again. "Uriel is an angel of God, not an imp of Satan. First, we must pray for God's guidance."

Robert prayed for a release of tension, to know whether Bess trusted him with the Dutch mission, even if the knowing was not to his liking. His body tensed to escape if a horned devil appeared in the mirror with an answer.

Dee, his hands still prayerful, called again on Uriel to appear.

"I yet see nothing," Robert said, and though the doctor had cast his horoscope and Elizabeth's, he thought perhaps Dee was going too far into witchery with his scrying glass.

"You must look deeper into your heart, repeating your question again and again. Let your body float. Allow Uriel to be your guide into the light."

For long minutes, Robert tried to relax his tense body with no success, but gradually Dee's soft, resonant, insistent voice crept into his head and he felt a kind of floating numbness, like a too-large draft of brandy flooding his empty stomach. As he stared into the candle's many reflections, he felt as if he were taken by a hand and led into the light and sensed that he was following the light.

An unearthly voice echoed through his mind. "I am the angel Uriel. I stand in front of God's throne with the archangels. What do you wish to know?"

Robert gripped the table, fearing to be pulled into the mirror. He feared nothing that was earthbound, but this! Yet he had come for an answer and he must not cower. "Will the queen appoint me to lead her army to save the Dutch, or will she choose some other man? A certain Walter Raleigh?"

No answer came for some time. Finally, the voice echoed again: "Death will come to the cursed."

Robert drew back, breaking his sight line. Was he cursed?

Dee's hand was on his shoulder. "Steady, my lord. Uriel has not finished."

Robert looked into the light again, though only the most distant light still shone bright.

He heard the spirit voice, faintly now. "She will live long, but so cursed, she will lose all."

"Who?" Robert demanded. "Not Elizabeth."

"No, the other," Uriel said from beyond the last candle, which went out, leaving the glass dark except for Robert's own faint reflections.

Robert shook himself. "I don't understand. If not the queen, who is the other?"

Dr. Dee went round the room relighting all the candles, then returned to Robert and sat in a near chair. "My lord, I have found that these things come clear when we pray about them."

Robert shook his head, stood and walked about the room, even behind the glass, suspicious and still only half believing. He was relieved that no smell of brimstone filled his nose.

"The answer will come, my lord."

"I yet do not have an answer to what I asked."

Dee bowed his head and plucked at a loose star on his robe. "I have also found, my lord, that it is usually the answers we are afraid to hear that are slowest to reveal themselves."

At that moment there came a cry at the hall door. "Make way for the queen."

The door was unlocked and opened. Robert and Dr. Dee both bowed as Queen Elizabeth swept in, motioning her ladies to remain in the hall.

"Majesty," Dee said, and Robert heard the doctor's voice shake.

Robert bowed again to hide the dozen thoughts that must show on his face, his mind thinking of several possibilities, all of them not in his favor. *Is Dee in league with Raleigh and this a trap to accuse me of consorting with Satan? Calling demons?*

"Robin," the queen said, her voice private and petulant, as if Dr. Dee were not in the room. "My lord Leicester, I called for you and you were not in the castle. My pensioners looked everywhere. I thought you gone to your manor of Wanstead against my orders."

Robert felt worry leave his face, because it was clear by Elizabeth's expression that she was both jealous and relieved to find him. "As you see, most gracious Majesty, I am in the palace. Wherever I am, I am always near to you," he added, looking into her eyes, which were now growing bluer.

Elizabeth's face relaxed. It was the answer she needed. "You will not find my decisions in my good philosopher's glass. Not even Dee's angel knows my mind. Come," she added, taking his arm with a tug of authority, "we'll have supper together in my chambers."

"A great honor, Your Grace," Robert said. And it was. Very few people were invited to dine with Elizabeth. She preferred to eat alone and in private except for state banquets honoring some foreign ambassador or suitor, although there were no suitors left now that she had passed childbearing age. Praise be to God. He would no longer have to fear losing her to a foreign prince who would see that he was dismissed from all his posts of influence near Elizabeth. Or have him murdered.

Even a queen regnant had to obey a husband, since it was God's will that women, no matter how high, obey their masters. It was the order of things that God Himself had created, and so it would have been had Bess married him . . . as she had known.

Their supper was regally served, but finally the queen's attendants were dismissed. He was alone with Bess in the room that held many of their life's memories. In this room he had hoped to make her his wife, coming close, many times . . . so close. And in this room she had refused him until it was too late. After that glorious summer at Kenilworth ten years earlier, he had accepted that she would never marry him and had rushed to marry Lettice for his last chance at an heir, hoping to love her enough to find some happiness.

The queen's privy chamber was lit by the fireplace and a many-stemmed candelabra on the table, the light dancing over the queen's face as she nibbled at her food. When he was honest, he had to admit that she had lost her soft, youthful beauty, but the remarkable woman beside him had taken the girl's place. God help him! He loved both, the young princess with the love of a youth, aching heart and stiffened cock, and the woman and queen he knelt to and served with his heart and all of his body, mind and soul.

Although he was weighted with such memories, Robert had a hearty appetite, having consumed but one bite earlier in the day. He tried to eat sparingly, as Bess did, but his belly growled at him and he took another helping of apple tart, full of vanilla bean and spices, as the queen liked it.

As usual, Bess did not neglect her cautions about his health. "You must promise me, Rob, to eat sparingly of the rich Hollander food," she advised, frowning.

He swallowed the last of his tart and promised, though he reminded her: "A soldier marches upon his stomach, Bess."

"Then you will march the entire length of that besieged country on yours."

He bowed his head and she covered his hand with one of hers in gentle apology for her chiding. With her other hand, she caressed the Turkish carpet covering the table, obviously loving its weave. At last she gave him her orders, the red wax royal seal hanging from it. "Promise me, Rob, you will not hazard a battle without having great advantage and good care for yourself. Do not go in front of your men."

"But, Majesty, I cannot play the coward while I order my men into battle."

"Promise me, or I will choose a more cautious man to lead them. Jesu knows, I have them about me in plenty."

His shoulders sagged. This was his first defeat of the campaign. "I promise to keep myself safe as I can in honor, Bess." He leaned down and kissed her hand where it lay upon his, hoping she would not notice the less than complete promise he had given her.

"Now go, my lord of Leicester, before I change my mind, for I sorely miss you already."

He did not remind her, because he didn't need to, that it had always been her choice, never his, that he not be on the throne and in her bed at her side forever. But he could not bring himself to say it. "Bess," he whispered, "my heart is always with you."

She released his hand slowly, then turned her head away from him, never able to see him close the door on her. He stood and bowed, his hand on his heart, and murmured, "My long love," then backed away to her outer chamber, his hand still warm from her touch. He was quickly in the hall leading to his own apartment next to hers. *She loves me still, though Raleigh will quickly grow in favor while I am away. Like her father, she needs, always, to feed on the thrill of adoration and the new. I must show her such victory that she will turn from Raleigh when she receives news of what I have wrought for her and for England.*

Victory seemed less likely later as he strode toward his quarters and quickly opened and read the royal charter. He was to fight a purely defensive war, ensuring that the Dutch paid for much of it. *But they can't pay for a smaller war now!* He did not allow the wrathful complaint to escape his mouth. All palace walls had ears and eyes.

Bess had also laid claim to two prosperous Dutch towns, which were to be taxed for the war and to repay her treasury. "S'bones!'" he yelled at poor Tamworth, as soon as he reached his quarters, where all peepholes had been plugged and all doors were guarded, by his own men, against spying. "This is a plan for total failure!" He read on with a sinking heart. Why did she do this? Was it her natural caution in war, or was it deliberate? Did she not want him to succeed? He tried to deny the thought, but doubts rose even though he struggled to hold them at bay.

The queen had named him a lieutenant general of her forces, but he was also to endow the Dutch assembly with full powers. It was a sure formula for conflict.

He drew in several deep breaths before he read further. *We command that by no means are you to accept any title from their assembly other than the one we gave you and on pain of your sovereign's unalterable displeasure are you to accept their throne.*

So that was her fear! She had not allowed him to be king beside her, nor would she allow him to be king in any other country. She would tie him to her forever.

The charter also limited him to one thousand cavalry and six thousand foot soldiers against the Spanish Duke of Parma's army, one of the largest and best trained on the Continent.

Robert groaned as he and Tamworth immediately began to cloak themselves for travel. "She has no liking for this cause. She gives me few troops and less money and authority than I need. Victory is almost impossible."

"Nay, my lord, Her Majesty thinks that you of all her lords

can work miracles for her because you have her in your heart. When you return to England the port of Calais that her sister, Queen Mary, lost, she will—"

"Stop! There was ever only one thing that I have wanted from Bess and that is all past and done."

Tamworth did not reply, but Robert knew what his servant thought. And he thought the same. Past, perhaps, but never done.

He dared not wait the night and risk Bess's mind-change, for her mislike of this cause was plain both spoken and written. He would be on the road at night with torchbearers going before to light the way to London.

With a retinue of only twenty men, he left Nonsuch in the cold night, looking back to see if Bess was at her window. He was certain she was wakeful, but she did not watch him leave, as she never had. He could not be sure that she was unhappy at his leave-taking, though she had claimed the sight of it to be beyond her ability to bear. Sometimes Robert believed one thing and sometimes the other, and he wondered if that was true of all those who loved too much and in vain.

Once away, he heard Dee's angel's voice in the beat of horses' hooves all about him: *No, the other.* What other? Another woman? His wife, Lettice? Had Uriel seen into the darkest suspicion of his heart and answered it?

Robert reached London and clattered across London Bridge just as pale dawn broke over the city and river fog swirled low in the city streets. The tradesmen were out in front of their ware benches, displaying their knit caps and vests and raised pattens, the overshoes that protected expensive boots and slippers from street mud and refuse. Carters filled the streets crying their fresh fish, the last of the fall fruit harvest and fresh-baked bread, some of which was undoubtedly yesterday's. Serving maids were at the wells filling their wooden buckets, yelling strong words at his men when their horses splattered them with street rubbish.

They stopped near St. Paul's to water their horses, the Tower looming nearby. Though London had almost doubled in size in the last twenty-six years of Elizabeth's reign, little else had changed since he'd ridden behind Bess in her coronation procession down this street toward Westminster Abbey. Although she had already been queen for two months since her sister, Mary, had died, she was finally to be anointed and proclaimed England's queen by God's priests.

CHAPTER 7

❦

QUEEN ELIZABETH'S CORONATION DAY

EARL OF LEICESTER

January 15, 1559
London

*L*ord Robert Dudley paced in the hall outside the royal apartments in the Tower, where every English king and queen, by custom, spent the night before their coronation. He had dressed carefully for Elizabeth in his new heavily embroidered black velvet suit, snowy white ruff and cuffs, a cuirass of polished, beaten silver spanning his chest, a fur-lined cape thrown over one shoulder and his feathered cap atilt over his right eye. Scarlet knit hosen outlined his long legs, and his feet were shod in black Spanish boots oiled to a bright sheen. The polished steel mirror at the far end of the anteroom showed his full image to his great satisfaction, reflecting the jewels on his sword hilt as they sparkled in the torchlight. He was satisfied that he would make a grand appearance that day, the most important of his life as well as Elizabeth's.

He waited eagerly to be summoned by the newly reigning queen of England. He had not been alone with her since they'd left Hatfield, her childhood home, where she'd received news of her sister Queen Mary's death along with the coronation ring and tales of rejoicing in London. Bells had rung from each steeple, bonfires flared in every major thoroughfare and tables loaded with food and ale were set in the streets for all comers.

After accepting the royal ring and thanking God, Bess had immediately sworn all to allegiance in the great hall at Hatfield. She named Lord Robert Dudley her Master of Horse and Revels, a position which they both knew would keep them always close.

As he had knelt before her, she had raised him before all. "We do not forget, Lord Robert, that you comforted us in the Tower and that you sold your own land to give us money when we were kept in penury by our sister, the late queen. Therefore, we command that you be always near to us"—she lowered her voice to a playful whisper for his ears alone—"both day and night."

He had almost jumped up, hope rising against all experience, even against his married state, that she would say more, but the queen continued with business, naming others to high posts in the realm while he offered a quick prayer that Amy forgive him for his most private wishes. God alone knew that he wished her no harm, though he wished as heartily not to be married to her. He would be free to marry Bess, ever his real love. Although he had gained the property and income he had desired— indeed, had to have after his father was executed—he had also gained a clinging wife who wanted him to settle into being a minor country noble, always within her sight. The thought of that life left him as cold as did Amy's bed.

At Hatfield, Elizabeth continued her appointments in her royal voice that had seemed to arrive with the coronation ring. Her words carried to all, including the new Lord Secretary, William Cecil. "My Lord Secretary Cecil, our first decree as queen is that all our subjects, Catholic and Protestant, be free of harrying for their beliefs. We would make no windows into men's souls."

She had not stopped with this queenly concern for her subjects, but had further decreed that her coronation was to be held in both English and Latin.

Robert nearly laughed aloud. A clever compromise for those who wished her to declare herself either Catholic or Protestant, and so like Bess, who always said, "Take the middle ground."

Then she had announced in the regal tone that he granted came easily to her: "The word of God and His apostles should be hidden from no man." And it was clear to Robert that she meant to change the Latin services, as she had once told him privately, to English ones in every church. She meant to return the Church to the one her father had decreed.

The Catholics in the hall were not pleased, but they hid their consternation until Elizabeth further announced that at her own anointment with the holy oil as queen there would be no elevation of the host. Ah, this was defiantly Protestant.

Their faces grew dark at that, but Robert knew that they did not dare challenge her right as governor of the Church of England, at least not yet. But they would. He was not the only one present to understand that this woman meant to take her father's place in all matters of the realm. Some of the bishops present planned already to defy her in Parliament. They believed that a woman could not rule unless she was guided by men to right courses, whether church, marriage, or realm.

They did not know Elizabeth Tudor as he did, although she

could still surprise him, as she had when she named her councilors so fast he knew she must have been thinking of whom she wanted as advisors for some time, maybe for her life long.

Robert was recalled to the present by John Carpenter, a gentleman in the queen's guard. "My lord Dudley," he announced in a newly ponderous voice from the doors leading to the royal suite. Upon Elizabeth's arrival in London, she had named the former Tower guard who had once befriended her during her imprisonment to her personal retinue. Like her father, Bess never forgot a hurt or a service.

The guard called Robert's name again. He marched quickly through the open door and knelt before his queen, who was wearing her crown, lined with crimson velvet, encircled by a starburst of rubies, diamonds, sapphires and pearls.

For a moment, Robert was breathless at first sight of her in her golden, ermine-edged coronation robes. Was this his Bess, little Bess of their childhood games at Greenwich Palace, Bess of their breathless rides in Windsor Great Park and Bess of their youthful stolen kisses? Bess, who was soon to be his anointed queen?

His throat tight and full enough to make swallowing difficult, he filled his eager eyes with her . . . the queen of his dreams and now queen of all. "Majesty, I always believed that I would see you thus in your rightful place."

"Sweet Robin," she murmured, and gave him her hand to kiss. With a little laugh, she curled her fingers around his chin, stroking his mustache with her forefinger.

He captured her fingers and kissed them one by one. "Bess, I am beyond happiness this morning, as I hope you are."

"Yes, Robin, how could I not be?" she asked, retrieving her

hand and stretching from having posed so long. "Surely this is the Lord's doing."

He grinned. "Bess, you helped the Lord as no one else could. All these years, you kept your lovely head and they could not break you even in the Tower dungeon."

"Nor imprisoned at Woodstock for the next year, suspected of every crime against God and my sister, the queen. Now I am in the Tower again, but not awaiting my end—"

He interrupted. "Your beginning."

"Aye, Robin, where I belong, not in a traitor's cell, but in the royal apartments."

Robin knew that Bess thought of one queen in particular, Anne Boleyn. But the daughter never said her mother's name. Still, he knew with that dead queen's daughter on the throne, no one could defame Anne Boleyn without harsh retribution. Englishmen would have to watch their tongues or have them slit. For the first time he noticed a quiet painter at work in the corner.

"She is painting a miniature of my coronation portrait," the queen explained.

Robin stood and went to look at Levina Teerlinc's work. The woman trained in Flanders had already been appointed miniaturist to the queen, and for good reason. "Mistress Teerlinc, you have captured the soul of Elizabeth, queen of England." He looked back at the queen. "Majesty, I must have one for my own to look at when I have a sudden need."

Robert heard the queen laugh at his obvious meaning. Elizabeth had a liking for raucous humor and knew she could now indulge it with no one to object.

Readjusting her coronation robes in a sweep across her lap, accentuating her small, jeweled waist, she thrust her hands through the opening, one hand holding the orb and the other the scepter. She nodded to Teerlinc to continue and he was dismissed.

He bowed and backed away from the queen, observing royal courtesy. Before he was out the door, she said, "You will ride behind our canopied litter to Westminster. We will be content and safe when we can see you close to us."

He bowed at the door. She was showing him great favor, and from the warmth of her hand . . . its slight tremor when he touched it . . . he knew enough about women to sense longing. She expressed every delight in him. He wondered if she'd pull away if he tried to test her womanhood too closely. He would be careful and look for an invitation. He smiled to himself, knowing that soon he would be admired openly by the ladies at court. Jealousy was Elizabeth's only weakness.

Did she allow him to see her need for him because he had a wife that made Elizabeth safe from her own desires . . . safe from her own scarcely hidden fears of marriage and childbirth? All women feared childbirth, but Bess had the greatest fear he had ever known, since her stepmother Catherine Parr had died after birthing a daughter in great pain, only for both mother and daughter to die days later. It was a dread for which he couldn't find an answer, perhaps didn't want to find an answer. And because of Amy, his sworn wife, he didn't need to find one. Did he? His own thoughts ran in ever tighter circles.

If he hadn't married in youth for a few parcels of land and a small manor house and, yes, to come to a woman in his bed whenever he liked, would Bess have been his? He doubted her brother or sister would have consented, certainly not their councilors. He pushed the question away a moment later, feeling suddenly disloyal to Amy, though they had seldom lived together and she had proved barren. She'd clung to him until his boyish affection was suffocated.

His thoughts flew here and yon, always coming back to the same question. Henry had made divorce possible, but would Amy agree to it? Would Bess? His heart seemed to skip beats as he thought of marrying Elizabeth. Would the realm accept a divorced man as their king? Not the Catholics, surely, who had never accepted Henry VIII's divorces. And not many of the Protestants, either. Yet could anything now stop Bess from what she truly wanted?

He acknowledged that his father and grandfather had been executed as traitors, but they had been accused by succeeding reigns they had not served, their heads offered up as retribution for past sins against the new monarch's allies. If he could get Parliament to rescind his forebears' sentences, or at least lift the attainders on their estates . . . He shook his head to clear such hopeless thoughts from his mind. Yet they lingered in his heart.

Robert descended to the courtyard near the west gates, mounted and steadied his great black horse. The coronation procession needed only its queen to begin. Within minutes Elizabeth appeared and entered the chapel of St. Peter in Chains, where her mother's body was buried—alongside her severed head—to pray alone. Bess's father had decreed that the grave would go forever unmarked, so to Bess, the entire church was her mother's marker.

Horses whinnied and stomped, a light snow beginning to fall as a long retinue formed. Gentlemen pensioners, close servants of the queen and the nobles of England, including the Duke of Norfolk, Earl Marshal of England, who was by rank the personal protector of the queen, stood ready to form a retinue. Norfolk did not nod to Robert, but ignored him completely. Robert smiled to himself at the man's obvious jealousy, but could not stop himself from a little bravado. "My lord Norfolk, if the queen's train moves too fast for those of you on foot, you will cry out to slow us, if it please you."

Norfolk did not turn his head, or answer.

The duke, highest noble in the realm, thought himself fully qualified to be king of England and, if not due to his already having a wife, to marry Elizabeth . . . at the very least to guide the young queen in all she did. But Elizabeth had already openly rejected his counsel on several occasions, making him the sullen man marching beside her today.

Robert knew the duke blamed Robert's influence and not his own arrogance for the queen's dislike. He was furious that Robert Dudley had been named to follow immediately behind Elizabeth's gold-brocaded litter and his brother, Ambrose Dudley, to lead her horse.

Robert saw Ambrose take his place, holding the lead reins of two white horses. The queen exited the chapel and with a look of solemn triumph on her face was assisted into the golden litter, open so that her people could see her and she could see her people. Pride swelled in Robert's chest. *This is my love who is now queen.*

The long train of nobles and knights, city officials and guilds proceeded through the length of London in the Procession of Recognition, down Cheapside, past Smithfield floating with the ghosts of Protestant martyrs and on to Fleet Street toward King Street that led to Whitehall and Westminster Abbey beyond. The streets had been swept, and citizens wore their best, except for the poor, who had no best but wore their everyday tatters joyously. Each towering, half-timbered house bent together over the streets was dressed in rich tapestries and colorful banners.

Citizens knelt streetside and called: "God bless our queen!" At every intersection, poems and prayers, even short plays, were recited for her, some practiced, some halting, but all heartfelt. The queen waved to all and stopped to listen. "Thank you, my good and well-loved subjects," she called repeatedly in the tender language she used to all her gathered people, as if she were a mother talking to beloved children.

She patted the head of a ragged little girl, who handed her a bunch of gray winter rosemary with her mitten-covered hands. The golden queen kissed the sprigs and laid them on her Bible.

It was freezing. Robert wondered how Bess could bear the cold even under lap furs. But when she looked back for him, as she did often, her face shone with all the joy she had been denied for her twenty-five years of life. As they passed Fleet River, he called: "Are you cold, Majesty?"

"No, my lord, I feel nothing but the firm weight of the crown on my head."

Robert rejoiced with her as four pageants were presented along the way. The last one allowed Elizabeth to show herself to the people at her best. Robert knew they would never forget it, as he would not. This was her stage and her audience.

She smiled and waved and said in a voice many could hear, "I shall continue your good lady and be as good unto you as ever a queen was unto her people. No will in me can lack; neither shall there lack any power. For the safety and quietness of you all, I will not spare, if need be, to spend my blood."

The cheers were deafening and Robert knew that she had locked herself into their hearts today as she had his long ago, and taken the key.

As they rode the last mile, he wondered from where such speech full of grandeur had come. Was it the magic of the Boleyn temptress combined with Henry's majesty that gave Bess the words and voice she needed just when she needed them, words that might live on when all on earth now were gone?

His own heart soared with her remembered phrases, though he knew beyond doubt that she loved England more than she loved him. His heart ached as if it would never stop.

Hours later, when they finally passed through the Holbein Gate at Whitehall on their way to the abbey, she was as upright as when she'd begun her journey to the throne. The little girl's rosemary remained on her lap.

Robert saw a thousand candles lighting Westminster Abbey for Elizabeth's crowning. The Archbishop of Canterbury had refused to speak the coronation service in English, so Elizabeth had chosen the Bishop of Carlisle, who had fewer scruples and a brighter future. He awaited her now at the throne of Edward the Confessor.

The long service and anointment was a blur of smoking candles and shuffling feet to him until Elizabeth, the anointed queen of England, walked back down the scarlet-clad aisle, her train carried by a sour-faced Duchess of Norfolk. Elizabeth wore a brilliant smile under her high-arched Plantagenet nose and carried her orb and scepter as if they had no weight at all. She had won, Robert knew. Escaped the ax her jealous sister had planned for her beautiful neck, escaped even those who had meant her good, like Thomas Wyatt. He had raised rebellion in her name and nearly brought her to the block.

As she reached Robert kneeling in the aisle, she slowed and he looked up. Her eyes were swimming with pride and emotion. He could not help but wink before she moved on. He would have taken her to his breast if such a thing were possible, but she had stopped in recognition of him. That was enough for now.

Still, Robert knew that Elizabeth was not safe on her throne, might never be safe. Disaffected English Catholics thought killing her was their assurance of heaven, and Protestants wanted her to go further in changing the Church than she would be willing to go, always treading the solid middle ground . . . making haste slowly. The poison cup and the dagger would be a constant threat. Outside her realm Spain and France coveted her island. Enemies crowded Elizabeth's England from within and without. He breathed deeply, knowing that he alone would be her chief guard, with his body between her and any assassin. At this moment of her glory he dedicated the rest of his life to her happiness and safety.

Yet, as queen of England, she had come this far and he did not doubt that she would cling to her throne with the strength of her father's right and for her mother's vindication. And at her side, he would stand tall.

That night at Whitehall Palace in the great hall the coronation dinner lasted until one in the morning. Norfolk had his moment when, as the fully armored Earl Marshal, he rode his horse into the hall and in an ancient ritual threw down his gauntlet: "I, the Earl Marshal of England, challenge any man to dispute Elizabeth Tudor's right to the throne."

Bess was delighted with the ceremony and raised her cup to Norfolk, but her gaze was on Robert. Now she had to hide nothing. Who could deny her?

But he couldn't rush to her and lift her from her throne, holding her close for all to see.

Robert Dudley had to hide everything.

CHAPTER 8

❧

ALWAYS THE SAME

---- ❧ ----

ELIZABETH

Early December 1585
Greenwich Palace

*R*obin had not been gone four days as her lieutenant general, but to Elizabeth it seemed forever. Why had he not returned? Did he think that she would truly allow him to go from her? She must have him by her side always. This sorry Holland business had been thrust upon her and she regretted having agreed to it.

She paced to the end of her privy chamber and back many times, her hands warming in a small ermine muff. Usually, she loved the plush white fur on her fingers, reminding her of Robin's soft beard, but today it was a poor substitute for the touch she really needed. Soon, she heard a small commotion in her antechamber and went to stand by her writing table, where Lord Burghley also stood. At last, Robin had returned!

The queen's gentleman usher admitted an exhausted courier,

who knelt as Elizabeth took a vanilla comfit from her pocket to sweeten her stomach and stared at her antechamber doors with a ready smile of welcome. "Master Crowley, does the Earl of Leicester follow close behind?" By the courier's face, she could tell he had news that would not be to her liking.

"Majesty," the courier said looking up. "When I reached Harwich, my lord Leicester was beyond recall."

"Beyond recall!" She began to pace to the huge fireplace and back, to stand with her hands on her hips, the spreading red on her neck showing its true color beneath the white Mask of Youth. "Beyond recall? No subject is ever beyond recall of his sovereign!"

Crowley cleared his dusty throat and shifted to his other knee, but lowered his head. "Your Grace, His Lordship with all his fleet had cleared the harbor and with a good following wind was beating for the Holland coast."

Elizabeth paced about and then advanced on the courier. "Are there no other fast ships in my realm? Why did you not have one sent after him speedily?" She stomped away and back again in a fury, and thrust out her hand. "Return my letter to me."

The courier shifted uneasily, opening a pouch and withdrawing the sealed letter. "Majesty, I tried first to deliver it to Leicester House on the Strand, as you instructed me."

Elizabeth's face swelled now, but before her temper rose further, Burghley, who had been waiting quietly leaning on the writing table, spoke: "Majesty, may I have your leave to question the man?"

She nodded, unable to deny her councilor. She swallowed her rage, Cecil's calm voice bringing her back from supreme displeasure and disappointment. She had never wanted Robin to go to war, to be beyond her reach for weeks, months. Could it be years?

The Lord Treasurer spoke softly, but his chain of office gave him authority. "Tell me, Master Courier, what you did exactly."

"My lord Burghley, when I reached Leicester House, I found the earl already gone some two days from London, with all troops, his company of horse and the baggage train. Although the countess said she would follow her husband soon and demanded the letter, I did not give it to her." He took a deep breath. "Many baggage wagons were packed in the courtyard, and a great gold-trimmed coach with four white horses, very handsome with gold-trimmed harness, stood at the door."

Her Majesty advanced on the courier, frowning. "Christ's bones and chains! She leaves for Holland?" The queen's color was now very high and her face seemed to swell, setting the courier to trembling. "And she dared demand my letter?"

"Aye, but Your Grace instructed me to give it into Lord Leicester's hands, and although the countess was angry, I left her and sought to reach the port before His Lordship sailed."

"But you failed," Elizabeth interjected.

"Aye, Majesty. He sailed early, loading men and horses immediately without rest," Crowley said, his shoulders slumping.

The queen's eyes narrowed. "Stand up, Crowley." She turned to Cecil. "My Lord Treasurer, will you help this man to a cup of wine? We can see he is near to falling down."

"Thank you, Your Grace," the courier said, needing to clutch a stool to help him stand, though he still wavered on his feet. He gulped the wine quickly.

"Get you to my kitchens, courier, and refresh yourself and thence to your bed," the queen said, in a softer voice. "We will need you no more this day."

When the doors closed behind him, Elizabeth sat down on her high-backed chair near the fireplace, resting her chin on her hand. "Did you hear, Spirit," Elizabeth said, her voice now soft as a whisper, "that She-Wolf plans to follow Rob?" She lifted her head. "We will not have it! If she goes, she will meddle in affairs to the ruin of our plans. Prepare a warrant forbidding her to travel."

Fearless after more than thirty years of service to her, Cecil approached, saying in his solemn voice, "Forgive me, gracious Majesty, but the people will surely wonder if a lawful wife is kept from her husband."

"Let them wonder!" she said, her voice rising, not yet ready to give up her deep, resentful anger for the woman who had taken Robin from her, though not often and not for long.

As Cecil began to withdraw, the queen yelled, "Hold!"

Cecil returned to her, his mouth relaxed by relief. "Yes, Majesty."

"You are wise, Spirit. Allow her to depart." Elizabeth wasn't finished and, with a half smile, added, "She is restricted to three baggage wagons, only four ladies and no coach. No coach, do you hear? That She-Wolf will not queen it on the Continent."

"It will be so ordered, Your Grace," he said, bowing, his hand firmly on his walking stick to ease his gouty aches. He walked a few steps, then paused. "Majesty, please pardon my old legs for halting on your service."

She rose and went to him, putting her hand on his shoulder. "My Lord Burghley, you are close to us not for your bad legs but for your good head."

Burghley bowed where he stood and walked out of the chamber, his step firmer.

Elizabeth called in her favorite lady-in-waiting, Anne Warwick, wife of Robin's brother, Ambrose, the Earl of Warwick. "Anne, bring my best paper, blackest ink and fresh swan quills."

While waiting, she tore the undelivered summons into smaller and smaller pieces and tossed them into the fireplace.

After her writing materials were brought, Elizabeth moved to her writing table and bent her head to the letter.

> *Rob, we gave you leave to go, but you had no date certain. It grieves us to our heart that you felt free to depart so quickly without a final farewell.*

Elizabeth paused, taking in a deep breath before she dipped her quill again.

> *We had a thought to speak to our brave soldiers before they sailed to do God's good work for the Hollanders.*
>
> *But we do heartily acknowledge that your haste proceeded from no evil intent toward us, but from eagerness to do our will in this matter. Do not allow Others who follow you to do aught whatever to bring disgrace to you or to my authority.*

She had pressed her quill so hard, its point was dulled. She laid it aside for a fresh one with its feathers dyed green. Her Eyes' remembered face rose before her, he always young and at her feet, and all her anger flowed from her heart as the ink from her pen formed the words that he would read. Would to God she could write all that was in her heart, the deep feelings of love that never changed.

> *Remember our multiple cautions to our ÔÔ in this matter before you departed so hastily, espe-*

*cially to have good care in all that touches the sub-
ject we do esteem to be more greatly devoted toward
us than ever subject was to prince. As you know,
always the same,*

Elizabeth R.

She called for a special courier for the letter, not wishing it
to go through Cecil's hands and be copied by a secretary for the
official record. As queen, she had little privacy, was constantly
surrounded by the court and her councilors, but by Christ's
wounds and bones, she'd have this much with Robin now.

Privacy for them always had been something to snatch in
moments, not hours. Although for a time, in that first year of her
accession with Robin at her side, she had thought herself free of
limits and criticism . . . a glorious few months, the best and most
liberated she remembered of her life.

CHAPTER 9

❧

THE FIRST MONTHS OF HER REIGN

---- ❧ ----

ELIZABETH

September 1559
Hampton Court Palace

*E*lizabeth glanced over her shoulder and laughed, taunting
Robin, spurring her horse, a swift hunter he had brought
over from Ireland for her pleasure. She stirred a stiff breeze that
lifted her gold-strand hair netting. It sailed behind her, landing
on the knoll she'd just o'ertopped.

Entering a small copse of old oaks, she pulled sharply on the
reins and slid from the saddle, throwing herself on the soft, mossy
earth, her legs tingling from gripping her hunter's flanks. The
horse trailed its reins and frothed at the bit. He needed a rest and
so did she, though she'd never admit it. Glancing back, she saw
Robin spear her golden hairnet, which he carried to her on his
sword point, waving the net in the air like a tournament winner
with his lady's favor. Her stomach tightened, but not from a lack
of breaking her fast that morn. Hers was a hunger of another sort

and she steeled herself to resist it as she always must, while all the time seeking to satisfy it as far as she could.

Robin reined in and jumped down, removing the net and sheathing his sword. He bowed. "Your golden net, Majesty, although I would rather my eyes saw your hair unbound, falling about you as it is now." He knelt and leaned close, whispering, "You should never be enclosed in any part, Bess . . . except by me."

She laughed at his overconfidence, though his meaning was clear and sent quivering warmth through her belly.

Overconfidence was part of his strength; her strength was to resist him no matter how much she wished to be o'ertaken by desire. She thought to give him so much, but no more, or risk the love of her people. He was married to that pale, sickly country wench and, though he was from a noble family, he had not enough rank for a queen's husband. Oh, the entire idea of marriage to Robert Dudley was ridiculous, as her councilors repeatedly told her at every opportunity. In her own majesty, she agreed with them. There! Settled at last.

But for how long?

She extended her hand for Robin to kiss in reward for the net's return, but he took her hand, holding it to his heart as she had feared. Hoped? Christ's bones! All was churning confusion in her overheated breast.

"Surely, Bess," he said, lying beside her with only crackling leaves to separate them, his eyes glittering just inches from her face, always with a dark Gypsy brilliance, "I deserve greater reward for so valuable a rescue. I can always kiss your hand before the entire court, but"—he smiled and she caught her breath at his fiery gaze, sensing her will weakening—"I cannot always kiss your lovely lips as I would do now."

She glanced quickly behind him; then she forgot caution, forgot everything. The limbs and leaves swaying above them made intriguing patterns on his face and she thought him quite mysterious. One kiss only. They were quite alone for once, so why not allow herself what she wanted? A sweet kiss . . . like another of her favorite vanilla comfits? Only one show of affection that other women took without thought. Who could deny her? She was the queen!

But she didn't have to give him permission; her body moved of its own will toward his. He took her lips and she could feel his man's flaring heat flowing through her, firing her need for him, a need that she could never completely allow, or completely escape. His hands went around her waist and she knew that he would have pulled her closer to him if the sounds of horn and hoofbeats had not been so near. He opened her mouth, his tongue touching hers. She moaned, her cheeks flaming as his lips moved down to brand her breasts where they arched out over her gown and riding doublet as if asking for his kiss.

"Sweet Robin, help me . . . help me to remember my royal self," she whispered, her voice ragged as she pushed feebly against his doublet. "We cannot be seen like this."

"How can I help you, Bess, when I cannot help myself?"

She took in a deep breath, lest she faint. "I am not as other women. I can't—"

"No, not as others, but a woman nonetheless, Bess, and you know it. . . . You feel it."

"Majesty," shouted one of her gentlemen, stopping upon the knoll looking for the queen, "word comes from my lord Cecil and your council that an emissary of Sweden's Prince Eric has arrived in court with presents, eager to beg for your hand."

"Robin, we *must* go."

He helped her scramble to her feet and she quickly brushed leaves and twigs from her gown and his doublet while he stood patiently, looking with soft eyes at her face.

They strolled calmly out of the woods with their horses, as far apart as the trees would allow. Robin knelt to help her into the saddle. She tugged the reins hastily to move her horse away just as all her ladies and gentlemen pensioners broke out of the woods and into the open.

She did not dare to look at Robin, for she would look at him as a woman, heated beyond hiding by his lips.

But as queen, she threw back her head and laughed. "Ho! Put spurs to your horses, my lords and ladies!" She shouted the words gaily to the courtiers, who could see her flaming cheeks, and she hoped they assumed it was from the excitement of a prince's courtship. "We cannot wait all the day. We have at least ten other ambassadors at court seeking our hand for their princes. Shall we have a tournament to choose the winner?" She laughed and, with her golden net hanging from the pommel, raced them all back to the palace. Elizabeth did not look over her shoulder at Robin, following her closely as her Master of Horse should, though she heard him call to her on the wind. She knew what she would see in his dark face and she did not want to see it. She had a royal marriage game to play and she would not stop it, even for Robin.

Elizabeth turned her face toward the palace, hoping to cool it as she neared the great gardens her father had built for her mother, near the tennis court where her father had played. She saw her duty and the snares that lay in her path, Robin being the chief one. She could not help the satisfaction she felt at being courted by so many of the greatest men in Europe, but she could not allow Robin to see it, lest he think he rather than the prince of Sweden had put the contentment there. And, Jesu Christo, he would be right to think it!

A prince of Sweden now sends an ambassador to woo me to his cold country. She laughed aloud now, not caring whether she was heard. This offer would drive Philip of Spain mad when his ambassador wrote the news, which Alvarez de Quadra, Bishop of Aquila, was probably doing at this very moment. A Protestant alliance with Europe was Philip's great fear, one that had compelled him to offer the queen of England his own hand, fearing all the while that he could be denied and humiliated before all Catholic Europe by his former sister-in-law, a heretic woman . . . girl, really, daughter of a witchy-whore. She laughed again. The news that Sweden courted Elizabeth, as did the Earl of Arran from Scotland and a prince of France, would bring a flood of jeweled presents from Philip, whose treasure fleets brought him all the precious gold and silver of New Spain for his coffers.

Cecil had intercepted Philip's letters and she knew all his fears. Satisfaction filled her. A few months ago, less than a year, she was buried deep in the countryside, exiled from all state affairs and from her people. Her jealous sister, Queen Mary, on her deathbed mourned King Philip of Spain, a husband who had ruled with her but never loved her. What would Mary think now that Elizabeth had taken her throne and could, if she wanted, take her husband? She could admit to some satisfaction, since Mary had wanted her younger half sister dead.

Mary Tudor had thought she needed a man's help to rule, but Elizabeth Tudor knew that she needed no husband to rule, nor would she ever be ruled by a husband, for she would never marry. She had decided that long ago. Childbirth was likely death. And with a king for a husband, a queen's will meant nothing.

She shivered at the thought of her mother standing below

Henry's window, holding her babe aloft, begging for her life so that she could care for Elizabeth. She saw Henry turning away from both mother and child, plotting to take the mother's head, another wife already chosen and in his bed.

No! No! The mastery of men that marriage brought to a woman was not for her. Yet she must give all such suitors hope, juggling their princely offers for as long as she could, keeping the Catholic rulers of Europe always wondering and jealous of one another, keeping them in hope and England safe.

As for Robin . . . The sound of his horse's hooves right behind her warned her not to turn to him, lest she lose her resolve to play her game of marriage hoodman-blind, first rejecting one prince, and then with a sweet, tempting smile engaging another.

Robin was not pleased that her court was full of marriage offers, but this marriage dance was a part of her reign, would always be a part of it, and to quiet her council, Parliament and people, she must dance the dance while keeping Robin at her side. She could not lose him. No—she squeezed her eyes tight and bit her lip—she could never lose him. She did not need him to rule, but she must keep him to breathe.

This very day Robin would have a new manor or some new office to show him her true favor. There was no other way she could calm him . . . no other way without the great risk she knew she faced every day and night whenever he went to his bed and she longed to follow. And sometimes . . . almost . . .

As she dismounted, Elizabeth set her mouth in a firm line, though she saw him stop behind her and fling himself from the saddle, throwing his reins to a groom. She could not send him from her sight and she could not hide what she felt when he was beside her. So let the court talk. She was queen and she would rule as the king her father had done, totally. But unlike Henry

VIII, she would rule with her court's love and only a little of their fear.

Yet let them dare try to deny her Robin, the only joy she'd known in her twenty-six years, and they would receive a blow such as they had never felt.

Her ladies holding tight to their gowns rushed after her as Elizabeth entered Hampton Court through the tiltyard, sweeping past gathered courtiers, her mouth set, her chin high, remembering how she had vowed at her coronation that she would be more than a woman. Elizabeth of England would not pay a price for the love of a man, as her mother and her sister had paid. She felt the strength of her conviction aid her spine. She would resist them all. Resist Robin. Resist herself!

That night the queen, followed by her ladies and ushers, arrived at her great hall to greet the Swedish emissary with all the ambassadors of other princes looking on, trying to catch her eye from across the great hall. She could see Prince Eric's envoy's admiration when she entered and he turned to bow from his position near her throne. As she had expected.

Elizabeth had dressed in a splendor to match any European court, first choosing pearl-encrusted oversleeves, then ruby-studded ones over a marigold gown and yellow stomacher of embroidered gold, which pushed her breasts higher. With her red hair loose as a maiden's about her white shoulders, she knew by the admiring glances she received that she had outdone herself.

Eric's emissary, Ambassador Guildenstern, tall and blond with an arrogant nose and eyes but a meek chin, bowed low. His prince was said to look like a Viking, but be easily led and more apt to spend his days in reading the Bible than in ruling. At least the Swedish prince was better favored by his portrait than the pox-ridden French princes, each one madder than the next, the oldest recently dead after awakening in a pool of his own blood to die screaming. Elizabeth was not enchanted with such a family, although Catherine de' Medici had many sons and would no doubt offer them up to Elizabeth one after another, since she was determined to unite France and England. And Elizabeth was just as determined the other way.

As courtiers knelt on both sides, Robin did not look up at her, but kept his head low. He was in a sulk, which she could no more allow than open defiance. "My lord," she said, stopping before him, her words shrill with displeasure, "do you not like to look upon your queen?"

"Majesty, I shall always adore to look upon England's queen, but never Sweden's."

She slapped her fan against his cheek, a stinging blow, which others could judge playful or not, as they willed.

Robin leaped to his feet, his dark face flushed, his Gypsy eyes like midnight on her. He turned on his heel to leave the great hall.

How dared he defy her by rising and leaving without permission before all the court and foreign ambassadors? She called after him in a voice that penetrated to the farthest corners, "You will remain here, my lord, until I give you leave, or you will have a quick river voyage to the Tower!"

He strode back to her, a hand on his hip, as haughty as any prince. "Majesty," he said, his face now heavy with memory, "I have lodged there before at your sister's displeasure. If it is your will that I be so caged again, at least let me know what action of mine merits such extreme censure. If you would imprison all your subjects who like not a marriage to foreign princes, then the Tower will not hold them all."

She glanced toward the Swedish ambassador, who pretended

not to notice and perhaps did not understand such rapid English.

Now, her voice was almost a whisper, not meant for the ears of all those staring courtiers looking from her to him. "Robin, do not do this. Your open defiance will leave me no way to avoid your imprisonment."

For once, she saw with relief, he held back his rash spirit and knelt, offering her his proud, bare neck. She longed to put out her hand and touch his hair, weave it around her fingers. Instead, she signaled her ladies and walked on to her throne, head high, smiling and nodding on either side.

As her musicians played softly in the gallery, Elizabeth received Prince Eric's gifts, some exquisite ermine furs, sparkling diamonds hidden in their folds, with apparent delight.

"Majesty," the emissary said in Latin, "I bring you ardent greetings from my prince, who is very much in love with your portrait."

"My lord, why did not Prince Eric come himself?"

"That's impossible, Majesty, lest he be rejected."

"If your prince is not enough in love with me to come and try his luck, even if he is doubtful of his success, I do not care very much."

Eric's man seemed at a loss for more words; then his face brightened and he found enough English: "We have heard much of your delightful English country dances. Will you teach me?"

The queen smiled her agreement, and answered in Latin, the common diplomatic language, loving to show her knowledge to her court. "To please the Swedish ambassador we shall dance the petticoat wag," she announced, looking toward Robin, who leaned against a pillar, seeming uninterested. She would soon change that!

It was not a difficult dance, but one lively and very much as its name implied, a skipping, leaping dance where gowns were raised above the ankles and waggled temptingly back and forth to great laughter.

The Swede made a halfhearted effort, looking politely interested and bored at the same time as only a man from a cold climate could do.

Elizabeth leaped in front of him, waggling her gown. "You seem not greatly amused, my lord emissary."

"But it is charming," he objected, "and I see that you like it very much. When Prince Eric and you are married, he will order the court musicians to play it often." His mouth smiled, but the smile did not reach his eyes.

Elizabeth's liking for the dance ceased as he spoke the words. Her eyes had caught sight of Robin leading out one of her ladies . . . her cousin and lady-of-the-bedchamber Lettice Knollys . . . that slut with her hands all over him, her full lips taunting him, using his desire that she, Elizabeth, had aroused. And had not satisfied.

"I am more in need of rest from my long morning ride than I thought," she said, and the relieved Swedish emissary led her back to the throne, where she signaled the music to stop.

Immediately, she told her ladies that she would return to her chambers and walked out quickly without greeting all the bowing ambassadors who wished to promote their own princes. Some held out jewels of every hue on pillows to tempt her, but she ignored them.

In her privy inner chamber, Elizabeth called for her ladies to undress her and freshen her with rose water. "Lady Lettice," she ordered, "bring my green robe and satin slippers." She would enjoy that minx groveling at her feet. She would keep her to the ladies' chamber tonight. She would not frisk and hey about with any man, especially not Robin."

Though she and Lettice were cousins of Boleyn and Tudor blood, and Lettice's father, Sir Francis, was a council member, Elizabeth could not abide her cousin. It was true, they both had King Henry's red-gold hair and the Boleyns' slanting dark blue eyes, but there the resemblance ended. Lettice had larger breasts, and thus they were too large and vulgar. Younger and wanton, Lettice would have a big belly soon, if a husband were not quickly found.

Although Elizabeth encouraged her ladies to emulate her virgin state, at that moment she determined to find a lord for Lettice and ship the hoyden off to some country house, nevermore to be seen in court.

Elizabeth called for wine and sank into a chair near the fireplace. Hampton Court was a warm palace, but she was cold, shivering.

"Bess," said Kat Ashley, "if you would dine more heartily, your flesh would keep you warm. Bones never will."

"Yes, yes, Nurse," Elizabeth said, looking fondly on the buxom woman who had been her only friend in childhood, caring for her, cooing over her as if the young Bess were her own babe. Although sometimes foolish and much too free with her advice, Kat truly loved her and had loved her when she was disgraced and living in the country without hopes for a throne. Elizabeth knew that truth as she knew the sun rose each morning.

"Bess," Kat said softly with her familiar Devon burr, taking the queen's hand as only she could without permission. She knelt before the queen's high-backed chair. "For the love of God, I beseech you *not* to utterly throw yourself away."

Elizabeth laughed. "What talk is this, Nurse?"

Kat's lips quivered. "They are saying that you and my lord Robert Dudley are thinking of destroying Amy Dudley and that you are already with his child."

Elizabeth sat up, rigid. "Who would say such things? Tell me and the truth will be racked out of him!"

"Bess . . . Bess, it is no one person, but common gossip throughout your court." Tears tumbled down Kat's wrinkled cheeks.

The queen gathered her old nurse to her breast and soothed her. "Kat, you should not listen to such low talk, surely coming from servants."

Kat shook her head vigorously. "Nay, Bess, 'tis on every lord's lips as well and I suspect even your councilors wonder if—"

Elizabeth stood suddenly, though careful not to overturn Kat. She began to pace, which always calmed her. "You know, my old friend, that you are the only one who could speak so to me."

"That is why I speak, because you are in danger," Kat said, struggling up on her short legs.

"You worry for naught," Elizabeth said, trying to keep from showing Kat how upsetting her words had been. "You of all people must know that Lord Robert would have no hope of being my husband if his wife died under suspicion. He knows this; I know this. Do the rogues think me without wits!"

Kat grabbed the queen's arm as she had when the child Bess had rushed headlong toward some folly, her voice pleading: "But, Your Majesty, don't you see that Lord Dudley's enemies—and he has many because of his traitorous family and your favor—can't you see his enemies know that, too? How many are plotting to entrap him into losing your favor with his wife's sudden death?" Kat was finally out of breath.

"You mean others would kill her, hoping for Robin's downfall?" Elizabeth didn't await her nurse's answer, but pulled away, the truth of what Kat said all too distressingly plain. She must warn Robin.

With a final embrace, Elizabeth spoke in Kat's ear. "Go now, Nurse. I would be alone this night. No one is to come to me."

"But, Majesty . . ."

"Ka-at . . ." The queen used her stern tone, one she rarely used with her old friend, but one which was not to be denied.

When Kat had retired to the adjoining large chamber occupied by the beds of the queen's ladies, Elizabeth locked that door; then she locked the one to her antechamber, first telling the gentleman pensioners: "We will brook no disturbance this night."

Eagerly, she stepped into her linen closet to its very end. Within the large cabinet was a hidden latch that opened to a narrow corridor. She hesitated, closing her eyes tight. She had resisted Robin all the day, and for all the years of days and nights before that. Surely, there must be a reward for such restraint. Not for Queen Elizabeth, who would never lift the latch. But for Bess, the woman, who would. The woman whose fondest memory of childhood was of playing games upon the Greenwich greensward with a boy named Robin. That woman would be rewarded.

The narrow opening revealed a large door leading to a wider hall. The door had to have been large to accommodate her father, who kept his current mistress in the apartment next to his own. Henry had shown it to her as a young girl, whether to warn her with his power or brag of his man's prowess, she did not know. Probably both.

She blessed the generous door. Although she did not wear a

wide Spanish farthingale, her heavily brocaded gown was not narrow and clinging, but had a train that was regal and flowing. She had to walk sidewise, swiping away cobwebs that the palace spiders had been weaving since her father's time. Were these webs the first set trap of her rule? She shook her head, refusing to admit that her loyal spiders had evil intent.

Giddy in her head, she was like any young servant girl running through the dark of night to the stables to meet a waiting handsome horse groom.

To quiet her breathing, she covered her mouth with a hand and leaned against the dusty wall. *It's not too late to turn back!* She stopped and then was pulled forward. *It is too late.*

She edged on toward a door at the end of the short passage. A key hung on the wall. She touched its hard brass surface, knowing that she touched the key in the same place as Henry VIII, erasing her father's fingerprints with her own. The key made no sound in the lock, which opened at her touch after all the years unused. Certainly her pious sister, Mary, and her even more pious younger brother, Edward, had never made use of secret lovers. Had Robin oiled the lock for just such a visit? Was he that man-sure of her?

She listened for voices until she heard Tamworth, Robin's servant, say, "God give you good rest, my lord." A door closed.

She held her breath as she stepped across the lintel and beyond the covering tapestry, embraced by the warmth of a log fire lighting the high-waxed walls of Robin's paneled room. He sat in his bed, the bed curtains open, his dark head propped on white bolsters, staring at her with a small smile on his lips. It could be welcoming or assured. She did not care.

"Bess," he said, his drowsy voice deep and soft, "I've waited every night for that door to open . . . to see you standing there."

He did not move from his bed. The churl expected her to come to *him*!

"I'm here to warn you, Robin . . . and for nothing else."

"Of course, Your Grace. I expect nothing . . . else." He threw back a satin coverlet and swung his legs from bed and she saw a long expanse of them from under his nightshirt, the finely muscled calves . . . and thighs of a horseman. He quickly donned a long black velvet robe without seeming to notice her attention and, offering her his hand, led her to the best chair of the two placed in front of the fire. "Majesty," he said after she was seated, "may I call for wine?"

"No," she said, and then fell silent.

He seated himself across from her and stared, very relaxed, his large, dark eyes glinting in the firelight.

"Robin," she said, "I am come on a grave matter." *I must keep a distance.*

"I can see that." He cocked his head. "You've decided to send me to the Tower. Should I have Tamworth pack a change of clothes and my second-best nightshirt?"

"This is no cause for jest," she said, wanting to scream at him, and yet her legs trembled as if she stood in freezing water.

He rose. "I can see that, too," he said softly. He took one step and was on his knees, lifting her slippered feet and kissing them, first one, then the other.

Elizabeth's hands clenched in her lap and she tensed her body to flee, but he raised eyes that held her. His eyes. Her ÔÔ. "Listen to me, Robin." She bent to his ear as if his door could hear, for far too many doors in her palaces had ears to them. She repeated what Kat had told her, her lips against his ear. A tremor raced through her.

He seemed to be unaffected by her whispering. How many women must have whispered entreaties into those ears?

"Bess, are you saying many in the court are speaking thus of me . . . that I would kill poor Amy?" He shook his head violently and leaped to his feet. "It is true that my marriage is no love match, not as I have come to know and want love."

She tried to ignore his meaning, although she stored it away to repeat to herself and savor later. "Robin, you know they would say anything of you, accuse you, kill you. It was always thus in every court for the favorite."

He returned to the back of her chair and put his hands gently on her shoulders, kneading. "Am I your favorite, my queen?"

She would have twisted to face him, but he held her. "Robin, you know—"

"But, Bess, I do not know. . . . I have every day signs of your favor. In every way it is shown . . . except for one. You have never said you would marry me if I were as free in law as I am in heart." His low voice enveloped her as a warm blanket on a chill night.

Her face flamed as his hands moved up to her neck, gentle, barely touching her. Then his touch wasn't there and she leaped to her feet, fearing that he had gone. But he was there and advancing around her chair. "Robin," she said, trying to bring authority to her voice, but his name left her mouth as a caress.

He enfolded her in his arms and kissed her as he had before, but never so deeply, never with his whole body as now, not since their youth. She returned his kiss, the second of her day, and two kisses more than she could bear. She took in a deep, shuddering breath. "We must not, my love. I cannot forget who I am."

"Nor can I . . . my wonderful girl, my Bess, my beautiful queen." He lifted her from her feet and carried her to his bed.

She moaned, her body's heat rising. "No, Robin. No. I

cannot. . . ." But she did not want to stop his next kiss, though the all-consuming warmth that spread everywhere in her body warned her that she must stop soon . . . but not quite yet.

His bed . . . his bolsters had his scent everywhere. She was drowning in the sweet oil of musk and civet he used for his hair. "Robin, we must remember that you cannot get a child on me. . . . We must . . ."

He pressed himself to her and she felt him to be fully aroused. "Bess, I will take care. There are many paths to pleasure."

His hand stole to her breast and he pressed it through her robe. She wanted to command that cloth to be gone. She ached for him to touch her everywhere, to kiss her everywhere. But just as she felt herself lost to all reason and found by deep surrender, he sat up on the edge of the bed, his head in his hands. As she reached for him to pull him back, he stood and extended his hand. "I forgot myself—and I forgot who you are. Yet I do see that this is inevitable between us. We are flesh and hot blood and young, Bess. . . ."

"My lord," she said, gathering her senses, which had betrayed her body as they never had before. "I will remember this night and how you had a great care for me."

"Will you?"

"I will never forget, my heart."

He held her hand, smiled and bowed, his dark eyes sad, though his breathing was labored. "To calm your worry, Bess, I will post extra guards about Amy's house and let it be known that I have done so. Not one of my enemies will try to entrap me with her death, lest his minion be caught and the truth racked out of him."

He laughed as she stepped toward the secret door.

"What amuses you so?" She was unexpectedly angry, though

she realized anger was a substitute for what she had denied herself.

Robin shrugged, though he looked pained. "Amy's murder would be useless. She is ill unto death, Bess, with a growth in her breast."

"Oh. I knew she was sickly—"

"I have consulted doctors and they tell me there is nothing they can do but increase the laudanum physick. She has not above a year to live . . . or less."

"Oh, Robin. I am . . ."

"I will not pretend, Bess. It is you I want. When I am free, will you marry me?"

"Yes," she breathed, hardly believing she had said it as she opened the secret door and stepped through. "I'm sorry for her, Robin." *And for myself,* she thought. *This is a complication that I cannot will away.* She slowly closed the door, her eyes upon him until he was not there.

She turned the key in the lock, vowing never to use it again or to be so forgetful of her own majesty. *I must try harder.*

Elizabeth stumbled toward the faint candlelight coming through from the linen closet. Hastily, she replaced the latch in the cabinet and unlocked her chamber doors. Slipping into her bed, she turned on her side to face the windows sending moonlight in diamond patterns to her bedcovers. She pulled the satin coverlet to her chin and drew her knees high against her chest. Her bolster smelled of rosemary, a sure defense against the plague.

But plague take it! She had no mastery over her own desires . . . as she *must*! Robin had kept her safe this night, when her own virgin will had faltered. He had always had a care for her before himself. Tomorrow, she would make him constable of Windsor Castle and keeper of the Great Park. And . . . why not? . . . knight of the Order of the Garter. Then in a year or so, she would grant him an earldom, give him rank enough for a queen. Robin would be appeased and happy.

But would Elizabeth Tudor marry him? She caught her breath before it became a sob, but such bottomless tears would have their way, and they fell onto the embroidered flowers beneath her head. "My heart," she whispered, "more than this can never be between us." She said it again and again to plant it firmly in her mind. Tomorrow, Robin would come and she must deny her promise, swear that he had dreamed it.

Elizabeth lay awake all the long night, her words echoing about her chamber and back again to taunt her, until the starlight ceased.

CHAPTER 10

❧

To Marry the Wrong Queen

---❦---

Elizabeth

Summer 1564
Hampton Court

*T*hrough the open doors of her antechamber, Elizabeth saw Robin brush past the hesitant guards at the royal apartments and stride boldly into her privy chamber. *I will give him what he wants; I will make him a king.*

She pressed her palms against her gown, readying herself for his outburst that she would have to punish. He did not kneel or remove his cap, unpardonable manners even for the newly made Earl of Leicester. *Does he not know that I am tearing out my own heart with this demand I make on our love . . . on his loyalty?*

Cecil and the Earl of Sussex, who had been studying warrants with her, both stood up from their chairs at the table, uncertain whether to stay or excuse themselves.

Elizabeth saw that they hesitated to challenge Rob, although both men had recently challenged him at the council table when his conduct was too outrageous even for the favorite. Yet now she knew they asked themselves: What wise man wishes to come between two quarreling lovers when the chance of being right is less than betting on a dice throw? Challenging him was up to her.

"What means this intrusion, my lord?" She kept her voice half-amused, though she allowed a warning undertone of temper.

"Majesty, you know well my reason," he said in a choking voice.

Elizabeth waved her two councilors toward the door, since they were edging there in any case.

"I warn you, my lord, this behavior is unpardonable—"

"*My* behavior?" Suddenly, he knelt, looking up at her, his Gypsy eyes and dark face clouded with pain. "Bess, how could you do this to me . . . to us?"

Elizabeth strode about and stopped behind him, unable to face him and in no doubt of what troubled him, knowing she must keep her own pain from her voice and her face. "Oh, yes, a terrible thing to make you a *king*, my lord! Offer you the queen of Scotland to wife. They say she is as tall as you and *somewhat* beautiful. Is this the honor that distresses you so?" She must keep her face lively, and empty her eyes so that he could not see into her torn heart.

Robin twisted about and then, obviously realizing he was groveling on the floor, he leaped to his feet and faced her, his hands on his waist as if in a vain effort to hold himself together, though she could see his fingers trembled.

She widened her eyes in feigned amazement. "Robin, I had no notion that men were so fickle. You have urged me to marry you since before you became wifeless. You have longed to be a king, my lord . . . and now I make you one. But do you kneel in gratitude?" She attempted a raucous laugh, but it sounded strangled to her own ears.

Leicester's words were choked past a full throat. "You mock me, Bess. I beg you, stop this charade. You know I want no queen but you in my bed, no woman but you."

She hardened her face so that he would not see that she treasured these words even as she was forced to reject them. "Yet it cannot be this queen, Robin, as well you know. So for the love I bear you, I will give you another queen." She paced away from him, her Gypsy, knowing she could not look at him and say what she must. "Listen well to me, Robin. Mary Stuart is half-French, once queen of France. The French want to send their troops to stand upon my border, to raise the clans, ever ready to fight England, to foment rebellion in my own north counties. She must marry someone whom I can trust. Mary cannot be without a husband, since she cannot control her lords, or marry one that means us ill."

Elizabeth raised her hands in resignation and let them drop. "Robin, I would finally know that peace would ever reign on my northern border. You are the only man in my realm I would trust to give this to me."

"But at the sacrifice of my heart!"

Did he think she didn't sacrifice her own heart? Every time she must be a queen and demand he take this other woman, this northern queen, into his arms and give her love and children, it was a misery beyond miseries for her. Still, she was anointed by God to reign for England's good and must keep to her purpose, though her heart was shredded into tiny pieces. She steeled herself to show anger.

"You dare not refuse your queen, my lord! Do you think England would ever know true peace if Mary wed a Catholic prince of Spain or France with their armies at her command?" She came close and tapped his chest with her finger. "And don't tell me that you do not see the great benefit I bestow on you."

She could see him gaining self-control.

"I do see it, Majesty, and I would ease your mind in this matter if I could. Yet my heart overrules my mind, as you see . . . though yours does not."

Elizabeth heard the pain in those words, but neither could nor would ease him.

Robin stood tall, his chest thrust out, the jewels on his doublet glittering as if stars had fallen out of the heavens to decorate him. But his voice was bitter. "Is that why you made me the Earl of Leicester . . . ? I hoped it was for yourself." He came close to her, took her hand and kissed it with the same passion as he had kissed her mouth in his bed and in other secluded places. "Bess, I love only you. I want only you."

Elizabeth longed to draw his head to her breasts, to feel his breath of life upon them, but she forced herself to keep her eyes hard, calling on all her resistance to him, of which she realized she had too little at this moment. "You will love another and want another, if I command it," she said, keeping her confident mood although her own words made her want to shout, *No, never!*

"Come, sweet Robin, you are a man born. Do you think I do not see the way you look on the ladies of the court and they look on you?"

"They mean nothing to me, Bess."

"Only so long as I am watching, but if I weren't . . ." The thought of how many coverlets would be pulled back for him, perhaps *had* been lifted, raised welcome anger she needed to resist her longing for him as if he were already gone from her. Now her voice was heated. "You will do as I say, my lord. You are my servant to use in any way I deem necessary for my good and the safety of my realm." When she saw no yielding on his face, she called on the heartlessness of her father, King Henry VIII. "Robin, you are not master here. Have a care, my lord, lest you find yourself in the Tower and this time without the love of Elizabeth."

Leicester said nothing, but his bold stare showed his unwavering defiance. He bowed and rushed past her and out her antechamber doors.

She shouted after him, leaving her yeomen guards and ladies of the bedchamber no safe place to look but, by turns, the floor and the ceiling. "By God's wounds, my lord Leicester," she shouted after him, "you will do as I give command!"

When Elizabeth called him to her that evening, she learned that he had left the court for his manor of Kenilworth, a rich manor she had given him with his earldom. Ungrateful wretch! Judas!

She flung cushions and everything easily at hand and of not too great value about her privy chamber, sending her ladies scurrying out of reach, but not before she ordered in a fury of frustration and, the worst wrath of all, regret: "Send a courier in all haste at once with six armed men to intercept my lord Leicester on the north road and bring him back to us. And in chains if he offers resistance!"

Her guards brought him in to her the next morning, dusty, disheveled, his face ashen with want of sleep and yet stubborn, his dark eyes haughty, his face unyielding.

Elizabeth smiled at him and he knelt. She couldn't help smiling.

He looked as sullen as a schoolboy caught out in some great mischief and trying to brave it before the schoolmaster.

"Robin, Robin," she said softly. She went to him, raised him up with her own hands and, taking his face, cradled it against her breast. Her ladies quietly crept from her privy chamber, every one blushing.

"Bess," he whispered, "how do you think I can bear to be without you in the cold north?"

"Isn't a throne worth some bad weather? And you will have a queen to warm your bed." She swallowed the hurt of those words, using the last of her will to drive him to Mary Stuart.

"Bess, a throne is worth nothing if you are not beside me; my bed is cold if you are not next to me."

"You sound like a poet, Robin, and not a very truthful one."

"No poet, Bess."

"What, then?" She knew his answer, or hoped she did.

"I'm a man . . . just a man, who loves a woman more than life."

"But not *just* a woman." She did not like to taunt him further, but each time she did, he protested his love for her, and that she did need in the deepest part of her heart. Had her father made it impossible for her to truly believe in a man's love?

She began to pace her privy chamber to find her answer in motion. Did he think this decision she made was not wrenching for her? Did she even know her own mind? Her duty pulled her one way, her heart the opposite. It was the worst of tortures; she was racking herself harder than a traitor in the Tower dungeons. How could she live without Robin by her side? An awful truth stiffened her resolve. This would not be the last time she would be called upon to sacrifice what she most desired for her throne; neither could she be seen to have a subject win his way over her before her court, or henceforth they would bow down to him. She must be always dominant. Always queen.

She picked up some papers and pretended to read.

He bowed, she suspected not deeply enough, and left her. She did not call him back. Either of them could say too much, too many words that could never be recalled. Better to let Cecil negotiate with Mary Stuart; then she would *order* him north. She must stay firm in her resolve.

That decision gave the queen's mind, if not her heart, a few hours of peace until the Scottish ambassador came to her.

"Majesty, I long to take my queen a token of your friendship, since you desire to strengthen the futures of our two countries with a marriage."

"What, would please her, my lord Murray?"

"You have a fine black-and-white pearl necklace."

Elizabeth smiled to think he thought her such a fool that she would give his queen such a necklace when Mary Stuart had sent nothing of like value. As long as he did think she was willing to pay anything for the union, she had the advantage and could keep him hopeful. "The necklace is very heavy, my lord ambassador, and your queen is somewhat frail, I hear, not as eager to exercise as I am."

"Majesty, you have been wrongly advised. My queen loves to ride and is tall and strong."

"Is she taller than we are, my lord?"

"Yes, Majesty, she is."

"Then she is very much too tall, because we are tall enough."

He bowed.

To put him off his desire for one of her best necklaces, Elizabeth went to her bedside table and opened her treasure box, thinking to give him an old brooch of some intricacy but no great value. Instead, he saw Robin's miniature atop her possessions.

"Majesty! But this is an excellent likeness of the Earl of Leicester. A perfect gift for my queen to wake her desire for him."

The idiot! He had said the very thing to seal her mind against any such gift. "Oh, no!" she said, snatching up the miniature. "My lord, I could never part with this."

"But, madam, you have the original."

"Soon, my lord, your queen will have him and this small portrait will be what we have left." As soon as she said it, she realized how hurtful the words sounded to her own ear and always would. Life without Robin was a high price to pay for peace. Could she pay it and still be the woman she was?

Months of negotiation followed and abruptly Robin acquiesced, indeed, more than consented.

"Most gracious lady," he said, kneeling at her throne in the presence room, the court looking on. "You do me great honor in the matter of the Scottish queen. I am most eager to do your will. When may I leave for the north and my beautiful bride?"

Elizabeth was enraged. How dared he turn from her before the court! What had been private between them would now be laughed about everywhere from the cellar kitchens to the highest lord's apartment. The Earl of Leicester was as faithless as all men led by their loins . . . and greed.

"You will do as we decide best, my lord." She could scarcely control her voice, which wanted to rave at him.

"Of course, if Your Majesty asks, I will give up my great desire for the northern queen."

"Ask? We *command* here, my lord!"

His head was bent in submission, but she saw the smile curl his rogue's lips.

She almost knew the future before it happened. She would continue to demand his obedience, leading to his renewed enthusiasm for Mary and her repulsion, and so round the Maypole they would go.

At last Robin's letter to Mary was intercepted and brought to her. "'Most gracious Majesty,'" she read, "'I am not fit to be your husband and so would not want to put myself forward to contend with higher men for your hand.'"

Elizabeth, her face red with fury, confronted Leicester in private. "My lord, tell me how you cannot be fit to husband her, yet you think yourself fit for *me*?"

"Bess," he answered quietly, "it is obvious that the queen of England prefers men, while the queen of Scots prefers boys and her Italian secretary, the singer David Rizzio. . . ."

"That is vile gossip."

"Perhaps, Majesty, but she has shown no liking for me. Have you forgotten what she said when at the French court?"

Elizabeth turned away, not wanting to be reminded of that slander.

Robin repeated what had angered her greatly when Mary had first said it: "'I understand that the queen of England will marry her horse master, who will do away with his wife to make a place for her'?"

She had not forgotten that hateful accusation, nor the laughter in the French court that was reported to her. "Leave me, Robin."

He bowed himself out with elaborate ceremony, obviously thinking he had won the tourney.

Within days word came to Elizabeth that another Englishman, her cousin, nineteen-year-old Lord Darnley, son of the Countess of Lennox, was already on his way to woo Mary, against his queen's express orders. Elizabeth was in a fury. "That traitorous family has been warned not to send their baby-faced son north. Order the countess to the Tower until her son returns!"

Elizabeth suspected worse was to come and was right. The Scottish queen warmed to the boy, no more able to resist his handsome face and form than she could resist any male temptation she tripped over.

The Earl of Leicester held Elizabeth high against his body that night while dancing the lavolte at a masque for the Austrian ambassador in the great hall. He had come to plead for her to sign the marriage contract with the Archduke Charles.

"Another suitor," Elizabeth said, looking down into Leicester's face.

"How exciting, Your Majesty," Robin said, his eyes showing none. "A Habsburg king for England. The people will rejoice."

He lifted her high again at the next leap, the lutes and citterns throbbing. "Sarcasm is not to be used by earls to queens. It is for little men, Robin."

"Tell me truly, Bess," he whispered, "are you sorry that I am not even now in Mary's bed?"

"Yes," she said fiercely, her head thrown back to avoid his dark eyes.

"Bess, you are the most beautiful, glorious, fascinating pretender from here to Cathay."

She frowned.

He grinned. "Pardon me, sweetheart. I meant in all the world."

She suppressed her satisfaction and the thoughts she held deep inside. Had she ever really meant to send him to another woman . . . even for lasting peace? Even for a moment?

CHAPTER 11

❧

HOLLAND HEADQUARTERS

EARL OF LEICESTER

January 1586
The Hague, Netherlands

*T*he earl stretched his boots to dry before a crackling fireplace, holding Elizabeth's New Year's gift near to his heart. He traced each pearl strand as if to imprint his love on it so that Bess would sense the warmth he enclosed.

In a length of scarlet silk, he carefully wrapped the pearl rope necklace with one hundred jewels, a huge table diamond sparkling in its center with a large ruby on each side. He gave it one last look of approval and tied the package with a gold-tasseled cord, readying it for a courier and a swift boat to Whitehall, where the queen held her Christmas court.

He had scoured the jewelers from Flushing to Amsterdam for the perfect gift. It had cost an earl's ransom, but Bess would adore it. *And know I love her no matter how far away I am.*

He smiled again, thinking Raleigh could not possibly afford

a better gift, not with all his New World plunder, potatoes, tobacco, gold and all, especially since the queen took one-third of all the wealth her sea dogs brought to the shores of England, all the while denying to Spain that she knew anything of such piracy.

He glanced at the doors and was relieved to see they were yet closed against any visitors. He would not have Lettice see this package and demand to know what he sent. Although the gift would bring more return from the queen's favor, Lettice would be furious at its cost. She was already angered enough that he had sold some of her dower lands and mortgaged the rest to raise twenty-five thousand marks to finance his troop of horse and was raising more to pay and feed his six thousand foot. She had become reconciled only when their welcome by the Hollanders had been more than even she could have imagined.

"Robert," Lettice had exclaimed excitedly as they passed under a raised arch, their horses treading on a profusion of flowers and boughs, "the people are kneeling to us as if we were their rightful rulers. And why shouldn't we be? Look at how they love us!"

"They love Elizabeth for sending us," he reminded her, trying to hide his own thrilled heart. Her excitement was such that he could see her ample breasts labor for breath. Now, she had everything that her banishment from Elizabeth's court had denied her. And more! And truly, many of the shouting citizens called, "Leicester! Leicester!"

All along their way to The Hague, they had been greeted by cannon firing, bells ringing, citizens bowing and great feasts and speeches of welcome. He had not expected this overwhelming greeting, and it all seemed to be for him.

Lettice had quickly grown accustomed to being seen as a

greater lady than an earl's wife, especially when her complaint to the officers of the States-General of having no adequate coach had immediately produced a huge gilt coach, with the arms of the king of Holland—assassinated a year earlier—carved in ivory on its doors.

Robert ran his hands for the last time over the silken wrapping of his gift. Of all the New Year's gifts Elizabeth would receive, she'd love none more than his, even if she had heard with displeasure of his elaborate reception by the Hollanders. Elizabeth brooked no rivals, but he was her man always. She must know that and not allow the thought of a crown of his own to distance him from her. Hadn't she once offered him Scotland's crown? Didn't she know that no crown would ever replace his Bess in his heart?

Robert handed his gift to the courier, who placed it deep in a leather pouch. "Haste!" Robert shouted after the man, who wasn't moving fast enough.

He took a turn about the room, then sat again and, almost as soon, jumped up. He laughed, imagining the look on Bess's face when she opened his gift. He wanted to be there to see her delight more than he had wanted anything of late.

His guards opened his chamber's outer doors, announcing, "Your countess comes, my lord."

Lettice appeared wearing a coronet, her train carried by two ladies, her sleeves expanded with wire to their absolute limit. She was out of her carriage for only a short time, he was certain. She spent hours being driven from one great house to another, at last receiving the full honors and attention that Elizabeth had denied her. "Wife," he greeted her, forcing a smile, though the words of Dr. Dee's angel, Uriel, were never far from his mind: *the Other*.

He must resist the thought of putting Lettice aside, no matter his suspicions. Though Bess thought she had his total love, she must never be so completely sure that she could be freely cruel. It was that small doubt that Lettice provoked in Bess that made him a man, since Bess would not.

"Robert," Lettice said, leaving her ladies behind and sweeping past the guards, "why are you not ready?" She stared at him impatiently, his boots off, his doublet comfortably open at the waist.

He felt his belly gripping, his old malady upon him again. "What must I be ready for now?" he asked wearily, the joy in his gift almost completely evaporated.

"For the delegation from the States-General!"

Since they had landed, Lettice had been insatiable. No honor or gift was enough, but only aroused her appetite for more. Although she was nearing her middle forties, she had kept her beauty and a girlish need for its constant recognition. He smiled to himself. In that she was not so different from the queen, her cousin.

Unexpectedly, Lettice knelt and helped push his boots higher on his long legs. She brushed at the wrinkles in his doublet as he stood and handed her to her feet. It was a rare sign of caring and he could not help but view it with suspicion. Unfortunately, she had not grown in affection as Bess had, his wife's face always inclined to anger when she was with him. He was the first lord of England, but that was not enough for Lettice, since she had been kept from the court by Elizabeth's anger. His wife was forever fond of reminding him of her banishment, as if it were all his fault. The queen had always disliked her. Their marriage had only increased dislike to loathing. Still, on occasions like this one, he was reminded of an earlier, gentler Lettice.

"Thank you, wife."

"Do not forget the delegation, my lord husband."

"God's bones! Another delegation from the assembly, Lettice? I've seen five this day. No more bibble-babble, I beg you. I'm weary of their incessant demands that I write to the queen for more money."

"Yes, another delegation, my lord husband, only this one comes with a difference . . . an offer and not a demand. Prepare yourself to be granted what your own beloved Elizabeth denied you."

He ignored her sarcasm. She could never hold tenderness long. "Another medal? I have enough already to an uncomfortable weight." Wearily Robert tugged his boots higher and closed his doublet, holding his anger inside. "My lady, what have you been up to?" He tried to make his tone light, but he wasn't completely successful.

She came to him and rubbed herself against him in the kittenish way that had once excited him, but now he only tolerated . . . without telling her. No woman liked to be told her charms no longer appealed. Not that Lettice would believe him. She still had young admirers in plenty, some the friends of her son Essex, who was not yet twenty years old. Robert steeled himself to smile at her.

"Your countess, my lord," she said with a coquettish curtsy, "has been at the work you should have been doing . . . seeing to our future, taking what is eagerly offered."

Before he could question her further, the doors opened and a guard announced: "My lord, a delegation from the States-General."

"You are most welcome," Leicester said as the Hollanders approached, all with grave expressions.

He exchanged greetings with each of the men and one

extended to him a document from which many large wax seals hung. "My lord, we have come to advise you that it is the will of the States-General as supreme governance of the northern provinces that you be quickly named our governor-general as was our late King William."

Leicester was alarmed but, he had to admit, not quite as much as he was intrigued. King? Or as good as king. The one thing that Elizabeth had denied him by refusing to marry him was now his for the grasping. But how could he defy her orders? "Sirs, my queen has named me captain general. More than that I cannot accept."

Lettice whispered in his ear, "Think you *she* will give you what you need to win this war? She grasps her authority to herself as she does her crown. If you intend to succeed here, you *must* have supreme authority."

He knew Lettice spoke the truth for once, though not for any reason of fairness or victory in war. Yet would Elizabeth accept any truth but her own? She had a great fear of being drawn deeper into continental wars than she wanted to be. She would put a toe in, but no more. Yet the queen would not accept his failure, either. Nor could he. This was his last chance to succeed as a battlefield commander, proving to her that he was her man in every possible duty. He must demonstrate that to her while there was time left in his life.

"May I have a private moment to think on this, my lords and gentlemen? Countess Lettice will serve you some excellent wine from the Brabant."

Without waiting for an answer, Robert walked into an adjoining chamber he used for a private office and softly closed the door. He circled the room twice, then stood looking out of the floor-to-ceiling windows over the square busy with carters selling the last of their wares before going home to a warm supper. For a moment, he almost envied them their porridge, beer and comfortable burgher wives and cottages.

He bent his head. "Lord Jesu, guide me," he prayed aloud for his own ears. Elizabeth had given him strict instructions, few troops and little money to win a war against Spain's best army and greatest general, the Duke of Parma. Leicester was already using his own marks to feed his troops, though now he could not pay them all even the few shillings due them without bankrupting himself. The Hollanders had been slow to grant him funds, hoping to force Elizabeth to open her treasury. But if he were their governor-general, their highest ruling lord, they would have to pay his troops and allow him the supplies to move against the Spanish before inaction further decimated his English ranks with sickness and desertion.

He dared not ask Bess for permission to accept the offered honor. She would deny him absolutely, leaving him without options. The only possible way forward was to present her a fait accompli that she would have to accept, or disgrace her own man in front of all Europe. She would not dare do that. Would she?

Leicester pressed his belly to relieve the pain that gripped him more and more often these days. He breathed in deeply, clenching his hands. He had no more lands to sell or mortgage. No earl could become a pauper and laughingstock . . . not even for his queen, who would then blame him for failure, since she could never blame herself. As she often said, she was the lion's cub, and as absolute in her right as her father, Henry VIII. And more, he knew, she had Henry's courage and physical vigor, but she also had his scheming mind.

Leicester walked back into his outer chamber, not looking at

Lettice. Her demanding eyes would probably anger him enough to change his mind.

He took the warrant firmly in his hands. "Thank you, my lords and gentlemen. You may advise the States-General that I accept this honor on behalf of Her Majesty, Queen Elizabeth of England."

He had made himself king of Holland in all but name, and that would quickly follow with his first victory. Elizabeth would have to see that this was the only way to success.

The delegates knelt. Their spokesman hailed him. "My lord, your investiture will take place on the morrow in the great square."

When they left, after kissing Lettice's hand and murmuring, "Majesty," Lettice was ecstatic, whirling through the chamber, triumphant. "Now, you will be who you were meant to be, and I will have a court of my own." She laughed—almost hysterically, he thought—and continued whirling, as happy as he had ever seen her.

"I must choose more ladies from these good people and see to a palace where we may greet our subjects as we should."

Robert felt a flush of fear. "Careful, wife. The queen may be accepting of this honor for me, when I explain that it is done for her, for her army and for her honor. . . ." He paused, taking in breath. "But she will not be accepting of too great a display of power."

"Display by me! That's your meaning, Robert. Say it."

"Display by you, Lettice."

Or by the Earl of Leicester, Robert thought. Bess could have married him and made him king at any time, but feared marriage and sharing her power, driving him, after twenty years of waiting, to marry Lettice in 1578. Would Elizabeth accept his advancement by any other hand than her own? Dark despair swept away any momentary pleasure he had felt. He was trapped between what he dared to do and what he dared not do, what would please Lettice and win a war and what would anger Bess . . . perhaps forever.

It was a week before he was able to write the truth to the queen that he had accepted absolute governorship of Holland. He sent his trusted secretary, William Davison, with the letter explaining his good reasons for disobeying her orders to obtain England's victory. How else was he to control events? It was unrealistic for Bess to think that there was any way to command a war in Holland from Whitehall Palace. Yet she did think so; of that he was certain.

Another week passed before Davison returned with the queen's answer, a week in which Robert, despite endless ceremonies and struggling with the States-General for funds, spent holding his breath. He was close to emotional exhaustion when his courier finally appeared at his morning court. He immediately took Davison to his private inner chamber.

"How did you find Her Majesty?" Leicester needed to ask, while dreading the answer.

Davison hesitated.

Robert called for wine and, after it was poured, he motioned Davison to the warming fire. He knew from his messenger's face that he would need to be steady on his feet. "Well, what were her words? Out with them!"

Davison gulped at his wine cup. "My lord, I fear she was mightily angered."

Robert closed his eyes against what was to come, but he could not hold back Davison's torrent of words, which swept over him like the smoke of a battlefield, making his throat ache and his eyes mist.

"Her Majesty denounced your actions, my lord, in most bitter and hard terms. She did not stop berating you for an hour by the clock." He slumped into a chair and held out a letter closed by the royal seal. "This was to be given into your hands and no other's."

Leicester took the letter, his fingers cold, his stomach still gripping him. "Thank you, Davison. You are a good man."

"My lord, there is another thing I must tell you. Secretary Walsingham took me aside the morning I left and spoke a message to you privily, not daring to put his words into writing."

Robert did not move, bracing for the next blow.

"He told me, my lord Leicester, that Her Majesty has opened peace negotiations with the Spanish. A delegation was sent to Parma short days after you sailed. The queen needed to show the Spanish that she was only halfhearted in this war. She is greatly concerned that Philip of Spain will come against England before her fleet is ready."

Robert heard his own weak laugh. "They will come when Philip is ready."

"One other thing, my lord. She also sends Francis Drake with several good ships to the Caribbean to harass Spanish shipping and take what treasure they can." Davison smiled at that.

"By God's chains! She will have it every which way and I am caught in the middle."

Davison bowed.

"Forget what I spoke. The queen has no more loyal—"

"I know that, my lord, and when her anger abates, she will remember," Davison murmured.

What else could the governor-general of the States-General say? This was ongoing treachery, but it was the queen's way. She hated war so much that she would sacrifice his honor and any man's life to shorten it. He looked at the folded, sealed letter in his hands, wondering if it ordered him back to England, and almost glad to think of it. If he could see her, if she could see him, all would be soon mended.

Davison started to leave. "Wait outside, Davison. I may have an answer for the queen."

When Robert was alone, he bent to kiss the royal seal, where her fingers had touched. Even an angry, obstinate Bess was yet precious to him.

He opened the letter, recognizing her handwriting. There was no greeting, no tender words, no *Rob*, but this abrupt opening:

> *How contemptuously we conceive ourselves to be*
> *used by you. . . .*

Robert groaned and sat down, squeezing his forehead and breathing deeply, before he could read on.

> *We could never have imagined that a man raised*
> *up by ourself and extraordinarily favored by us,*
> *above any other subject, would have in so con-*
> *temptible a way broken our commandment in a*
> *cause that so greatly touched us in honor. . . .*

He closed his eyes again, hearing her outrage as if he were kneeling at her feet and she were shouting the words in his face.

> *Therefore our express commandment is that, all*
> *delays and excuses aside, you do obey and fulfill*
> *whatever the bearer hereof directs you to do, or you*
> *will answer the contrary at your extreme peril.*

Robert got up, adjusted his ruff and doublet, calling to his guards. "Send for Davison."

"He is waiting here, my lord," the guard assured him.

When his secretary reappeared, Robert spoke clearly but softly. He would not berate the messenger for an unwelcome message. "Davison, the queen gave you verbal instructions for me."

"Aye, my lord." He looked down and clasped his hands in front of him, almost as if to pray. "These are her words: You are to go to the exact place where you were given this false honor and renounce it before the States-General and the populace."

Robert felt a hammer blow to his heart. "Impossible! Can the cheers be uncheered, the bells be unrung?" Desolation swept through him like a cold channel wind. Bess had raised his hopes and dashed them many times, so many he had no count of the number.

"Did she order me back to England?"

"Nay, my lord. Before I had reached Harwich, a swift messenger overtook me with new instructions from the Lord Secretary Cecil. Cecil and Walsingham had counseled Her Majesty and she had changed her mind. You were allowed to keep the title, but not to act on it."

Robert tried unsuccessfully to keep hurt and anger from his voice. "Is that all? I may be a puppet king, with all the duties and responsibilities remaining, but not the authority."

Davison bowed. "I suspect my lord Cecil advised the queen that such a public act on your part would weaken you with the Dutch and Spanish . . . doom the war before you could take the field."

"Exactly right. Is that all?"

Davison bowed his head. "I fear not, my lord. The queen demands your countess return with all her baggage and ladies to

London . . . but with no Dutch coach. Your wife is to return all gifts."

Robert looked hard at the man. "Did Her Majesty use that word . . . *wife*?"

"Nay, Your Lordship, she called her . . ." Davison was embarrassed.

"I know . . . 'that She-Wolf.'"

The man nodded, avoiding Leicester's eyes, his shoulders sagging.

"Off to your bed, Davison," Robert said, his throat tight, his words hoarse.

Davison bowed and the earl returned to the fireplace, seeking warmth that a fire could never give.

So, with Bess it was not as much the idea that her Rob would be king, but that Lettice would be a queen. That honor for her cousin, Bess could never abide.

He poured a cup of wine and gulped it to keep from laughing wildly aloud and being overheard by his guards and rumored a hysteric. He hardly knew which would be the worse: being humiliated in public before the States-General and the citizens of The Hague, or telling Lettice she must go home without her new gold-and-ivory-laden coach.

Jesu. He should have forced Lettice to stay behind with all her young admirers. He should have known that Bess would be angry, jealous and conjuring such images of her Rob with Lettice . . . that her terrible anger was the only possible vent.

It had happened before.

CHAPTER 12

❧

An Impostor in His Bed

---❧---

Earl of Leicester

Early Summer 1566
Greenwich Palace

*L*ettice Knollys, the queen's youngest lady-of-the-bed-chamber and close cousin, lolled against the wall outside the royal apartments across from the windows overlooking an inner court, the light shining about her to her great advantage, as she knew.

It was there Robert found her when he exited after an argument with the queen that everyone in Greenwich Castle must have heard, or soon would in great detail. Courtiers had long memories when it came to gossip.

He was in need of softer words from a woman and Lady Knollys looked much like Elizabeth, with red-gold Tudor hair, though her own yielding eyes were so different from Bess's that he could not resist their obvious invitation to tarry. And if that flirtation were reported to the queen, so much the better. Though Elizabeth would be angered, perhaps she should be.

"My lord earl," Lettice said, looking about her before she spoke more, "my cousin the queen uses you harshly today, though it is a certain thing that she will forgive you by eventide." Her mouth twisted a bit with amusement.

"Lady Lettice," he said, bowing. She was a sly one for her young years and Bess's least favored of her ladies, in fact not favored at all. "You do not agree with your queen's anger?"

The girl lowered her voice again, but raised her slanted dark blue eyes, her heavy golden lashes almost too languorous to follow. Robert knew she was desired by the men at court, and a flirt, but thus far had escaped complete scandal, though she was obviously inviting one now.

"Oh, nay, my lord Leicester. Her Majesty is never wrong." She smiled slyly and added, "Especially when she is in such temper. It was most startling of you to agree to a Habsburg marriage when the queen depends upon you to oppose all her offers. If she cannot rely on your opposition, then whose?"

"That is what Her Majesty said," Leicester added drolly, "as you must have heard."

Lady Lettice opened her eyes wide in practiced innocence. "My lord, as faithful subjects we must never add to our queen's trials, but offer her all comfort. I know you agree with me in this."

"I would never add to any lady's trials," Robert agreed, but he was intrigued by the seductive minx in spite of his spinning mind warning him against the trouble she posed for him, indeed for any man. He shifted his feet and shrugged his shoulders until his ruff scratched his earlobes. His blood heated. God's bones! Bess could not keep him a monk forever when there were ladies like this one eager for his company. He bent closer. "But if you *would* add, Lady Knollys, to her trials, I mean . . . what would you do?"

She shrugged, sliding away from an answer. "My intimate friends call me Lettice, my lord."

He grinned at her, knowing that he was treading in deeper water than he should, but his anger at Bess's capricious behavior— the queen angry if he opposed a foreign marriage proposal and now angrier when he supported it—such unreasonable resentment pushed him to plunge in further with this maid, and he repeated his question: "What would you add to the queen's trials, if you could, Lettice?"

She tapped him playfully on his cheek. "My lord Leicester, do you mean me a mischief?" She smiled, showing teeth still white. "Else how can you tease me so? If I say that I think the queen cruel to you, you will tell her and I will be dismissed from court or take a trip to the Tower for speaking ill of my sovereign mistress."

"Nay, Lettice, I would never say aught against you . . . as long as you take care not to involve me in . . . scandal."

She laughed and he noticed her laugh was unkind, and, though warned, he did not walk away. He knew he should, but this was a game he had won before.

"Ah, my lord, I always take care. I would not be sent from court before I have married well."

"I think you can be assured of that." He did not add, *as long as you keep your reputation.* He gave the expected compliment, never wanting to distress a beautiful woman, especially one who approached him . . . with such friendliness and intimacy.

She raised one lovely white shoulder, but her face told him everything. This lady had no love for the queen. Was he part of Lettice's plan to best Elizabeth? He must have a care. Bowing to her curtsy, he kissed her hand and walked away, putting her from his mind for the most part.

That night the queen called him to her privy chamber, as he knew she would, for she slept ill and needed company through the night. Her ladies remained near the walls in the chamber, sitting in their low chairs embroidering or reading by candlelight.

"Yes, Majesty, you called for me," he said, bowing formally at a distance from her great chair near the fireplace. She had spoken the harsh words to him and she would have to recall them with sweet ones.

"Robin," she said, "come and make me laugh."

She had said these same words to him as a young girl, shaking with fright at the king's dealings with her stepmothers, which she had come to know before she understood them. And she had ever understood Henry's heart, loving and cruel by turns until near his end he was quite mad. Would that be his daughter's fate?

Elizabeth raised a hand to her forehead and pressed. "My head aches with petitions and every man in the kingdom calling for an heir to the throne from me as if I were the royal brood mare."

He didn't mention the obvious, that she was England's only royal brood mare. "You will never give them an heir, Your Majesty."

"Won't I, my lord?"

She leaned her head against the soft tapestry chair back, weary to the bone. His heart softened as he looked at her, and he knelt and kissed her hand as he always did. And, Jesu protect, he always would.

"I was a named heir once," he heard her whisper for him alone, "and never so hated and feared. My sister, Mary, would have had my head on Tower Green if she could have borne a child of her own."

"Ah, but Bess, fortunately for both of us while you were in the Tower, King Philip could produce only Spanish tumors in her womb."

She smiled, then broke into laughter. "Robin! That is cruel . . . but true."

"Gracious lady, much truth is cruel."

Robert saw her body relax and he sat down suddenly at her feet, hugging his knees, a grin on his face, his jeweled earring glittering in the fire's reflection, casting flickering light on her face. He knew well that it created some mystery and, therefore, some uncertainty. "What shall we do to get you an heir for the realm, Majesty?"

She frowned a warning, casting a quick glance at her ladies.

"I have it . . . the very thing," he said, his proud head thrown back so that she could see the glint in his eyes. "Dice, my queen! We shall cast dice among the princes of Europe and the winner will—"

"Robin"—she laughed behind her hand—"remember decorum. You are an earl and a queen's favorite."

"Am I so fortunate?" he drawled. "Still a queen's favorite, I vow." He grinned and tossed his head to its best advantage.

Bess leaned forward and whispered: "You know you are . . . always. We are tied together since childhood not by blood, but by lo—" She clamped her mouth, then added, "By understanding."

He moved toward her until their lips were as close as they could be without touching, all her reading and embroidering ladies going rigid with concentration on their tasks. "Marry me, Bess," he whispered, "and put an end to this torment for both of us. It has been seven years since you came to the throne. Amy has been dead now these six years from a fall down two levels of stairs."

"You were absolved by two juries of any wrongdoing, but many still believe you guilty of her death."

"What do you believe, Bess?"

"As you do, Robin, that she killed herself to escape the pain of the tumor in her breast."

"But I could not make such known, Bess, or she could not have been buried in consecrated ground."

"I know." She smiled ironically. "You had more care for her soul than you do for your own."

He grinned, his face close to hers. He almost dared to touch her lips with his, but he stopped, though he saw a clear invitation in her eyes. He needed more from her, always more than she was willing to give him. "You love me; I know you do," he whispered. "I do not forget that you willed your realm to my care when you thought you were dying from smallpox."

"Yet God saved me—"

"With the help of the German doctor I brought you when your own doctors had reached the end of their skill."

Elizabeth turned her head from him, though she did not push him away. "You do not need to remind us of what we know."

"Bess"—he smiled—"I do not know that you always remember."

"Then you do not know me."

He loosed the top button on his doublet, his body much too warm. He was going very far and he knew it, but he did not stop himself. Now that he had begun, he would say it all. "Most beloved lady, I have waited until the council would accept me.

They no longer insist on a prince or a king for you; even *I* will do for them now, if you would only marry and have an heir . . . our son."

She looked deep into his eyes and he thought he saw her waver. "Hear me this one time, my long love. I would marry you, Robin, if I could marry anyone. But I cannot marry. I told you that long ago when I was but eight years old."

"I know, Bess. But you were in a shock when your cousin Queen Catherine Howard was beheaded. . . ."

"But there was a worse shock before Catherine went to the Tower. I saw her running through the halls after my father, holding out her arms, screaming his name and he would not turn . . . or answer her. I hear her fearful terror in my sleep."

"She was an adulteress several times over."

"She was a frightened, silly girl who had been allowed too much freedom by her dim-witted Howard grandmother."

"The king, your father, had doted on her."

She looked pained by that memory. "Aye, his 'rose without a thorn' he called her, but he turned from her with such anger and her foolish head was struck off on Tower Green."

Robin drew back as if she'd slapped him. "Bess, you cannot think that I . . . if I were your husband would ever—"

"Let us talk no more about it, Robin!" she said, her voice sharp. "It brings on my night terrors."

He knelt in silence, his head bowed, his heart emptied of sudden hope, as she obviously wished it to be. She whispered his name, her whisper so slight he could be dreaming it. "Robin, you would be the man I would marry . . . if I ever were to marry."

Hope burst suddenly into flame again. He bent to her and

laid his hand on the beautiful hair lying on her shoulders . . . praise God, fully restored after the smallpox had almost taken it all—hair, beauty and life itself. All the royal doctors in their masks had claimed there was no hope, and to the horror of her councilors, she had named Robert protector of England, with fifty thousand pounds a year. He had refused to give her up and found a doctor who cured her. She recovered and he had sat by her bed for many days and nights. "Are you saying you will marry me someday, Bess?"

"Oh, I do not know. . . . Yes, maybe." She blinked rapidly and he thought it was to keep a tear from falling.

"For now, cease plaguing me, Robin." Her head turned first one way and then the other; then her next words burst from her. "No, I will not. When I die, it is my wish that my monument record, 'Elizabeth, queen of England, reigning for such-and-such a time, did live and die a virgin.'"

He did not answer; he had heard her say these words to the Parliament, although Parliament men could never believe her and Robert did not want to. He knew that her body yearned for him. He knew.

"And now," she said, rising, as did all her ladies instantly, as if catapulted from their chairs, "I will go to my bed, for I must find a way to deny the archduke of Austria's proposal tomorrow." She smiled slightly. "While leaving the door ajar. And, of course, you will support me at the council table."

He bowed, meaning to step away and leave, but she put out her arms and pulled him to her so that he felt the heat of her body through her velvet dressing gown and lacy gold shoulder netting. He closed his eyes and felt her lips on his, for just the briefest moment, and then she twisted from him toward her bed as he backed to her antechamber. He felt himself shaking and fought for control. What did Bess mean . . . yes, no and yes again?

She was still a virgin, and yet she carried his kiss and her longing to her bed with the imprint of his body.

Outside the royal apartments in the corridor lit by torches spaced along the walls, he damned himself in most bitter terms. Once, that first year of her reign, she had come to him and he could have had her in his bed, but he had thought of her first and not himself.

He smashed one fist into the other. He would never make that mistake again, nor could he regret having once protected her in his bed. He laughed bitterly, the yeoman guards in the antechamber eyeing him curiously. He was as trapped by Elizabeth as the poor, hopeful Habsburg archduke. He, too, waited while she advanced and retreated, not able to commit to him, nor content to lose him completely.

Robert struggled that night, turning from side to side, too heated to sleep, though trying to quiet his mind. Bess was ever likely to do the unexpected. That was the one thing he could be sure of. Would she change her mind about marrying him? Tomorrow? Come Michaelmas? Never? He tried to stop such thoughts, but they came without his bidding until he had Tamworth twice bring him beakers of cooled wine. Knowing he would suffer a large head on the morrow and not caring, he finally drifted to sleep.

His bedside candle had burned very low and only a faint lantern light on a far wall lit his room when he was awakened by a woman's body covering his.

"Robin." It was the voice he heard in his dreams. It was her perfume about him.

"Bess! You've changed your mind."

"Yesss," she said, and laid her head upon his chest, her soft hair all about him, blinding him.

He was aroused as never before. She had not meant to dismiss him. It had been a game to control the whispers about them.

"Bess . . . Bess," he groaned her name.

She raised her gown and grasped his cock, eagerly sliding herself onto him. He swelled at once, ready from years of waiting and wanting. He filled her and, pushing hard, moved rapidly until she was rising and falling over him like a troubled sea.

As he suckled at her breast, he heard her moan and, looking up, saw her face clearly for a moment. Although it was Elizabeth's gown and her Tudor hair, it was Lettice's face looking down on him, her mouth slack, her eyes tightly closed.

But he could not stop. Could not even try to stop. It was too much to ask of any man.

And this woman, Lettice, was all the bed comfort that a man could ask.

She buried her head in his chest to muffle her scream of pleasure. He could not move, done in by the woman and his own needs.

"I love you, Robert."

For all her charms, he could not say the words she wanted to hear. Lettice must know that, or did any woman ever accept second best. Jesu! He was doing to her what Elizabeth did to him, giving her just enough to raise her hope of winning.

Yet how could he wait, tortured by Bess his whole life? Near her every day, but spending his nights alone, lying in his own sweat. Never to have an heir. And never to be the master of a woman, but always the servant. Could any man be happy with such a life? Could the Earl of Leicester?

Sometime after he fell asleep, Lettice departed, he hoped without being seen coming from his rooms. What possible reason could he give to Bess for such a night visit? In future, he must be very careful, but would Lettice? He had his choice of women in court, but she was most willing and unafraid. Did she want the queen to know? Was that her game? He knew she wanted a good marriage and he was a peer with estates and no heir. Nevertheless, he would be careful and tie on a sheath. He would not be trapped by this woman, no matter what he owed her.

The queen could not condemn him to life without a man's release, especially with a woman who was so like her. Such a temptation was beyond any man's ability to resist.

Eventually, there were no secrets from the queen, and would Lettice even want to keep theirs? She hated Elizabeth as only blood could hate blood. Had always hated her, for Bess had always what her cousin wanted. Besting the queen would be a triumph for Lettice, though the little fool, so full of her own womanhood, did not realize what a price she would pay.

That summer Leicester spent in great suspense, waiting for Elizabeth to hear of his affair with her cousin, since half the court was eager for her to know, but all the court afraid to be the messenger.

The decision was made for him, as it usually was, but this time by Lettice and not Elizabeth.

"My lord," Lettice whispered one night in his ear after coming to his bed, "I am with child. You must marry me. I would make you happy if you make me your wife."

"I cannot, Lettice. The queen would never allow me to leave her." He bit back the other reason, which she would laugh at: He still had not yet given up all hope of marrying Bess.

Lettice's answer was not carefully controlled, her voice rising until he feared the whole of Greenwich Castle would hear. "Robert, you mean you will not risk the queen's anger."

"Lettice, quiet yourself. I will think of something."

"You will think of a way to rid yourself of blame for this child I carry. The queen has everything and I have nothing, now less than nothing." Her voice caught on a sob. "Mark you, Robert, someday you will regret it."

He tried to comfort her, but he could not give her what she wanted. She refused to be calmed and fled his room in great anger, almost as immense as her Tudor cousin's. He would have to do something quickly. He did not think Lettice would tell the queen herself. It would mean the Tower for them both, and no chance for a notable marriage for her, or for him. She carried a lifetime of jealousy within her breast, but she was not rash . . . he hoped.

The next morning, Leicester strolled with Elizabeth in her walled garden, the ladies, including Lettice, who walked out with the queen gathering at one end. He picked flowers and adorned the queen's dress and hair until she could have been mistaken for a forest sprite.

"Robin," she said, laughing like a girl, "you weigh me down."

"Never, Bess. I only ornament you as God would have, had he thought ahead."

"Robin," she said, pretending shock, "you come much too close to blasphemy."

He put his hands in a prayerful position and she grabbed them, pulling them apart and placing them on her cheeks. "You are in a very cheerful mood this day. Still, I do not expect you to be my fool and entertain me."

"I will always be your fool, Bess," he said, knowing he spoke truth as he looked up into her eyes, his heart beating fast against his doublet.

Pup! Pup! She made the sound with her lips that showed some irritation.

Did she suspect? Did she know?

He plunged forward, having no other choice. "Speaking of fools, I beg you to find a husband for your cousin Lettice Knollys."

She eyed him narrowly. "Has she been a fool, Robin?"

Her face was more aware than he liked, but he had to be bold, or be trapped once more. "Nay, my only queen, but she is ripe for the marriage bed and not prudent."

She strolled down one gravel path in the geometric garden centered by a fountain with a statue of Poseidon atop it. She turned toward him at the far wall espaliered with Spanish orange trees. "Do you have a husband in mind, Robin?"

Her voice was soft, her face unknowable.

Robert kept his own features from appearing too innocent, too easy for Bess to read. "That is for you, Majesty, to decide, but I think Walter Devereux, the Earl of Essex, looks on her with favor."

"Do you think it?"

"I do."

She walked on and he caught up to her at the center fountain, offering his arm. Bess took it, holding tight to him. He relaxed. She might suspect, but he was certain she did not know. Or did not want to know. Elizabeth had the ability to accept or reject what she wanted to know according to her own needs.

Robert gave the Earl of Essex and his bride a handsome wedding gift of gold plate. The queen gave them the manor of Chart-ley near his own Kenilworth, but far enough away to keep them from chance meetings.

Breathing deeply with relief as Essex and Lettice drove away, the Earl of Leicester attended Elizabeth in her apartments that evening as he always did and was met by her fury, a precious vase thrown with queenly precision from across the room.

"Never think me brainless, my lord." Her irate voice filled her chambers.

He fell to his knees, shocked and speechless, not compre-hending immediately what had angered Elizabeth.

"Majesty, I—I am . . ." Not knowing how to answer, he heard his voice trail away like that of some cringing lad who had thought himself more clever than he was.

She stood above him, her face so wrathful he could not im-mediately regain his usual poise, the ability to look her in the eyes and not blink.

"I rid you of your whore. Shouldn't you humble yourself in thanks?"

She knew. "And you also rid yourself of your hated cousin," he dared to say, regaining at last the pride that had deserted him when he had needed it most.

"We did not give you leave to rise, my lord," she said, her words spit in his face. "Down, we say, if you would serve us longer!"

"I would serve you with my death, if you desire it, but not my manhood. You cannot keep me a monk in a cloister, refusing to marry me while retaining me as a pet . . . and making me run mad in my need for you." He felt the fury of his guilt and anger and desire, the years of frustrated waiting, rage through him. Enough! He had had enough of crawling before her. He walked away through her antechamber.

She screamed after him, "You are banished from our court, my lord earl."

"As you see, Majesty, I am banishing myself."

"And do not return!"

"As you will, my queen," he said, leaving Bess and her shocked ladies gasping.

Immediately, he rode with his household retainers to Leicester House on the Strand in London. She sent no rider after him, as he'd expected she would, and his heart was heavy as granite as he walked through his empty and echoing rooms.

It was a week before she came, but only two days after he had taken to his bed with a recurring fever.

"Robin—Robin," she said, rushing into his bedchamber. "I am here."

"Bess, my love," he whispered hoarsely, speaking truth, "I was praying you would come to heal me."

"Always . . . always, Robin." She stroked his fevered forehead, a tear falling on his lips.

He captured it with his tongue, knowing it would make him well . . . for a time.

Late Summer 1566

It began as an adventure during the queen's annual summer progress. Leicester saw that Elizabeth had tired of the pageants, speeches, dinners, honors for local knights and magistrates and gifts requiring more speeches at each village along their route, the largest one at Cornbury, where they stopped for a few days to rest and take the curative waters.

On their second evening at the spa, they sat in one of the cool shaded alleys, the queen's ladies at some distance, watching some village dancers.

Robin knelt before the queen on a Turkish rug where her feet rested. There was mischief in her eyes, a reckless spirit he had not seen often since the first years of her reign, when her sense of freedom and her constant affection had given him such great hope that she would marry him.

"Sweet Robin," she said in a hushed voice, "come closer."

"Majesty, I am at your feet. If I come closer, I must touch you and there would be talk."

"Let them talk! Is a queen never to know the least affection that her subjects know? There are times when I would be a simple woman with a man she—"

"She what . . . Majesty?" His heart had begun to pound loud enough to be heard by everyone near.

Elizabeth raised her hand as if to dismiss him, but allowed it to drop with no signal.

Still on one knee, Robin bent forward until his doublet touched her satin gown. "Bess," he whispered, "would you have the courage for an adventure this night?"

She frowned. "I have courage enough for anything at any time."

"Then when it is full dark, meet me in the woods behind the hot springs. We can ride to my nearby lodge at Rycote for a midnight supper."

He waited while yes and no flickered across her face, not once, but several times. He raised her hand to kiss, stood and stepped back to bow and leave her.

He waited in the woods well past moonrise, leading his horse back and forth to quiet him and make the time run faster. It was close to ten of the clock before he saw a cloaked woman running from tree to tree. Almost at once, he knew it was Bess, thinking to disguise herself, as if she could. Who could miss that erect, slender figure of above normal height, her gold-red hair glowing in the moonlight?

She ran up, a little breathless. "Where is my horse?"

"The path is rough and winding, Majesty."

"All night paths hold their dangers."

"For your safety, you will ride with me and I will hold you," he said, trying to keep the excitement from his voice.

"My lord, I can keep to the saddle on any horse. You take a great liberty."

It was time for boldness. Without asking, he lifted her into his saddle and mounted behind her. "But not, I think, madam, a completely unexpected liberty."

She laughed, her desire for adventure already crowding in.

He took up the reins and kicked his horse into a canter, turning its head onto the path to his lodge. His arms were about her and she rested her head against his chest.

After a time, she shouted into his ear, "Robin, I will eat your supper with good appetite. Expect no more."

He knew that she had now had time to regret her rash acceptance of this adventure, but not enough time to stop herself completely, nor would she now.

Tamworth met them at the lodge door, holding up a lantern, bowing low to his queen, though she swept past him without acknowledgment. Robert smiled. She would pretend that she was not here. Only Elizabeth could command her mind and memory as she desired them to be.

A supper of steaming brawn broth, a pigeon pie and a custard with a pitcher of ale was already spread upon the table in the great hall before a fire hot enough to erase the night's chill.

Savory aromas rose from the broth and meat pie, but Robert's senses knew only Elizabeth's special delicate perfume. Dismissing Tamworth, Robert served her himself, kneeling before her and bowing his head as if all the court looked on.

"Robin, if this is a mockery . . ."

He raised his eyes, fearing they might be moist. "Bess, why would I mock my heart's only desire?"

She bit down on her lip. "I know well the devious ways of men."

"But not of sincere men, a man who has loved you since a boy."

"Ro-bin."

Her voice shook and so did his hand. He was forced to place the soup bowl back on the table and lay his head upon her lap. She stroked his face and he kissed her hand, then her arm as high as his lips could reach. "Bess, Bess . . ."

She stood abruptly, trembling like a deer encircled by hounds. "I cannot bed you, Robin. You know that I . . ."

He stood, brushing against the length of her body, and put his arms about her. "Sshh, Bess. On my honor, I will not harm you . . . or do aught but what you permit."

Her gaze roamed the great room, as if looking for escape, but came back to rest on him.

She allowed him to lift her and walk to the stairs, climbing to the second-floor gallery, her head nestled in the hollow of his neck. He kicked at the door to his bedroom and found it off the latch. A fire had been lit and fresh linen covered the bed. He set her down there, removed her buskins and unrolled her hosen. She stopped trembling, hot color rising to her face as he fumbled with the ties of her kirtle and gown. "Bess, you are wearing no corset. Did you . . ." Had she planned to give herself?

"Don't question me, Robin."

He lifted Elizabeth to her feet and kissed her, opening her mouth with his, hungry even for her breath. She hid her face against his cheek, allowing him to drop her gown and shift to the floor, where they settled in billows of satin, lace and Flemish linen. Firelight danced across her slender body, while he flung off his doublet and shirt and dropped his trunks where he stood. Her eyes were tightly shut in denial of what she was allowing.

She trembled as he curled his naked body beside hers. Putting his hands on her smooth hips, he whispered, "My queen, you are beautiful."

"I have less flesh than most," she said, trying to cover herself with her delicate hands.

"You are the more beautiful to me." He kissed her stomach, vowing to himself that he would not take her without her asking, without her begging. Yet he was not at all sure that he could abide by his own pledge, and Bess was not helping. She moaned as he kissed her everywhere, licking at her nipples until she cried out and pushed her body against his. "Robin . . . Robin, do not torture me more. . . ."

Bess had asked, or as close as she could ask, enough for him. Her legs parted and he entered her, slowly, slowly, pledging anew to hold himself back. She would never forgive him if he got her with a babe.

But he could not stop himself and plunged ahead until he met the obstacle that told him he was her first lover, the first for all time.

She cried out in an ecstasy of pain, his release mingling with hers; he fell upon her breasts until their breathing quieted.

"I love you, Robin," Bess whispered into his hair. "I will marry no man but you."

"When?"

"Soon. But we must never mention this night again until we are wed, never think of it."

"I will not speak, but I cannot promise not to think, to dream."

They remained flesh in flesh until Robin reluctantly roused himself. "Sweeting, we must return to Cornbury before the dawn and you are missed. Who is sleeping in your chamber?"

"Two bolsters under my blanket," she said, laughing like a girl.

He smiled down at her and saw her suddenly frown.

"What is it, Bess?"

"Was Lettice better . . . ?"

"Sshh, my love. I would never compare you to another woman. You are a goddess, Diana, Gloriana, Elizabeth Tudor. There is no other woman like you . . . nor will there be, tomorrow or ever."

CHAPTER 13

❧

WITHOUT ROBIN

---❧---

ELIZABETH

October 1586
Whitehall Palace, Westminster

*E*lizabeth banished her ladies, Anne Warwick, Helena Gorges and Philadelphia Scrope, to the far reaches of the grand gallery overlooking the tiltyard. She walked alone under the mural of Moses on the ceiling, her footsteps sounding hollow against the stone expanse beneath. She prayed for Moses' wisdom, knowing that with or without it she must make all of England's hard decisions, without Rob's support. With him still in Holland, she was alone for now, and she felt his loss as if she were half-empty, incomplete. She had the power to make all decisions, but was the throne worth the price she had paid for it? She clenched her fists, trying to throw off the strange, questioning mood that had filled her all the day, the emptiness that being without Rob had always brought . . . an emptiness she could never reveal, not even to him. Especially not to him.

A cool autumn breeze swirled leaves through the open arched windows and into the gallery's corners. Her memory of a young Robin walked with her, Robin in the tiltyard below in an Accession Day tournament astride his white charger, the dust spurting from its pounding hooves, his leveled lance, as straight as his back, aimed at his opponent's shield. He conquered all challengers whom he rode against . . . as he had conquered her. Once more she saw him raise his helm to her as she acknowledged his victory with a wave and a smile she meant to outdo, the applause for him from the overflowing crowd of Londoners in the two-shilling bleachers. His black hair was matted with sweat, his compelling dark Gypsy eyes looking up at her with . . . Was that love or triumph she remembered? Maybe both.

And why not that same eager young face greeting her again when he returned from Holland, the years magically fallen away? Perhaps sadly, without triumph, since the Duke of Parma's army had outgunned Robin's poor soldiers.

This was in no way a fault of hers. She had England's treasury to consider and the power of her peace offerings . . . and, perhaps, Philip of Spain's memory of her as the young princess he'd spied on in her bath while his wife died of a growing tumor she desperately insisted was a royal babe. Almost thirty years ago now, so he could have forgotten his humiliation over Elizabeth's refusal to marry him almost the moment she took the throne. Did a man, especially the king of half the world, ever forget the rejection of his person? The queen of England had chosen no prince of Europe, preferred no royal man to him. Instead—she stopped to stifle a laugh, then walked on—the queen of England had preferred Robin, son and grandson of traitors and a minor lord, a man so poor he mortgaged manors to clothe himself for court. Could the greatest king in the world ever forgive such an insult to his royalty and person?

Elizabeth turned quickly at the end of the gallery to march back. She could not care about Philip's embarrassing memories. Delay, delay, delay was the battle tactic she used against him and the mighty fleet he was assembling. This was the strategy she most favored and which she had found most useful, whether against a marriage proposal or a foreign enemy. For every month of delay Rob might gain in the Low Countries, her sea dogs could harry Spanish treasure fleets, while she could use the gold they brought to add to her own navy's readiness. She prayed her ships would not be needed, but if they were . . . if Philip dared . . . England would be ready, due to her careful diplomacy and watch on her money.

Against all the warlike hotheads on her council, her objective of keeping Spain's King Philip at bay with both her army and her peacemakers had worked and was still working. Parma's peace commissioners remained at Ostend. As long as they talked, the armada would not dare sail. England was kept safe. Though rumors of an attack had been two a penny all summer, the Spanish fleet had stayed in its harbors and not come up the channel.

Elizabeth reached the end of the gallery and, avoiding her ladies' faces, she turned sharply and marched away, her mind turning as well. How could she wait longer here in her palaces, alone with all the burdens of rule? And without Rob she was always alone, though surrounded by guards, servants, ladies, courtiers, ambassadors, councilors and Parliament and . . . Raleigh, the handsome rogue. She clasped her hands in a prayerlike attitude. If she recalled Rob, that She-Wolf would have to spare him in service to the queen of England. Lettice must accept that her queen would have him here by her side!

Elizabeth whirled and was about to return to the gallery's other end, a little breathless. She must slow her pace and breathe deeply to escape light-headedness.

As queen, she had no substitute comforter for Rob, as gossip whispered Lettice had now, with her young son's friends swarming about her like drones around the queen of the hive and, perhaps, around her bed. No, nor could favored courtiers, kneeling before the English throne, claim Elizabeth's attention if Rob was absent, for in her heart he was never missing. She compared them all to him and found them wanting his understanding, his true devotion and care . . . all she had ever known since her mother had been so cruelly taken from her, a comforting warmth she remembered only when Rob held her close in those few secret moments they had.

God's bones and thorns! She needed him here. Now! She had a dreadful decision to make, since Mary, queen of Scots, had been condemned by England's peers at Fotheringay. Elizabeth alone must sign the death warrant. Her mind rebelled at the thought. How could she order the death of a queen anointed by God, as she herself was? The Earl of Leicester must be by her side to support her in this terrible duty, and here she would have him.

A new general must go out to hold the Dutch northern provinces. She would order it at once! Her happy decision quieted her heart, though she knew it would be weeks before he would be with her.

Elizabeth looked down at the tiltyard again. The cool autumn wind now raised nothing but the dust of its emptiness.

A commotion down the gallery revealed Lord Burghley and Sir Francis Walsingham passing despite her waiting ladies' objections. The two men hurried toward her, bowing before they stopped.

The queen sighed. Troubles. Always her Spirit and her Moor

brought solemn difficulties. Rob was the only man who knew how to make her smile at bad news, but all problems could not wait for him. She prepared herself for what was clearly visible on their grim faces. Mary, queen of Scots, was condemned, and yet she lived on, everyone looking to Elizabeth to sign a death warrant against her cousin. Did they know what they asked?

"We have no wish for more delays," Elizabeth said irritably. "You come to tell us that Mary Stuart yet lives and not one of our good and loyal subjects can remove this horrible necessity from us . . . a queen to kill a queen . . . because her men fail her. Why has no one loved me enough to spare me? What think you, my lord and gentleman, of such subjects?" she demanded.

They seemed reluctant to answer her question, both of them Puritans and unwilling to have a queen's blood on their hands, the same blood they readily cast on their sovereign's. Her voice was rising and she sought to bring it under her tight control. "You perhaps think us daintier in our aversion to the ax than our father!"

"Majesty," Walsingham said, "I know you do not hesitate with other traitors."

She clenched her fists against her bodice, wishing to show them her displeasure and suspecting she had been successful. "Well, what news have you brought to delight your queen?"

"Majesty," Lord Burghley said, his voice strained through the effort to hold himself erect with his stick, "as you know, the trial of Mary Stuart has been concluded and she has been judged guilty and sentenced to execution, as is the law for treason. I have prepared the death warrant for your signature and seal."

"What! You dare to do so without my permission?" Her face flushed and her breathing grew ragged. *I will not be pushed to this, a deed which will outrage every prince in Christendom and God in*

His heaven! "Now you approach us on so grave a matter as an anointed queen's execution . . . while we are so grievously concerned with the Holland business . . . so worried. . . ." She knew she was sputtering, but she could not let out her full rage, since her worthy Spirit sagged as if to fall.

Walsingham put an arm about Burghley's back to support him.

"Sir Francis," the queen said, "call our guards and have my lord Burghley taken to his rooms. And send our doctors to him."

Burghley put up a hand to deny his condition.

Elizabeth feared for her Lord Treasurer and for herself without him. Without Rob. God's bones! At every turn she was alone. "Dear Spirit, you must get you to your bed. We will come to you later."

"Madam, do not trouble yourself."

"Guards!" Sir Francis commanded.

Two yeomen hurried forward, trailing pikes. The queen ordered them to take Burghley to his apartment. "On a chair, good yeomen, to spare his legs."

"At once, Majesty."

With eyes on her stern face, her guards gently overcame Burghley's protests and carried him away.

Walsingham remained, his face grave. "Majesty, I have reports from Holland."

"Yes, Sir Francis, we planned to speak with you on this matter."

"Madam, there has been a great battle at Zutphen. Many were slaughtered, both English and Spanish."

She swallowed the breath that caught in her throat lest it sound as a groan. "The Earl of Leicester?"

"Not injured, Majesty, but nearly so. They came upon the enemy suddenly through a thick mist and were caught between cannon on the city ramparts and heavy musket fire from the trenches. The earl led the attack most valiantly, it is reported, hacking and hewing with his sword in the thick of the enemy with the courage and energy of a young warrior, though often his captains lost sight of him and communication was impossible. Now, His Lordship's heart is breaking—"

"But not—"

Walsingham shook his head. "Nay, Your Grace, he is well enough, though full of grief. His young nephew and my son-in-law, Sir Philip Sidney, was wounded by a bullet in his thigh, having given his leg armor to another. That brave knight then gave up his water to his men, who, he said, needed it more. He is now dead most painfully and slowly of a terrible suppuration of the wound. The doctors thought to amputate, but he was too weak to bear the pain."

A line from one of Sidney's sonnets rushed to Elizabeth's mind, a line she had often clung to: *Desiring naught but how to kill desire.* He had been madly in love with Lettice's daughter, Penelope, when young, but that daughter of a She-Wolf had turned him away most cruelly. Alas, all desire was dead for him now, though Elizabeth had still to find a way to manage her own.

"We are saddened to hear of his death, Walsingham, and we offer our regret to you and his wife, your daughter. We will write to Lady Sidney." Elizabeth put out a hand to the gallery wall and steadied herself. "He will be buried with all honors at St. Paul's and we will mourn him publicly and keep him in our private prayers." She bowed her head.

Walsingham murmured his gratitude and began to retreat.

"Is that all?" Elizabeth said, looking up, hoping to hear of Rob without asking further.

Walsingham stopped. "Majesty, the earl says that he will try to recapture some of the smaller towns to provide his valiant soldiers and his queen with some victory. . . . Then he begs you to recall him with strong words: 'Would to God I were rid of this place.'"

Elizabeth leaned against the carved stone pillars flanking the window opening. She could not be angry with Rob for leading his troops even against her express wishes. How could he not and retain what had always made him the man he was . . . her brave Eyes?

"Sir Francis, is there further word from our commissioners negotiating with the Spanish at Ostend?"

"There have been no meetings of late, Majesty."

"What say you? Why are they not continuing?"

"Majesty, my spies tell me Parma negotiates with the French and the States-General as well. I believe it to be an attempt to lull all sides until Philip's ships are provisioned and manned for an attack on England."

"Yes, yes, Sir Spymaster, so you have warned many times. But we hear the old Spanish king has more care for his soul than for his fleet. It is said he takes communion four times a day to be ever shriven in case death comes between. But we have more immediate business than Philip's soul. Come to us within the hour and we will have a private letter for the Earl of Leicester to go by swiftest courier to Holland."

Before Sir Francis bowed and backed away, Elizabeth was moving toward her privy chamber, her ladies hurrying to keep her fast pace. Once alone, she pulled her silver-trimmed writing cabinet to her and took out fresh parchment and a sharpened quill. To calm herself and allow her mind time to think clearly, she drank a few sips of watered wine and nibbled one of her favorite vanilla comfits before beginning.

How to begin? A queen did not apologize or explain. Still, she had to show Rob her heart to reassure him that she . . . Jesu, to give him as much reassurance as was possible for a sovereign to a subject.

> *Rob, I am afraid you will suppose by my wandering writings that a midsummer moon has taken large possession of my brains.*
>
> *But you have never been far from my thoughts and now I think to recall you from your labors in the field and urge you to come to me in England as soon as you can finish your affairs and those speedily.*
>
> *There is much trouble here and I am threatened by plots, assassins and spies of every hue and stripe. You know of the recent Babington conspiracy that planned my death and that Mary, queen of Scots, was part of it, agreeing to my assassination in writing and therefore condemning herself. Those men have met the traitor's end they deserved and Mary has been tried and condemned, though I have not signed her death warrant.*
>
> *Plots and plotters are always with me and I need all my loyal men at my side.*

She stopped and closed her eyes, seeing his face, pierced by his eyes yet unable to go on and admit that her previous angry letters had been too harsh. Mistakes were not for queens, not for this queen. Her heart wanted to speak loud, but all that she could do was allow it to murmur through her swan quill:

> *Now, will I end and do imagine that I talk still with you, and therefore loathly say farewell, ÖÖ, though ever I pray God bless you from all harm, and save you from all foes with my million and legion of thanks for all your pains and care. As you know, ever the same,*
>
> *Elizabeth Regina*

In November, the first hard snow of winter fell outside Whitehall Palace when the queen, at work reading Walsingham's latest stack of spy reports from France, Spain, Holland and Scotland, heard the words she had so longed to hear.

"Majesty," her gentleman pensioner announced, "the Earl of Leicester craves audience."

She pulled another warrant to her without looking up, though her hand shook so that she pressed it against the table. "Inform my lord Leicester that we are very busy, but will call for him within the hour. He is to wait in our antechamber."

"At once, Majesty."

As soon as the guard retreated, she regretted her words, but they were said and now must be kept. Always she must thrust her throne between herself and Rob. Though she longed to see him with her own eyes, to see for herself that he was as always her faithful Rob, she could not be seen to scurry down the halls of her palace to him like any milkmaid to her stable boy. She refused to allow herself to think how near she was to being that milkmaid, making herself a fool, to be run by her heart. No, not after all the years since Rycote that she had resisted such folly.

"Anne," she called, and her favorite lady of the bedchamber, the Countess of Warwick, appeared instantly from an antechamber. "I will change into my black-and-white gown, ermine trimmed with the gold embroidery." She smiled to herself. "And I will have my ivory fan with the Earl of Leicester's badge."

Anne nodded. "Majesty, the fan is very old and yellowed. It was one of the earl's first gifts to you as queen."

Elizabeth shrugged. "I will have it, nonetheless. And wear my lord's New Year's gift. Have it brought from the jewel room at once."

"Majesty, the necklace is in the Tower wardrobe."

"Send a swift courier downriver at once to retrieve it. It will suit the gown well."

Anne nodded and smiled. "Majesty, in my eyes it would suit any gown."

Elizabeth returned her smile, her heart lighter than it had been for . . . She tried to think back to the time, but always came to the same place, the night that she and Rob had supped together before he had left for Holland.

She was quickly dressed and perfumed with the special musky rose fragrance her perfumers made for her from a flower and herb garden grown for just that purpose at Hampton Court.

Her face was freshened with new white powder. And still there was a half hour to wait. She settled into her fireplace chair with her treasured Latin copy of *Plutarch's Lives*, but her eyes kept going to the big case clock where the hands crawled as if held back by Dr. Dee's angel, reminding her that, though a queen, she could not command time. Returning to her book, she reread the words again and yet again because she immediately forgot them, if she had seen them at all. Finally, she put the book aside and began to pace her chamber to release a hurly-burly spirit that could be tamed only with exercise. She took a deep breath and whispered, "I fear I will have to walk to Norfolk—"

Anne was next to her with her necklace and clasped it about her neck. "Majesty, I hope not so far." She smiled her sweet understanding. "Shall I call for the Earl of Leicester, Your Grace?"

Elizabeth held her temper, always angry when her thoughts could be so easily recognized. But of course Anne could read her mood. A beggar at the palace gate could read it.

"Majesty?" Anne questioned.

"Yes, yes, my lady, call him to me."

Anne curtsied and stepped to the door of the chamber where he waited, opened it and spoke quietly to the gentleman pensioner.

After almost a year apart from him, Elizabeth prepared herself to see a change in him. She felt her heart beating against her bodice as she saw he entered still with the same proud stride of his youth, but with more effort and many more white hairs in his beard. As he knelt to her, he winced.

That sign of pain propelled her to step quickly to him and signal him to rise. "You are most welcome here, my lord."

"Majesty, I thank you for your kind greeting to your old soldier." He smiled, making a handsome bow, and again grimaced.

"Rob, are you ill?"

The queen noticed that her ladies were gathered at the door, watching the tableau with interest soon to be whispered throughout the court. "We have no need of you," she announced. "Withdraw!" Realizing she was as shrill as an old shoe seller in a London alley, she added, "We pray you, my good ladies."

They were gone at once and she led Rob to her own chair,

which he accepted gratefully. She poured him a cup of her watered wine, which he drank, though he wrinkled his nose at its weak nature, as he always had.

"My queen, I am well enough. Do not be overconcerned. The channel was choppy and my poor stomach, my old complaint, is still uneasy from it. I came straight on to Whitehall without stopping."

She was pleased at that. He hadn't gone first to his country house of Wanstead, or Leicester House on the Strand. He hadn't seen that She-Wolf first.

"Rob," she said gently, "I will send for Dr. Dee to prescribe my potion for you and feed it to you with my own hand. Your old rooms next to mine are always made ready for you."

The earl attempted to rise from the chair, but she put her hand lightly on his chest and pushed him back. "Nay, Rob, I'll have you well before you take up your old duties."

"Then I am still your Master of Horse and Revels, on your council and—"

"Yes, Rob, you are still everything." Her voice shook a little before she could bring it under her control, especially as his eyes misted. "Everything," she emphasized, "and always will be. Why would you think otherwise? The Lowlands have done you ill. But I'll soon have you to rights."

"You are my physick, Bess," he said, looking full into her face. "You do your old Eyes too much honor."

"Nay, Rob, I but have a care for my own." *My own.*

He took her hand and, though she closed her eyes, she felt his kisses cover it, *softly, softly,* as they had that night that she could not forget.

She looked down upon his head and thought she saw the Robin of old, his dark hair against a fancy purple-and-green peacock feather swirling about his black velvet cap. And for a moment or two, her stomach ached again as it had in those days, wanting him to bestride it, love her, ease her. It was as if she had two heads, one a woman's and the other a queen's. She had always denied the first and still must. Always she must deny her woman's wants, a queen outside, a woman inside.

She straightened her back and stepped away. No man, not even Rob, could ease a queen. There was no ease to be had. Only duties and troubles . . . one of which, Jesu help her, she was about to shift onto him.

"When you are recovered, my lord, I will have a task for you, a task only you can accomplish for me. All my other lords have failed me, but they do not love me as you do."

"Anything, Bess. Give me one night of rest and I'll lead an army against your enemies."

"Nay." She laughed to see once more her eager young Robin looking at her. "It will not take an army . . . only you, and you will not fail me."

"Jesu, Bess, tell me what you would have of me. I am too old for suspense."

"Perhaps too old to serve me?" she taunted him, already uneasy about how much she must ask of him, how much she must reveal of herself.

"Never, Bess. As long as I draw breath I will live to serve you. Tell me the task I must do."

"Later. Now you must rest. I will come to you as soon as Dr. Dee has given me word that you are at ease from your ills."

He bowed and swept his hand from his heart to hers and so left, stepping as firmly as ever. He had said she was his physick. Now, he would be hers and help to lift her burdens as he had always done. She smiled to think of it.

Dee came to her later after her lone supper had been served with all royal formality, with which she would never dispense. Whether she was alone or at an official feast, the ceremony of her father, King Henry, must preserve her royal dignity as if every foreign ambassador and English subject looked on. Regal dignity unobserved was no dignity at all.

"Yes, my good Doctor, what news of the Earl of Leicester?"

"Majesty, His Lordship suffers from a gripping of the stomach and fever, an old ailment of his. I bled him for the fever and reduced the meat in his diet, which brings heat to the stomach. He must have five grains of mastich every night at going to bed. I also left the earl a dram of galangal powder to take with his breakfast wine."

"And—"

"Majesty, he is already much improved."

Elizabeth felt heavy anxiety take flight at his reassurance. "Thank you," she said, giving Dr. Dee her hand for his kiss, an honor he had earned.

After he left, she called her ladies and went to her chapel, where a priest in his long white alb, cinched at the waist, lit altar candles which were tended day and night, much to the anguish of her Puritan courtiers. So the practices came from the old religion, yet she found them comforting to think on. . . . When all the world was dark, God's priest on earth kept these little lights always shining. Kneeling at her private altar, she thanked God that Rob was not seriously ill and again gave thanks to God for favoring England and keeping the Spanish at bay.

She sent her ladies to their beds early. "We have no more need of you this night," she announced.

Anne delayed. "Majesty, do you want me to sleep on the trundle as before?"

"Nay, Anne. Off with you! Take your rest." Elizabeth put a gentle hand on her arm to take the sting out of her urgent words, and as soon as she was alone made her way with one yeoman guard to Leicester's rooms. She was met in the hall by a few startled people, who were surprised to come upon the queen without her long entourage of lords, ladies and peers preceded by announcing drummers and trumpeters. She had thought to use her father Henry's secret entrance as before. Then quickly, she had thought better of it. She was no heated young woman stealing through the night to a lover, but a queen showing particular care for her general and loyal subject. Nothing more.

Tamworth opened the door to her yeoman's knock. "Majesty," he said, startled into a hasty bow.

"Your master, John. How does he fare?"

"Much better, thanks to Your Majesty's care, since you are ever my lord's best physick."

She smiled at Tamworth, faithful, silent Tamworth. "We will see for ourselves."

He crossed quickly to an adjoining chamber and opened its door, announced her and bowed her in.

Rob struggled up from his bolster.

She raised a hand. "Nay, my good lord, do not disturb yourself. Rest while we talk."

"But, Bess, it is not fitting for me to lie abed while you—"

"We say what is fitting here, my lord!" She had not meant to be sharp, but her mood would brook no delay. "Rob," she said quietly, covering his hand with hers, "I had to see for myself if Dee told me true."

"True indeed, Bess, but I would not have you worried for my sake."

His ruffled hair gave him an impossibly boyish look, like the

Robin she'd first known as a young girl in her father's time, when she had not been a merry child, but young Robin had shown her how to be merry. She bent and kissed his hand.

"Bess." He said her name in that somewhat broken way he had said it when she was first in this room. Was he thinking of that night during her first year on the throne?

The fire still burned in the grate, though the chairs that they had sat in were replaced and the bed hangings were new and even finer. She wanted to lay her head alongside his again, feel her body covered by his. Was she mad? *Enough!* she commanded herself.

He smiled up at her. "What troubles you so, Bess?"

Elizabeth wondered if he could read her mind, their old mutual stars still at work in the heavens. "You must save me from a heavy duty," she said.

"Anything, Bess. You have only to ask. You know I will do all in my power. . . ."

She stood, losing the heat of his hand deliberately, because she feared it could lead to the need for more . . . closeness. "Mary Stuart is condemned, Rob. My Parliament, councilors and even Londoners in the streets demand her head."

Leicester nodded. "Aye, and rightly. Those who plot the death of a sovereign are traitors and—"

"Yes, yes, quite true, but not all the truth. Perhaps not even the most important truth." She shivered as if the ghost of the king, her father, who had condemned two wives to the ax, had crossed her grave. "If she dies by my hand, I fear that her son, James, may be urged by some in his court, or in Europe's courts, to come over the border and make war on England. I would not fight a war in the north with the Scots and in the south with the Spaniards."

Leicester sat up, healthier color rising to his face. "I am on good terms with His Majesty, King James. I will write to him and speak privily with his ambassador. You will be out of it. Believe me, Bess, James greatly desires to be your heir above all. He would not risk your enmity for a mother he does not even remember. A mother, as I recall, who conspired in the murder of his father and abandoned him for her paramour, Lord Bothwell, a mother whom Scotland refuses to take back as their queen now that her son reigns."

"Perhaps, perhaps," Elizabeth muttered, "but that is not the worst of it. I cannot . . . *cannot* by my hand order the death of my cousin and an anointed queen. I, too, am an anointed queen. If one queen can be executed, *any* queen's death can be so ordered. The pope has already absolved any English Catholic who takes my life. I need eyes behind me everywhere I go, even here in my castle and in my gardens." Her voice lowered to a fearful whisper. "How many of my Catholic subjects would like to see me dead and still achieve heaven?" She came near to his bed again and sat down, shaking with dread. The dark cloud of assassination followed her like a swarm of angry bees.

"Bess," he said quietly, and swung his legs over the side of the bed. His nightshirt did not cover his long shanks. She could not help but notice that those legs were thinner and corded with little muscle and outstanding veins, rather than the strong, shapely legs in purple hosen she remembered dancing with her at her masques.

"How can I help you?" he pleaded. "If the Parliament demands her death and your people beg for it, you have but to allow her sentence to go forward. Let it happen."

She straightened at that. "We rule here, my lord, not the Parliament, nor the people."

"Then how is this festering sore to be lanced?"

Her voice was low, but its intensity filled the room. "You could be my surgeon, Rob. Take her life for me and end this misery. My other *faithful* servants are too dainty for the job."

Leicester's head sank into the hands he clasped before him. "And you think this is work for me, Bess? Ask of me *anything* . . . but not this."

"This is all I ask."

"I have faced brave men in battle . . . killed with sword and pike . . . but I cannot murder a woman."

"Sir Amyas Paulet, Mary's keeper, will not do it, neither Burghley, nor Walsingham. I dare not ask Raleigh, for I do not fully trust him. Oh, that I had ruled in a better time!" Her face reddened and she hit one fist against the other. "How did Henry II get good Englishmen to step forward to rid him of that saintly troublemaker Becket? Are there no such brave and loyal men to serve *me*?"

Rob stared at her as if he'd never seen her before, and did not speak or move.

She had counted so on his understanding and desire to do her any service, to save her from awful necessity. Her last hope gone, she was enraged, feeling as betrayed as when young Robin had married his Amy. Before she could stop herself, if she had even thought to, her hand left her control and slapped his cheek hard.

His head fell back.

"Oh!" She looked with horror on the hand, but could not recall her cruelty or yet stay her righteous anger, which allowed her to say anything, even the unthinkable. "What? So delicately formed are you now, my lord Leicester? You were not so when you thought I would marry you if you were only rid of your wife! And then miraculously . . . you were!"

Jesu help me, she prayed silently. Could she have thought this monstrous thing deep inside herself all these years?

He jerked as if she had struck him hard again, though her fist was only clenched in anger. "You know I am innocent of Amy's untimely death."

Still unable to admit to fault, she lashed him again. "Oh, no, my lord, it was timely, very timely!"

Finding his pride, never far away, he lifted his head. "I was proved innocent by two juries. You could accuse me of nothing to wound me more. I truly believe Amy wanted to die and killed herself not from the pain of the tumor, but from the pain of my love for you."

Her anger dropped from her body like a fallen cloak. "Rob, Rob," she whispered, thinking to go out and reenter this room to start anew.

He did not answer her, sliding back under the coverlet, twisting away from her.

Tears came to her eyes, but she would not allow them to fall. She had nothing left to say. No appeal to make. Rob would hate her now and she would be truly alone, always. She moved slowly toward the door, trying to think of some words to salve his wound, but she could not and retain her dignity. Then she heard his strangled laugh.

"Majesty, even after our life together under the same stars, I am still all amazed by the twists and turns of your mind. You want me to kill Mary, queen of Scots, when there was a time when you ordered me to marry her . . . *ordered* me to it and all my begging would not stay you."

She closed the door softly behind her, her thoughts racing back to the agony of that time. Always she had fought to keep England safe from invasion, and Rob was to have been her painful sacrifice upon that altar. But had she ever truly meant to give Robin as husband to Mary Stuart?

CHAPTER 14

❧

"I am resolved to marry. If there be no foreigners
agreeable to me . . . I shall then choose no other
than the Earl of Leicester because of his merits
and virtues which I know him to possess."

—*Elizabeth I to Fenelon, the French ambassador*

———————————— ❧ ————————————

EARL OF LEICESTER

Autumn 1572
Hampton Court

While the queen was being dressed for an audience in
the presence chamber, the Earl of Leicester looked
out from her antechamber windows upon Hampton Court Palace. The cluster of brick towers and cupolas, the shady cloisters
and sunny loggias were as grand this day as on the day Henry
VIII had admired them so much that its builder, Cardinal Wolsey, was forced to give the palace to him. Henry would not have
borne his servant having a better palace than a Tudor king and
Wolsey knew it. The cardinal fell to his knees and Henry received

Hampton Court as a gift . . . on the spot. Was that why Bess favored this palace, because it was royal as a result of her father's power?

Robert had been in Henry's court as a boy and was able to summon the scene to his mind all too clearly. The huge king would have towered, intimidating Wolsey, a powerful man in his own right, yet in no way touching the king's supremacy. The king's vast bulk and florid face containing all the authority of his person and his realm behind it would have inspired any subject to please him and not make Henry wait a minute longer for his desire.

Would Bess feel the same about his own manor of Kenilworth? He doubted it, rather hopefully, since she already complained of the cost of upkeep on all the palaces she had inherited with her throne. And, Jesu knew, it cost him a treasure of gold marks to maintain and embellish his manor.

His planned addition of a great wing for Elizabeth's next visit had already put him in debt, not that he was ever out of debt. He had always lived far above his means, borrowing from one estate to add to another. For what purpose? None but to honor Bess and show his love. "And damned if I change now," he murmured.

"Sorry, my lord. Is there something I can bring you?"

"No, no, just thinking aloud." He saw that it was Sir Christopher Hatton speaking beside him, one of the dozen or more gentlemen pensioners, men of good family and some wealth who stood guard about the queen. Hatton was tall and well made, with blond, curling hair, a man whom women would find handsome. Bess found him handsome; Robert had no doubt. He felt jealousy rising within him, always there when the queen looked fondly on another man. And she kept no man about her who was ill to look upon. She adored youth and beauty, which he would inevitably lose. It took a moment of strong will to keep his face from showing what was seething inside him.

Since their night at Rycote, they had kept their promise never to speak of it again, though he had never ceased to remember. At times, he thought he saw sweet memory on her face, but he was never certain.

Was Bess's will to remain a virgin queen so strong that she could truly forget? Could she bewitch herself? He had proposed marriage time and again. Sometimes she had said yes, only to evade or deny the promise hours later. Sometimes she had not answered at all, leaving him in hope, or in anger and ultimately in despair. Yet, no matter how many years had passed, he had not forgotten the night they . . . He dared not think of it, lest it show on his face. He called on the endurance that life with her demanded, since life away from her grew no easier.

"Announce me, sir," he said when he heard Elizabeth entering her privy chamber, although there was no need. Bess had long ago granted him entrance into her bedchamber upon a knock whenever he wanted, the only one of her courtiers so honored. His desire, now, was to immediately put Hatton in a less exalted place as a servant . . . mean natured, but thus Robert must be to closely guard his place in Bess's court—and in her affections—or be lost in an instant and lonely hell.

"My lord of Leicester is come, Your Majesty," Hatton announced rather too self-importantly.

"Yes, yes, Kit, we see him."

So it was Kit now.

Hatton bowed. "Majesty, may I have your leave for the afternoon? There is a contest. . . ."

"A contest?" The queen, who loved games of skill and tournaments, looked interested.

"Aye, madam, at the archery butts in the near village of Molesey." He bowed and added, "With the prize being a kiss from the prettiest maiden. I am woefully out of practice at the butts," he said.

Elizabeth laughed. "But not at the lips, I vow."

Robert frowned at Bess's coquetry. It rubbed his heart raw to hear Bess jest so with anyone but him, though he had to hear it and bear it, as he always did, or leave her service if she would allow it. It was hell with her and an even hotter hell away from her.

At any rate, he didn't believe Sir Christopher was not prepared for the contest. The man was excellent at tiltyard practice. If his bow was as talented as his lance, Hatton would be impressive.

"Ah." The queen smiled and then sucked in her cheeks and pursed her lips, as she did when thinking. "Yes, go forth, Kit, and win your kiss."

The gentlemen pensioner bowed, his hand on his heart, and stepped backward to the outer chamber, closing the door softly.

Bess looked to be in a light mood, smiling and playful, almost skipping to the window where Robert stood. "Ah, a village . . . delightful. How long since I have visited a village?"

"Last month on your progress, Majesty," Robert said, trying to keep his tone from sarcasm and obviously failing.

Bess gave him a sharp look, missing nothing. She disliked being questioned in the least way. Agreement was her favorite sweet, even sweeter than her vanilla comfits.

Quickly, he smiled and knelt, looking up at her, knowing his features were none the worse for the soft morning light shining on them. "Would you like to walk in your perfume garden, Bess?" He had it in mind to have musicians playing behind the hedgerows for a special surprise.

"Later in the evening, perhaps, Robin, when it grows cooler. I have much work today . . . my marriage. Always my Parliament plagues me for marriage." As she ever did, she gained the advantage in this old and to him threatening conversation.

"Then until the cool of the evening, Bess, I take my leave."

She placed one hand fondly on his hair and gave him her other hand to kiss. He turned it palm up to imprint his lips, noting with satisfaction that she trembled slightly and turned her face from him as he left. She knew he could read desire in a woman's face. Had he put it there? Or had Hatton? Robert clamped his mind around such a thought, unwilling to allow it to escape and torment him all the day. He was never sure; he was never unsure, but suspended in a vast space between. He caught his breath, his chest sore from holding so much inside.

Robert stopped in the outer chamber and frowned. She never refused a walk in her favorite garden on a sunny, breezy day. What had changed her? He stepped closer to her bedchamber doors.

"Anne." He heard Elizabeth's excited, slightly shrill voice. "Anne, I will dress as your maid and go to the archery contest."

He heard a breathless enthusiasm in her voice.

"But, Majesty, you have many warrants from Cecil—beg pardon . . . no longer Sir Cecil, but now Lord Burghley, since you made him a baron this year."

Pup! Pup! "My new-made Lord Burghley can wait for a few hours. It will be an adventure that I do not read in a love sonnet, but live for myself! Come, Anne, do you seek to deny me some small amusement?"

"Nay, nay! Of course not, Majesty . . . but shouldn't we take a guard for your safety?"

"A royal guard would most certainly be recognized and that

would quite spoil my quest. Dearest Anne, you are growing old and fearful before your time. Come, we are yet young. Adventure with me!"

The excitement in Bess's voice echoed in Robert's head as he spurred his feet to race toward his rooms, only to find one of the Earl of Shrewsbury's sons, Lord Gilbert Talbot, blocking his way.

"Sir, I am hurrying to change and gather my favorite bow and truest arrows. Will your errand await a better time?"

"My lord," Talbot said, bowing, "I think not. For a beautiful lady awaits you."

Robert frowned at this presumption and the scarcely concealed amusement on the youth's face.

"What lady?"

"My lord earl, I may not mention her name, but she is one you know well and"—he bent forward toward Robert's ear—"I believe is far gone in love with you."

In spite of his better self, he was intrigued. "And her name?" It could be someone he did not suspect of such regard.

The youth's voice became a whisper. "Lady Douglass Sheffield."

Oh, Douglass. A beauty, true, but her husband had returned from Ireland, Robert knew, and she must leave court for her home. He quite liked her and for the past two years had soothed her loneliness and even at certain times had a real affection for her, but he could not stop now. "Talbot, tell my lady Sheffield that I will attend her later. I am now on an . . . urgent errand to the aid of Her Majesty."

"Lady Sheffield says, my lord, that her need is also urgent." He smirked.

"Later," Robert said rather overloudly, but needing to move fast away from this curious lad who thought to collect more court gossip for his father, the Earl of Shewsbury, and his wife, Bess of Hardwick. Rumor had it that the earl, who guarded Mary, queen of Scots, was almost overcome by her charms . . . charms that had proved fatal to better men. A fleeting moment of clarity made Robert angry as well as hurried. How different was he from poor Shewsbury, both chasing the heart of a queen?

"Fortunate man!" the forward lad called, but Robert was already rounding the corner.

Douglass was lovely and fair and of a gentle nature. She had all but thrown herself into his bed, how many nights he could not count. Was he a eunuch to turn away from such willing beauty and satisfaction? He came from Bess every night scarcely able to sleep. Even a queen could not expect to keep his aroused manhood caged!

But he was on more urgent business and hurried on down rush-lighted corridors. "John," he shouted to his servant Tamworth as he flung his antechamber door open, found his longbow but not his arrows.

His man rushed from another room.

"Where are my arrows?"

"They are with the fletcher, my lord, their feathers needing to be renewed from long lack of use."

"Hurry. Get them at once, or ones as good with straight shafts and sharp points . . . three fletches at the nock, mind."

Tamworth was almost out the door on his last word. "Wait, John. Afterward, hurry to the stables and have my best Irish hunter saddled, then discover which way Sir Hatton rode, so that I can ride another way."

He dressed in a suit of tight green velvet, the doublet embroidered with his arms of standing bear and double-crooked staff, a pair of purple-and-yellow hosen tight on his long legs held by the garter of a Garter knight, topping all with a peacock-feathered hat. He would be Robin the Hood this day and win a kiss from a maid . . . a particular maid . . . in disguise.

He downed a glass of wine and rushed to the stables, his stomach churning with excitement. It was just such an act of boldness that might topple Bess's stubborn desire to remain unmarried. She loved surprises and daring, gallant men in equal measure. Today he would give her both.

At the stables, Tamworth held out his arrows, and when he sighted along their shafts, they looked to be the best. He waited impatiently while a groom handed him the reins of his favorite hunter. "My lord," Tamworth whispered in his ear, "Sir Christopher took the west road. If you take the southwest road, the stable master assures me that you will arrive at nearly the same time."

"Has the queen left yet?"

"Aye, my lord, in her second-best carriage and in a great hurry."

Robert nodded and, grim-faced, leaped onto his saddle, gaining the stirrups and galloping through the south gate. He spurred his mount along the southwest road, scarcely wider than a path and not well traveled. He raised an arm to protect his feathered cap when hanging limbs grew too perilously low.

It was cooler on the wooded path, while Hatton would arrive sweating and dusty from the road. Robert, the Earl of Leicester, had not kept his place as supreme favorite with Elizabeth without practicing all the clever arts of courtship at his command. Though neither a poet nor a musician, he was the most practiced man in the courtly arts in this realm. Or perhaps any other, he thought, smiling to himself. He gave constant attention to every detail of dress and every opportunity to outshine Elizabeth's minor favorites . . . and there was always a new man in the ascendancy—yesterday Heneage, today Hatton, tomorrow another, although Elizabeth did not put away old favorites, or get rid of them as Henry had done. They were promoted, if she deemed them clever enough, and kept in service near her, collected like the treasures in her bedside treasure box to remind her that many men sought her favor. Adoration was as necessary to Bess as breath itself. She would never get enough to fill the void of emptiness her early years had left . . . in fear of her father, without a mother, alone with her servants, suspected of participating in every threat to the throne, alternately bastard, princess and simply Lady Elizabeth, each title more than once. But she remained a princess in her own heart, knowing that one day she would be queen. Those who sought her downfall suspected it and could not dislodge her faith in her own destiny. The long travail had made her strong . . . perhaps too strong for any man.

His jaw tightened and he raised his proud head. The Earl of Leicester would never be collected into her treasure box. He would be her partner. Bess could not resist him forever . . . she loved him. He knew when a woman loved and wanted him. He had always known that about Bess, as she did about him. Although they could shake each other's surety with others from time to time, love was always renewed when the hurt and emptiness of their separation could no longer be endured. Perhaps it was time to make her less sure of him. A man always there, like the little dogs that ran after her, was doomed to be less regarded . . . as a chair she didn't need to look for before sitting.

Robert straightened in the saddle, spurring his horse through the woods and out upon the edge of Molesey to see Elizabeth's empty carriage hidden just inside the trees. He rode on through smoke scented with roast ox. In moments, he reached the common grazing green and pond. An ox was indeed on a huge spit, and from the number of tethered horses, it was clear that the archery contest had drawn entrants from around the countryside. A kiss was not the grandest prize. . . . Winning and reputation were. But young men could always be in hope that more could follow a kiss. He grinned, knowing that about his own sex . . . and about himself.

He galloped onto the green, skidding to a stop, his great horse almost on its rump. No one missed his arrival.

Leaping from his horse, he threw the reins to a village lad and unfastened his bow and swiftly strung it. He stretched his shoulder and back muscles and sent a silent prayer to God that his archery skills had not faded since his last too-infrequent practice. And why should they? Once learned, the bow was like a galliard. A man just needed to call the moves to mind and his body would answer. Pray God and all His saints!

Surveying the crowd surrounding the green, he easily spotted his sister-in-law, the Countess of Warwick, looking straight at him without surprise. He bowed to her, removing his cap and smoothing its long peacock feather of green, yellow and purple. A tall serving maid hid behind Anne with a basket over her arm. A reddish curl peeked from under her rough hood, though she wore new satin slippers that no serving maid would ever be provided by a mistress.

To Robert's eyes, Elizabeth, without her Mask of Youth and fine gown, looked much as she had in 1550, at seventeen in her brother, Edward's court. There, she had assumed a demure, almost Puritan dress and demeanor meant to thwart the ugly rumors of her seduction and pregnancy by Lord Admiral Thomas

Seymour, Catherine Parr's husband. The admiral had high ambitions: to marry Princess Elizabeth, to overthrow his brother Edward Seymour, Lord Protector of England, and to rule England himself, eventually to be a king. By 1550, when Robert and Bess were together at Richmond, Thomas Seymour was an admiral without a head and Elizabeth was cautious with male admirers, though not with Robert Dudley.

But on the Molesey green, the Bess who was now Queen Elizabeth was no longer used to hiding her true self. Robert could plainly see that her bearing was certainly not that of a lady's maid. There was no way she could disguise that confident carriage of head and body.

"My lord," Hatton said, bowing, "I did not know you were shooting today."

"Sir Christopher, I decided it was time I practiced as every knight should."

"I never miss practice myself, Lord Robert."

"Admirable," Leicester answered, the word pushed between his teeth.

Hatton bent and strung his bow. "May the best man win."

"Indeed, sir," Leicester said, galled at the probable double meaning behind those words and ready to teach the upstart a lesson. Robert made ready to walk toward the lineup of archers.

"My lord," Hatton said, daring to put a hand on Robert's sleeve, "I would hope to be your friend."

"My friend, sir?"

"Aye, we have much in common."

"How so?"

"We both love and serve Her Majesty and want only her good. Is that not so?"

Robert stared at him to see if he saw any devious notion on

that too-handsome face, but there was not. Could the man be so naive? It was their mutual love for the queen that made them natural enemies, not friends.

Hatton saluted with his bow and left Leicester to take his place in the line, undecided if here was a rascal or a true man.

Robert, as was his right by rank, took first place ahead of Hatton. He adjusted his arm guard and studied the course. It was laid out in the ancient way of roving marks, where each archer would shoot to a mark and then shoot from that mark to another, gathering points along the way, depending on how close to the mark his arrow lodged.

Stealing a glance at the queen, he saw she had advanced to Anne's side and watched him with a faint smile. She would be seeing the black ribbon around his shooting arm from which dangled a large white pearl. Bess would know that he intended it as her favor.

He raised his bow, fitted an arrow nock into the bowstring and took a wide stance, his left foot slightly ahead of his right. Pulling the arrow back strongly with three fingers, he let fly and hit the post, burying his point deep in the wood. He resisted a prideful smile, waving a hand briefly to acknowledge the applause.

"Twenty points for the Earl of Leicester," shouted the archery master.

There were cheers from the villagers and other archers. The lady's maid on the edge of the green stepped forward to see better.

Sir Christopher shot next, taking a bold stance, raising his arrow to his nose before loosing it, but it flew to the left and landed within three feet of the post.

Robert applauded politely with the villagers as the master shouted, "Seventeen points for Sir Christopher."

"Good shot," Robert shouted.

Hatton bowed. "Not as good as yours, my lord."

The man sounded sincere. Perhaps . . . just perhaps they could be, if not friends, at least honorable enemies. Jesu knew he had a surfeit of the other kind.

Robert strode to the post and sighted his arrow on the second mark, a red flag. He waited for the breeze to pick up the flag to give him a wider shot. But the breeze died to calm as he loosed and his arrow landed within the three-foot circle. The master awarded him seventeen points.

Sir Christopher took careful aim this time, sighting the arrow lower, and hit the flag, pinning it to the ground.

"Excellent shot, sir," Leicester shouted, determined to be chivalrous. They were even in points and so it remained around the marks until the last shot, the most difficult of the day. The mark was a dovecote in the village church tower.

"Difficult mark, my lord," Hatton said at his shoulder.

Robert shrugged. "I spent my boyhood shooting at birds. I know their habits."

Hatton bowed, his face pleasant. "For one unpracticed, as you say, I honor your skill, my lord." He was either a playacting flatterer or too good-hearted for royal service where goodness was seen as an Achilles' heel. At that moment, Robert felt his sincerity . . . strange for a Tudor court. If he was as he seemed, he would need an earl's protection against those who would take advantage. Robert warned himself against such foolishness. When did a true courtier come to aid his rival if he were not a fool!

He saw Elizabeth leaning forward in anticipation of his turn, her face clear of white paste and red cochineal, looking as young and fresh as a true village maid. She saw him and must know he saw her, but her eyes avoided his and he turned to the target.

The dovecote was thirty feet in the air, doves cooing and flapping about their roosts as if to celebrate another day they had escaped a village cook pot.

He tested the wind with a wet finger. The breeze had picked up again. He would have to gauge the crosswind and the doves' habits of bobbing up and down, suddenly going back inside the cote or unexpectedly fluttering off their perch. He had killed them as a boy and proudly taken them to his mother's cook for a meat pie. But that was many years ago. He briefly but carefully watched the birds and their habits and picked the fleshy one in the middle who seemed quieter. And it was the best shot. If he missed it, he'd have a chance to hit one of the other two off its perch.

Glancing again toward Bess, he saw that she had stepped in front of her "mistress" and was drawing the curious glances of the villagers. A plain gown could not hide this queen. The countryside would be buzzing with talk of Elizabeth in her disguise, the tale told for years. And Bess would savor it.

Shaking his head, he dislodged the image of her and looked down, carefully placing the arrow nock on the bowstring. Here was another tale to be told around their cottage fires.

He sucked in breath and tensed his stomach muscles, raised his bow knowing he must release the arrow at once. He loosed. The arrow flew true and the shouting began, but his bird ducked inside the cote to its nest a brief moment before the arrow reached it. The villagers groaned, or was it his own voice he heard?

Village boys were already on the tower climbing to the cote.

One retrieved his arrow and held up the pigeon by its legs, very much alive, frantically fluttering over his head.

"Nay, lad, the bird lives," he shouted. "It fairly dodged my arrow." He bowed to the villagers and they cheered him politely, but the lady's maid had turned away. Bess was embarrassed for him. She knew nothing but winning.

"A good shot, my lord," Hatton said, bowing.

Since there was no trace of triumph on his face, he meant to be chivalrous. "Sir Christopher," Robert said, returning the bow, "I pray you a better aim."

And, of course, God granted his prayer, when he had been denied so many others. The skewered bird fell at Hatton's feet to hearty applause. He handed it to a beldam for her supper.

Shouldering his bow, the handsome gentleman pensioner walked straight toward Elizabeth. "From this maid I will take my prize," he shouted. Taking her in his arms, Hatton kissed her soundly to raucous cheers and a flute and drums playing a lively country tune. Elizabeth smiled up at him.

Now the villagers would talk endlessly for years of that kiss while the great Earl of Leicester looked on haplessly. Robert bowed to the master bowyer and leaped to his horse. S'blood, he could not, would not, watch longer. Was this what Elizabeth had come for? His stomach churned and he forgot all his kind thoughts of Hatton. Why not call him out on some pretext? What would Bess do if her Robert disobeyed her law against dueling and killed another favorite? Would she dare send him to the Tower after what they had endured there together?

His chest burned with held breath, heated by resentment he could no longer feel for Hatton. He had nowhere to aim it but Bess . . . and yes, he could be angry with her even after his own misdeeds. Did he not reap kisses elsewhere?

Robert galloped from the village and onto the cart road for Hampton Court. He cared nothing for the heat and dust; he cared only to get away quickly. Losing the contest meant embarrassment, but losing even one of Bess's kisses to another man meant much more. He told himself he was being foolish, acting like a jealous lad, and not a man who took love where he found it. But it did no good, as it never did.

That night he dressed for a masque in the great hall. He was in no mood for it, but if he were not in his place, some other man would eagerly fill it. His heart was in his boots as he approached the great hall until he heard the sweet, high voices of the Chapel Royal boys singing:

> *When we two are parted*
> *All the world is gray.*
> *Star and moon and sunshine*
> *Go with him away.*

His fast-beating heart flooded with hope. He stepped inside to see if Elizabeth waited for him and this was her tender greeting, her signal that Hatton's kiss meant nothing lasting.

The queen, her jeweled gown sparkling in the candlelight, saw him. He was certain. She immediately called for a galliard and stepped out with Hatton. So the sweet song was for the gentleman pensioner and winning archer . . . deliverer of sweet kisses. Not for him. He tasted bile and fought to keep his face a blank but he knew his jaw tightened, his eyes grew blacker and his mouth became harder.

He could see how well Hatton danced, living up to the name

some wags had bestowed on him, "the Dancing Pensioner." Did she seek to humiliate Robert or show her trim ankles to another man?

Robert felt his face heat with anger, but he made a stiff bow in her direction, so brief it was nearly an insult. Walking toward a group of ladies against the rear wall, he stopped in front of the Baroness Douglass Sheffield and bowed low enough for the queen. "My lady," he said, removing his glove and holding out his hand, "I am free to attend you now." Douglass was not a dancer of Elizabeth's skill, but he would make her look better. She was already good to look at with her blond hair, fair face, pointed chin and large green eyes that he swore could see in the dark. Her sister, Lady Frances Howard, stood beside her, her lovely hazel eyes flashing angrily at Douglass.

The sisters were each in love with him. He would dance with one, then the other, and Bess would regret her treatment of him.

Robert began to feel himself again.

"My lord Leicester, I am honored," Douglass said formally for the benefit of those around them.

She took his hand while Frances pouted and he found the hand heated, as was the red growing on her neck and face.

"I thank you, my lady," he said loudly, as if meeting her for the first time. "I have long wanted to make your better acquaintance." He probably fooled no one, but that was the court game everyone played.

He guided her closer and closer to Elizabeth and Hatton, knowing that the queen was perfectly aware of him and of the attractive lady with whom he danced.

"Robert, don't take me near the queen. Please!"

"I must. I have no choice, or she will be suspicious." *Not more than she is*, he thought, but did not voice it.

Elizabeth looked at him with surprise, as if unaware of his presence. "Here you are, Robin. I called for you but you were not in your apartments and not in your place beside me. You grow lazy in duty to your sovereign." She stopped dancing; the music ceased and every courtier turned an interested face toward them.

He knelt to his queen and bowed his head to hide his angry face at her reprimand in front of Hatton.

"Come," she said, holding out her hand for him to kiss. "Rise, Lord Robert, stay your brooding and sit with me." She smiled at him, amused, as if he were a young lad in a sulk for not having his way . . . and perhaps he was, but he would not be treated so before the court, not even by Elizabeth. Every day, he must watch her bestow her favor on other men. Let her watch him with another woman!

As the years had all slipped by, now twelve since his wife, Amy, died and six since Rycote, he and Bess could have married and had princes. And waiting had not become easier but more difficult and far more wounding. They said that the heat of youth burned lower with the years, but it had never been so with him.

How much longer could she keep him waiting? Did she think that serving her was enough for a man? Maybe for a Dancing Pensioner like Hatton, but not for the Earl of Leicester. He wanted to laugh, but it would not come out. He knew his response would be a mistake, but he refused to stop himself.

He stood. "Majesty, excuse me, but I am most occupied with the Baroness Douglass in the galliard."

Elizabeth's turned red as she filled with rage. "There is no music, my lord, and there will be none!"

"I am sorry for that, Your Grace, since you were dancing so skillfully with the archer." He lowered his voice until only Hatton and the queen and Douglass heard him. "By your leave, madam, I will make my own music."

He tightened his hold on Douglass Sheffield's arm.

"My lord, get me from this place," she urged him in a nearly breathless whisper.

He steered her out of the great hall toward her own room, expecting Elizabeth to demand his return at any moment, but she did not.

"I seek sweet company tonight, my lady Douglass." He exhaled slowly. The war of words with Bess was always exhausting. "Shall we walk in the perfume garden together?"

"Are you running mad, Robert?"

"I may walk with whom I choose, Douglass."

"Not in the queen's court, or in her privy garden. You will have me in the Tower." She looked to escape from him. "I must away. She will know if she looks at me again, already suspicious."

"Know what . . . that we walk in her garden? Must I have permission for that? Jesu, I can walk and piss where I please!" He only half heard her quavering response, wondering instead if Bess would call him to her tonight, or wait to punish him tomorrow.

"Rob, please—"

"Don't call me that."

The woman, always so sweet and docile, was now demanding and difficult, as sooner or later all women were no matter how they loved you.

"My lord earl, I am with your child."

"What?" His response was so loud that others going toward the great hall stopped to look at them.

"How could that be? I wore a sheath. Your husband?" he asked softly, but hopefully.

She shook, her teeth chattering with fright, and would not look at him. "I have not been with him for three months. He will never believe a six-month babe. Never!"

She was near hysterics, but of sadness rather than fright.

"Come, calm yourself." He took firm hold on her shaking shoulders and steered her toward her chamber. He knew the way.

When they were inside, he took her in his arms, her servants quietly slipping away. "Have you thought of . . . well, an abortive? Dr. Dee would help you, if he is at court."

"Burn in hell if I abort your son? For so Dee has assured me is the sex of the child by my stars." She shook in his arms and he damned himself for his words, but Bess could not learn of this, although the word *son* rang in his head. Bess must never know!

"Then go to a wise woman for pennyroyal and tansy. If not, you must go home, Douglass, and quickly."

"No, no, Robert, I do not want to return there. John will divorce me. There will be a scandal. Her Majesty will be furious with me."

Nothing to what she will be with me.

"What then?" He was weary of trying to please women.

"I will try for a divorce so that we can marry."

He closed his eyes and took a deep breath. "That can never be."

She began to sob, her pale complexion becoming mottled red and her beautiful eyes swelling. Why did women think tears would bring a man to agreement, when it only made their faces lose their attraction?

Robert helped her to a chair and knelt in front of her, gently taking her shaking hand, for he truly felt sorrow. "Hear me, Douglass, for I may say this but once." Even as he said the words, he knew they would need to be repeated many times. "You must know that if I were to marry you, it would result in my utter ruin. I would never regain the queen's favor and would be completely overthrown."

Her voice quavering, she looked full in his face. "You mean that I am nothing to you and the queen, who has ever rejected you, is everything?"

Robert would have never put it that way for the affection he felt for Douglass, but she was exactly right. He did not want to hurt her, but he had never lied to her or promised her anything but his regard, and she had that. "Go home at once to John Sheffield, your good husband, but know I will ever care for your child . . . and for you."

He left her sobbing. There was nothing more he could say or do.

He required three large glasses of wine to sleep that night.

Elizabeth did not call for him later, nor all the next day. Although he attended her in council, she looked past him to others for advice as if he weren't there.

Bess was deliberately breaking his heart. He knew what Douglass suffered and had known it for much of his life. He answered a message from her after dark and saw her tearfully off to her husband in the north on one of the Howard estates she'd inherited, after the queen had granted her written permission to return to her husband.

Robert's dragging footsteps echoed in the halls outside his chamber. He was unsure whether he should retire to Leicester House on the Strand, or stay and face Elizabeth's anger and probable dismissal.

Tamworth greeted him outside his door, whispering: "My lord, the queen waits for you in your bedchamber."

Robert was suddenly so completely exhausted, he doubted

he would be at his best appeasing Bess's outrage, which must be great indeed if it had brought her to him in private. He slipped quietly into the room, ready to humble himself or accept angry blows . . . anything. But there was no need. The queen of England and Wales was curled up on his bed, which, praise God, had been freshened this morning. She was fully gowned and bejeweled but apparently asleep. Her breathing was shallow, her eyes tight shut.

He carried a chair to the bed, sat down and took the hand that trailed over the bedside. Her lids flickered and she sighed.

"Good night until the morrow, my love," he whispered.

"You don't love her?" It was a whispered question, her eyes still closed.

"Never. Only you, Bess. Always you."

Thus, he knew he was forgiven his interest in Douglass, though he did not think it would last more than six months. Elizabeth had studied mathematics diligently.

He must win the queen's hand before that calamity.

CHAPTER 15

❧

"What! Shall I so far forget myself as to prefer
a poor servant of my own making to the first
princes in Christendom?"

—*Elizabeth I to Kat Ashley, who
urged her to marry Leicester*

———————————— ❧ ————————————

Elizabeth

A February midnight, 1573
Leicester House on the Strand, London

To the sound of the drummer in the prow, beating time
for the oarsmen, a sound Elizabeth usually loved, her
foot tapped the deck, but not this night. Tonight, she had en-
joyed none of her usual pleasures, not the soft, silken touch of her
shifts, not the stiff brocade of her gown and oversleeves, nor the
yielding warmth of ermine, a fur that only a queen could wear.
This night was not a night for sensual pleasures, but her firm
resolve to confront Robin once and for all time. Seven years had
passed since their one night together at Rycote. She had steeled
herself through the nights of those years, never to repeat the

hours when she had come so close to setting aside her throne for love. Tonight, the Earl of Leicester would be a fortunate man, by Jesu, to escape the Tower, or banishment, or at least a tongue-lashing that would bring him to tears.

The royal barge, its lights glaring into full dark, landed at the ice-covered dock of the Earl of Leicester's town house across the river from Whitehall. Elizabeth strode ahead of her guard to the earl's back door, her empty stomach churning. She would bear Rob's deceptions no longer. He had promised to love and serve her in everything, and by God and all His saints, if Rob had failed her again, she would . . . She clenched her fists inside her ermine muff, forcing her mind away from all it could think and her mouth from what it could say in anger and never recall.

She passed the garden pavilion Rob had built, where they had spent lovely summer evenings protected from ill breezes blowing from the tanneries and the eyes of the curious. Evenings never to be repeated now.

"Knock!" she commanded, and her guards pounded loudly with the butt ends of their pikes.

The rush lights inside appeared to have burned low and there was no immediate response.

"Majesty, they are all abed," her captain said, turning back to her, uncertain.

"Break it down!" ordered the queen in full throaty voice, her rage barely controlled.

Quickly, the guards who carried short pole arms advanced and took turns skewering the door with their ax blades.

Elizabeth stepped back and saw lights beginning to blaze one by one from many windows. She noted Rob's windows up the stairs were among them. He would be readying his lies . . . and his knees for submission. But this night she was in no believing mood. She swallowed bitter laughter, making no sound.

Her guards began to break through, just as a man shouted, "Who assaults the Earl of Leicester's house?"

Elizabeth recognized Tamworth's voice. "By Jesu and his holy spear wound, open this door to your queen, John, or we will make you a head shorter by sunup!"

Both doors were flung wide-open and Tamworth threw himself to his knees. "Majesty . . . Majesty . . . had I known . . ."

Other servants cowered in their night shifts behind him, the hall now ablaze with light.

"Don't stand there gawping! Take me to my lord of Leicester at once!" Her voice, her presence and her high color would convince him if her menacing pikemen did not.

"Your Grace, this way, if it please you," John said, bowing and holding his many-branched candelabra high to shine light in every corner for her.

"You . . . you," she said, pointing to her guards' captain and his lieutenant, "follow me."

She climbed the great, sweeping staircase, narrowing her eyes as her youthful coronation portrait appeared at the top. A show of loyalty, but no real devotion. She expected Rob to come into sight at any moment . . . on his knees, by Jesu and his holy wounds, if he knew her temper.

But he stood in the door of his bedchamber, one bare foot crossed over the other, smiling his welcome with drowsy eyes, a stubble of beard on his usually clean-shaven cheeks. Was he growing a full beard? Heaven forbid! As she had often noted, the less men trusted their manhood, the more they grew their whiskers.

She brushed past him as if he were a post. "Search this place," she commanded the guards. As they rushed to do her bidding, she yelled after them: "And under the bed!"

He must say something, she thought. But he bowed and, with a wave of his hand, and a shrug that lifted his high robe collar even higher, invited her to look wherever she would. The arrogant fool. All the while appearing so tousled and boyish in his blue velvet night robe embroidered with his coat of arms, as if no one knew who he was in his own bedchamber! She tried to calm her breathing. Why did the sight of him cause her great anger to wend around and pierce her own spirit? Had Rob won his archery match after all, skewering her heart as he had not the dove's?

He bowed, a bemused smile on his mouth, his full lower lip slightly lowered in a way that made her wish she were on sweeter business. She clamped her mouth against such thoughts lest they escape into acts.

"Majesty . . . Bess, as you see me, I am alone here and yet eager to be at your service. What would you have of me?"

Elizabeth rounded on him in the middle of his anteroom. "My lord, do you think me brainless?"

"I would never think so, Majesty. And I am puzzled by the question."

She clenched her fists and he saw. Clever man, but she was the more clever, as he should know. "I had word this night that the Baroness Sheffield was brought to bed two days ago with a healthy boy."

She watched his face closely. What man would not give himself away at news of a son, especially Rob, who had no heir? Were all men alike? Her father had been the same . . . exactly the same. He had raged about Greenwich, canceling the tournament he had ordered planned in honor of his son, who had been born a daughter, good only for cementing ties with a foreign prince. It was said he cried aloud so that half the court heard: "Is this what I destroyed a church for?" Well, she, Elizabeth, had shown him that his daughter was stronger than a girl, strong enough to rule England as well as any son, better than the son, Edward, he finally had of his third queen, Jane Seymour. Oh, if only she could see her father's face in heaven and read what astonishment she had put there.

But Elizabeth, queen of England, ruled her emotions as her father never had. Except for Rob. Was she strong enough to rule herself away from the Earl of Leicester?

By this time Rob had had good time to gather his wits. "Majesty, I must congratulate my lord John Sheffield," he said, controlling his voice, his face and her . . . or so he must believe, as any clever man would.

"Too late for congratulations, Rob."

"Too late?"

She narrowed her shortsighted eyes to see him better in the dim light of candles and fire. "It seems the lady's husband, Lord John, was at the very moment of birth on his way to obtain a divorce." There! That would be enough to show on even his practiced face. But what was this? He looked truly shocked.

"Majesty, I am amazed to hear a man would turn away from the birth of his own heir."

Pup! Pup! "Enough of this dissembling, Rob! He found a letter from you to his wife that she oh so carelessly dropped on the floor for him to find! He was prevented from a divorce action." Did she see a look of relief on his face?

"Prevented?"

"My lord Sheffield was on his way to London to obtain a

divorce when he died of dysentery in an inn on the north road. There is already rumor abroad in London and the court that you had her husband poisoned." She watched him closely.

Leicester shrugged, but his face reddened and his jaw went rigid. "They must think I do nothing but poison husbands, since I have been accused of killing how many others before tonight?"

The queen, changing from cold to hot at his arrogance and the truth in it, grabbed a vase and threw it, but he nimbly side-stepped the missile. Elizabeth saw it then: the visage she had expected. He could not help himself. He was damning the Lady Douglass for bringing this on him. How like all men Rob was, only worse because he had a queen to love . . . and he chose a brainless jade like Douglass, who would part her legs for him at every chance.

The guards crowded back into the anteroom, having found no hidden lover.

"Leave us and wait below," she commanded, and watched as they shut the door softly. She was relieved that he did not have a woman every night, but even angrier that she could be made to seem foolish and rejected. Well, she refused to be so. He was at fault here and he would admit it or go to the Tower . . . well, maybe to his new manor of Wanstead.

"Majesty," he said, dropping to his knees, "come sit by the fire and warm yourself. I would not have you shivering for my sake."

"I shiver not for your sake, my lord," she said, the words rasping from deep in her cold throat, "but my own. I would know how many ways you make a fool of yourself . . . but not of me. That dishonor I will never accept."

He rose without her command and poured some wine in a cup and held it over the edge of the fireplace to warm.

"Bess, please come, sit, and drink this. I worry for your health."

"Worry for your life, my lord," she said, straightening her spine. It was an old threat that she would never carry out and she knew it. But he did not. Or did he?

He stood in front of her, and though she was tall for a woman, he was taller yet by a head. He held the cup out, until she must either take it or knock it to the floor. He moved it an inch closer, his dark, uptilted brows showing his concern. "Rob . . ." She heard his name pass her lips. S'blood! Her anger was draining from her like rain from a sluice pipe. And he would see it and know, as such practiced men always knew, that she desired him and fought it.

"Bess, dearest . . . sweetest, I am here in my bedchamber this night waiting for you . . . always waiting for you."

As she sagged toward the floor, she heard him drop the wine cup and felt its contents splash her shoes, felt his hands on her. He picked her up and carried her the few steps to a chair by the fire. He knelt and rubbed her hands with his warm ones. He removed her slippers and rubbed her feet, kissing each in turn until she ceased to feel the cold, but did not cease shivering.

Elizabeth felt her eyes mist and turned her head away. "Is the babe yours?" She whispered the words into the fire, merrily burning the logs away as his faithlessness was burning away all her heart's love for him. She could never forgive this! Never! She had forgiven him for Lettice because she believed that he bedded the woman thinking she was his queen . . . but not this time. . . . No more forgiveness was in her.

He laid his head in her lap, holding her tightly, his hands curving around her waist to her hips, the heat of them burning through her gown and shifts to her skin. He kissed her stomacher, bringing on a familiar ache of yearning that she had followed to its end only once, just once, that night in Rycote, seven years earlier. At the memory of that night, she was cold no longer. Her hands went of their own accord to his head and she buried her fists in his thick black hair.

"Bess," he said, and looked up at her.

She was lost now in his Gypsy-dark eyes, so close to him, so close to losing him to that frivolous Douglass, who could give him what she would not . . . and surely never could again.

Hearing herself make an excuse for him was the last thing she intended, but she heard her own voice saying the words of understanding and forgiveness. "She came to you in your sleep. You believed it a vivid dream. You do not love her. . . . Tell me. S'blood, tell me that much." She gripped his shoulders. "Rob, I command you!"

"Bess," he said, almost choking on her name. He started to bury his head in her breast, but she held him away.

"I will see your face to know if you speak truth to me."

He took a deep, shivering breath and looked into her face. "This is my truth, my only truth. I love you as I never loved another woman, as I never will love another . . . but . . ."

She bit her upper lip. "But you are a man with a man's hot appetite. Is that what you were going to say . . . again? Do not say it! I hate the words. I have heard them before and I will listen no more. I am queen and I deny myself everything . . . husband, children . . . nights like this. . . ."

"But you have favorites other than me who would give you anything you asked. I would give you anything . . . everything." He withdrew his hands from her and she abruptly had no anchor. She gripped the chair arms to keep from falling toward him, and he saw. Standing, he drew her to her feet and, still holding her, put his lips softly on hers, working her mouth open and finding her tongue.

She heard a sound rising in her throat, a woman sound, a starved sound. "Robin . . . my Eyes," she whispered his old, tender names.

"My queen . . . my Bess." He bent slightly and picked her up.

She did not stop him. She could not stop herself. She would know a little of what other women . . . what Lettice and Douglass knew of him. Only a little. She would know the joy that the least village woman in her realm knew. She would know the joy of that one night at Rycote again, or as close to that joy as she could ever allow herself to go. She could not speak of the summer night while on her summer progress they had escaped to his hunting lodge at Rycote, the one night they had completely loved, but sworn never to speak of more. Though that oath could never stop her from thinking of it, of feeling his hands upon her breasts, of knowing what it was to be a woman loved.

He turned slightly as he entered his bedchamber, his broad hand protecting her head, and then she felt his bolster under her hair, the spicy scent of him all about her, all about her forever. At once she was frightened as she never had been. "Rob, do not get a babe on me. . . . I . . ."

But he was kissing her and pressing his body against hers. She could call her guards. She could stop him . . . but could she stop herself?

He lay so close that his body's warmth came through her gown, her stomacher, her shifts. She felt a trembling begin inside, heat making its way to her womanhood and gathering there until the flames nearly o'erwhelmed her. She must cease this!

"We do not think the better of you for Douglass's babe," she said, her voice made cold to put out the blaze.

"I do not think the better of myself, though I have not claimed the boy."

"Douglass will nevermore come to my court."

He opened her ruff and kissed her neck and her anger was blown away like a great storm at sea carrying all ships before it. She allowed herself to cling to him, to arch to him . . . just one more time. It had been so long since she had felt the length of him against her . . . weakening her will, burning it away until her cheeks and the woman part, the part her father had hated because he had desperately wanted a male heir, were rapidly turning to enticing flames.

"Marry me, Bess. There is still time for us . . . for you to have princes, heirs to this realm . . . our princes. We two, together like this every night of our lives, while there is time."

"Beloved Robin, we will have many years yet."

"No, Bess, I will not make old bones. No one in my family lives long."

"They lose their heads." She immediately regretted uttering those words, true though they were.

"I could lose mine. You are queen and your love can one day turn upside down to hatred."

She wrapped her arms about him to keep him close, continue his warmth. "Never, Robin. My love for you is so much a part of me . . . head and body . . . that if you were to lose your head, my heart would die." She felt a brief annoyance sweep over her. "Have I not told you that I am married to England and if I married any man, it would be you?"

He kissed her lightly. "Yes, you have told me, but the words make cold bed comfort on a winter's night."

"Rob, after all these years, do you not know my heart?"

He laid his head on her breasts, his lips kissing the rounded part that fashion dictated she expose. "Dearest queen of my love," he whispered, "it is the years themselves that make me doubt you . . . some days . . . and many lonely nights."

She was irritated again. "Your nights appear to be less lonely than mine."

He sat up and looked at her, his black eyes catching candle-light and holding it. "Bess, don't you see what you do? Whenever we are close like this, you choose anger to stop your woman's desire. Do you think I do not know?"

"That is false!" She trembled with the truth of his words.

"Is it?" He reached for her.

She did not roll away from him. Her head told her to, but her body did not obey. And she was queen! How much less could an ordinary woman resist this man's body?

He lay atop her, bearing most of his weight on his forearms. He kissed her, opening her lips, or finding them open. Oh, he was very practiced! But her anger did not rise. Her body did. She could not stop it. She did not wish to stop it! She rose to meet him, finding the ancient rhythm again, a rhythm that had wak-ened her on too many nights of dreaming that he was atop her. Now, through her gown and his night robe, she felt him grow strong, again her dream come true.

"My long love," Rob whispered above her tight-shut eyes, "where you are empty, I will fill you."

Elizabeth heard a triumph in his voice, which may or may not have been there. She no longer could tell what was true or untrue.

He rolled from her and put his lips on hers; they were firm . . . hard this time. His hand was at the hem of her gown, reaching under, from satin to satin to fine linen to lace until he found her. She groaned as she felt his hand on the inside of her thigh reaching higher.

"Bess . . . Bess . . ." His voice trembled under the words. "Allow me"—he took a quick breath—"to give you pleasure without harm. Only delight, my sweet queen."

"No . . . no," she said, but took his hand and pushed it to where she was burning. As he stroked her, he moved against her leg.

Her breathing came hard now as she responded to his caresses in fiery spasms. "Ro-bin!" His name, breathed so softly into her pillow for so many nights, filled the room as an anguished cry.

"Bess, my love. I must—"

She clasped him to her, smothering her cries against his shoulder, and Rob's mouth muffled sound against her breast as he shuddered against her.

Elizabeth felt a great weariness and she wanted to rest, to sleep without moving, to forget that she was . . . No, no, she could never forget that she was a monarch. No Tudor queen could be a simple woman, loving a man. The least brown-faced cottage girl in her realm could leave her fields and love a man, lying with him every night like this, but the queen of England could not.

Unexpectedly, she wondered if there would be a day when Robin would not be with her. Would she know endless regret? She shivered as if someone had trodden upon her grave.

She put her free arm about his shoulders and held him close for a long time until she felt him rise again.

She stirred, lifting herself to sit, and he rolled away.

"What do you want, Bess? You know what I can give you . . . long to give you."

"Yes, many times yes. They say that I am not a real woman,

even that I am a man or some crippled mixture." She gripped him. "But I am a woman with you, Rob."

"You are that, Bess. I know it even when you look at other men . . . like Kit Hatton."

Wrenching herself more upright, she said: "And I know it when you look at other women. Do not think that I am not watching every time, that my heart—" She stopped her mouth with her hand, knowing her words gave him too much power.

"You must go now," he said, smiling up at her.

She saw the first hint of dawn creep around the drawn tapestries on the windows. "Yes, I must leave," she agreed, and slid from the bed, arranging her gown and hair, fluffing her flattened neck ruff.

His voice was low and breaking. "What if you did not have to leave . . . never had to leave?"

"I must wait for that in heaven, Rob."

She turned in the doorway for one last look.

"Perhaps my sinful ways will keep me from heaven," he said, his brilliant smile wavering.

She drew herself up straight with the help of the doorposts. "Then, my lord of Leicester, you must mend your ways, for I refuse to be without you."

*I*t was a hot September day that year of 1574 when the widow Baroness Douglass Sheffield arrived at Richmond Palace to answer the queen's summons, the mullioned windows of the royal antechamber casting diamond patterns on the marble floor.

The baroness, pale and with faltering steps, as if she walked to her scaffold, knelt three times as she approached Elizabeth, seated on a small dais with the royal cloth of gold raised above her head. Only one of the queen's ladies, Anne, Countess of Warwick, stood behind her, ready to serve.

"My lady Douglass." Elizabeth greeted her heartily and noticed with admitted delight that Douglass had not quite regained her slender figure.

"Majesty," Douglass said, kneeling again in a too-tight gown.

"We give you belated commiseration on the death of your husband, Lord John. How cruel he did not live to find joy in his son."

"Yes . . . most cruel, Majesty, in a lonely inn where I could not nurse him," Douglass said, at last gathering her courage to raise her face to the queen.

"And you named the boy John, after his father?" Elizabeth watched her as she would watch a chained young bear being baited by a larger bear many times champion in the arena, watched her eyes dart to every corner, but nowhere finding any escape.

"No, Majesty."

"Not John? What name, then?"

"Robert." She bowed her head and the name was almost buried between her ample milky breasts.

Robert! How dare she be so forward, so barefaced?

"It is an old family name, Your Grace."

Oh, no . . . a new name, I'll wager.

"I wish you delight in young . . . Robert, is it? . . . my lady, and I will not stay you at court. You may return north to your brother Lord Howard of Effingham's manor as soon as your carriage is readied."

"My dutiful thanks to Your Majesty."

She was almost at the doors and moving fast.

"Oh, my lady," Elizabeth said, fixing her nearsighted stare on Douglass's face. "Tell me, is there any truth to the report that you have married the Earl of Leicester?"

The woman's knees began to buckle before she could straighten them. "None, Majesty . . . I . . . I am a widow in mourning for . . . for my dear husband."

"We are certain that my lord of Leicester will say the same, will he not?"

"Yes, Majesty, exactly the same."

"We must send young Robert a christening gift. It will follow soon, my lady."

"My humble thanks, Your—"

"Yes, yes . . . Douglass, you may retire."

Lady Douglass backed the last two steps to the antechamber doors, almost stumbling in her haste to leave her queen.

"Anne," Elizabeth said softly after the doors had been closed.

"Yes, Majesty, I am here."

"See that she is sent a basin for her babe."

"Silver or gold, Majesty?"

"Neither, we think."

"Neither?"

"Pewter. It is fine enough."

Anne hesitated. "Aye, Your Grace. I will make it happen." She started for the door.

"You think me cruel, Anne?"

Anne turned and curtsied. "It is not for me to think anything . . . but to obey my queen."

Elizabeth sighed. Not even Anne could understand, for she did not know what a queen must endure in silence. "We will be alone until the supper hour."

Anne closed the doors quietly.

Elizabeth removed a vanilla comfit from her pocket and nibbled on it to sweeten the acid taste of treachery in her mouth. Walking to the fireplace, which had burned low, she pulled a letter from underneath a pile of warrants to be signed.

The letter was addressed to Douglass in Rob's familiar hand. All letters sent from the palace passed through Walsingham's office, and a clerk eager to gain his queen's good opinion and perhaps special favor had carried it to her in secret. He had gained a gold pistole, but not her good opinion. Who could trust him?

Elizabeth had read the letter once, silently. Now she read it aloud so that her ears would believe what her eyes saw.

"'My dear Douglass.'" Then there were salutations and other greetings. *Get on with it, Rob.*

> *We are not legally married. There are no witnesses, no priest to be found. Thus you must put aside any idea that you will be the Countess of Leicester and cease from calling yourself by that title and demanding its privileges. Yet know that I will always care for you and in time acknowledge my son.*
>
> *You must think it a marvelous thing that forces me thus to the ruin of my own house to refuse a legitimate heir when I have none and am not like to have one. It is simply for the queen's favor and love that I do this, for as I have assured you, I would utterly lose both if I were to marry. Nor will I shirk my duty to you and young Robert, but I offer you seven hundred pounds per annum if you would marry one of the suitors you have so far declined for my sake. It would not be honest for*

*me to forbid you marriage with another. If you
marry, you shall find me a most willing and ready
friend to you and your husband.*

Robert, Earl of Leicester

At that moment the door opened and Kit Hatton announced: "My lord of Leicester, Your Majesty."

"Ah, yes, my lord of Leicester, come in. I have something of yours."

Rob walked quickly to her and knelt, his head bowed. "You have my heart, Majesty."

Worry was written in his face. He had surely heard that Douglass had been called to the queen and he feared to wait for a summons, wondering every moment what the queen knew. He need wait no longer. She held the letter out to him.

"We believe this belongs to you, my generous lord. We suggest you send it by a safer courier." She was satisfied that he paled. "If all my earls had to pay so much for their bastards, they would soon have to mortgage all their lands."

"Bess . . ."

"No, Rob . . . not this time."

"You are ordering me from court?"

She felt her throat closing and feared that she might give way to tears like some ordinary woman. "No, my lord, stay and be witness to the consequences of the disloyalty you have wrought. We wonder, my lord, how many furrows you plow in our court."

Robert moved closer, bent and kissed her slipper.

She trembled to remember other times when he had done so. "Leave me," she ordered.

"I can never leave you."

Elizabeth walked from the room into her privy bedchamber, leaving him before she tasted mixed salt tears, some sad, but some of joy, finding their slow way down her cheeks to her lips. *He truly does not love her.*

CHAPTER 16

❧

Home to Wanstead and Lettice

❧

Earl of Leicester

Christmastide 1586
Wanstead

*R*obert Dudley, Earl of Leicester, rode at the head of a
small entourage of twenty men through the thick carpet of fallen leaves on the edge of Epping Forest and came out
onto the sweeping lawn of Wanstead, his country manor.

The formal knot gardens were sharply outlined in a dusting of
white snow to show their careful patterns, and the gardeners had
diligently cleared the wide carriage road leading to the entrance,
which he had recently made grander with marble columns.

The sight of Wanstead for the first time since his return from
Holland did not bring him the happiness it once had. Since his
Noble Imp was taken from him, he had dreaded Wanstead's
empty, echoing halls and rooms once filled with the laughter and
play of his boy, now gone from this earth.

Yet he was as pleased as any landed lord to see his country manor well tended and must remember to compliment Lettice, who was strict about the servants' duties, as she was with everyone . . . except her young son, Robert Devereux, the Earl of Essex, who had grown to young manhood instilled with his mother's sense of frustrated privilege. The boy was a secret credit to his own blood in every other way. Yet he feared for him under the influence of Lettice, who was determined he get the recognition that she lacked.

Had the love he bore his queen forced his wife to become so grasping and now firmly intending to achieve everything through this impressive older son that her husband could not give her? He sucked in a deep, steadying breath; he could see no way to give her what she truly wanted, since he had never had a choice but to love Bess.

Lettice had never forgiven him for not marrying her when she had first become pregnant by him. Had that cost him his young Imp's life? It was a suspicion he did not often allow himself, but he could not always escape creeping doubts or the words of Dr. Dee's angel. He tightened his knees against his horse's flanks to speed the animal. The sooner there, the sooner away again and back to court, back to his queen.

He accepted that he would have no legitimate heir now, one that he could own before the queen, court and country. He had two living sons who carried his first name, though not his last. One Robert from his liaison with Lady Douglass Sheffield and another Robert, now a young man of almost twenty, his earlier son with Lettice, the pregnancy that had forced her marriage to Lord Devereux, Earl of Essex. Both sons carried other men's surnames. They were fine boys, but he could not claim base sons and give them his name and title, hoping eventually for a legitimate heir. Now, his youngest Robert, his beloved Imp and rightful son, was gone and the Dudley name had died with him. Since his brother Ambrose, Earl of Warwick, had no children, Robert would bequeath his title, Earl of Leicester, to young Essex, as Lettice wanted. He would give her that.

To avoid the great hall from which he could hear the sounds of rollicking music and shouts of young laughter from Essex and his friends, he walked to a side door and took the back servants' stairs to his chambers off the grand gallery. Then he threw off his fur-lined seal coat that kept rain but not cold from his body. He sat at once in front of the fire, hoping to warm his bones, which ached from hours in the saddle. He closed his eyes and waited for Tamworth to remove his boots, though he often looked to his door as if expecting to see his Imp run through it to clutch his knees. Would he never escape this mourning?

"My lord, if you are weary, I will send to tell your lady that you will not attend her. The continued and late sessions of the council—"

"Nay, say nothing. I would greet our guests . . . later. Bring me spiced rum and I will change into better clothes and go down." He would have to make a pleasant appearance before telling Lettice that the queen had commanded his return the next day. That Bess spared him from the court for one day of Christmastide she considered generosity enough. He laughed aloud. The queen would never change and in his heart he thanked God for that. At her side in a royal palace was his natural place, and he knew it, as did Bess. Though Lettice would never accept it in her great jealousy of the queen's ability to command the Earl of Leicester and bring him running.

He drew a large diamond ring from the pocket tied about his waist and looked at it again. It had value enough for the queen. Lettice demanded equality in his gifts to her, or she tossed them aside. Would he ever be able to appease her anger at being second-best in his life?

He turned the ring this way and that, catching the glow from the fire and watching its lights dance against the walls. His wife would love this stone so great in size that she would have difficulty bending her finger. She would be forced to leave it extended for all to see and for a time she would be at peace with him. As he grew older, he longed for a house of tranquillity.

Tamworth returned with his rum and knelt to heat it over the fire, while Robert thought of Lettice's finger extended to draw all admiring eyes to her diamond and laughed aloud.

Tamworth turned a puzzled face to him. "Are you so happy to be away from court, my lord?"

"Always the country air refreshes my spirit. The queen would not have her aching heads and lung miseries if she were not breathing the noisome air of London and Westminster." Robert frowned. There were times when Tamworth became a bit too knowing. "And why would I not be happy to be home and away from my heavy duties?"

"No reason, my lord," his servant muttered, offering him the heated rum. "Though I would wish you had more rest from your cares."

"The council will meet at Whitehall again tomorrow afternoon and I will be there in my place, as always."

Tamworth dressed him with freshly sponged, perfumed and brushed clothes.

Robert liked the new, longer, tighter trunks and beribboned garters now all the fashion, much warmer against the wintry breezes sweeping through the halls of Wanstead, despite a chimney in most rooms.

Escaping Tamworth's brush, he descended the staircase toward the great room below. He heard Lettice's laughter. . . . *The other one*, he thought, remembering Uriel's words, although they were never far from his mind. He had tried to push what had been said in the scrying mirror out of his mind. Yet those words came back to him whenever he was with his wife. He had tried not to divine what the angel had meant, thrusting doubt from his mind. He could not live with the suspicion that his wife had killed their only legitimate son. She was ambitious for her older son, the Earl of Essex, and wanted him to have Leicester's earldom, too, but only a monster could . . .

After their young son's death, Robert had named his nephew Philip Sidney as his heir, but he had been lost in Holland. Now, Lettice plagued him to name Essex, so he would give her that.

His stomach gripped again, and not from his old ailment, but from the awful suspicion that he tried to push away, though it returned like one of the bouncing Spanish balls from the New World. The black-beard explorers said the natives' ball game had ended with a human sacrifice. The gripping came again, harder this time.

God's bones! He must guard his wandering mind, lest it drive him out of his wits.

He was so deep in such dark thoughts that for the first time he did not stop on the stairs to admire his paintings, everywhere hung on the walls in elaborate gilt frames. His last inventory counted sixty paintings here at Wanstead, with many more at Leicester House on the Strand and even more at his manor of Kenilworth. Only the queen owned more paintings, a balance he carefully maintained. Bess didn't like her lords rising above her in any way and was quick to show her stinging disfavor if they did, and her disfavor, once shown, could last a lifetime, as Lettice had learned to her sorrow.

He smiled, remembering the young attendant who had worn a gown better than Elizabeth's. The next day the queen had donned the dress and paraded about. "Is this not a fine gown?" she asked the lady.

"It is too short for you, Majesty."

"Too short for me and much too fine for you," the queen snapped.

The young lady never had worn the dress again.

The sound of happy young voices and music, feet pounding out a country dance on the polished oaken floors of his great hall, greeted Robert at the turn of the stairs. He moved forward quickly and gracefully, showing them that his knees were still young. The musicians saw him first and halted their lutes, harps, drums and citterns to offer him a trumpet fanfare. He walked down the line of bowing dancers toward Lettice, warmly acknowledging his stepson Essex and Christopher Blount, his blond young friend, then row on row of handsome and wealthy mischief makers not yet in their majority. His countess delighted in their youthful company and attention. Had she bedded any of these young fools, as rumor suggested? At first, he had dismissed such foul gossip, knowing all beautiful women were suspected of wantonness. Though her daughters did not carry his name, their connection had been close enough for the always-eager gossips.

Lettice smiled at him, flanked by her beautiful Devereux daughters. Both were married and beyond her control, beyond even the control of their husbands. Penelope was wed to Lord Rich, but lived openly with the aptly named Lord Mountjoy. Dorothy was said to be a party to raucous evenings at the Cardinal's Hat, a brothel in Southwark. They had achieved the station in life that Lettice wanted for them and then had thrown it away in riotous behavior. No wonder his wife wanted better for her son, Essex.

An enormous blackamoor servant dressed in new gold-trimmed finery stood behind Lettice's chair holding a bowl of apricots, considered the most efficient aphrodisiac next to asparagus. Robin was dismayed at such a wanton display.

"Welcome, my lord husband," Lettice said.

He must change his disquiet into a handsome gesture, lest he face her wearying anger when he announced his intention to stay but the night. Though there was no real attraction left between them, Lettice wanted everyone to think Leicester was still dazzled by her.

She held her hand out for his kiss, which he dutifully gave, slipping his gift onto her finger, where its sparkle put to shame all the candles and torches in the great hall.

For once, she was speechless, and he was pleased. Perhaps he would escape her usual harangue against the queen's exclusive use of her husband's time.

Robert knew that she did not really want him here except to taunt him with her handsome boys, but she needed to be the one to send him away. And he had admitted to himself long ago that she needed to punish him for not marrying her when she was pregnant with Essex and he had forced her from court. Lettice, like her Boleyn cousin Elizabeth, could carry a grudge forever.

"My lord," his wife said, not taking her gaze from the ring, "I did not expect anything so grand. This is a jewel fit for the queen. She will be jealous."

"And you will take delight in that," Robert murmured for her hearing alone.

Lettice laughed. "You know me well, my lord husband."

When she laughed, Robert could not help but admit that she was still beautiful, and so much like Bess that it took him some time in his wife's presence to become used to the near resemblance again. It had intrigued him from the first. Jesu, more than intrigued! It had led him to this marriage in 1578, when Lettice returned to court long after her husband, Walter Devereux, had died of the flux in Ireland. All his hopes of wedding Bess had fled by then, but his marriage had almost cost him the queen's affection. Yet it was a marriage without choice. By 1578, Lettice carried his babe once more and this time without a prospective husband other than the Earl of Leicester. If he wanted a son and heir, he had no choice but to wed her, though he kept it from the queen until he could find a way to gently inform her and convincingly plead his truthful, unending love . . . a delaying scheme, as it proved, unworkable in the Tudor court. Bess had been told by the spiteful French ambassador, de Simier, who thought Robert opposed the queen's marriage to the Duc d'Alençon. Although the queen had gone very far in these marriage negotiations, she had never really meant to marry the pockmarked young son of the monstrous French queen Catherine de' Medici.

The French marriage matter had been resolved when Elizabeth sent her suitor off with enough wealth, both real and promised, to satisfy his honor; then Elizabeth's full fury had fallen on Robert and Lettice. The queen had threatened them with the Tower, but on Burghley's strong advice the queen had relented and banished Robert to Wanstead and Lettice to Leicester House on the Strand.

Elizabeth's wrath had nearly broken his heart and he had fallen ill almost to death, bringing the queen to him by fast carriage from Richmond Castle. For three days she had nursed him

with her own hands, her heart seeming to shatter. They had secretly reconciled in this house . . . in his chamber above, although
for appearances he had not gone back to court immediately.

His mind had wandered, but Lettice brought him back.
With little sounds of pleasure, she turned her hand from one side
to another to capture all the light she could reflect from her
jeweled ring. "Is this a consolation gift, my lord husband, or does
it mean you have succeeded in urging the queen to invite me to
court as she would any other peer's wife in the realm?"

Robert caught the groan in his throat before it was expressed.
Lettice would never cease from gnawing that old bone. He bowed.
"The queen is so burdened with grave matters that—"

"*You have not pressed her!*"

Knots of chatting young men turned toward them to stare.
They had nothing else to do, since Lettice had allowed few young
women but her daughters, always needing to be the queen in her
hive.

"Have a care, wife. I will not be tormented in my own
house."

She made an obvious effort to control her anger and he advised her in soft tones: "The time was not right, my lady. If I did
not know how and when to approach the queen, I would have
had no such long position in her court as I have had."

"Ah, yes, my lord husband," Lettice said, her hands clenched
about the arms of her chair, "you are courtier everywhere except
in your own home with your own wife."

He saw it was useless to talk with her when she was in such
a mood, knowing Elizabeth's blood cousin Lettice had received—
along with her red hair, her Anne Boleyn slanted eyes and her fair
skin—a full portion of the Tudor temper.

Robert bowed to his wife and her daughters, turned, walked from the room and climbed to the great gallery and his rooms, where he could seek some warm quiet and peace.

He was to have the warmth, but not the peace.

As he climbed the short steps into his bed, Tamworth parted the heavy tapestry curtains that would shut out the night's cold. Within minutes Lettice entered his room in a diaphanous night shift that brought a blush to Tamworth's face along with his hasty exit.

"Husband, make a place for me," breathed Lettice, her curled red hair shining in the candlelight beside his bed.

Knowing his wife to be a passionate woman, he was not surprised. He lifted his Bruges satin tester and she slid under and stretched herself close against his side. She was wearing Elizabeth's rose perfume, which made him silently damn her for a scheming tart.

Yet he was a man and easily aroused as always. Since he willed her to be Elizabeth in his bed, she had to be. If he thought of his wife as *the other*, there was no way he could raise his cock to do its duty, a duty he had once longed for to ease his aching for another woman.

As he began to mount her, she squirmed about and turned her back to him like a Bankside bawd afraid of the French pox.

Oh, no. Roughly, he turned her about to face him. She would know that it was her husband who gave her pleasure.

It wasn't to be that night. After enough effort to raise a sweat, he threw himself down beside her. "I'm too tired," he announced.

"Husband . . . dearest Robert . . . let me help you be the man I know you to be, the man of our secret trysts." She bent, the candlelight casting shadows of her curved arse onto the ceiling. She took him in her mouth. Though she had always given him that, her tongue now played the tricks of a slut in the School of Night, or a boy whore in Smithfield's Cock Lane. Had Lettice been performing with her daughter Dorothy in brothels? He tried to care, but could not. He gave himself over to a vision of Elizabeth bending to him in complete surrender.

Lettice made the appropriate sounds of delight and triumph when she brought out his manhood, though when he could think on it later, he didn't believe her ardor, although once he had . . . eagerly.

"Husband," she whispered, snuggling against his chest. "If you cannot gain the queen's consent to show your wife the honor due her at court, then take our perfect son Essex—"

Robert wrenched himself away from her. "You demean our Noble Imp!"

"My lord," she said in a soothing tone, "we cannot deny he was imperfect. One leg was shorter than the other."

"He had yet to grow into it," Robert argued, and knew he was denying a truth he could not bear.

But Lettice would not silence herself. "My dear lord husband, take Essex to court and introduce him to Her Majesty. She has not seen him for many years."

Tired almost unto death, Robert roused himself. "Not since Kenilworth in 'seventy-five, when, as I recall, he refused to kiss her when she asked."

"He was but a boy and frightened of so grand a lady."

"He was willful and ill taught."

She laughed against his chest and he could feel her hot, wet breath radiate on his skin. "He is yet willful, but better taught. He knows how to charm a woman . . . even the queen, who has been charmed by masters of the art."

She meant him and he stirred, holding himself farther from

her. "I will think on it, wife. The boy did well in Holland. He does not lack courage, but he does lack judgment. He does not know how or when he should let a thing rest." Like his mother, he thought, speaking without thinking through to consequences. "He pushes until he gets the opposite of what he wants and then is certain he has been ill treated. Elizabeth will never tolerate or mother him."

Lettice was silent for a breath. "Do not be so certain of her, husband. She is still in love with the boy you were and she will surely see the likeness."

Robert's chest tightened. "Then it is too dangerous, wife. Her Majesty never forgets a suspicion. Although young Essex has my dark coloring, he has your reddish hair and is taller and thinner and not of my temperament. . . . Still, she—"

"Husband," she said, taking his cock in her hand though it did not stir, "he must begin making his way in the world, and an earl's place is in the court and on the queen's council. Perhaps he can bring her to call me back to her service better than you. I have suffered enough exile even for Elizabeth," she said, her hand sliding up and down.

There was a time when she could have brought him to stiffen again, but not tonight. He pulled away and opened the bed curtains for her.

"I remember a time when you did not want me to leave you in your bed alone."

Did he see real sorrow or playacting in her face? He did not know, but he felt some blame and thought to ease her. He placed his hand gently on her shoulder, smiling up at her. "Wife, you have exhausted me with your bed sport."

"Husband, please," she begged. "I would have one child, one

son, who would make me proud and take the place at court that I am denied."

Robert opened his mouth to answer her, but she put a finger on his lips.

"Sshh, husband. Do this one thing for me. I will ask nothing more." She left quickly, for once knowing when she had said enough, and for once he understood her desire.

Robert lay back on the bolster, the scent of Elizabeth's perfume in his nostrils. Lettice had it made from the queen's own recipe to taunt him. Though he knew her design, the scent worked on him as she had thought and he closed his eyes, wishing it were Bess's head on his bolster this night. But she was safely sleeping at Whitehall. *Sleep softly, my queen*, he prayed, his lips touching the pillow. *Softly, softly*.

He pulled the coverlet up to his chin against the cold. There was no denying that Lettice spoke truth about Essex. It was time for the youth to be introduced at court . . . and Lettice's first husband, the man who had thought Essex his own, had been tall and dark very like the boy. Pray God that was enough to quell Elizabeth's suspicious mind.

*T*he earls of Leicester and Essex entered through the city gate, cantering through snow turned gray by mud and the many sea-coal fires of London. They made their way to King Street, through the great Holbein Gate and into the Whitehall Palace mews. It was January 1, 1587, and as soon as they changed from their muddied traveling clothes they went immediately to the presence chamber. Everyone of any importance was gathered to bring their yearly gifts and hope to receive Elizabeth's approval.

"Have a care, Essex," Leicester cautioned. "This is the most important day in your life." *And perhaps in my own.*

Queen Elizabeth sat upon her canopied throne receiving her customary homage. She wore a gown of embroidered black velvet, dotted throughout with large white pearls, with seven ropes of pearls about her neck reaching to her knees. Her pet ermine perched on her sleeve above a fine Flemish lace cuff, completing the black and white of her virginal costume. Her gold-and-diamond crown shimmered atop her red hair.

Robert saw with some relief that she was as he had left her. There were times when he feared for her, since England's enemies surrounded her realm. He pulled a silk-wrapped New Year's gift from a large pocket. "Majesty, all my time with you is precious to me, but I would be pleased to know that you counted those hours, too . . . with this."

"A riddle, my lord?"

"Answered, Your Grace, on opening my poor gift."

She spread the silk on her lap and looked at the bracelet of small, very fine glowing emeralds, then held it up to look closer at the face of a small mechanical clock in its center. Then she smiled and clapped her hands together in delight. "The hours," she said, obviously elated, "hours to wear upon our arm. We have never seen such."

"It is the smallest clock ever made, for the greatest ruler." He thought the cost worth it to see her pleasure. He had paid a great price for the intricate piece and it had taken the best clockmaker in the Royal Exchange a near year to make the miniature mechanical parts. It had been even more expensive than Lettice's large table diamond.

Elizabeth smiled, a little sadly. "When we look on time, my lord, it is always passing."

"Yet over years you grow in power and beauty, Majesty."

Robert could sense Essex's awe as he knelt beside him, head bowed to the sovereign, listening carefully to every word passing between them. *That is the way you speak to a great queen*, he thought to show Essex, *especially this queen, who is surer of her power than she is of her person, a more powerful queen, than woman. Never, never touch her scepter or her idea of her own youth and beauty. She will forgive neither.* It had taken him years of being near her to come to this knowledge of Bess. Some men, to their grief, never learned.

Elizabeth turned a blank stare on Essex. "So, the little boy has learned better manners since the summer at Kenilworth."

Essex lifted his head higher. "Majesty, had that young boy not learned of your glorious grace and forgiveness of an overawed lad, he would not dare kneel before you now, a grown man showing you his strong desire to serve your good."

"Very pretty words, my young lord. Stand up. Let us see how the boy has grown to almost a man."

Leicester felt Essex bristle but for once control his pride. Even this mother-spoiled boy knew that his self-importance could not o'ertop Elizabeth's on her throne. Pray he always remembered that.

Essex turned about on his toes, his boots gleaming, as if he danced the popular brawle, a country dance that ended masques. His steps showed his fine long legs to advantage and drew all female eyes in the presence chamber.

Leicester knew it was exactly the kind of flourish that the queen liked in her courtiers . . . the very thing he would have once done himself to catch her eye, though her face showed nothing of what she must see. Must guess!

"How old are you, my young lord?"

"Almost twenty years, Majesty."

Leicester could see the queen mentally counting back the years.

The queen stood. "My lord Leicester, we will speak to you in our privy chamber. At once!"

He followed her entourage, preparing himself for the tempest that would surely follow.

When they reached her privy chamber she angrily dismissed the yeoman guards, gentlemen pensioners and her ladies busy with their duties and embroidery. "Close and guard my doors," she shouted, and turned on Leicester. "Down on your knees, my lord liar!"

She did not come near him, where he might try to draw her into his arms, but paced about before she finally came to the table and took a chair. "Do you think to make a fool of us in front of our court, my lord of Leicester?"

"Majesty—"

"Do we not have eyes? Though others may think him sired by the Devereux husband, dead these fifteen years, do not count us as one so easily duped. We see you as you once were, in his face, his movements . . . his carriage, his eyes. . . ."

Leicester bowed his head.

"He is your son by that She-Wolf. She whelped him of you while yet a maid! Admit it."

The queen stood and came to him, her gown brushing his legs, her fists beating upon his head. "Do not lie to us!" When he did nothing to protect himself, her hands dropped to her sides.

"How could you so betray me?" She lowered her voice but he could hear the scarred-over old wound opening, a suspicion flowing out that she had covered over for nearly two decades without allowing herself to recognize it.

Leicester straightened his spine. "Because you had turned from me to Kit Hatton." It was not the whole truth, but true enough.

"God's blood! You blame me? Admit your guilt!"

He looked up at her, his eyes begging for an understanding she could never give. "Yes, it is true. Essex could be my son . . . could be *our* son in my heart."

She seemed to freeze. *"How do you dare say that to me?"*

"My queen, he will need you when I am gone."

"Do not speak of such things to me," she said, her voice hoarse.

"I must. He lacks judgment and will need your guidance and understanding. Bess, will you give it for my sake?"

He bent and kissed her feet. That she allowed it gave him courage to rise from his aching knees. "Love him, Bess, for me. Do not hate him for the father's fault."

"I will love him or hate him for his father's sake. Maybe both."

She was shaking and he put his hands on her arms and then drew her to his chest so his soft words could reach her ear. "The truth now, my love. Lettice came to me one summer night wearing your gown and scent. I thought . . . I thought it was you, Bess. I had waited every night for you to come to me again."

"And I did not come to you."

"You did not, but I thought you had. I wanted to think it. I *had* to think it!"

Elizabeth stiffened and he thought tears stood in the corners of her eyes.

"Bess, when Lettice told me she was pregnant, I did not know whether to believe her or think it a trap to take me from you . . . to win me from you. She knew where my heart rested."

"You did not want to marry her?" Elizabeth's usual confident tone was missing. She needed his reassurance.

"Never! That is why I suggested Essex to you."

"And why we stopped the night at Rycote on my progress that year," she said, putting her still-trembling arms about him, though they could not move closer. "Have you forgotten I made that happen?"

"You knew about Lettice even then." He tightened his hold on her fragile body. "Bess," he whispered, knowing the answer. "My sweetest lady, Rycote is never forgotten. It will be my last thought on this earth. But, Bess . . . Bess, you wouldn't take me in marriage, even after that night." He still ached from the weight of that truth after all the years that had passed.

"Yet you continued to ask me by word or by look almost daily for years until you finally married that She-Wolf without my permission." Her eyes closed in pain at the memory of the struggle between her heart and her head. "I had much practice in denying you. You did not give up until—"

"Kenilworth," he said, his head nestled next to hers, his breath on her neck.

She trembled slightly. "Kenilworth." She repeated the word as if it were part of a sacred litany.

CHAPTER 17

❧

KENILWORTH

—————————— ❧ ——————————

ELIZABETH

July 9, 1575
Kenilworth

*I*t was near the last of the day's light when Queen Elizabeth motioned for her baggage train to stop behind her, not an easy thing when three hundred carts and several hundred courtiers on horseback followed. She didn't doubt that some careless carter, slow to respond to shouted orders or asleep at the reins, plowed into the cart in front of him. She frowned. S'blood! If any of her furniture or her precious wardrobe were damaged, she would have the carter straddle a cart on his last drive to Tyburn!

Most of her belongings and the entire government, plus many in the court, trailed her from castle to manor while on summer progress. This was the time she could show her regal self to her people, who might know her only by a portrait, or not even that, and incidentally lower the strain on her summer purse by bringing her court to her nobles' manors.

Behind them, Richmond Castle would be sweetened of all noxious odors left by her courtiers and servants. The scullery, scalding house and flesh kitchens in the lower levels alone took weeks to scrub, and the common jakes . . . She didn't want to think about that work. And so she wouldn't.

She looked forward to ending her progress at Oatlands, her curiously built but restful hunting lodge, a series of attached cottages built to form a wall around an old castle keep and great hall. There she would spend the late summer shooting its abundant red deer. And perhaps some dozens of waterfowl to serve the lodge. That much meat, at least, she would not have to purchase, which she would not do, by Jesu.

Lady Anne Warwick rode up behind the queen, asking: "Majesty, would you have me send to discover if there is damage behind us?"

"Aye, Anne, but tell us on the morrow. We will not have our entrance to Kenilworth spoiled, since we have long looked to it as the best and last of these summer progress days."

"Your Grace, my husband says his brother, my lord Leicester, has abundant surprises prepared."

"Don't tell us, Anne," the queen said, smiling on her friend and chief lady-of-the-bedchamber. "A surprise known has no pleasure in it and we delight in astonishment. There is little enough in our life . . . unexpected."

Usually, foreknowledge was her choice. She did not like to be taken unawares with no prepared response . . . a habit of childhood and now of a lifetime. As a child in Henry VIII's court, she had thought twice and thrice before acting or speaking. Around every corner lurked her father's ill temper and another banishment from court. Every word of hers had consequences, a lesson she had learned early and well.

Quickly, she snatched herself from old gloom. She had nothing to fear; she was going to her dear Robin. "Come, follow me!" she shouted.

Several gentlemen of her personal guard wheeled their mounts at her command and she spurred onto a track leading to the Earl of Leicester's Kenilworth, where she would stay for more than a fortnight while on progress through the country northeast of London. She had heard fantastical stories of the fete Leicester planned for her, but surely they were exaggerated, as were most such carried tales. Yet Rob, ever ingenious, always seemed to know the best revels to entertain her.

At the thought of him, she felt a warmth that owed nothing to the summer heat, but everything to her sweet memories of his loyalty to her in everything. Annoyed, she pursed her lips. *Pup. Pup.* Loyal in almost everything with the exception of Douglass and that strumpet Lettice, who, gossips said, had come to him again as soon as her husband left for Ireland with the new title of Lord Marshal. But Lettice would not dare to be at Kenilworth.

Elizabeth's little troupe trotted along the forest cartway, cooler now under the trees, the sun splashing bright ribbons on her path. She began to hear music and smiled. Ah, sweet Robin meant his entertainments to start immediately.

A wildly cavorting green man covered with leaves and twigs held together by moss jumped into her path, causing her horse to shy and rear.

"No hurt! No hurt!" she cried, to stop her guard from attacking the man, who was sputtering out some poor poetry on his knees.

"Majesty! Majesty!" One of her men tried to grab her reins, but she had the horse firmly under her control.

"Stop your shouting, man!" she ordered in full voice.

The green man, kneeling in the dirt, continued to sputter his poetic tribute, but he was so unnerved he couldn't remember his lines in their right order, tying his tongue in several knots as leaves drifted from his costume.

Elizabeth threw back her head and laughed. "Very appealing, Sir Wild Man," she said, and put out her hand to calm him. "We are well pleased, but beg you, recite no more."

She rode on, not stifling her laughter. She'd give the man her mirth if not a commission to publish his elegy.

She emerged from the path near a great lake. The mere, fed by several springs, surrounded two sides of Kenilworth, which was much enlarged since she had last seen it. Robin was indeed a great builder. This old castle dating from Plantagenet days was now an imposing modern, fortified country manor. She heard the rumble of carts and many hooves beating the earth behind her as her great train began to arrive and was ushered by Kenilworth servants to a tent village raised in an adjoining field.

Robin, magnificent in green-and-gold slashed velvet doublet and trunks with matching embroidered hosen, walked across a great columned bridge and bowed to her. "Welcome, Your Grace, to Kenilworth. I delight in seeing you in my humble country home."

"My Eyes," Elizabeth said, smiling. Humbleness was no part of this manor, or of this man. Indeed, here was a man, she thought, to make all other men ashamed to own their sex. At forty-two, he had that still-handsome lift and confident turn of his head, the same as the cocksure boy she first loved so hopelessly during her brother's reign and next loved in the Tower. And now needed the strength to resist loving.

She slipped her hand onto his and put out her arms to be lifted from the sidesaddle. He grasped her waist as she held to his shoulders, but he did not whirl her about as in the lavolte, somewhat to her disappointment.

Elizabeth gestured to Kenilworth. "Robin, you make wonders here."

"The wonders are waiting for you, my ageless queen. I have enough spectacles ready for a lifetime, all given to you in the coming days. For the rest of your long and healthy life, for which I hourly pray, you will compare all your delights to these and find them inadequate."

"You are very sure of your delights, my lord," she teased.

"Would you have me otherwise?" he whispered, bending to kiss both palms of her gloved hands. She felt the pressure of his lips, but missed their warmth, always missed it when she could have had it forever. She brought herself back sharply from such dangerous reveries. In this place with this man, dreaming must be strictly controlled. She had once again resumed her intermittent monthly flux, for which her doctors could give her no reason. Fertile again, childbirth, a danger for any woman her age, was a possibility. Though she continued marriage negotiations with this prince or that one, she would always be a celebrated virgin queen who would remain without children . . . and immortal.

Yet she took his proffered arm as a Lady of the Lake on a torchlit island came floating into view, declaiming in a loud voice that King Arthur had sent her to welcome the queen.

"The great king, your ancestor," Robin shouted in her ear, having supervised her genealogy leading back to Adam. He raised his arm and the fireworks and cannon began their flashing, thundering welcome.

The bridge shook on its pillars and Elizabeth grasped his arm tighter. "My lord," she said, "this is a greater display than I have ever seen."

"Majesty, I have imported Italian fireworks makers for your pleasure . . . pleasure I plan to increase for you daily."

"You sent so far?"

He tightened his grip. "For you . . . to the ends of the world."

His voice ended on an up note as if he left much unsaid. She looked at his face and it held the questioning eyes of a lover. He was courting her again. Still. And she loved him for it. Robin meant to tempt her to him and knew all the ways that drew her woman's body . . . was born knowing these ways. Unable to stop her mouth, she smiled, showing him how she loved his efforts. "My lord, you have outdone even your past triumphs." *Jesu, let him be satisfied with that much.*

With a flourish, he led her through the tall gatehouse into a large entry court. "Majesty, I have planned a fete that all England will learn of and in all time hereafter remember forever how I honored you." He bowed his head and, serious now, led her into the enormous courtyard with radiating sand paths, geometric gardens and fountains splashing everywhere, one with great fish swimming in its lower pool.

Elizabeth could not take her eyes from such a display, knowing it must have cost Leicester dear. She had been right that he was trying to woo her, not just with this overwhelming attention, but with his fortune. Yet why should it not come back to her, since she had bestowed it?

Robin bent to her. "It is near full dark now and I have a hunt planned for early on the morrow after Sunday prayers. Would you like to see the new wing and chambers I had built for you in the Italian manner?"

Elizabeth starred at him. A whole wing! "What riches have you spent, Robin?"

"All I have, I give for you," he said, his dark eyes flashing in the torchlight.

Did he love her so much, or still hope to be king . . . to *buy* a throne, by Christ and all His saints? But she could not hold such a loveless thought for long. This was a fairyland of love and he had made it for her.

He whispered, perhaps reading her mind as he too often did: "It came from you and now goes back to you transformed from gold into moonlight, from silver into stars . . . by my love. Come, Bess," he added, slightly pulling on her hand, holding it high and yet tenderly as if it were the most fragile thing he had ever held.

Up a wide stair into a wider gallery, she passed bowing gentlemen and ladies. The Sidneys, especially young Philip, already a poet of some distinction, she recognized with pleasure. Others with not so much pleasure . . . Lady Douglass Sheffield and her own cousin Lettice, Countess of Essex. *Why, Robin? Do you have them here to remind me that other women love you?* Before she could gather her outrage, Lettice pushed forward a beautiful young boy.

"My son, Majesty, Robert, Earl of Essex."

Elizabeth bent to the lad, her heart seized by his beauty and the still-soft curves of his face. "You may kiss me, my pretty young lord," she said, offering her cheek to him.

The boy drew back sharply, alarm clear in his eyes.

Robin murmured, "The lad is o'erwhelmed at the honor."

"He is but eight years, Majesty," Lettice murmured.

Elizabeth walked on. "We see your two paramours are here for *your* entertainment," she said aloud, not caring who heard, her body rigid with the anger of such betrayal and the boy's refusal of the honor she bestowed.

"Nay, Bess," he whispered urgently. "I love, have loved and will love only you. All the gentles and nobility from the near countryside gather to honor their queen as is their duty. Lady Essex lives just a few leagues distant at Chartley, the estate you gave her on her marriage."

She knew he was reminding her of her own folly, but for once, she was not angered by an unhappy truth, nodding once to show she heard and was already tired of this subject.

He spoke urgently into her ear. "I see no lady here but you, recognize no lady but you. I have built all of this for you and no other." His words vibrated with his desire to make her believe him.

And she did.

The queen in her quickly stepped forward, silent, fearing he would draw from her all her welling affection in front of the gathering. Her head half believed him against every gossip; her heart fully accepted his words as true. Of necessity she had been a good judge of men from a very early age and could smell the sharp odor of deceit no matter what the distraction of gifts or handsome faces and forms behind them. Or, she admitted, she had such skills with all men, but perhaps not with Robin.

At the end of the gallery, servants threw open huge doors and Leicester led her into chambers flooded with rising starlight and the setting sunlight through ceiling-to-floor glass windows set with rubies and emeralds shimmering in candlelight. Almost dancing, he turned her about on rich velvet woven Turkey carpets, fine enough to hang on her palace walls. He guided her into her adjoining bedchamber with like windows bringing in bursts of fireworks to light up a soaring ceiling of tracery stone.

Laughing, Elizabeth ran to the windows, then whirled on Leicester, not pleased. "But, my lord, I cannot see a garden from my windows. What good are these windows if I cannot view fountains and flowers all the day and night?"

He did not hesitate. "I will remedy my oversight. You are my queen and your wish is everything to me."

"Robin!" she exclaimed, laughing. "Your speech is ever extravagant. But now I would rest from my journey. You may leave me . . . but not to go far."

He acknowledged her words and meaning with a warm smile. "Everything is here collected as you would wish it, my queen. Your watered wine is on the side table. Your bitter ale will be there for your morning thirst. If there is anything I have forgotten for your pleasure, you have but to command it."

Elizabeth laughed like a child with a new toy house. He knelt and kissed her hand, looking up to her face. "I mean it, Bess. . . . *Anything* and I will cause it to happen."

He backed from the room while her ladies were exclaiming over the richness of the fabrics on the floor and on the elaborately carved bed. The overhead tapestry, embroidered with the Leicester emblem of double ragged staff and bear, read, *Droit et loyal.* A tapestry with the same design covered the chairs with an elegance even a queen did not expect.

Later, as she lay alone on woven silk sheets, she read the words over and over again. *Just and loyal.* She believed Robin had been loyal to her except in his need to bed willing women. She pulled the tester tight against the lace nightcap tied around her chin and turned over, making the disturbing words above her disappear. She turned her face to allow any tears to fall into the bolster and be lost, undetected. She had long ago accepted that she could not keep him from satisfying the natural needs of a man with other, all too eager women. Men were not like queens with the will to deny their urges. If men were seen to do so, they would be laughed at, even thought to prefer one of the pretty boys frequenting Cock Lane in Smithfield. Though she'd been furious that Robin went to other women, she could not forever deny him what she would not give. Could not give . . . at least not forever, as he wanted. She had tried to keep him for herself, as any woman would, but in that she had not succeeded. Perhaps she had not wanted to succeed. Such success created an obligation for a woman, especially for a queen.

"Oh, sweet Jesu," she murmured, and she didn't know if she said a prayer or a curse.

She was awakened the next morn with sun streaming through her jeweled windows and her ladies running to her. "Majesty," said Anne, "please come and see . . . please."

Having slept well for once, Elizabeth did not want to rise early, but finally could not resist the astonished cries. "Anne, what is amiss . . . ? Please you, my morning robe."

She walked to the windows, wrapping her satin-soft robe tight around herself, her ladies parting so that she could look out.

"Isn't it amazing, Majesty?"

Elizabeth took firm hold of her mouth, which wanted to drop open, but finding the effort too much for an early morning, she let it drop. Spread below under her window was a garden of gravel walks, arches with flowering vines and a center fountain. Robin, covered in dirt, but the more handsome for it, stood with his foot on the lower fountain bowl looking up at her. He bowed, sweeping his workman's hat from his head, and placed a hand on his heart. *And her heart.*

Robin had done this to fulfill her wish. She was awed. She was delighted. She waved a greeting.

Anne at her ear whispered: "Majesty, how could he have worked this magic during one night?"

"Discover the tale of it for me. Quickly, Anne, question the porters."

Elizabeth turned again to look down on him, seated now at his ease on the lower bowl, trailing his hand in the water, motioning her to come down and just escaping a drenching from the water being spewed from the fountain. She laughed, her heart as easy in her breast as it had ever been. He had done this for her. Performed a miracle. Had he summoned witches or ancient gods? Hercules?

Anne rushed in, talking as she came. "Majesty, most amazing news. Lord Leicester stayed up the night through, calling in all his servants and men from villages around, more than a hundred in number, to make the garden. It is said he offered a gold mark to each man who worked quickly and silently and instant dismissal and three days in the stocks to a man who made a single sound."

Elizabeth looked down again at a garden that appeared as if it had grown there since Eden's time. "The fruit trees? The fountain? The flowered borders and paths?"

"Aye, Majesty. All."

Anne saw what the queen saw, shaking her head in disbelief. "It is a tale that will be told everywhere and put any other man to shame before his dear wife or sweetheart."

"Or both, if not the same." Elizabeth's eyes were wicked before she squinted, being shortsighted, to look at her friend. "What do *you* think, my lady?"

Anne was pulled sharply from her reveries. "My apologies, Your Majesty. The magic ruled my tongue and gave voice to my thoughts for, alas, my own dear husband would never think of such a thing."

Elizabeth nodded, accepting her friend's reason, no doubt

true. Though Robin and his brother Ambrose, Earl of Warwick, were of the same blood, they could have been born from different wombs. Ambrose was sober-minded and settled with a wife. His younger brother, Robert, was fun-loving, with a roaming eye, even while he waited for a queen to marry him. At first passion Elizabeth had been furious with Robert for the other women and they had had many roaring arguments; each time she banished him, only to recall him. She had forgiven him and all between them had been as before. She could live and rule no other way than with him beside her. When she tried, her need was proved true again.

Grooms brought horses into the courtyard, and the queen was quickly dressed by her ladies for hunting in a gown topped by a doublet and a brimmed red hat, the latest fashion from France.

She raced down the wide stairs and stopped to step regally into the courtyard to meet proud Leicester, bathed and dressed, holding a splendid white hunter with pinkish eyelids and startling blue eyes, trembling eagerly to the sound of the hunt trumpets. Lord Leicester knelt and handed her the reins.

"He is called Whiteboye and he is yours, my queen, foaled by the most famous Irish bloodline I could command . . . and that is the very best."

Magnificent, both horse and man, Elizabeth thought. "We thank you for him and we thank you for our garden," she added with a slight tremor in her voice. He bent his head to her and she could not resist stretching a hand to tickle his neck. He shivered and raised his head, his eyes swimming with love, dark eyes that pierced her heart like hot quarrels from a crossbow. She must . . . must be on her guard against him. Against herself.

Elizabeth was quickly in the saddle and the huntsman's horn called her to the chase. Laughing as of old, they raced out of

Kenilworth into a slanting sunlit morning, followed by a pack of dogs, and onto Leicester's great greensward deer chase said to be twenty-six miles long. Deer were everywhere for the shooting.

"Majesty," Robin called loudly to be heard over baying hounds and pounding hooves, "I have set aside a special buck with a great rack for you."

"Take me to him," she cried, excitedly spurring her horse, the great stallion leaping under her, tireless and wonderfully strong, his flank muscles rippling with each stride under her demanding hands and prodding feet.

The stag was indeed magnificent, bounding away from them, but, experienced and wily, he turned an abrupt circle and headed back toward Kenilworth, the dogs and hunters after him.

The queen braced herself and pulled on the left rein, and Whiteboye began to turn immediately in a shorter arc than any other horse she'd ever ridden, the perfect hunter.

They all dashed pell-mell after the stag, Leicester next to her, his hunter taking a stride for each of hers, all the court, servants and huntsmen pounding after them. Ahead Kenilworth rose high on its hill as the stag reached the mere and with no hesitation plunged in and began to swim, its head and horns sailing over the lake like a great ship on the ocean. The dogs swam after it, nipping at its hindquarters.

Elizabeth came up to the lake and reined in her horse so fast that the front hooves skidded into the water. Robin was right there to grab her horse's head.

"Have a care, Bess. I will send my huntsmen to drive him to you for a fair crossbow shot."

The queen watched the men in several boats turn the stag toward her until it stood half out of the water, so weary its body trembled, its breath whistling past its flaring nostrils. She took the loaded crossbow, its quarrel big enough to sink deep into this huge beast, and sighted it at the stag's heart. Her finger tightened, but refused to pull. Why? She did her duty daily and sacrificed her love to do it. In the forests of her realm, it was the duty of this deer to die for her entertainment and meat. Still, the beast looked straight at her, unafraid. *He is king here and will bow to no one. We are rulers together, given life and title by God.*

Nay, she silently commanded herself, and spoke aloud to the stag. "Sir Beast, I grant you a royal pardon and long life in honor of your strength and courage."

The people around her were silent for a moment and then burst into applause.

"He loves you and thanks you, Majesty," someone in the milling hunt crowd offered.

She laughed. "He is a male and loves a woman who pursues him," she shouted back over her shoulder, wheeling her great horse.

"Call off the dogs, good Robin. See that my stag lives long. Such strength and bravery should replenish your herd and you will have the finest hunting in the realm."

He bent to kiss her hand, but she heard his words as clearly as if he had shouted them in her face. "Just as we would have the finest sons, my Bess."

She retrieved her hand, but gently, and tugged on her reins, turning Whiteboye's head. "To prayers now, Robin. I think them needed, don't you?"

"Majesty, I never cease to pray . . . for Elizabeth, queen of England."

As they cantered across the bridge over a dry moat and through the gatehouse, Elizabeth knew that Robin had determined to make

Kenilworth his last and greatest wooing of her. It was obvious at every turn.

She looked up at the entry tower, puzzled. "My lord, your great clock has stopped."

Leicester jumped from his horse and ran to help her from hers. As she slid into his arms, he whispered, "No, Bess, I had the mechanism halted on the moment you arrived. Time stands still for me when you are near. There is no hour, no day, no night . . . only you, the queen of all my time."

She smiled, keeping her mouth firm, so that he could not possibly guess how deep into her heart his words had reached. "My lord Leicester, after prayers I will keep to my chambers until the cool of evening."

The queen escaped Robin in the heat of day at Kenilworth to read, write, consult with her council, but in the cool of evening, she was always with him, hunting and hallooing through the forests before returning to Kenilworth, heart racing and eager to see the surprise Robin had planned for her that evening.

One night she was met by a swimming mermaid talking of love, another night a huge mechanical dolphin, large enough to contain a six-voice choir and several musical instruments serenading her with love songs. On successive nights, the pantheon of Roman gods greeted her and she delighted in their offerings: Diana, the huntress, brought her a brace of fat pigeons; Triton brought her greetings and fat fish from Neptune; and Flora presented sprays of flowers. Always, imported Italian tumblers and contortionists made for a merry entrance into Kenilworth after hunting.

Every night a feast of three hundred dishes was set in the great hall, with musicians, dancers and merry tumblers. One night she watched a village couple wed in a rustic ceremony, another night a re-creation of the slaughter of the Danes at Hocktide.

"Enough, Robin," she told him on her last evening as he led her into a shaded bower scented with her favorite perfume. It sat so very near to the mere, she felt as if the water lapped at her toes. "There can be no more entertainment in the world than what you have shown me." She chose a cherry, red and ripe, from the tray of gilded fruits and comfits placed by her side.

"If I had a hundred days, I would call on a hundred gods to entertain you," he said. He smiled down at her as a servant waved a huge feather fan for cooling and the island in the mere floated toward her, full of musicians playing her favorite William Byrd fantasias.

"What now, Robin?"

"Wait and see, my queen," he said.

Two actors, a man and a woman, stepped out until their toes almost touched the lapping water and the music softened.

The man, dressed for court, pronounced, "My lady, I am Deep Desire!"

"I am Ever Virtue," responded the woman, wearing a flow-ing gown and a crowned red wig.

Elizabeth sat up very straight on her cushions, no longer easy. Since she and Robin shared a birthday and nearly the same horoscope and were of the same air-water nature, he knew she was inspired by a flow of emotion. *Too clever, Robin. If she were captivated, why would he not be?* She laughed slightly and looked to Leicester to see if he heard her, but the music had his atten-tion. *Ah,* she thought, *he has no fear of emotion. He relies on his manly difference.* As the greatest minds of the age thought, the sexes were set apart even before they were born, the female devel-oping on the weaker left side of the womb nearest the heart and the male on the stronger right side nearer the liver. God's bones! He may think his heart more powerful than hers, but she would prove him wrong as she had done since a girl.

The island floated nearer and Desire looked full at the queen before turning to Virtue, speaking with his hands on his hips, his voice deeply resonant and urgent:

> *Queen of all my desire,*
> *I wait here upon England's shore,*
> *Lit with your royal fire . . .*

Elizabeth watched intently although she knew that Virtue could not hope to win at Kenilworth.

Desire spoke again, stepping closer to the woman.

> *And though you close love's door . . .*

He lunged forward and knelt.

> *It will open and give me more.*

Virtue threw up both hands to stop Desire, pretending horror.

> *You are wrong, untamed desire,*
> *I resist or lose my crown,*
> *My virtue, the gods require,*
> *Never to be thrown down.*

Elizabeth smiled. Virtue might win after all.

Desire rose and pulled Virtue to his body, kissing her full on the lips, until she fell limp in his arms. He turned to Elizabeth and imitated Leicester's voice perfectly:

If it be wrong to love a queen,
Then there is not desire, nor ever been.

At this time, the isle slowly sailed away and Elizabeth saw Virtue in a swoon that looked real enough to unsettle her, one hand trailing in the water. In spite of the obvious nature of the speeches, the dusk, the last twittering of birds, the rising moon, the applause, the intensity of the actors and the stillness of Robin beside her . . . all jangled her nerves.

Elizabeth stood and applauded the actors and musicians. Robin was again standing by her side. "Delightful, my lord, although you overuse your tired poet." She lifted her skirts to step onto the beaten path running beside the mere. "My journey begins anew tomorrow to end at Oatlands. I will go to my rest now."

"Ah, Majesty, I had hoped on your last night at Kenilworth you would like to walk in Elizabeth's garden one time. Seeing a small garden from your high window is one thing, but walking in the special garden I have made for you, amongst its cool, evening-scented delights, is quite another. It is the last of my tributes." His eyes, midnight dark in the deepening dusk, implored her and she could not break his heart. After all, it would be ungracious following such extravagant entertainment. And she was ready with answers to his pleas, quite well rehearsed over the years.

He led her forward as if in a delicate dance and she a nymph found in a beautiful glade deep in the forest. They stepped through a rose-covered trellis onto a terrace that led in wide steps down onto a torchlit garden, while behind her, she heard ushers urging everyone to their duties in low voices. It was indeed glorious to walk down the garden's sanded paths shimmering with gilt in torchlight, between its obelisks and columns with Robin so close that she could hear his breathing. She bent to smell some rosemary and then some lavender, then on to a rose that had a sharp, spicy scent that stung her nostrils. Water tumbled from the fountain to the lower bowl where fish splashed their tails. She was surrounded with waves of soft sound and scent.

She took deep breaths, then hastily moved on toward the sound of birdsong. "Come, Robin, I would see your aviary."

They walked on toward the jeweled cage the size of an adequate bedchamber. Many strange, colorful birds squawked, chirped and flapped within and at their approach flew about, swooping and dodging.

"Robin, ask me."

"Tell me what you would have me ask, my queen."

"My lord of Leicester, no more of this. Let us get to it."

"I hardly dare."

"S'blood, Robin!" She heard herself sounding impatient. She was not schooled in waiting. "All these days and nights lead to a moment when you ask me to marry you. I suspect you have locked your two former bedmates in the old dungeon."

Robin smiled, rather ruefully. "I sent them home immediately they paid you homage, Bess."

"And your bed has been empty this fortnight?"

"I have been waiting for my eternal queen."

She felt no more need to jibe at him. "So Virtue wins in the end."

"Oh, miserable Desire, deeper than ever before!"

"Why, my lord? We both know that I love you and cannot

live and rule without you at my side. But I will never share my throne. Let what is be enough."

He bowed and walked away to the fountain, sitting on the rim of the lower bowl. She thought that he was like those great fish, swimming in a circle getting nowhere, except growing older.

She came to him and he knelt before her. Since he was to be nothing more than a subject, she saw that he was determined to behave as one.

"Robin, stand."

"Nay, sweet Majesty. This is my proper place, at your feet."

"Then this is my proper place." She knelt in front of him, heedless of her gown spreading in the wet, golden sand, heedless, too, of what those at Kenilworth's windows could see in the torchlight and whisper about.

"Bess, why do this? Is it some mockery of me?"

"No, sweet Robin, it is to show you that we are already one. Though our bodies must be apart, in every other way we are together. Let it be enough for now and ever."

"It will never be enough for me, Bess, but I will let it rest at last. I am tired."

The queen believed him. He would ask her no more for marriage and a seat on her throne. That part of her life and his was over and she felt some relief, though relief was fleeting, followed swiftly by regret and a sense of lost youth. She bent forward and put her head on his shoulder. Finally, he stood and lifted her up. They walked arm in arm about the garden silently, except for the sounds of the aviary birds sensing day in torchlight and the scraping of their feet against the golden sand in unison.

CHAPTER 18

❧

TO KILL A QUEEN

❧

EARL OF LEICESTER

February 6, 1587
Whitehall Palace

*E*lizabeth's perfume filled the stuffy council chamber, sending Robert deep into a memory of the Kenilworth gardens, when they had walked there that last summer together and she had finally freed him from all hope of their marriage.

Outside Whitehall, a winter storm howled, hail rattling against windows, icy winds sweeping down every corridor. He saw Elizabeth shivering but refusing to admit to any weakness of body, and rose from his seat next to hers at the council table, placing his own fur cloak about her shoulders. He whispered for her ear alone: "I cannot see you cold, Bess."

It was winter outside and inside at Whitehall, but she would never admit to it in front of her council, just as she would never acknowledge their love to the world by marrying him.

Robert looked in the faces of the greatest lords of England

and thought the queen's often-repeated maxim, *Make haste, slowly*, was ringing in their ears. Though unsaid this day, the words were there amongst them as they waited and waited for Elizabeth's decision to execute the condemned queen of Scots and prepare for the Spanish attack that was sure to follow. Indeed, King Philip's fleet was already being gathered in the ports of Spain and Portugal.

Cecil sat calmly observing her every expression, every flicker of an eyelid, as he always did at the other end of the council table, waiting to see which argument prevailed, cautious from long experience. The same guarded look was worn by both Walsingham and Hatton. Lettice's father, Sir Francis Knollys, kept his eyes on his ledgers, as a good vice chamberlain should.

"What is this?" the queen asked, picking up a document from the pile in front of her.

Robert thought she knew very well what it was, since Parliament's seals dangled from it.

"You do try my patience, sirs!" Elizabeth had read no more than a few lines and threw it down the table, where it skidded to a halt in front of Mr. Secretary Walsingham, the man who had done more than any other to capture the queen of Scots' most recent incriminating letters begging King Philip to send his armada at once to save her head. Now from Fotheringay, though under a death sentence, Mary promised to disinherit her son, King James of Scotland, and make Philip's daughter, Isabella, her heir if he would rescue her from the ax with an immediate attack on England.

Mary Stuart had plotted to overthrow Elizabeth's government and take her throne for nearly twenty years, even now plotting her covert death. But Mary, reading the English queen well, had been careful never to openly threaten Elizabeth's life until the last

great plot laid to kill the queen and all her ministers was uncovered. The assassin, Sir Anthony Babington, a Catholic supporter,
had been quickly caught and had gone with his coconspirators to
a terrible traitor's death at Tyburn last September. Yet Mary lived
on after she had been charged, convicted and condemned to beheading, a noble traitor's death. Still, Elizabeth hesitated.

Knowing his queen could forgive almost anything but a di-
rect threat to her person, Walsingham and his agents had cleverly
trapped Mary Stuart into agreeing in writing to Elizabeth's assassination. Then Mary, not content with plotting the queen's death,
had breathlessly promised Philip to have the Protestant religion
thrown down and Masses said everywhere in English churches
within three months of her accession. These messages written
and signed by her hand had condemned her to execution . . .
now four months overdue. Unlike Mary, Bess could not quite
bring herself to execute a fellow anointed queen and kins-
woman.

All of Elizabeth's advisors, peers and gentlemen of the realm
bowed their heads while she stared angrily about the table, not
wanting to catch her eye and be battered by her tongue as they
had been for months.

"We will not have it!" she shouted, her face swollen with
anger and sleeplessness and, Robert feared, the dropsical illness
she was prone to suffer when under so much nervous tension.

When Elizabeth next spoke, her body strained forward under
the weight of such a great decision. "No more importuning us to
take off the Scots queen's head, my lords." She lowered her loud
voice to not much more than a raspy whisper, which held extra
menace for those who knew her temper so well. "We see heads
in plenty here, my lords, heads that disobey our orders and yet
remain on their too-proud necks!"

No councilor, not Sir Christopher Hatton and not the Chancellor of the Exchequer, old Sir Walter Mildmay, said a word, their eyes sliding away from her face. Robert had rarely seen her in such a state since . . . ah, since her father had beheaded his foolish young Howard queen. Henry had made Catherine Howard in his mind his "rose without a thorn," though when out of his sight she was far from thorn-free. The Tudors hated to be wrong, and therefore never were.

Bess lived under the shadow of Henry's famous Holbein portrait wherever she resided, proving to all the world that she was the great king's legitimate daughter. Yet there must be some deep hatred in her heart, too, born of the helpless fear of him she had known as a child, losing mother and surrogate mothers, one after another, until she was almost a woman grown.

Did she deeply hate all those who sought the head of a queen? He studied his hands, adjusted his jeweled rings, but finally looked full on her, hoping by the worry in his face to remind her of her better self, the one that honored the men who spent their lives serving her.

"And you, Sir Puritan," she said, mocking Walsingham in his plain black garb. "You have had much to say before. Have you no words of council for me now that I ask for them? You would have me kill a queen, but you offer no alternatives to spare me from such a miserable undertaking."

Walsingham turned his long, narrow face to her, his mouth almost smothered by his full, much-grayed beard. "Majesty, I but take the council of your own words and hold prisoner my tongue while I have a head to jail it in."

Robert saw Elizabeth's lips twitch. Even when angry she appreciated a clever rejoinder . . . as long as it was humble. Walsingham was master of the right humble word.

The spymaster picked up the warrant for Mary's execution and appeared to study it, though, having supervised the writing of it, he needed no review. And then Robert saw him dare what many greater men would not. "Your Grace, all appears in order here. The Scots queen has been found guilty of treason for plotting your death by twenty-one of your own lords." He cleared his throat. "She has betrayed your long . . . hospitality. Since it is treason to speak of or wish for the death of England's monarch, your Parliament but calls for the sentence of execution to be carried out, as is their duty to the Crown." He took a breath after a long sentence for a man who usually said much in a few words.

Elizabeth leaned forward, her black-shot blue eyes losing all traces of the gentler color. "In truth, Walsingham, if I took your advice, Philip would have his armada sailing past our south coast by spring. Does not one of my councilors see the danger in beheading a Catholic queen when our navy is yet in a state of unreadiness?" She spoke in an exasperated tone to all, but her eyes were on her spymaster.

Robert was happy that Walsingham did not mention that Elizabeth had not been generous enough to build up her navy. The man was a consummate courtier and never said the unforgivable.

Walsingham picked up one of his many reports. He had spies everywhere in Europe; it was said he even had an intelligencer inside Philip's palace, the grand Escorial. "Majesty, my agents in Spain advise me that the armada could not possibly sail this year. Their commander, the Marquis de Santa Cruz, is dying and it's rumored that Philip will next choose the Duke of Medina-Sedonia, a timid man with no experience as a soldier and who, it's said, is prone to seasickness."

Though Walsingham did not attempt drollery, Elizabeth

could not help but smile, allowing every lord at the table to be amused: "Philip was always fortunate in his choices. He married my sister, Queen Mary, didn't he?"

Since that marriage had been no less than disastrous, smiles broke into the open.

"Majesty," continued her spymaster, "there is also plague aboard the ships and there have been many desertions. They must recruit more sailors and soldiers from their prisons, which are jammed with criminals and heretics who would choose any other death over the stake. More naval stores must be requisitioned and they are building their supply of shot. We will have good time to prepare our navy and drill our army of village trainbands. Though"—Walsingham took a swift breath—"madam, word comes that Pope Sixtus V has offered Philip one million gold ducats after he attacks England."

"Jesu in chains! So much as that!"

"The pope is determined to return England to his religion, though he admires you."

Robert looked up, holding a smile. He read from the paper in his hand. "'The pope has been overheard to say: "She is certainly a great queen, and were she only a Catholic, she would be our dearly beloved. Just look how well she governs! She is only a woman, only mistress of half an island, and yet she makes herself feared by Spain, by France, by the Empire, by all . . . if we had married, our children would have ruled the whole world."'"

Elizabeth laughed. "Then we must marry at once!"

All her councilors laughed with her, though she quickly frowned, making her *pup! pup!* sound of annoyance. "So the pope with his deep coffers thinks to inflict my realm equally with the tyranny of Rome and the violence of Spain. We will not allow it! My father would have fought them and, by Jesu on the cross, we will defend against them." Her fist pounded the table and Robert believed her. "If their armada were in the center of Spain, I would go against them!"

Robert stood and put one hand to his heart and the other to his sword. "All Englishmen stand ready to fight with you, Majesty."

*Aye*s echoed around the table.

But Elizabeth, ever cautious, had already drawn back from the brink of war. "Sir Francis, how do we know your intelligencers are not already turned to Philip's service and are now trying to mislead us? We spend our treasury on equipping a fleet and an army and . . ." Her words ended, swallowed by her natural wariness.

Robert knew that no one would speak now until they could soothe Elizabeth's humor, and not a man knew how to do that as the Earl of Leicester could, though he had no idea how he would do it this time, or turn her wavering mind toward inevitable war. At the council table, one simply agreed with her or was silent. In private, he might be able to help her to reason; then Bess could announce her change of policy as if it were her own idea. By that time, it would be.

Walsingham spoke again, no one able to read his bearded face. "Majesty, I know which of my agents are loyal and which are being used by Spain to play me false. I make use of both." He said now, seeming careless of his head, "Majesty, there is less danger in fearing too much than too little."

"You seek to instruct your queen, sir?"

Though she'd said a dismissive thing, she was stopping to consider his words. He had made them all reflect in a new way.

The queen looked about her council. "Cleverly said, my lord spymaster." She paused, then spoke her final words, standing as she said them: "Yet we will steer the middle course. There are no shoals in the middle course."

She motioned for Mary's death warrant, threw it on the floor and trampled it on her way out, her ladies hurrying after.

Every man, after rising from a deep bow, turned to Leicester.

"You must dispute with her, my lord," Burghley said.

Walsingham nodded. "You are the only one who can convince her and keep your head."

Knollys, no friend of his son-in-law Leicester, nodded in agreement.

Robert shrugged and spoke the truth. "Her Majesty has many other ways to punish me."

"My lord, you *must* quiet her fears so that she will sign the death warrant, or England faces disaster from within and without. If not this year, Spain will come next year and try to raise the northern Catholics and put Mary on the throne. Do it for our queen, my lord. The next plot against Elizabeth might succeed."

Although Walsingham spoke the words, all the councilors nodded.

Robert bowed to them. "For the queen, I will try. As long as Mary lives, all our heads are in danger from the Spanish."

"All England is in danger, General," Lord Burghley amended.

Robert pulled down his doublet and squared his shoulders. They reminded him that he had headed England's army. He took a deep breath, needing to fill his lungs. "My lords and gentlemen, when Her Majesty has set her mind to a course, she is a much more formidable foe than all of Parma's army."

Walsingham moved closer to him and spoke softly. "Her Grace must realize that there are now shoals everywhere. Mary schemes from Fotheringay trying to save herself from the block.

King Philip gathers a huge fleet in Cádiz harbor to attack us. There is safety only in swift action, not in caution."

Burghley leaned on his stick, standing close. "My lord Leicester, the queen yet hopes that her negotiations with Parma . . ." His words were muffled by his own skepticism. "I pray she is right and we are wrong."

Robert nodded. "I think we must all pray, but find a way into her mind with a difficult truth that she will mislike."

Walsingham nodded grimly. "Then I will ask God to guide your words, my lord."

When Robert was alone, he walked to the map of the world across from the queen's chair, the known and the imagined unknown, although there was less of the latter since Sir Francis Drake had sailed around the world, returning in 1580. Robert stared at the very short distance between Cádiz and England, tracing it with his finger. Parma's resupply coasters sailed up the channel from Spain to Holland in less than a week, hugging the coastline of France. In good weather with a north and westerly wind the channel could be crossed at its narrowest in a few hours, certainly less than a day. *Jesu Christo!* All of England's south and east coasts were there for the black beards to take. Although King Philip pretended his Great Enterprise against England was meant only to restore the true religion, not even the pope believed him entirely. Philip meant to expand his empire and with England and Holland in his grasp to encircle his ancient enemy, France.

"Bess. Bess." Robert heard his own pleading voice. Mary of Scots must die or foment dissent among English Catholics, and England must prepare for war. He knew that he must make these twin dangers clear to Elizabeth and he needed help. He hated to admit it, even silently, yet he must have help from a rogue, but a rogue who was a sailor. Though it pained him to know it, Raleigh was one of Bess's new favorites. She could not resist a handsome young face . . . an adventurer who wrote love poetry to her. Robert had hoped his son Essex would supplant him, but so far the lad was not polished enough to make his way toward the front of the courtiers.

Elizabeth would never gain enough attention from young and handsome men, but the ones she had were too ambitious to urge her to action. Had he been so himself when a youth? God forgive him if he had ever acted in any way that did not serve Bess.

Robert leaned his forehead against the map, tired from too much truth, from the struggle to hold his body as straight as a youth, from the effort it took to be Bess's old Robin. He had fought in many tournaments, but never one that had exhausted him more than the one he fought with his queen.

He left the council chamber and went to Raleigh's rooms, being stopped many times by bowing courtiers, not a few who begged Robert for favors. He found Raleigh in and was announced and greeted with obvious surprise.

"I see you well, my lord of Leicester." He bowed handsomely. "This is an unexpected, but most—"

"Sir, I come for your aid in a matter important to the realm." He did not like the man and would not pretend.

Raleigh, whose handsome face had also caught the eye of one of the queen's favorite ladies-of-the-bedchamber, Elizabeth Throckmorton, had obviously been interrupted.

Leicester heard the swish of a gown and a door closing in the next chamber, which explained Raleigh's hastily tucking his shirt inside his paneled trunk hose, padded and boned to a fashionable degree with a smaller-than-fashionable codpiece. Robert smiled to himself. Many young men used it as a pocket, enhancing whatever manly part nature had given them. Raleigh was more self-assured. He meant to draw a woman's eye with his own true part . . . and easily did so. The novelty of the man's self-assurance was more attractive than an engorged codpiece.

Leicester clenched his teeth, regretting the need to ask Raleigh for any help involving the queen. He would never have done so except for the queen's good.

Sir Walter bowed with his hand on his heart, making a great and graceful production. "If it please you, my lord, take this chair, which is my most comfortable." He motioned to a servant. "A glass of my best Portuguese Jerez sherry for His Lordship."

Leicester sat, but leaned forward, tense and uncomfortable. "I come only on a service for Her Majesty."

Raleigh bowed again. "My lord, ask anything of me and you shall have it to my small power."

"I am sorry for interrupting your other guest, Sir Walter."

The man had been at court just long enough not to show surprise or embarrassment, but Robert had made them equals. . . . He had a favor to ask; Raleigh had a secret to hide.

Leicester did not bother to smile or repeat endless pleasantries. "As you know, sir, the queen is reluctant to sign the order of execution for the Scottish queen."

"My lord, I do know that the business troubles Her Majesty exceedingly."

Robert had some difficulty understanding the man's thick Devon accent, the same that Bess loved because it reminded her of her adored childhood nurse, Kat Ashley, dead now these twenty years. "Her Majesty is beyond troubled, sir, and unwilling to see that as long as Mary lives, England must be in a state of readiness for a Spanish invasion. They will come upon us with all force, sir, and your head is on their list as well as mine and the queen's."

"I am with you, my lord, to save all our heads, but more to take some Spanish gold. What can I do?"

"Mary is the first business. Her Majesty must sign the Scots queen's death warrant and I must see it carried out." Robert stopped and stood facing Raleigh. They were of a height, though Sir Francis was somewhat younger—damned upstart!—twenty years younger, with a young man's body and carriage.

Robert tightened his hold on such thoughts. His errand was too important to make a greater enemy of Raleigh than their rivalry had already made. "Sir Walter, I have a plan to ease the queen's fear of an immediate Spanish attack, which would remove one concern regarding Mary's death. Let us take Her Majesty on a river trip—the Thames is clear of ice and the sweeter air flowing up from the channel will do her good."

"Why would you need me, my lord . . . unless you seek out my company?"

Raleigh's air was of amusement, but Robert could see that Sir Walter was curious to see what would follow. "I mean to stop at Deptford. There are new ships building there; the *Golden Hind* is in dry dock and the *Ark Royal* readies for sea."

"Her Majesty would know that the fleet prepares to fight her enemies even if her captains have to pay for it," Raleigh said, immediately grasping the idea.

Robert knew he had struck the right chord with Raleigh, who always looked for any possible adventure that might bring him advancement. He longed to be on the privy council, but Elizabeth chose her advisors from less reckless men. He longed to be an earl, which he would never be. The queen, clinging to her power, had created few nobles during her reign, but ambitious men were always full of hope. The Earl of Leicester was an example of that to every courtier. England was without a duke since the Duke of Norfolk was executed in 1572 for his plot to wed Mary Stuart.

Why not Robert, Duke of Norfolk? Would Bess ever allow Lettice to be a duchess and lead the wives of peers in every procession? His mouth twisted in less than a smile, knowing the answer.

Raleigh bowed, merry in return. "We will show Her Grace that her navy is strong and growing stronger."

"You take my meaning exactly. Better to see it than hear it."

"My lord, I will send at once to Hawkins and Frobisher and Lord Howard of Effingham to meet us there. And Drake, who has been longing to take a small fleet into the port of Cádiz and wreak destruction on the Spanish Armada where they gather. Drake can bring in sailors from shore and we will show her a ready fighting navy—"

"Exactly!" Leicester nodded and left quickly. Raleigh was no friend, but for Bess's sake Leicester would make plans with the devil himself.

The next day after dinner, with a sense of an early thaw in the noon air, Robert escorted Bess to the royal barge tied up at the Westminster water stairs, royal flags flying. The tide was coming in, making the trip under London Bridge easier, since they would not have to shoot between the bridge's center pillars, though the downriver trip tested the strength of the royal oarsmen. Leicester thought it appropriate to this mission that the men row against the tide.

They watched the marshy shallows slide by, swans and other

waterbirds tucking their heads under their warm wings. A brazier's coal heated the queen's three-sided cabin in the stern while musicians played forward, occasionally splashed by the oars.

The queen's oarsmen in red-and-black livery with an embroidered rose on their backs bent to their task and kept the barge steady in midstream.

Leicester sat in the open cabin with the queen, under fur robes, heated wine in their cups. Raleigh chose to stand in the prow, his foot on the rail, his profile silhouetted to his advantage. Leicester remembered when he had done much the same, the queen knowing then as she knew now who was supposed to be impressed.

"Rob, do you see yourself in Sir Walter?"

He swallowed his annoyance, but sat straighter. "Should I, madam?"

She was merry, laughing for the first time that day.

"What have I said to amuse you, Bess? If you tell me, I swear I'll repeat it."

"Nay, nay, rest yourself, Rob," she said, her hand covering her mouth. Then she relaxed and leaned back against the pillows, her body at a rest he rarely saw. "S'blood, you men are amusing creatures. Though I am yet a virgin maid"—her eyes flashed at him in the torchlight, daring him to deny what she wanted to believe—"I know the endless games men play."

"And women play no games, Bess?"

"Never, my lord," she said, even more amused.

"Yet I think you take pleasure in our labors to draw your eyes."

She shrugged. "Of course. I am a woman."

"But you are also a queen."

"Rob, you need not remind me. My duty is always in the vanguard." She laughed and added, "Almost always. But that does not require me to turn away from a handsome form."

"Bess," he said, his voice and gaze all for her, "I could never turn away from you. To me you are beautiful . . . ageless."

Elizabeth liked to be reminded that she was forever young in his eyes. He wondered if she really understood that it was no mere courtly compliment, but what he truly saw, the girl, the princess, the young queen . . . all the women he had loved, still loved, more deeply as the years passed and their time together became more precious.

Robert sat silently for the rest of the trip to Deptford, though Bess's hand stole under the furs to clasp his own. They looked west down the river all the way, Bess nodding her head in time to the music, a lively country tune, their hands growing warmer.

As they approached the Deptford main dock, Robert could see that Raleigh had done his work well. Lord Howard, Drake and Hawkins stood bowing, while sailors lined the rails of the queen's ship, *Ark Royal*. Armed merchantmen were swinging on their anchors and busy pinnaces darted from ship to ship. To their left, the five-hundred-ton *Golden Hind* stood in dry dock, where it had been on exhibition for seven years since Drake had returned from sailing around the world, claiming much of it for England's Queen Elizabeth. Robert was heartened to see several new keels were being laid, and several others were more than half-finished.

Lord Howard knelt and stretched his hand to help the queen to the quay. The sailors on the ships sent up a frenzy of shouted *huzzah*s. Several small guns were run out and a salute fired in the queen's honor.

"We thank our loyal seamen and pray you always find safe harbors," she shouted back at them, and they hallooed all the more to their Good Queen Bess, waving their dark caps against the white of sails unfurled from yardarms, to be mended.

Leicester heard her mutter: "No Spanish harbors for my sailors."

"Your Majesty may be assured of that." He couldn't help himself: "Spain will come to us."

Surprisingly, her anger was controlled. "My lord of Leicester, you know my mind on this subject."

"Aye, madam, I do know it, but I ever hope that you would pray on the matter."

She gave him a sharp look. "We are ever at our prayers on all matters touching our realm, my lord."

He bowed and she turned away with a flick of her fan, probably not to forgive him for the rest of the day.

"Sir Francis," Elizabeth said, recognizing Drake. He was a short and solid man with a light beard and the wide-legged stance of a man more used to a rolling deck than dry land.

"Welcome, Your Majesty. This will be a fleet to keep England safe and make Spain wish they had never come against us," he said, his weathered sailor's face proud as his gaze seemed to look beyond horizons.

The queen glanced at the new ships being built and frowned. "What manner of ships are these, Captain, that take so much from my treasury?"

"A wonderful new design, madam, race-built and low in the water, for speed. They will outsail any lumbering galleon of Spain."

"But they have no forecastles and only a single deck. Where

would the soldiers be? How would they grapple and board the towering Spanish ships?"

Drake bowed, grinning widely, well pleased with himself. "We wouldn't, Your Grace. These ships will lay snug to the water, stand off and fire from a distance." His voice rose as he warmed to his subject. "They will sail better to windward, always staying upwind. We'll fire at the Spaniards' waterlines, while their galleons' cannon shot falls short."

Elizabeth looked puzzled. "But, Captain Drake, if they board you they would overwhelm your small crew."

"Pardon, Your Grace, they cannot board us, for we will fire at will from beyond their range."

Elizabeth thought for a moment, then smiled. "So these ships are not floating forts for soldiers, but ships for my good fighting sailors and their new cannon."

Drake beamed. "Exactly so, madam. Good English ships for sailors and cannon that take the same ball, not a dozen different ones." He took a breath. "All of these new ships will be ready before summertide."

The queen turned to Leicester. "My lord, did not Mr. Secretary Walsingham say that the armada would not come this summer?"

Before Leicester could answer, Drake spoke, too excited to observe royal protocol. "My pardon, Your Lordship, but some of these new ships will be ready by April and I would like to test them. Majesty, with your permission I would take a small fleet and lay off Cádiz harbor in April, taunting the Spaniards to come out." He clapped his hands together in his eagerness. "And if they do not want to face *El Draco*, I will sail right up the Spanish king's arse—begging your pardon, Majesty."

Elizabeth thought for a moment, smothering a smile. "Indeed, *El Draco*," she said, trilling the name in the Spanish way. "You would go right into their midst in their own harbor?"

"Aye, madam, that is my meaning. Take them where they least expect us."

The queen's face was as alive as Drake's. "And then wait for their treasure fleet off the Azores. Building new ships such as these and provisioning them for war is costly, sir."

"My idea exactly, Your Majesty. What better way to test our new ships than by fighting them?"

"What better way to pay for them," Elizabeth noted, highly amused, "than with Spanish gold."

Drake bowed again and kissed the hand Elizabeth offered. "We will make Philip regret that he ever eyed England, or thought to come against her navy."

"Will we, indeed?" she asked herself, but with a sparkle of mischief infused. "We thank you, sir, and wish you Godspeed, though I will deny all knowledge of your mission." She gave him her hand to kiss.

Leicester heard a lift in her voice that had been missing since his return from the Holland war. He wished that he had put it there, but he was grateful to Drake.

The wind came up off the Thames, tugging at their clothes. They faced into it and walked down the wharf toward the *Ark Royal*, careful of the uneven planking. Robert offered Elizabeth his arm and she turned to him as a shot whistled over their heads, followed by a puff of black powder from the lower deck of the *Ark Royal*. Although Robert tried to hold her up, the queen sank slowly to her knees.

He knelt, clasping her to his chest, fighting for breath against a pounding heart. "Bess . . . Bess, sweetest? Are you wounded?"

Around them, men formed a protective circle while other men ran toward the ship.

"Get that man!" Lord Howard called after them, pointing toward a gun porthole, where a smoking harquebus disappeared within. Drake and Hawkins unsheathed their swords and ran for the ship.

Elizabeth shivered, her teeth chattering, but she could still force words from her mouth. "Rob, Rob—"

"Where are you hurt, Bess? Where—"

Raleigh knelt beside them. "Majesty, my lord of Leicester, I think it is but my poor cloak that is assassinated." He lifted his expensive embroidered velvet cloak, one finger poking through a bullet hole.

Elizabeth raised her head and laughed, shaky but gathering herself together, always queen where her people could see her. "Good Sir Walter," she said, her voice a little too high, but strong, "I think that is two cloaks you have lost in my service."

"A price I'd pay many times over." Sir Walter bowed and the crowd of gathered ship's carpenters relaxed at the queen's laugh, though Robert kept tight hold about her shoulders. "Your Grace," Raleigh said, "I think I prefer losing a cloak to a muddy puddle than losing one to an assassin . . . since it cost me a gold mark."

"Your gold mark will be repaid." Elizabeth tried to smile, though she leaned on Robert as she stood erect.

Raleigh had lost a cloak, Robert knew, but had probably gained a manor with grazing rights for his Devon sheep.

Lord Howard returned down the dock, a bloodied sailor stumbling with his arms bound in front of him pushed along by Howard's guards.

Raleigh stepped up. "May I have charge of this prisoner,

Majesty, and I will see him to the Tower and show him no mercy in the dungeons."

The sailor screamed at him, "Do as you will with me. I am a Catholic and a priest ready to meet my God, who will welcome me as Queen Mary Stuart's loyal subject and the slayer of a heretic bastard queen!"

Robert shouted at him. "You fool! Murderers are not welcome in heaven."

"At Douai, I was taught that the pope says—"

"We are lawful queen here! Who are you to doubt it?" Elizabeth shouted, gulping deep breaths, but keeping her voice from trembling.

"My name would mean nothing to you and I would not have you murder all my family. They know nothing of this." The fear on his face as he frantically looked about for some escape told Robert that he had realized his bravado about meeting God was about to come true, and, if he were lucky, quickly.

Elizabeth stood tall and shook off Leicester's assistance, not wanting to appear to need it. "Raleigh, take him and see to it that you have the Lieutenant of the Tower devise a new and most horrible torment for this man who would slay God's anointed."

All the way back upriver to Whitehall, Elizabeth lay quaking in his arms while he comforted her.

"Don't leave me, Rob," she whispered over and over. "Don't ever leave me."

"Bess, dearest, you are always safe with me," he whispered, "though not from Mary Stuart as long as she lives . . . as long as she lives."

That night when he came to sit at Elizabeth's bedside, he carried the warrant for Mary's execution with a quill already dipped in the blackest ink. She signed her name without hesitation, yet still could not quite bring herself to allow Mary's life to end.

"Do not send this warrant until I agree to allow that it be delivered," she said, turning toward her ladies while they soothed her face and arms with rose-scented water.

Leicester bowed and took the death warrant to Burghley and Walsingham, who were in Walsingham's closet, lit with many candles, the spymaster's secretaries working late into the night on coded dispatches. "One thing only I must know," Leicester told the Lord Treasurer and Walsingham. "Did either of you send that murderer to Deptford to force the queen's hand?"

"My lord!" They both said the shocked words at the same time, but Robert knew he would never know for a certainty, nor did he want to know as long as Bess was safe. He doubted that Burghley would harm Elizabeth. His method was to threaten to resign, though he was careful to do it only when resignation was certain to be refused. Of Walsingham's shadowy nature, Robert was less sure.

But Walsingham was staring at Robert with a question on his dark-as-a-Moor face. "I fear that if we hold this warrant as Her Majesty wishes, my lords, she will rescind it after she sleeps. We will be back as we were."

"Send it!" Robert said, knowing he was the only one who could survive defying Elizabeth. "Let it be done tomorrow. The queen must be safe from Mary's danger." He turned to leave. "I will be by the queen's bedside this night. She will have need of me." As he hurried back to the royal apartments, he passed William Davison, his old secretary, wrapped in a cloak. "Are you for Fotheringay?"

Davison nodded.

"You must deliver the warrant before the queen gains knowledge of Mary Stuart's execution. Godspeed you, William, now and later," Robert said.

"My thanks, Lord Robert. I fear no punishment; I carry this order for England and my queen, may God preserve her."

Robert embraced Davison, who would need God's help on both his long night ride and later, when Elizabeth discovered her order had been executed upon the Scottish queen's neck without what she considered her final permission. But this time she had come close enough so that those who cared for her could act. He doubted he would escape her furor. He knew it only too well. He might even be sent to the Tower after that poor deluded Jesuit thirsting for martyrdom, but he would return to her. She could not live without him by her side, just as he could not live without her. God must be an almighty jester to play such a trick on two people who could not have, but could not leave each other.

Once before, the full weight of Bess's anger had landed on him. Eight years earlier, when she had learned from his enemies about his secret marriage to Lettice . . . Before he could explain his reasons, before he could save himself from being thought her worst betrayer, she had banished him.

CHAPTER 19

❦

ROBIN . . . MARRIED?

───────── ❧ ─────────

ELIZABETH

January 1579
Whitehall Palace

*A*n elegant, many-ringed hand parted Elizabeth's tapestry bed curtains and, as she half started upright, the hand gently lifted the nightcap from her head.

"Do not be alarmed, most beautiful queen," the man whispered in his courtly, accented English. His face peeked through and it proved to be the rather handsome emissary and friend of the Duc d'Alençon, who had come to woo Elizabeth in his master's stead. Jean de Simier lingeringly kissed her stolen nightcap, his black eyes dancing with roguery. "I will send it to *le duc* to sleep with. He will kiss it before and after he sleeps . . . and perhaps during." His drollery ended on that expressive up note the French affected that promised so much to come.

Elizabeth laughed, delighted with such arch gallantry. She

was considering marriage negotiations with the *duc*, a younger son of Catherine de' Medici, the French queen mother, who in her ever-sly wisdom had sent this charming man to court the English queen in her ugly, pockmarked son's stead. And de Simier was a very fine substitute. Though well made, he was a small man, but a giant of *amour*, with the archly mischievous manner she loved. "Ah, de Simier, my handsome Monkey." She sighed, teasing him with her play on his name, though she should be outraged that he had entered her privy chamber uninvited. Yet he was such a playful monkey, she did not want to discourage his games.

She knew that many in her court were disturbed that she had given such a fond name to an enemy negotiator . . . for the French were always enemies . . . except—she sighed—when they gave her this much delight.

"Ever your own Monkey, my queen, though my face cannot approach the beauty of my master, *le duc*."

She adored playing these love games, especially with one so skilled. "We think you do yourself no justice, sir, since we have not heard many good things about the beauty of your master . . . though we grant you, gossip can be cruel . . . especially English gossip about the French." She poked him with a truth to see him cleverly defend it. How delightful to wake to such a man.

He knelt beside her bed and kissed her nightcap again, holding it against his cheek as if it were the most precious thing to ever touch his flesh. "Majesty, when I think that *le duc* will have this in his bed"—he took several hasty and deep, gulping breaths, seemingly overwhelmed with ardor—"I know that he will swim to you across the water that parts our countries. If he were here this minute, he would die to be in your bed."

Elizabeth drew back, pretending shock. "Monkey, you go too far."

"Your gracious Majesty, can love's hot longing ever go too far?"

It was all a game. De Simier thought it his, but she knew it was her game. How often she'd played at it! Perhaps too often, but once only when the game overtook her heart. *Robin!* Where was he? He would be hot with jealousy if he saw this.

Elizabeth jerked the tester to her chin. "Still, de Simier, you go very far!"

"Not so far, Majesty," he whispered, "as I would like."

Does he speak for his master or for himself? She had to reprimand him to quiet the gasps of her ladies, all of them idle, staring and too much prone to gossip amongst themselves and too often overheard. Though true, the man had gone very far. . . . She grinned into the coverlet . . . then made a dismissive gesture as if annoyed. *Pup! Pup!*

He fell backward. "I am prostrate with grief that I caused you one tick of yonder case clock's unease. I would never do you harm . . . for I am your love monkey."

The queen laughed aloud. This man went to the edge of insult and then most charmingly drew back. He was indeed a merry monkey and she could not chastise him too greatly. De Simier was sweet relief from constant council meetings, and Robin's strange distance of late. And always more death warrants to sign when young English Jesuits trained at Douai in Spanish Holland were sent to work against her and her law. They had tried to kill and would try and try again. Now they worked inside her realm to turn her people against her.

If they would not recant their allegiance to the pope, the law said they had committed treason and must die. She had been a tolerant queen. Why did they come against her when they knew she had sworn to preserve her father's church? And worse, insist on martyrdom and a terrible traitor's death at Tyburn?

"Leave us now, Monkey, for we must make ready for the presence chamber and our morning walk."

De Simier rose in one fluid motion without seeming to use any energy. "Can your Monkey dare hope to walk with you this morning? My master would have me see you in every guise and report . . . in detail . . . to him."

"Your master is curious about my walking? He need have no fear that I could easily pace him in walking or riding."

"Majesty," he said, and threw himself to his knees again. "You may slit my tongue if I implied any other thing. You are the mistress of all activity. I have told him that you dance like a goddess on Olympus, float on the water like a nymph of the sea, hunt like Diana in the night woods—"

She laughed at his delightful exaggerations. "Monkey, begone! I have no time to spare for the entire pantheon this morn."

He started to leave and then ran back and snatched up her handkerchief from her bed table. "This, my beautiful queen, is for Jean de Simier!" And waving his trophy in the air, he danced from the room without another word and she felt as if he had sucked the room's air out with him. She did not wake ready to joust, but such an exchange was . . . Would the duke be so loving when he rose from her bed? She shivered and put her arms about her body. "Build up the fire," she ordered. "We are afflicted with winter in our own palace!"

When a fire roared in the giant hearth, Elizabeth stretched, stood, dropped her night shift and spread her arms to be bathed with rose water and dressed in fresh linen shifts and a gown sparkling with diamonds and rubies like all the stars in the night heavens. Her favorite ladies, Anne Warwick and Kate Cary, attended her on rising, as did her ancient tutor and loyal lady from childhood, Blanche Parry, weak and nearly blind now, but insistent on doing her duty until Elizabeth ordered her taken to her bed.

The queen closed her eyes and sighed as her body was refreshed with cool water and her own special Elizabeth perfume, made from herbs, damask roses from her Hampton Court garden and musk from a ripened deer that she had shot with her own bow. She breathed in deeply, bringing her summer garden aroma to her nose. Opening her eyes wide to the pale winter-morning sun lighting her east windows, she noticed at once that Anne had a frown line between her eyes.

"What troubles you, dear Anne?"

The line disappeared. "Nothing of importance, Your Grace."

"Is it de Simier?"

Anne bowed her head to tie the queen's oversleeves to her gown and, Elizabeth knew, to escape her question. "Monkeys are harmless, comic creatures, Anne."

"There is talk, Majesty."

Pup! Pup! "There is always talk. What else would they talk about if not their queen?"

"He is very bold."

"He is French!" Elizabeth laughed. "They must all be bold or lose their reputation as lovers, which they care for above all things."

Anne smiled, but she did not look quite satisfied.

"Anne, I have been courted forever and know the rules. If I have not been ensnared before this . . ." Her voice trailed away before Robin's name came unbidden to her lips or Anne's. For that matter, what if she were to marry young Alençon? Could she still have an heir for England? She had submitted to a doctor's examination and they had informed her and her council that she could bear children. But what did men know? Her courses had been erratic and of short duration in late days. She was nearing . . . Well, she was growing older. She shivered.

Humbly Anne knelt. "I worry for you, Majesty."

Elizabeth drew her up gently. "What worries you, Anne? Tell me and I will order it resolved this day."

"Forgive me, Your Grace, but I must speak. I worry about this proposed marriage . . . and . . . and childbirth."

Elizabeth had to dispute Anne. This was her own great fear and she would not be reminded. But a modern queen did not show fear, not Elizabeth. "Anne, would you have me never know the blessings of motherhood?"

Anne stiffened and retreated without moving a step away. "Your Majesty will do what is best. Forgive me my presumption. It was said out of love for you." Anne added, hurriedly, "Your Grace, I would never question—"

Elizabeth turned her face away toward the lightening windows, her chest tight, tears daring to form in the corners of her eyes. "Anne . . . Anne, courtship is always a . . . a balm to me, reminding me that I am more than a queen . . . when little else does." She kissed Anne's cheek. "Sweet Anne, quiet your heart. I will break my fast now with ale and vanilla comfits." Elizabeth smiled and waved all her ladies but Anne from her bedchamber. Although these were her most trustworthy attendants, nobody should know her mind . . . until she knew it herself. She laughed lightly at the change in her mood. "Anne, I know you love me. There is no need to concern yourself. And remember, if we were deeply allied with France, both Spain and France, our great enemies, are neutralized."

Anne curtsied. "Gracious Majesty, you know best."

Elizabeth's pearl strands were brought and looped about her neck. "Anne, you know above any woman here that love has been cruel to me. If not for my realm, why would I wish it?" *And why would I wish to love another when I have my loyal Robin forever?*

Anne bowed her head and Elizabeth said no more. Each had spoken her truth as friends should do.

After a quaff of bitter ale and a nibble or two of a vanilla comfit, Elizabeth put several comfits in her pocket and called for the captain of her guard to form a procession for the presence chamber.

Her dear Sir Christopher Hatton strode in and knelt for his orders. His gold breastplate was shining and he wore her portrait miniature on his waist cord. "Good morrow, Kit. How is my good Mutton today?"

He wore a little gold bell about his neck on a chain to portray his other nickname, Bellwether. It tinkled as he bowed his head. "Majesty, never better than when I see you well of a morn. The sun does not rise for me until I know how goes it with my sovereign."

She smiled at him and allowed him to retain his lips on her hand just a moment beyond necessity. He was yet a handsome man, tall as all her guards must be, and handsome, also a requirement, his beard and hair sparkling from sprinkles of gilt. He was vain, but a clever man could be vain without offense; otherwise false modesty was cause for great suspicion.

The procession was formed, the trumpets sounded, drumbeats began and, leading her lords and ladies, Elizabeth walked slowly to the presence chamber, stopping to recognize and raise up those who deserved it, ignoring those who did not.

Robin she raised and he escorted her to the canopied throne

while Kit took his place nearby as captain of her guard. Robin knelt . . . always there. Her world was in order. She motioned Burghley forward. "Good Lord Burghley, you have come from a committee meeting about the Duc d'Alençon's contract of marriage. What news?"

Burghley bowed, favoring his gouty knee. "Majesty, it is my duty to inform you that your council does not agree to the large life pension that the duke's emissary demands, nor that he would be crowned king the day after your marriage."

"What! They demand so much, my lord, when we have yet to meet. Do they think of fortune only or our person? Look upon us! We have no defect of nature." She glared about her and saw only agreement. "It has pleased God to bestow upon us many gifts in good measure! Let France show us this Duc d'Alençon and we will decide if *his* worth equals ours!"

De Simier stepped forward at once, bowing, now dressed in blue velvet reflecting candlelight on its surface, his slender, handsome face a picture of distress. "Gracious Majesty," he said in his soothing English, "I have just received communication from my master that rescinds all former conditions. If you grant him a passport, he wishes to come to you incognito, if you will receive him . . . and his gifts." He bowed again. "I have told *le duc* that he will find you at the height of your beauty." He smiled. "And it is well-known in my country, madam, that Englishwomen born under your sign produce children into their middle years. Tudor rule could go on forever."

There was light applause from the gathering, but after she smiled at de Simier, the applause remained light. Few present wished for a French marriage. "Let us think on this new offer, sir. We will decide soon if *le duc* may come . . . with his gifts."

Elizabeth saw Robin wince. His eyes were haunted, as she

remembered they were when she had offered him to the queen of Scots. He would never learn that a queen must sacrifice for her realm. If it required taking a poxy little Frenchman to her bed . . . then he must bear it, as she must. Nothing would change between them. Nothing could ever change.

That afternoon Elizabeth was in an explosive mood. Walsingham had reported that crowds in London streets were proclaiming loudly against a French marriage. One man on King Street not far from Whitehall had announced a return to the days of Queen Mary and King Philip's Protestant persecution and that the Smithfield burnings would begin again.

The queen was incensed. "Have these same Londoners and all the Parliament not been begging me for marriage now these twenty years? I am ruler here!"

"Majesty," Walsingham reminded her in his dry voice, "you have always sought and have had the greatest love from your people."

"Speak up, sir. Do you warn me that I could lose their love for having their best benefit in my heart?"

"Majesty, London gamblers lay two to one against the French duke."

She waved him away.

He stood his ground. "Majesty, I beg you. I think the people's mood is one of hatred for an ancient enemy and fear of childbirth for you . . . at your age."

Elizabeth was furious. "I am but forty and six . . . in my prime!"

Walsingham spoke quietly. "Madam, your subjects know well that high ladies die more readily than low women . . . from the care of learned physicians."

"So you count yourself above my physicians now, Sir Francis?"

How dared he speak of her age! Her voice was cold, which would have withered a lesser man, but Walsingham's face never changed, nor did his dispassionate tone.

"Your Grace, the common people are anxious for you. They do not understand that great doctors who wrap a woman's belly in the skin of a freshly skinned sheep have skills beyond their poor midwives."

The queen did not know if he mocked her doctors or her people. Maybe both. She dismissed him without another word and he crossed the chamber to join the Earl of Sussex, who was also against the French marriage, though he had begged her to marry for twenty years. But Walsingham and Sussex were soon replaced by her Monkey. She smiled with relief. No more grave matters and frowning councilors with news she did not care to hear.

De Simier bowed and presented her with a miniature prayer book no bigger than a child's hand, its binding sparkling with jewels. "A tiny gift, Majesty, from my master, *le duc*, begging a great queen to remember him in her prayers when he starts his journey to you."

"We have not agreed to his coming."

"He says that God's words in these pages will change your heart."

"God's word always changes my heart."

He bowed most elegantly. "I am confident that God will speak to you, Majesty, but I fear that one certain lord with a loud voice speaks against your marriage, fearing it more than his own."

Elizabeth frowned. "What lord fears my marriage more than his own?"

De Simier appeared startled. "Madam, I may have spoken wrongly. I will say no more."

"We command you to say more of what you mean."

Both Sussex and Walsingham hurried forward, begged her to delay his speech until they returned to the royal apartments.

When the queen, trailed by her ministers, reached privacy, de Simier knelt, his forehead almost touching the Turkey carpet. "Most gracious and beauteous queen, I speak of the Earl of Leicester, who was married for this past year to Lettice, former Countess of Essex, but has not told you, which is the duty of any peer."

Elizabeth felt her hands freeze so that she could not lift them to slap de Simier's lying face. "Leave us," she said, the words dull and flat. *Robin?* No, Robin would never deceive her in such a way. Yet, deep in her heart, another voice spoke. Lettice's husband, the Earl of Essex, had died in Ireland these two years past . . . and Robin went often to Wanstead near Chartley and Lettice.

Her heart cried out against such false trickery, but her head . . . her head told her a different story. He had been bewitched years ago, and the slut had done it again and this time must have forced marriage on him against his will. She rose and paced the room from hearth to outer doors and back, and forth and back again. Wed a year ago! Yet he had not been with her at the hunt, in the masques and in her garden as a married man, but had been hers . . . as always. All the court had known, while she was kept in shadow, made the laughable fool. Or had she . . . had she resisted knowing, willed herself not to know? Bile spilled into her mouth and she motioned Lady Warwick to bring her wine. But that lady did not move fast enough. "At once, my lady! Must we always wait? Always be last!"

Quickly, Anne brought the cup, but Elizabeth dared not try to swallow and threw the drink against the wall, bringing Walsingham to his feet to take a distraught Anne from the room.

Sussex approached her and knelt. "Majesty, what can I do?"

"Nothing! You all knew and you did not tell me. You are all traitors to your sovereign."

Sussex bowed his head, which had turned from blond to white in her service.

When had he become old?

"What would you have me tell you?"

"The Earl of Leicester. You all knew of his . . . his disgrace and yet did not tell us."

"Madam, we thought it the earl's duty to tell you."

Elizabeth's voice was trembling and heavily sarcastic. "You did not wish for our wrath to fall on you."

He nodded and she knew he had nothing to say that would appease her. She was full of fury now, but not against Sussex. Robin had betrayed her . . . betrayed their love. Never would she trust him again . . . or trust love. A man's love was false. Always false. She held her throbbing head. *Rob . . . married? Another woman's arms about him? Another woman's body warming him in the night? Her face on his bolster, where a queen's once rested?*

"Quickly!" She faintly heard Sussex shout the word as she slumped to the floor. "The queen is in a swoon."

Lady Anne rushed to her with a cloth soaked with a balm of vinegar and pennyroyal.

Elizabeth heard them talking, the sharp scent of vinegar forcing her eyes wide-open to a truth from which she wanted desperately to escape.

Walsingham and Sussex helped her to a chair, while Lady Anne hovered nearby, tears scribing her face. "My lord Sussex," Elizabeth croaked, "send them both to the Tower immediately."

She saw the disagreement on all their faces and drew in enough breath to let out her fury. *"Jesu on the cross!"*

But Sussex spoke softly, pleadingly, kneeling before her, his old face earnest. "Most gracious Majesty, you know I am no friend of the Earl of Leicester. But the Tower . . . It would do grievous injury to you, I fear. Praise God, if this affair could be kept quieter. Allow the earl and his"—she saw that he struggled with the word *wife*, which would strike her like a just-sharpened sword—"uh, woman to depart quietly. Banish them if you will, but I beg Your Majesty, quietly."

Elizabeth listened without wanting to. Lord Sussex had always been suspicious of Robin, thinking he had too much power and resenting it. On a sickbed once, when he feared for his life, he'd warned the council: "Beware the Gypsy!"

She bowed her head, believing he spoke for her own good this time. "Banish them," she said, the words muffled by her hand covering her quivering lips, "but not together. That She-Wolf is to go to Leicester House on the Strand, and he is for Wanstead."

Sussex stood and bowed. "At once, Majesty."

As he moved backward toward the doors of her privy chamber, she added: "We will not see him, nor accept his letters."

"As you will it," Sussex said, the doors closing on her last words, though they rang through her head.

One week later
Greenwich Palace

Elizabeth busied herself with preparations to receive the Duc d'Alençon in early April, when the channel waves were in a better mood. De Simier was his usual charming advocate for *le duc*, but she no longer warmed as easily to his substitute lovemaking. Even her vanilla comfits had lost their sweetness. Nor did she watch her still-frosty gardens, impatient for the first signs of spring. At night, she sat up with her ladies playing cards, and even though they allowed her to win every game, winning did not bring its usual enjoyment. All pleasure had rapidly drained away from her life.

One night, as Anne prepared to sleep in the trundle bed nearby, Elizabeth sat sleepless against her satin bolsters, trying to concentrate on her prayer book. Several times she reached to open her jeweled treasure box at her bedside before she would allow her fingers to finally open its clasp. There was Robin's miniature on top, as he always was in her mind, young and handsome, his mouth with its more prominent lower lip slightly curved in a smile, as if he held back an amusing surprise, his brows tilting up at their inner edges as if to say in his man's way: *Bess, look no farther for what you want.*

Had she driven him to this unfaithfulness? Her chest and throat ached as if her heart weighed more than the eight pounds, which was the heaviest of standard weights she had authorized in her realm. Did her own body flaunt her law? Could a heart actually grow heavier with the grief of betrayal? Could grief be weighed? Tomorrow she would call on Dr. Dee to examine the subject with his strange science.

She breathed in deeply, gulping air, her lungs never feeling full until they hurt. Pain was the only sign to her that she was alive and could feel emotion. Other than her heavy heart, she was emptied of everything, the desire to eat, to hunt, to laugh, to dance . . . to live.

"Your Grace," Anne whispered, "how may I serve you?"

"There is nothing you can do for me."

"Should I call your doctors?"

Pup! Pup! "They can mend bones, but they cannot mend a heart broken by a faithless man."

Anne drew in a great breath. "He is no better for it, either," she said hastily, and put her hand on Elizabeth's, an unbidden touch which would usually need pardon.

The queen felt her own hand tighten on Anne's. "How no better? He has that She-Wolf and she has him at last."

"Madam, if you'll allow me . . ." Since Elizabeth did not object, her chin sunk to her chest, Anne closed her eyes as if in prayer and said in a voice scarcely above a whisper: "He is very ill with his old fever, Your Majesty. His doctors have called my husband, his brother, to his bedside. . . ." Her voice broke.

Elizabeth clutched her hand in alarm. "Why did you not tell me?"

Anne bowed her head.

Because I have forbidden his name to be spoken in my hearing. Oh, what a fool . . .

"Quickly," Elizabeth said, swinging her legs over her bedside, "dress me, but say nothing to anyone. You will go with me."

"Lord Burghley, Sir Walsingham?"

"Send one of my gentlemen pensioners to tell them I am going to the country to rest and will receive no messages."

"Yes, Majesty."

Elizabeth arrived at Wanstead as the next sun rose behind the morning ground fog, her white coach and four white horses mud-splattered, their flanks heaving, their hides rippling with weariness. She was handed to the ground by her coachman and stood on her jarred, bounced and stiffened legs for a moment until full life returned to them. Then with Anne at her side, she started for the wide front doors of the manor.

The coachman knocked and rang the outer hanging bell until the doors opened, a servant standing there, half-dressed and blinking, with a candle held high.

"Wait in the great hall," Elizabeth told Anne, and brushed past the servant. Snatching up a many-branched candleholder, she ordered it lit and swept on up the stairs, past an old nurse in a stained gown who slept nearly falling off a chair in the hall. "Why are you not with Lord Robert?"

The crone did not open her eyes. "Who asks?"

"Get out at once, or by God and all His saints I will have you whipped!" Elizabeth cried, rushing past the woman, who smelled of strong ale but was now suddenly awake, scrambling to her knees and then as soon gone. The queen threw open the heavy oaken door.

The candles had gone out, as well as the fire. "Robin," she whispered hoarsely.

"Bess, is that you or . . . am I transported to heaven?"

She parted his bed curtains. "Is this the care your servants give you?" she said, eyeing the damp, dirty sheets he lay on, white faced with feverish red cheeks.

She rushed back to the door and shouted to the crowd of servants now standing in the hall, their eyes wide with fearful expectation. She would not disappoint.

"Where is the Earl of Warwick?"

"Majesty, he was called away yesterday noon to deal with thieves on my lord's sheep runs."

"Call Lady Anne from the great hall. We need her at once. Send to the cook in the flesh kitchen to bring hot mutton broth, and from the bake house, fresh manchet bread. Now! And send a maid for clean sheets. The best. Haste, you all!"

Several servants ran in as many directions.

"Now you," she said, pointing at a man in a heavy leather apron, "build up the fire. You," she said to another man, "bring the best fresh ale from the cellar."

She hurried back to Robin's side and took his hand, bending to him. "All will be put to rights. I am here." She wrung a cloth from a basin of cool water and, sitting by his side, wiped his face and chest, while his fevered eyes glistened in the candlelight.

"I see my gracious queen and hear her, but I think I am inside a dream."

She squeezed his hand. "No dream, Robin."

"Then it is sorcery. It cannot be you."

"Why? Am I not flesh and blood and . . . human?"

"No, I see a goddess, a divine angel sent to snatch me from death's grip."

She bent and kissed his hot, damp cheek.

He groaned. "Now I know I dream. I feared never to feel your sweet lips again."

Pup! Pup! She ignored his dire meaning. "You have had your old fever many times and returned to good health. I will pray for you. God listens to the queen of England."

He produced a small smile with a trace of his old impishness.

Maids came to put fresh linen on the bed, which the queen oversaw, allowing no slipshod service. "Put some fresh rose water in the washing basin," she ordered, and it was quickly done.

Anne brought in hot mutton broth and a spoon. "Majesty, shall I feed my lord Robert?"

"Nay, Anne, rest from our trip. We will feed the earl."

Anne's eyes widened, but she curtsied and left them.

"No, Majesty, I cannot allow you this menial service." Robin tried to sit up, but fell back against the freshened bolster.

"Open," she ordered, and, after blowing to cool it, she spooned liquid into his mouth.

"I am not hungry," he said.

"You will eat for strength, nonetheless."

Obediently, he opened his mouth again.

After several spoonfuls, she whispered, "Why, Robin . . . why did you do it?"

He stared straight ahead, a muscle jumping in his jaw. "Lettice was with child and I was without an heir. All my brothers are dead except for Ambrose, and he has not sired a child on Anne all these years. All my line—"

"Your legitimate line. Don't forget the Douglass Sheffield whelp," Elizabeth corrected bitterly. *If I had married him, I would have two heirs, not Douglass nor Lettice.*

He nodded at her jab, looking at her with some understanding. "As you say, Majesty, all my legitimate line will be gone when I die."

She winced. "Don't talk of such things. . . . This is only a fever."

"Fevers kill, my gracious queen."

"Not this one. I am here and my will is that you recover and soon. I shall speak with God." He sank deeper into the bolster and she noticed a vein throbbing in his neck. She wanted to kiss it and so she did.

"No, Bess, I could not bear it if I gave you this fever."

"You did that, Robin, long ago," she whispered.

His laugh turned to a cough and breathlessness.

She put her hand lightly on his chest. "Quiet now. Rest. I will be here when you awake."

"Bess, that is all I ever wanted in this world, and you give it to me when I am too weak to take full advantage." He smiled, tightened his hold on her hand and closed his eyes. "Do you mean to allow me back into your service?"

She hesitated but knew she was no good at pretense with this man. All her emotions were on the surface with him. "Yes," she said softly. "But not the She-Wolf. She will not come to my court as long as I live."

Robert's eyelashes flickered, but he did not open his eyes. "No, Bess, she will not come to court. When I am with you, I want no other."

Elizabeth wanted to believe him and it was enough. It had to be enough.

CHAPTER 20

❧

On the Royal Barge to Greenwich Palace

———— ❧ ————

Elizabeth

February 11, 1587

On the Thames

*A*t first, Elizabeth heard only the river sounds, waves lapping against the Whitehall water steps as she climbed into the royal barge. Watermen seeking morning passengers shouted, "Eastward, ho!" as they ferried still-drunken men from the Bankside taverns and the Rose Theatre to the city piers. From the city side, other watermen shouted, "Westward, ho!" to encourage late revelers from the city to hire them for the Bankside. Wherries piled high with cargo goods took advantage of low tide to shoot under London Bridge, hurrying toward the merchant ships anchored downstream.

The river, always the busiest highway in her capital, on this day had people lining the riverbanks, caps off, loudly cheering the royal barge as it passed, flags flying, drums beating, trumpets sounding, although they could not see their queen or her ladies who had gone into the lower cabin. Bells were ringing in the city side and in Bankside.

"The people seem in a festive mood and are in good sorts this morn," Elizabeth muttered into her fur-hooded robe.

"Aye, Your Grace," agreed Lady Carey, keeping her head low in her collar.

"Last week they were yelling for Mary's head in the streets. Today they are cheering at sight of me. The people are so changeable."

No one responded. They were not in good sorts this morn.

"Add more coal to the brazier," Elizabeth ordered a servant. "All my ladies are cold."

It was done quickly, but still none met her gaze. They were hiding something. Some scandal? A belly where none should be? Jesu help the maid if it were true! A queen could not abide indecency in her court. A virgin queen must have a court without blemish. She determined to question all her ladies one by one after they reached Greenwich Palace and had finished setting up her royal apartments and she had returned from the council meeting, where she would be urged again to release Mary's death warrant. Jesu Christo! A busy day faced her and her sleep had been poor in the last few nights and full of night terrors. She must rest a few hours before the banqueting hall tonight, though her confectioners would by now be busy below with their tarts, puddings and her favorite comfits. Her teeth ached from the thought. S'blood, she would soon have to call in the tooth drawer again.

Past London Bridge and the looming Tower she looked to see if she could sight the carts that had gone ahead before first light with Robert, Earl of Leicester, in command. Rob sat so tall on his horse of over seventeen hands that she would not miss him as he headed the long royal train. And she needed to see him this morn, needed his special comfort.

She frowned. He had been strangely absent from her presence in the past two days. He was hiding something from her because he could not look in her face without showing it. He knew his queen would have to recall the death warrant she had signed . . . too hastily, to please him and to stop the constant pleas of all her councilors, her Parliament, her people. Jesu on the cross! All the court had begged her for Mary's head while both the French and Scots ambassadors had all but threatened her with war if she were to agree to such a severe action. And then there was her oath. She had sworn that she would never execute a God-anointed queen, though if Mary Stuart lived in this world another plot would form to put the Babington plot to shame, and another and another, each more desperate, until one would inevitably succeed.

Elizabeth could hear her father laughing at her. He would have had Mary's head off on the first suspicion years before, while the daughter of his blood had hesitated before all the world when she had evidence of Mary's treason written by her own hand! Did God demand Elizabeth sacrifice her own royal self for another queen, a queen whose own people—indeed, her own son—did not want her back? No, never would she believe such a thing. She had served God and had seen to it that her realm served him, taking a moderate stand between Protestants and Catholics, only to see neither pleased. So much for moderation as an appeaser. Zealots were never appeased. Yet she would take no other course were she to start anew as young Elizabeth new-come to the throne of England. *I regret nothing, my lord father. Nothing.* Sovereigns did not have the luxury of second-guessing, or all future commands could be questioned. That could never be. God did not allow his anointed to be wrong.

"Mulled cider, Majesty?" Anne, Countess of Warwick, held out a silver cup to her and she took a warming sip, returning her face quickly inside her fur hood.

Despite her lady's cold fingers, she ordered: "Play upon your lute, Anne. We are all many times too solemn this morn."

The music soothed her as music always did. When there was music, her mind could rest from worries and labors, the notes weaving in and out of her thoughts, acting like strong wine to calm her wits. Yet this day she could not turn her mind completely to pleasantries.

Cecil, Walsingham, Raleigh and Rob, too, along with the rest of her council, would be confounded, but what she commanded must be. She had urged them to free her of the necessity to behead a queen, but they had refused. Even Robin, the last man in the world who she thought would deny her, had not helped rid her of Mary, the Scots menace, whose plots had threatened her throne and her person for almost twenty years. Now, they would have Mary dead, but they must learn that they could not force their queen to do anything against her sacred rights or her own reputation with the crowned heads of the Catholic countries.

The river became very foggy the closer they rowed toward the channel, and Elizabeth was gladdened to disembark at the great Greenwich water gate and be assisted up the slimy steps.

She hurried through the entry court past bowing servants with the barest of greetings, leaving the white gloom behind. Moving rapidly through teeming halls full of favor seekers toward the warmth of the chapel with its perpetual candles, she threw off her cloak and knelt to say a hasty prayer, begging God to protect England and England's queen this day. This was her duty and one she never shirked.

Minutes later, she moved swiftly on through the sweet-smelling palace, knowing it would stay that way a bare few days before the jakes and bodies unwashed in winter overwhelmed the herbs and flower-petal sweetening until even her perfumed po-mander would not come to the aid of her nose. She stopped at the council chamber doors. Her ladies hurried to a halt near her, barely having breath to keep a proper distance.

"Remain here," Elizabeth ordered, and motioned for the guard to open the council chamber door. She would not have Anne Warwick or Lady Carey accompany her to a contentious meeting touching so many great decisions. . . . Women were too emotional to deal with matters of execution and war. "Here, Anne, care for my little dog while I am in council," she said, pulling the tiny sleeping creature from inside her ermine muff.

Her councilors rose and bowed, avoiding her eyes. They were plotting something. Like little boys planning to raid the confectioner's pantry, they could not hide their devious desire from their faces.

"Sit you, my lords and gentlemen. Why so glum? The lack of winter sun has turned you all to pale faces and downcast eyes." She sat in the chair Rob held for her and motioned them all to be seated.

Not a man answered her jibe, not even Walsingham, who generally had some droll rejoinder to lighten her mood. Rob tried a weak smile as he returned to his seat beside her, though it did nothing for his eyes, darker yet with . . . what? . . . apprehension, triumph. . . . She could not divine his mood.

"Come, what of import has happened? We are no weak, fainting woman to be protected from truth. Have the talks with

Parma in Holland been quit by the Spaniards again?" No one spoke. "Out with it, my lord Burghley," she said, her tone not to be ignored.

Burghley stood, leaning against the table to support his gouty knee, which was always worse in the winter. "Majesty, the queen of Scots has been executed upon the findings of your court of lords and your own signed warrant of execution."

The screamed words that echoed in her own ears came from her soul, though she had not realized her mouth had opened to let them loose. "Treason! Betrayal!" She pulled in shivering breath after shivering breath and yet remained gasping, her lungs empty. She put her hands flat upon the table to hide their shaking. "You are all traitors! My orders were to hold the warrant until I released it." She knew her face was red with fury. "How dare you disobey your queen!"

Burghley bowed. "Majesty, the sentence had been passed and—"

"What is that without your sovereign's order?"

Baron Burghley raised his head, his old eyes holding sadness but no fear. "We had your signed warrant, Your Grace."

"You deliberately disobeyed our spoken order to hold the warrant. Who did this? Who is responsible?" She turned to Rob, but he looked straight ahead, at one with them. He was against her. They were all against her.

She almost hissed at them like one of the big cats in the Tower menagerie when cornered. "What manner of deep disloyalty is this?" she asked, hearing her own voice rise to a shriek. "Do you all seek to suddenly grow a head shorter?"

No man, not even Hatton, turned his face toward her, and none uttered a word.

The queen's voice fell now to a growl. "When we asked for

your service to spare us this dishonor, you refused; your stomachs were *too* fragile. You each know who you are. Yet, when we would spare Mary to save our reputation in the world, you cut off her head. . . . God's anointed queen! Do you not know that if one queen can be executed, then no queen is safe? You have put us in terrible danger. You can no longer call yourselves our councilors . . . our supporters . . . we will no longer believe your protests of loyalty and love."

Elizabeth fell back into her chair. "Who carried the order to Fotheringay?" she asked, regaining control of her body and her voice.

Rob stood and looked at her with . . . what . . . compassion? How dared he pity her, or have a care for her when he, too, had not helped her when she had lowered herself to beg him for . . . one small favor?

Rob spoke in a low, but penetrating voice. "Majesty, William Davison—"

Elizabeth felt her face hot with anger. "If he carried the warrant, we order him to the Tower to await our pleasure."

"He carried the warrant on orders from your Lord Treasurer," Burghley said, regaining his seat from apparent exhaustion, though his spirit was still strong in his face.

The queen looked about the table. "And you, Mr. Secretary Walsingham?"

"Your Grace, it is no secret from you that I agreed the Scots queen must die for her many treasons against you. And if not for that crime, for many others. She was a whore and a murderess. She was an adulteress who conspired with her paramour the Earl of Bothwell to blow up her own husband, Lord Darnley, your subject, Majesty. But that was not her only foul deed. She then married her husband's murderer, and when her people rebelled against her for a witch, she fled to you and you gave her refuge, which she used to plot against your throne. I cannot—nay, my queen, will not weep for such an evil woman."

How dared they justify their treason? "Out of our council chamber! Out of our palace and sight, the lot of you! We cannot bear to look upon such servants. And away with you, too, my lord of Leicester. Your treason is written upon your face and strikes us to our spirit!"

They left quickly after bowing with their hands over their traitorous hearts, Rob trailing behind and turning to bow again at the door.

"Stay a moment only, my lord."

He returned near her and waited silently.

"Did the Stuart queen die quickly?"

Rob hesitated and Elizabeth was not sure she wanted to hear the truth. But she would know sooner or later. "Rob?"

"Majesty, not at once."

"How many strokes of the ax?"

"Three," Rob said, his own voice scarcely above a whisper.

Elizabeth put her hands to her face to cover the horror there and shivered throughout her body. *Three! Oh, God and all His saints, forgive me. I wanted it . . . but I did not want it.*

She caught a deep and steadying breath. "Now," she said in a low voice, "don't you wish she had been your bride, Rob? You would be the king of Scotland alone on the throne in the north."

"If I had lasted so long, Bess. Her husbands did not live long lives. Yet that is not the reason, on my heart. Better a dead Stuart queen than I should have spent one day apart from you."

He put out his hand and touched her shoulder. She could not shrink from him, not Robin's warm hand, the only warmth she had felt that day. She remained still for a minute, then two, needing to have this memory while he was gone.

"Leave us now, but return in a fortnight. I will have greater need of you with the others gone, for I do not wish to forgive them for a time. I shall order my court into deep mourning and I will throw myself into a fury of weeping and praying. I must not give Philip or any of my enemies cause to come against England until we are ready. They must be assured that I abhor this act and had no part in it . . . and I do abhor it, Rob."

"I understand, Your Majesty."

"I am not so certain you do, Rob. It is a sovereign's burden alone, but it must be . . . it must always be my burden."

"If you will it, Bess."

As he turned to leave, she whispered: "Robin, I have no doubt that you did this for me and that you probably saved me from some future dagger in the breast or poisoned tart."

"Majesty, do not mourn so long that you forget the biggest threat building in the harbors of Spain."

Rob said no more, but opened the doors and left. She was certain that he would quit Greenwich Palace before she returned to her apartments, readied for her by now with all her possessions placed just as she wanted them. The Holbein portrait of her father would be hanging in her antechamber, guarding her, proving to the world that she was the rightful queen. Although he himself had labeled her bastard, she had proven her right to rule. Did he know that from his place in heaven? Did he have pride in the useless girl his Boleyn queen had given him? She would never know until she reached heaven, and she was in no hurry for that answer.

Her mind whirled with questions and few replies. Would

Rob go to Leicester House on the Strand in London and to Lettice's bed for his comfort? She forced her mind not to admit that vivid picture.

When she asked Kit Hatton that night, she learned the Earl of Leicester had left word he could be found at Wanstead when she required his presence. It took all her will not to send a swift courier along the north road to order him back to her.

Hatton lingered. He was now her Lord Chancellor and principal representative to Parliament. She was not feeling receptive to reports of endless debate between Commons and Lords. And she had dismissed him with the rest of her councilors. Was he defying her?

He did not begin a report. His bright eyes were dulled with some sickness. His kidney again? "Mutton, are you ill?"

"It is nothing, Your Grace. My old ailment. I know I have your permission to rest at my house in London until recalled."

"Yes, rest yourself and it will hasten you well and back to our service in good time. I will send my herbal tonic with you."

"My thanks, Your Grace. I pray to Almighty God that I will yet be on this earth when you call for me."

Her Mutton was growing old, his blond curls and beard showing gray, his back not so straight, his belly not so flat, his feet not so fast in a galliard, no longer her Dancing Pensioner. Did he see her as she saw him, see under her whitened skin and red beeswax and cochineal lips and cheeks the deepening wrinkles radiating from her eyes and mouth? She would ban mirrors in her privy chambers. A queen should not have to see what did not please her.

Sir Christopher stood before her, frowning, and did not take his leave.

"Out with it," Elizabeth said, knowing a problem to be solved when she met with one.

"I do not wish to add to your worries, now that you are in mourning for the queen of Scots and . . ." He took a quick look at the big case clock that followed the queen everywhere in its special cart. "The prayers for the dead in the royal chapel are to begin within the quarter hour."

"They will begin when we arrive. Now, out with it, Kit," Elizabeth said, a little irritable. It was not like Hatton to shilly-shally.

"Majesty, you were kindness itself to give me residence in Ely Palace when I am in London—"

The queen's eyes narrowed. "And the money to do renovations."

"Yes, Majesty, I do not forget. But now word comes that the Bishop of Ely refuses to convey the deed to you."

"Refuses? Refuses his queen! That was our requirement until we are repaid monies owed."

"Yes, Majesty, I—"

"Guard!"

She was sorry to alarm poor Kit and she doubted he had been party to the Scots queen's execution, but she could not explain every action. She would never finish in time to show herself in her chapel praying devoutly for Mary's soul, which she thought would have need of many prayers—endless prayers, if she were guilty of half that charged to her soul.

"Yes, Majesty," a gentleman pensioner said, bowing, his gold breastplate swinging loose, having been untied for comfort and not retied.

"Call my secretary, and fix your uniform if you wish to continue in your position as a royal guard. A child could penetrate your armor. We will have no guards who do not strictly observe our rules."

"Aye, Your Grace," he said, bowing and tying simultaneously.

The secretary appeared with paper, quills, a small writing desk and sealing wax. "Majesty, how may I serve you?"

"With this," Elizabeth said, and began to pace and dictate.

> *To the Bishop of Ely,*
>
> *Proud Prelate,*
>
> *You know what you were before I made you what you are. If you do not immediately comply with my request, I will unfrock you, by God.*

Kit and her secretary bowed low and left. She had the last word on the matter, as she would have. If all her councilors and Rob disobeyed her, the Bishop of Ely would not now or ever.

On her knees in the royal chapel while her choirboys sang of peace in heaven, she prayed God that He would not punish England for the sins of her councilors. But Philip of Spain should take no comfort that she had sent them away. Elizabeth of England could have them all returned to her side in a day's time.

*I*n mid-June, Elizabeth surveyed her council, now in their places at her council table, with satisfaction. They were all nicely humbled and more loyal to her than ever. "My lords and gentlemen, you are all the better for a rest from your labors for my realm and the fresh air of your estates. We forgive you for the wrong you have done to us."

All of them bowed their heads, acknowledging that they

were much recovered, and grateful to have heads to bow, Elizabeth vowed. "So, my good councilors, what news?"

"Good news, Your Grace," Walsingham said quickly, obviously excited, his gray beard almost dancing with his exhilaration. "Sir Francis Drake and his new ships have won a battle against the Spanish fleet gathered in ports along their coast. Would that I were with him to share in the glory!"

Elizabeth smiled. They were all such boys with toy ships in ponds and wooden swords in the tiltyard, braving it amongst their playmates. "Yes, yes, tell us, Walsingham, since we can see you are bursting with news, although you should all know that while you were gone to rest on your estates we gave Drake permission to *interfere* with Spanish shipping bringing supplies into Cádiz for Philip's vaunted Great Enterprise against England. We would make certain, Walsingham, that your spies are correct and the armada does *not* sail this year."

All her councilors looked to one another in surprise. She hid her pleasure. *They thought I could not act, lacking their guidance! After all these years together, they yet think I am a weak, womanly creature who needs their advice to rule!*

The Earl of Leicester, hand on his sword like a great warlord, strode to the map on the wall behind Burghley and traced a finger along the Spanish and Portuguese coast. "Drake arrived off Cádiz late in April and cannonaded the Spanish fleet and their port city. He boarded their ships at anchor, thirty-seven in all, and took their supplies in great quantity before sinking them. He then attacked and plundered the city, throwing their land and naval forces into a panic. It was surely a glorious thing to see."

"And his losses?" asked the ever-cautious Burghley.

Rob's eyes shone as he looked about the council table. "Minor compared to the havoc he wrought among the black beards. Then he sailed up and down their coast from Lisbon to Cape St. Vincent, taunting them to come out and fight while capturing ships and destroying supplies meant for the armada."

"As I ordered him," Elizabeth said, nodding.

Rob bowed to her and continued. "One sunken ship carried barrel staves; the sea was reported full of floating staves and hoops. They will have to use green wood now on their food and water barrels, which will be sprung quickly at sea to let in air. They will live on weevils and rot ere they sight the English coast. I hope they never catch Drake, or his death will be slow and horrible indeed."

Elizabeth clapped her hands in delight. "They fear our *El Draco* and our great English fighting sailors! With such men as these we will teach King Philip a lesson no Spaniard will ever forget."

"Aye, Majesty," Walsingham added as Rob returned to his seat beside her, "but there's more to Drake's tale."

"Treasure ships full of plate from the New World?" the queen asked hopefully.

"A great carrack of a thousand tons, the *San Filipe*, laden with gold and silver valued at one hundred and fourteen thousand pounds."

Elizabeth made a quick calculation. Over forty thousand pounds for her treasury. She grinned, well satisfied. Drake's triumph was hers and England's, as well as his. "We will name Sir Francis Drake as vice admiral of our fleet."

The councilors, even jealous Hatton, even Burghley and Walsingham, clearly felt a spark of lost adventurous youth, aching for such fame and wealth. They each nodded their agreement to Drake's advancement, enthusiastically. Even Rob's face was alight, though he obviously felt disregarded. She knew those eyes and could see through them to his thoughts.

"My lord of Leicester, we name you lieutenant and captain-general of our armies to guard against Philip's soldiers landing on our shores."

"Majesty," Rob said, trying to suppress a look of success, "I am honored to have your trust."

Elizabeth stood, bringing the meeting to a halt. "Walsingham, send our royal courier to Plymouth at once and order Vice Admiral Drake to court . . . with his gold . . . as soon as he docks."

CHAPTER 21

❧

"I have the heart of a man, not a woman, and
I am not afraid of anything."

—*Elizabeth I*

───────────── ❧ ─────────────

EARL OF LEICESTER

Late May 1588
Leicester House, London

Lettice, you must take your daughters and their families to Kenilworth, where you will be safer than in London. Parma is a general to be reckoned with and will bring his
troops up the Thames to capture London . . . if he gets past me
at Tilbury." Leicester rose from his worktable in his library and
moved to another covered with coastal maps. His doublet and
cloak hung from the back of his chair and he had rolled his shirt-
sleeves to his elbows as a sign to her that he was hard at work.
"They will want to capture the queen," he murmured, almost
unaware that he uttered the thought foremost in his mind.

"Think of your *wife*, Robert!" Lettice's tone was close to hysteria.

"Of course I think of you and your safety, Lettice. That is my duty as a husband."

"How sweet. I do not usually come first in your thoughts . . . or do you want me out of your sight so that you can run to Elizabeth?"

He closed his eyes to rest from the sight of his wife in such ill humor. It took all his strength to withstand the envy of two women forever fighting for his every thought.

"I want you and yours to be safe. Isn't that enough?"

She shrugged, turning aside. "How can I leave all my gowns and—"

How like his wife to think of her gowns before her country. "Take them, madam. Whatever you like for your comfort, although Kenilworth is not without its—"

Her face grew hard. "I shall sleep in the queen's bed," she announced, as if expecting him to deny her.

"If you like," he replied, knowing the bedchamber he'd built for Elizabeth had long ago lost any trace of her perfume. He had not been able to enter it himself for years now. The memory of her standing there with the light on her face and hair, and of those enchanted days and evenings they had spent together, the sound of her voice, her delight in the hunt, the garden and her soft, loving whispers . . . But he could not trouble himself now about what was lost. He was facing a great battle which must keep Bess and England safe. If the Spanish ships were not stopped by Drake, Howard and Frobisher, they would land with tens of thousands of King Philip's troops. Whatever else might be, he would get Elizabeth to safety if he had to take her to the New World. His mind began to race ahead of that thought and an image of Bess with him in a savage forest, looking as they once had in their youth, riding furiously over every obstacle they confronted, throwing themselves under a tree, laughing and . . .

"My lord husband, you are not listening to me!"

He drew himself to his full height. Quarreling with Lettice drained him, sucked the energy from his sick body. His old fevers were upon him again and he desperately needed all his strength for the fight to come.

Robert approached Lettice and kissed her hand, knowing that soon it would lie on the arm of another man, his son Essex's great friend Christopher Blount, thirty-five years Lettice's junior. She thought her husband ignorant, but he was simply and quite completely without caring as long as she was discreet and did not sully his name.

He had to admit that she was still quite beautiful enough to attract a younger man, but her hurt pride and hatred for Bess had drawn lines on her face that had not been there when he had married her ten years earlier.

"I will take my white carriage with its four white horses," she announced spitefully, spitting the words into the silence between them. She knew that the queen hated her to drive around like royalty.

"Yes, madam, do take all, if it please you." He wanted to sit, but he refused to show even a small sign of his weariness, his constant fever. She was like a jungle animal, in that weakness made her the more fierce, and he must be away to see the queen as soon as he had good news to give her of his drawing together an army for England . . . for her. He must soothe Lettice in some way. And he knew just what would do that.

"Lettice, my dear wife, I would have you know that I have drawn my will, leaving all my estates, but trifles, to you." He had carefully acted the good husband, knowing that he must protect Bess's reputation even from his grave, knowing what the rumormongers would have whispered if he had treated Bess as his wife. God knew she was wife in his heart . . . and he, husband in hers, though she would never admit as much.

Lettice embraced him and pressed her body hard against him. "Dearest Robert, what a good husband you are." Then she pulled her head back and looked up at him, her eyes wide and, to her mind, innocent. "Trifles! What trifles? As your wife, should I not have all?"

"I must recognize my servants and . . ."

"Her?"

"The queen has given me many estates for my service to her these thirty years. It is my duty to remember her."

Lettice smirked at the word *service* and he knew what she thought, but did not dare say. Instead she looked only mildly curious: "What is this trifle?"

"You will know when I am no longer here."

As any good wife—a game she liked to play, though usually in company—she repeated by rote: "Pray God that time is many years hence."

He did not think she would have to wait so long, but he would seem to accept her caring, since it was so rare and he was too tired to listen to further envy.

"Robert . . . husband . . ." Her hand went to his arm, almost caressing it, her face softening. Her mouth opened and then closed tight.

It was unlike her to hesitate. "Yes, my dear, what is it?"

"Nothing . . . a foolish fancy." She shrugged, as if to emphasize a trifling thing, kissing his cheek in farewell.

As the door closed and the sounds of servants rushing to do their mistress's bidding replaced his wife's retreating figure, for a moment it troubled him to think of what she could have said and he could have answered. But that moment was replaced by an image of Lettice and Christopher Blount walking in the Kenilworth garden, the garden he had made for Bess when they were still within sight of their youth.

*W*ithin two days of Lettice's departure, Robert was on his way to Richmond Castle to lay his plans before the queen. He knelt before her on a thick Turkey carpet.

The queen sat on her raised dais, wearing a shimmering silver gown woven through with silver metal threads and like knitted silk hosen he could glimpse above her shoe. She caught the light of every candle about her. He was enveloped in the wafting scent of her sweet rose perfume as he knelt, his head bowed, but his mind was drawn back to so many strolls in her perfume gardens. Ropes of deep-gleaming pearls were draped about her shoulders and waist to dazzle all eyes.

"My captain-general," she said, gesturing toward the carpet with a smile tugging at her lips, "I have had a care for the knees of my many faithful advisors."

"I am certain others bless you for it, Majesty," Robert said, glancing at Lord Burghley and Sir Francis Walsingham seated at the queen's table, "although I have no such need." He stood quickly and straight without pausing or wincing, though he felt his knees creak and prayed Bess could not hear them. Never would he show her that he was not fit to command her army, to keep her and the realm safe from Spain's soldiers crammed in the holds of their armada. He was her devoted servant until his last breath, creaky knees, fever and griping stomach or no. Only God could keep him from his duty and from her side.

Bess must always think to rely on his strength, the same strength he had shown so many times in the tiltyard as she watched from her gallery, her eyes shining on him.

Realizing his body was leaning toward her, he straightened his back. "Majesty," he said, holding up the rolled maps he carried, "allow me to show you my plans."

Elizabeth preceded him to her chair at the table and motioned for him to spread his maps before her.

"Your Grace, Lord Burghley, Sir Francis," he said as they crowded around while he smoothed flat the heavy vellum, "the sea-bound southern counties, here at Sussex, and here at Hampshire and Kent, should muster their troops on the coast to repel any southern landings by the armada. A series of fire posts must be set upon every hillock to be lit at the first sign of the Spanish fleet off the Straits of Dover."

"Order it, my lord."

"Aye, Majesty. The southeast must be readied to harry any vessels trying to land troops for a two-pronged attack, one from the south and one up the Thames. Yet I do not believe the enemy plans to fight their way north to London." He straightened.

"Where will they strike then, my lord?" the queen asked, frowning.

He pulled another map closer to her, since her near vision was excellent. "It is my belief that Parma's men will plan to come up the Thames"—he punched a finger at the river opening from the channel—"and thereby take London . . . and you, Majesty, the greatest prize of all. I advise Your Grace to go inland to Windsor, where you will be safer."

Both Burghley and Walsingham muttered agreement.

The queen sat very straight in her chair. "S'blood, my lords, do you think me a shrinking girl? I will don my cuirass, take up my sword of state and fight them myself if all are killed about me. They will not capture me to parade about Europe and Rome."

Robert held fast to the table. "Your Grace, you must keep safe, whatever happens."

She traced a finger across the counties to the west and stopped at Wales. "Needs be, my lords and gentlemen, we will fight from the rocky mountains of my ancestors in Wales, or better yet, from my forebear King Arthur's castle on the Cornish coast at Tintagel!"

Walsingham muttered into his beard in his dry way, "England is blessed to have such a queen."

"Do not doubt us, sir."

"Majesty," Walsingham answered, bowing from his chair, "I never have and never will."

Robert's hand moved across the map toward Elizabeth's to reassure her, but he stopped himself, knowing that any doubt of her strength would enrage her. "Majesty, they will never proceed so far as London as long as I live. They will have to march over my body to get to you."

Elizabeth frowned. "Then we will remain at Whitehall with our people. If you do not fear, then we may not. If we do not, our people will not."

Walsingham cleared his throat, becoming impatient, Robert suspected, at a drama better played at the Rose Theatre in a Christopher Marlowe play.

But the queen argued no more. Robert knew that she would do exactly as she pleased, and it pleased her to give no sign of timidity, determined as always to be her father's heir in all things.

Baron Burghley spoke next in his reassuring way. "Your

Grace, no one in all the realm doubts your courage, but your person must be secured for the sake of your people."

The queen sighed and raised her eyes to Burghley. "My Lord Treasurer . . . dear Spirit . . . we yet hope Lord Buckhurst will be successful negotiating peace with Parma." The words were followed by another sigh, this time of resignation, as if she knew that even a queen could not stop this war so long desired by Philip and delayed by England's brave sea dogs.

Robert continued lest Bess weary of such caution by her servants. He jabbed at the map, ignoring Bess's constant hope for negotiations. He knew this was no marriage contract she could complicate forever. King Philip had spent a fortune on his armada and it would sail, perhaps already had sailed. "Majesty, I will make base camp here"—he touched the map by the bank of the Thames—"at Tilbury, with a muster of twelve thousand troops and horse. The trainbands from Essex will march to London to guard the city and Whitehall. The city must provision them."

The queen smiled. "My lord mayor will not be fond of such an outlay."

"Better marks and pistoles spent now on good English stomachs than taken by the black beards to fill Spain's bottomless coffers," Robert said, his voice showing irritation that masked exhaustion. But he smiled before continuing. "Here, Majesty," he said, pointing to the Thames estuary, "I will build a chain boom stretching across the Thames, to stop any of the armada's ships from coming upriver."

Elizabeth stood, motioning Burghley and Walsingham to return to their seats. She walked to the oriel window, its diamond panes spaced by rubies, and looked out upon her walled garden, bright with the late flowers of summer. Though she did not turn back to them, they all heard her words. "I mislike war. It brings uncertain outcomes." She shrugged her shoulders as she rounded on them. "But no king of Spain and no pope of Rome may take this island from its people and its rightful queen."

Burghley and Walsingham bowed and moved backward to the door, which was softly opened and closed behind them. Robert began to roll his maps together.

Elizabeth was suddenly by his side, speaking softly. "Rob, have you been taking the herbal potion we sent you?"

"Aye, Bess," he said, making a face at the bitter taste, "and thinking of you each time I spoon it."

Her voice was stern. "We order you to continue it. Good potions are not supposed to taste of confection."

"Aye, my queen," he answered, purposely looking a little like a naughty boy, which pleased her.

She shook his arm and smiled, then showed her most serious face. "We beg you not to place yourself in any danger."

"I will do my duty to you, Bess."

"I know," she whispered, and allowed her hand to remain on his sleeve, "and that is what I fear."

He looked down at her hand, feeling its warmth go through doublet and shirt to his skin. It was the hand that wore her coronation ring and he bent to kiss it, feeling its raised edges sharp on his lips. "Bess," he said, his voice breaking like a hairless boy's, "I want you to remember—"

"No, Rob!" she said sharply, clasping his hand to her breast, "I will have no leave-taking between us. You have promised not to leave me and I will have no less. Do you not know my heart at last?"

"What man could truly know your heart, Bess?"

"You want me to say it again, Rob? It should not be necessary after all these years."

"Bess, after all these years, it is more necessary than ever." He knelt and she pulled his head against her stomacher and laid her arms about his neck. Her ladies must have begun to slip from the antechamber when such intimate talk began, because he was aware of doors softly closing. He wrapped his arms around her waist. "I can hear your heart beating," he said, his ear to her breasts.

"It should be thundering," she whispered, and pressed her body against him.

"Say the words, Bess. Let me take them into battle with me as my armor."

She could not say the words aloud, but they came in a whisper that surrounded him. "I have loved you above all men and will . . . until my last breath."

He stood and would have pressed her close to his heart, but she turned away, trembling.

"Rob, I cannot rue and repent now. . . . It grips my heart and I will need all my strength. Let that be enough between us, as it has always been."

He thought, but did not say: *No, never enough!* Instead he bowed and backed from the room.

"Stay safe," she said in a whisper he barely heard.

"And you, sweetest lady."

*I*n a sweltering, storm-clouded late July, the camp and fort at Tilbury were at last ready to repel a Spanish landing, or as ready as Leicester could make them with less of everything than he needed.

Gradually, he had forced order to emerge from chaos. He had spent weeks training the officers to drill the soldiers new-come from their fields and forges to fight for England. Although the law mandated they muster with all equipment, few common men had the means to do so and much of what they brought was not the latest in firearms. Many were equipped with ancient broadswords, cast-off pieces of armor, a few axes, crossbows and pikes. When a man came into camp with a matchlock, or more rarely a new flintlock, Leicester immediately dubbed him a sergeant.

Today, Elizabeth's captain-general looked down the neat rows of tents, pennants flying, men drilling in the wide alley between, and knew the troops were ready to confront whatever soldiers the armada or the Duke of Parma sent against them. Better good, stout English countrymen than all the Spanish soldiers dragged from prison to serve in foreign wars, half-starved in the hold of a galleon for a month.

Robert Devereux, Earl of Essex, rode up quickly, his yellow silk suit ruined by rain, sweat and dust. He knelt for Leicester's blessing, but began speaking as he rose. "Father, the signal fires have been lit. The armada has turned from the Lizard on the Cornwall coast and is coming up the channel."

"Are you certain of your information? All manner of rumors have been reported of late."

Essex smiled. "Father, I was with the queen when the news came to her."

"How is she?"

"Demands I play cards all night. I get no sleep until the birds awake."

Leicester smiled. "Then Her Majesty likes your company."

Essex stood even taller than Robert, if that was possible, since Leicester was the tallest man in Elizabeth's court. "Her Grace sees less and less of Hatton or Raleigh, if I take your meaning."

Leicester nodded, but said nothing. This was what he had

planned and hoped; still, now that Essex had pleased Elizabeth, he was not as happy as he had thought to be. She knew the young earl was Leicester's true son. Did this mean that she had forgiven him that long-ago dalliance, or did she seek to make him pay for it still with jealousy of his own child? He shook off the thought. He could not be jealous of his son, a son he loved.

"Drake is already at sea," Essex continued. "He has three squadrons of one hundred and eighty ships in all sizes from pinnace to galleon, he in the *Revenge* and Lord Howard in the *Ark Royal.* Drake placed one squadron at Plymouth in case more Spanish come to the south coast and two squadrons at Dover. According to Walsingham's spies, the Spanish commander, the Duke of Medina-Sedonia, is set to meet Parma and his troops off the Holland coast and then cross the channel to attack. Drake sends out ships to search the coasts off the Bay of Biscay, questioning every northbound ship. He knows the armada has left Corunna with a good following breeze and should be upon us any day."

"Bless Walsingham. England is ready with good intelligence," Leicester said, catching his breath on a sudden stomach pain. He reached into his pocket and withdrew the stoppered bottle Bess had given him, taking a single swallow. Since it had poppy in it, he dared not take too much. Though it dulled the pain, it also dulled his head.

"Does your stomach ail you again, Father?" Essex said, his voice anxious.

"My old fever. It is nothing to concern you."

Essex sighed. "Then here is something that does concern me and will cause you grief."

"Out with it!"

"We captured a Spanish spy and know what they plan for England."

"They will impose Catholicism."

"More, Father, they say they will kill all our people over seven years."

"A baseless boast. Englishmen will fight them."

"Philip expects to be greeted as a rescuer from the bastard heretic queen."

"He was deluded when he was husband to Mary Tudor and now is a royal hermit. He knows nothing of this country, or this queen."

"There is more, Father. The queen insists that she will come to Tilbury and fight with her troops. She was marching up and down her antechamber with a sword in her hand as I left her."

Leicester laughed. "How like her."

"Can you forbid her to come, Father?"

Leicester laughed harder. "Forbid Elizabeth? Easier to forbid a tempest from blowing. If I tried, she would dismiss me and take command herself! Don't you know her yet? This is her way of showing her father that she is worthy, as if Henry would have admitted that any woman was ever fit to follow him without a husband."

"But . . . but she must be kept safe."

"I will ready a manor to house her and her ladies a few miles inland from here and surround it with troops. Her barge will be all times at the ready."

Essex dug his boots into the sandy soil, his voice a little angry. "Is she mad to come among rough soldiers with a battle nearing?"

"No, not mad . . . a queen of England." He frowned with

concern. "My son, you do not know her as you think you do. Learn to know her and do not think to rule her, or it could be your downfall."

Essex laughed the superior laugh of the young who think their elders are fashioned from old cloth.

CHAPTER 22

❧

To Tilbury

------------------------------- ❧ -------------------------------

Elizabeth

Early August 1588
Tilbury on the Thames

Elizabeth was impatient. "Quickly, quickly," she commanded the oarsmen edging the royal barge up to the planked pier below a small manor near Tilbury. "Anne," she said as her ladies gathered on the deck, "have my rooms prepared at once, for I must away to Tilbury. Can you hear them?" she asked, her voice full of excitement.

"The cannon?" Anne asked.

"Of course, the cannon. They must be fighting in the channel as we stand here shilly-shallying. Now hurry or we will miss the battle." She ignored Anne's look of alarm and, placing the great sword of state over her shoulder, she marched up a small hillock to the manor. At once she saw it was secure with a troop of horse surrounding it on all but the riverside, and that guarded by two demicannon with a mound of large stone shot by each. Rob ever had a care for her safety.

She walked into the great hall, which was not great at all, but would do. The owner bowed low and his goodwife curtsied. "We will trouble you little," Elizabeth said, though she thought her ladies and guards would likely consume their larder to the last rabbit and loaf of bread. "We will have Lord Leicester send provisions to you."

"I beg you, Majesty, give all to our brave soldiers."

The queen smiled her gratitude. "These are my good English people," she said, standing even taller. "Now, Anne, we must prepare for my entrance to Leicester's camp."

"This way, Your Majesty," the goodwife said, and led them up the narrow stairs to a gallery bedchamber.

"Quickly, Anne, we must be dressed and attend our army at Tilbury."

"Majesty, is it safe?"

"That is not a question for a monarch," Elizabeth said, her voice sharper than she intended. Gently, she took Anne's arm and spoke low to her. "We are the symbol of this realm, and if we are afraid, then how can our troops have the courage to face a strong and determined enemy?"

Anne curtsied and went immediately to the chest being unpacked. She returned with Lady Carey, both carrying a beautiful white gown shot through with silver thread and studded with gleaming pearls. Elizabeth stretched her arms wide to aid them in dressing her. "My cuirass," she said, and although she saw a grim tightening about Anne's mouth, she did not laugh at her worries, knowing they came from love of her. "Dear Anne, we will fight with our troops as our father did in France, even if we must lay down our life into the dust." *Have you all forgotten that*

I am Henry's spawn? And Anne Boleyn's . . . a name that does not pass my lips, but is forever on my mind? Who can doubt the courage of a woman who faced the ax by lifting up her long hair with a smile?

Anne sighed, but helped tighten the leather straps of the gleaming silver cuirass from the front breastplate to the back plate and added the gorget that protected Elizabeth's throat.

"Wait here for my return," the queen said firmly.

Anne's mouth opened as if to argue, but Elizabeth flashed a glance at her to tell her not to dispute even for love of her. "I am determined on my course, Anne," she whispered, and was off in a flash of white and down the stairs to the great room, calling loudly for the captain of her guard.

He knelt before her, head bowed, one hand on his sword hilt. "Majesty, what would you have of me?"

"We will take no guard with us."

She thought the captain turned as white as her dress. "Majesty, I beg you, do not go among such numbers of new men who could harbor treachery."

"My loving people?" she said in disbelief. "Send at once to Lord Leicester to tell him his queen—" Before the words were fully spoken, Rob appeared at the door, filled it, his helmeted head coming near the top of the frame.

He stepped swiftly to her and knelt, removing his helm, his hair damp and sticking to his forehead as it had at the tourneys in the tiltyards of earlier years. Though his dark hair was now shot through with silver, the face that looked up at her was still her young Robin's in her eyes. "We meet in this place, my lord, and go together to fight for England. Is all in readiness?"

"Aye, Your Grace, now that you are here. I came to you as soon as I heard you had arrived."

She laughed, whirling about, her face animated with pleasure. "These days apart have passed too slowly. But you are in good time, my lord. Let us away to Tilbury!"

"You want no guard, Majesty." It was not a question. Rob knew her too well.

"Only those necessary to my dignity. I will have Lord Ormonde walk ahead with the sword of state, a page to bear my helmet on a velvet cushion and my captain-general to ride by my side." She held out her hand to him.

He rose, took the hand and whispered, "You have your captain-general by your side always."

She tightened her grip to let him know she had heard.

He led her to the hillock outside and stopped at a large gray gelding, which he helped her to mount. "Though gelded he is still spirited, Bess."

She laughed. "I would have no other mount than one with potency . . . unmanned or no."

He grinned and sprang into his saddle.

She wondered what that show of youth cost him in pain, but knew his pretense was for her love. *Ah, Robin, we are both growing older, but will make no admission of it. If we were like the man of this manor and his goodwife, we would be sitting by our fire tonight warming our cold bones and lying to each other that we looked no different from on our marriage night.*

Their small band was quickly formed and they rode the two miles to Tilbury, topping a hill above the camp.

Elizabeth showed her pleasure at the orderly scene below her, although her attention was held by the roar of ships' cannon shooting fifty-pound balls carried on the wind. "Rob," she said quietly, "would that I could see the battle."

"Bess, you cannot put yourself in danger."

Pup! Pup! "I have been in danger all my life."

They rode slowly down the hill and were met by the Earl of Essex, who took his place near the queen as her new Master of Horse. As they reached the sprawling camp near the fort, a great cry went up from the solid ranks of men confronting her. Elizabeth trotted her horse to the front of her entourage and raised her arm, shouting: "My loving people."

Men broke ranks and crowded closer to hear. Leicester reached for her bridle, but she removed his hand. "We are not afraid of our soldiers, Rob."

Elizabeth raised her voice. By Jesu and all His saints, she would speak with so great a voice that her sailors fighting at sea could hear her. She sat very straight in the saddle and knew her gown shimmered and her crown gleamed. She meant to show these men that she was every inch her father's daughter and if needs be could lead them into battle. "I am come amongst you, as you see, at this time, not for my recreation and disport, but being resolved, in the midst and heat of the battle, to live and die amongst you all; to lay down for my God, and for my kingdom, and my people, my honor and my blood, even in the dust."

Cheers rang in her ears, the men dipping their standards or raising their pikes in salute, but she spoke over them, acknowledging, perhaps, what they all thought, had always thought of a woman ruler. "I know I have the body but of a weak and feeble woman," she shouted, her fist on her breastplate, "but I have the heart and stomach of a king, and of a king of England too. . . ." *I am your rightful queen, the great Henry's heir. It is his strength I carry by birth in my heart and in my bones!*

"I know already, for your forwardness you have deserved rewards and crowns; and we do assure you in the word of a prince, they shall be duly paid you. In the meantime, my lieutenant general shall be in my stead," she said, gesturing toward Leicester, "than whom never prince commanded a more noble or worthy subject. . . ." More cheering erupted and Leicester's name was shouted with hers. She held her hand up for silence and the message quickly traveled back to the rear ranks. "Your obedience to him and your valor will shortly"—her voice rose to reach to the last rank—"give us a famous victory over those enemies of my God, of my kingdom and of my people!"

If any soldier did not hear her words, they were soon repeated to the least man, and as she rode down the ranks opening for her, she felt their love sweep over her like a warm wind, as she had not felt it since the day of her ascension to the throne of England nearly thirty years earlier. She had forsaken any marriage but to England and any children of her womb. Her people . . . these men . . . were all the children she had desired. For all but a few of her nights.

Later in Leicester's tent, though the cheering still erupted outside as her words were repeated again among the men, Elizabeth and Leicester had a supper together, this time Rob eating little, while the sea air blowing up the Thames had sharpened her appetite.

"I am sorry, Bess, for this rude meal, but this is an armed camp of soldiers—"

She laughed. "Rob, if I am ready to die as a soldier, then I am surely ready to eat as one. I will have nothing that they do not have." She dipped a piece of bread into the cold mutton pie and sopped up congealed gravy. "Delicious," she said, chewing it with an imitation of soldierly gusto. Jokingly, she wiped the back of her hand across her mouth.

Rob reached across the trestle desk now become a dining table and, turning a branched candelabra toward her, dabbed at her chin with a fine lace-edged handkerchief he took from his sleeve.

Elizabeth caught his hand when he would have removed it and held her bread sop to his mouth. He turned his head away.

The words quivered in her mouth. "Are you ailing, Rob? Tell me. I demand it!"

"Nothing of concern. My old ailment."

"And fever?" she asked.

He shrugged.

"And fever?" she demanded.

"Yea, a little."

She felt his face. "More than a little. Are you taking the herbal potion I had made for you?"

He nodded and removed it from his pocket. "Every day, but sparingly. I must keep my head clear for the attack. The armada's first duty is to escort Parma's barges full of troops to the Thames and on toward London. My duty is to stop them here."

"Your chiefest duty is always to your queen," she commanded, using her softest voice, her private voice that only he had ever heard. "I demand you take greater care of my general. I will not be robbed of all happiness now. Do you not understand me at last? Without you, my days would be all pretense."

Essex appeared at the tent opening and entered hastily, bowing. "My pardon, Your Grace, but there is news from Drake. A fast pinnace has just come up from Gravelines north of Calais."

She rose, tense, her voice hurried. "What news?"

"There is a great battle being fought at this moment. The captain of the pinnace is waiting outside."

"Summon him, my lord Essex."

The man, his face drawn from sleeplessness, entered and knelt before her. He grasped at the table to steady himself.

"My lord Leicester, give this man some wine."

The captain emptied the cup in three gulps. "Thank you, Majesty . . . my lords."

"Tell us about the battle. Leave out no detail. Do you come from Admiral Drake?"

"Aye. He sent me."

"Then deliver your message, Captain," the queen demanded. "How does my fleet fare?" She stood abruptly, motioned the captain to his feet and began to pace, the man's eyes following her.

"First, Majesty, our fleet caught the armada in Calais harbor and sent in eight large fire ships, their guns packed with powder exploding as they came. None of the Spaniards caught fire, but they panicked, broke their crescent formation, cut their anchors and came out, where we fell upon them one by one. The Spaniards have taken great damage. The battle lasted nine hours, until our shot was almost gone and we were fighting with musket and harquebus. We were always to windward and had the advantage, and"—he stopped to breathe deeply—"our gunners were superior, our rate of fire much faster."

"My good sailors!" Elizabeth shouted, picking up her pace. "Continue!"

"Their admiral the Duke of Medina-Sedonia was in the *San Martin* with the *San Mateo*, *San Felipe*, all large galleons and galleasses, their holds full of galley slaves at the oars. The *Maria Juan*, a galleass, came up and sailed right into our fire. It went down with all hands. We heard their wounded screaming." The captain sagged with fatigue.

The queen pointed to her chair. "Sit, man . . . there."

He sat, leaning against the back to rest, heaving in breath. "Majesty, the wind began to blow to the north and the enemy could not slow themselves against it because they had cut their anchors and had no drag. Then they were trapped against the Flemish shoals while our ships blocked their way to open water."

Leicester poured the man's cup full again. It was gulped down as fast as the first and he continued: "Then a gale blew up and scattered them north. All their hulls were shot full of holes, but . . ." He stopped for breath.

"Yes, yes, go on," Elizabeth said, ceasing her pacing to stand in front of him, her hands on her hips.

"A miracle, Your Majesty. Drake's ship *Revenge* took some damage in her fight with *San Martin*, but hardly another English hull was damaged. If their shot hit us, the stone balls were so poorly made they broke into little pieces."

"Aye," she said, her eyes shining, "a miracle indeed, and just what we prayed for. God has answered us, sending His wind."

Essex bowed. "Majesty, if the gale dies, they could put into a Danish or Norwegian harbor and refit. And there are yet stragglers coming up from the Dover Strait. Drake is waiting to engage them."

Elizabeth raised the tent flap. "Look at the pennants and flags. The wind is blowing a gale to the north. Yea, this is God's wind. Nothing can stop it. Not Philip, nor the pope."

Leicester, who had been standing all through the captain's report, frowned. "Madam, we must prepare for all possibilities. Drake will need more shot if a Spanish straggler comes up with shot and powder unspent. Captain, I will give you every shot that I can spare."

Elizabeth nodded. "You must haste your return to Drake and tell him his queen is well pleased."

"Aye, Majesty, as soon as my crew has a hot meal in their empty bellies, we sail on the outgoing tide." He bowed and was gone.

Leicester spoke to Essex. "See that the captain has all he needs."

Elizabeth waited until Essex had left and guards outside the tent were deep in camp gossip, then went to Leicester and took his hands. "Rob," she said, her voice low and passionate.

"Yes, Bess, what is it?" He showed some alarm at her intensity.

"I would see the last of this battle. Henry's daughter cannot sit ashore while others fight for England. My father would have been in the prow of the lead ship. And do not remind me that I am but a woman. I know that better than you."

"But . . . but, Bess, this is madness. You must not . . ."

"*Must not* are words never to be used to a sovereign." She gripped his hands as tight as she could. "Rob . . . Sweet Robin, I would have this adventure as we once would have in our young days. Though no one will ever know it, we will. Let us go down the Thames with the pinnace and back again before we are missed."

"Bess, that is not possible! You would be missed by your guards, your ladies. . . ."

"Send for Anne of Warwick. She will wear my dress and rest in your tent with orders to your guards to not disturb, as the queen ails. We could return before daylight."

"Bess, once we're in the channel the wind is against us. The captain will have to tack again and again to reach Drake. And you risk being taken by the black beards, giving them the victory that your navy has already won for you."

"I have the heart of a man, not a woman, and I am not afraid of anything!"

He knelt, his hands still in hers. "I beg you . . . on our love, do not do this."

"Get up! Are you a player at the Rose? This is your queen

requesting your aid, as you have sworn to give it to us." Her expression was not pleading or demanding, just so sure of her right that any man living could not but agree. "God is on our side. He will protect me."

Her words did not erase the worry from his face.

Her hands were on her hips again, her legs in a wide stance. "Where is my adventurous Robin? Did I lose him in one of the years we have passed together?" She was out of breath, so slowed herself and spoke evenly. "I must do this. . . . It is what my father . . . what all my ancestors would have done . . . and did. I can do no less. Placate me in this, Rob, and I will ask nothing more as long as I live."

He rose, his face amused though a muscle jumped in his cheek. "Bess, you may always ask of me what you will, but now I wish you would listen to your general. . . ."

"In all things, but not in this. No one will ever know." Her eyes demanded his obedience. "You were not always so opposed to night adventures," she said, knowing he would understand her meaning.

He smiled, a memory plain on his face. "I will send for Anne and tell the captain of the pinnace that I will be coming aboard with a servant, though I doubt you will make a very good one."

She laughed. "I have played a servant before. Remember the maid at the archery match?"

"I remember her well . . . and the kiss I didn't win."

She drew near and he bent to her as if he could read her intention, and perhaps it was clear. She rose up on her toes and kissed his lips, quickly and sweetly, her deep blue eyes open on his dark black ones. "Remember when we used to hide from my brother, Edward, and Princess Mary at Greenwich, holding each other as they called for us?"

He smiled. "We were children then."

"Let this be our last adventure together, before we grow too old for games."

"You never will, Bess. You are eternal."

Elizabeth threw back her head, the diamonds in her crown flashing in the candlelight. "That is close to blasphemy. God decides such things."

He caught her to him, a wistful smile on his mouth. "No, Bess, the people have decided on your immortality before now."

"Jesu and the bones of all His saints! If the Spaniards heard you speak thus, they would burn you in Smithfield."

"They will never hear it and you would never allow my harm." He grinned. "Remember, we will retreat to the Welsh mountains and fight on from there, side by side."

"It will now not come to that, thanks to Drake, Hawkins, Frobisher and my lord Howard. With you as my general on land and such men at sea, England will never be conquered. Now, enough. Quickly, call for Anne to take my place and get me a groom's clothes before the fight is over and I have missed it!"

It was done swiftly over the protests of the Countess of Warwick, but Elizabeth would not be denied. With her hair covered by a stocking cap and her face scrubbed clean, she swaggered after Leicester at a servant's distance to the Thames pier. The pinnace, under full sail, was just disappearing around the first bend.

"Jesu Christo! Am I to be denied my dearest wish? Send a swifter boat after and recall them, Rob."

Leicester's face was stern. "The captain was forced to take the tide." His face softened as he saw her disappointment. "Boy, would you deny Drake his cannon shot? Do you not want him ready to fight if a Spanish galleon comes upon him? He has two hundred and fifty good English sailors aboard who would needs fight the black beards' cannon with swords and pikes." He dropped his voice to a whisper. "Bess, think what is best for your loyal seamen and the army here gathered to serve you."

Elizabeth wanted to argue against his advice. As wise as she knew it to be, she was not used to being denied what she so dearly wanted. Her shoulders sagged within the too-large doublet. "I did say that I would lay down my blood. . . ."

"Now, Bess, you are asked for something far more difficult than fighting. . . . As any commander knows, making a right decision that does not allow you glory is often hardest of all."

She walked at his side up the hill to the encampment. "You learned that in Holland, didn't you?"

Leicester did not answer her and she knew he thought it unnecessary.

Elizabeth was quickly dressed as queen again and a relieved Anne was escorted back to the manor by Essex. The queen sat once more across from Leicester, taking a cup of wine with him. "Rob, how long will you maintain this camp at Tilbury?"

"Until I have good news that the armada is not returning."

"The channel storms of fall are early this year."

He pushed the candelabra toward her so that he could see her face in the darkening tent.

She spoke, her eyes shining. "We shall have a procession to St. Paul's to thank God for our victory, grander even than our first entry into the city."

He nodded, but she could see his sagging shoulders and his eyes puffy from lack of sleep.

"You must rest, sleep if you can."

"Majesty, I must wait for more news."

"You must take my herbal potion and sleep. I command you!" She pointed to his narrow camp bed and, as she knew, he was too tired to dispute with her.

He removed his boots, unbuckled his sword and dagger, placing them at the bottom of the bed. With a tired groan, he slipped beneath his cloak.

Elizabeth looked down at him, knowing every feature of his face, having seen it change over time from a boy's to a man's. "Rob, you will ride on a white horse beside my carriage to St. Paul's so that the people may know you are ever my trusted captain-general."

His drowsy, dark eyes opened wider. "You would share your triumph with me?"

We have shared our lives! "Before the celebration, I command you to take the waters for a few days at Cornbury near Rycote in Oxfordshire."

Half asleep, he muttered, "Rycote. Always Rycote."

She put her hand in his.

"But, Bess, I should be by your side if the Spaniards come around Scotland and try to land in the west or take Ireland with the help of the rebels."

"I can easily recall you. You will always be by my side." She put her free hand on his face, almost pulling it hastily away. "You are burning, sweet Robin. This very hour, I will send to White-hall for my doctors." He did not answer and she thought he had fallen into an exhausted, feverish sleep.

"Guards," she called. "Bring a basin of cool water."

Almost at once, she had the basin and tore a soft linen cloth from her undershift, dipping it into the bowl. Removing a small vial of her perfume from about her neck, she sweetened the water. Did he smile? Yes, she thought, he knew that she was near.

Elizabeth took the cooled cloth and traced the outlines of his face, the wrinkles fallen away, a pink glow of youth upon his skin. She bent and touched his lips lightly with her own. "Sweet Robin," she murmured, remaining beside him through the night hours, seeing his face in the dim light, watching the rise and fall of his chest until the candles burned low.

EPILOGUE

❧

LOCKED INSIDE THE ROYAL APARTMENTS

❧

ELIZABETH

September 9, 1588
Whitehall Palace, Westminster

Robin is dead. The words echoed through her as Elizabeth stumbled over the threshold to her privy chamber. Once inside, all celebration of the armada's defeat, all praise, all pleasure became hollow. Elizabeth rasped, her voice breaking, "Leave me . . . all of you." She pushed those words out, but when she saw Cecil and her ladies hesitate, she screamed, "At once, by Christ's wounds!"

Cecil bowed, his lined face full of care and uncertainty. Anne Warwick reached out her hands and, Jesu forgive, Elizabeth turned her face from her old friend and faithful lady. Behind Anne, Kit Hatton loomed, and Elizabeth screamed again for them to leave her sight, her voice now so high it became a tortured squeal. *I have no thought or love in my heart for anyone but Robin. I am not my father, feasting and caressing another, celebrating Anne Boleyn's death before she is cold!*

All love was dead to her. Love was a face inside her head, a hundred—nay, a thousand pictured memories. Without Robin, there was no other love in her.

Cecil bowed and closed the doors to the royal antechamber and Anne did the same to the ladies' tiring-room. She scarcely heard them, though her empty chamber echoed with the silence that she would now live with forever.

Elizabeth looked up later, knowing not how long she had lain in her bed trying to gasp breath into her empty breast—seeing that she was alone, understanding at once what alone would mean.

Raising herself, she stepped on the soft, vibrantly colored Turkey carpet, stumbled to each door and drew its heavy bolt. She would see no one and no one would see her like this, brought lower than the lowest wretch of a woman in her realm.

She was no sworn wife, but Robin was the only man she had ever loved as a husband . . . though not as much as her crown and throne. That truth tore at her breast, turning her about in circles, because he had known . . . he had known that his love was greater than hers. Though it was not, she never could explain rightly. No man understood, or wanted to understand, that he was not everything to the woman he loved.

Her legs shook. She was suddenly kneeling on the marble floor, hard and cold, to open his letter, her hands shaking so that she placed the page flat upon the floor to hold it steady.

Her gaze swept across the familiar handwriting once, twice. He told her that he mended much better from the good herbal potion she had sent to him by young Tracey than from anything his doctors prescribed. *Of course, their physicks were worthless.*

"But, Robin, my potion was *not* good enough, either!" She heard her voice speak the words aloud as if he could hear them. She bent and kissed the page his hand had last touched. Had he kissed this page? She grasped it to her cheek.

Reading on, she scanned the letter again and again for some private word, a word for her alone, not for the queen but for the woman, some memory only they had shared. But he could not dare that. Even with his last breath he had a care for his virgin queen.

. . . with the continuance of my prayer for Your Majesty's most happy preservation, I humbly kiss your foot. From your old lodging at Rycote . . .

Rycote! Not her lodge, but where they had journeyed to be alone one night long ago. Had he died in that room? In that bed?

Elizabeth looked up to the coffered ceiling of her privy bed-chamber as if to find heaven there. Was this all . . . the end of a lifetime together from early days in her father's schoolroom at Greenwich for his children and the children of his high councilors? Jane and Catherine Grey had been there, and Elizabeth's half brother, Prince Edward. Yet all her mind pictured, would ever picture, was one boy, Robert Dudley . . . young Robin at eight years, then no taller than she, but with a manful stride and boy's sword at his side.

She thought him then and always the most handsome of all young gallants. At play, he was lively and full of fun, ready for any game, always inviting her to take part with him, even when her father named her bastard and banned the use of her royal title for all time. Even then he had whispered the word *princess* in her ear.

Had she loved Robin then, or had her love grown through so many years of terror and companionship? Who knew the hearts of the young? Still, somehow when she came at last to womanhood, her love for him was there, waiting to awaken her full-grown body.

She sat back on her heels, cursing the wide gown and shifts that nearly smothered her. His letter fell from her hand to the floor.

And separated!

Two pages? She snatched up the one unread and found it blank. Why a blank page?

Almost at once, she knew the answer and pulled herself to her feet, catching the heel of her cork shoe in the hem of her gown, sending seed pearls flying across the floor.

Of course! Lemon and alum combined were invisible until turned brown by heat. They had used such a device to shield their private messages from Cecil's men and other prying eyes before . . . so long ago now, when young at the beginning of her reign, unable to be parted for an hour.

Elizabeth, her strength of purpose holding her upright, walked to the hearth and collapsed into the soft upholstery of her chair. There was a candle on her side table. With shaking hands, she passed the flame near the page and, as it passed and heated the precious words, they turned brown and visible.

Scanning swiftly, Elizabeth breathed in every word past a full throat. Over and over, she read the lines until they were as much a part of her as any God-given organ.

She slumped against the chair back, not for comfort, but for support. Her bones were melting with grief . . . she had to be held by something, since Robin would nevermore hold her.

The room darkened but she was scarcely aware. Her candles, unattended by her ladies and gentlemen of the bedchamber, had gone out one by one. She was stifled by the dark and found new candles in the linen closet and lit many until light flooded into every corner, brighter than the flashes of fireworks still exploding in the city and from outside the city in the liberties. Even the pick-a-pockets and whores celebrated there this night.

She looked away from the celebration.

On the far wall by the big case clock, she saw Robin as he had been when first she was queen . . . his stance proud, one leg thrust forward, his jeweled velvet cap crowned with a sweeping peacock feather, his hot, dark Gypsy eyes alight with some new planned mischief or delight for her. He wore no gloves on his strong hands and he held them out to her. She saw his veins pulsing his need for her as she had known them to do . . . so many times.

Was this an apparition sent by God to torment her, a vivid memory, or the result of little sleep and no appetite when he was not with her?

She held out her arms to him, arms that he had always filled. "My Eyes! Come to me, for I cannot come to you."

He smiled and Elizabeth knew that the path between them was one-way and she could not make that journey yet.

She raised her hands in prayer: *Lord Jesus, I have borne wars and the Tower into which my sister, Mary, sent me to die, but I cannot bear this. I bore my own father naming me bastard; the near loss of my right to succession and suspicions of treason, but I cannot bear this. I bore Robin's marriage to that She-Wolf because he wanted an heir, but I cannot bear this.*

Elizabeth opened her eyes and stared into the corner that held him as he had always been in her heart, only to see him slowly fade into a wraith, a chimera. She called to him, "Robin, wait yet awhile!" But he could not wait.

From somewhere, she knew not where, sudden anger filled her and she struggled, dizzy, to her feet and raged at him, raged at cruel death. "How dare you desert us without our permission! We will not have it!" She pounded on her councilors' table, but no one heard. She whispered a command, the whisper trailing into nothing. "Do not leave me, for I cannot live without you. . . ."

Frustrated, she tore at her gown, spraying still more carefully sewn seed pearls in every direction, and watched with satisfaction as they rolled across the floor. Her temper not spent, she looked about her chamber to see what else she could destroy . . . as she was destroyed.

A faint voice Elizabeth recognized as Anne Warwick's came to her: "Your Grace . . . Majesty, I beg you, allow me to help you . . . please."

"Help? There is no help. . . ."

Only his last letter could console her, and so she sat, unmoving without food or drink, by the dying fire until it had long been cold ashes—how long she did not know, though night turned to day and night again—reading the ciphered page over and over until her memory of it raced ahead of the written words. Dazed, she vaguely heard rapping on her doors and Lord Burghley's voice . . . her Spirit . . . pleading with her to take food. She did not answer but snatched up the original page and wrote across the outside: *His last letter.*

She rose and stumbled to her treasures box beside her bed, and under Robin's miniature, the one Mary Stuart had coveted, she slipped the page. He would stand guard over her as he had done so many nights when she was ailing. Elizabeth returned, then, to her chair by the cold fire and read the cipher one last time, his words already fading to a light brown, soon to disappear:

September 4
From our lodge at Rycote

My sweet Bess,

It is very late at night and John Tamworth has given me enough of your potion to ease me, though it does not ease as much as your coronation portrait hanging across the room from my bed. A lantern shines on your dear face and yet does not relieve me as much as my dearest memories of the night we two lay in this bed together. Not one minute of the night has passed that I have not known again the sense of you in my arms and under my hands. The first faint light of morn creeps through the windows as it did that night when we were at Rycote and at last as true a husband and wife as ever any man and woman churched in the greatest cathedral in the realm. It is what I wanted so many years, though now I see it was always unnecessary. No woman and man were more wife and husband to each other than we, dearest lady.

Elizabeth looked up as a new rising sun spilled light into her chamber windows, her eyes filling with the tears she seldom shed, though she knew they would return whenever, in years to come, she allowed herself to remember these words and that stolen night. She had never quite forgotten, but they had never spoken of what had happened that night, as he had promised, not even in their most private moments, the few rarely snatched from duty. Yet she had seen him remember, seen the remembrance in his face and his body more than once years later. Still he remained loyal to his promise.

Bess, sweetest, I will never fully speak of this, but I cannot promise to forget. Do not ask of me what is impossible for any man.

Had she promised to marry him that night, only to think better of it the next day when they returned to Cornbury and she was again Queen Elizabeth and not a girl frolicking with a handsome, beloved boy? Of course she had promised. What woman would not promise anything that her beloved wanted when the length and weight of his fine body lay over hers, his hands caressing her aching breasts even as she begged him to have a care while arching to meet his thrusts, abandoning every caution in her need to know him completely. When he had asked her to be his wife, she had not denied him. That came later, as it always did.

As queen, she had stopped her summer progress through Oxfordshire in 1566 to take the waters at Cornbury and they had escaped to Robin's lodge at Rycote . . . for one night, a night that must remain hidden from her subjects and which, through her great resolve, she had almost managed to hide from herself.

I know I promised that your old ÔÔ would ever be by your side, but today I must leave you. God is hastily calling me to Him and I feel my soul draining from me. I have no choice, sweet Bess, just as I had no choice but to love you. Though it cost me everything, it gave me everything I value. Still I must leave you and all on this earth and you must rest content with your remembrance of me and of my love for you, the truest I ever knew.

Our years have passed too swiftly, Bess. Was it so long ago we were children hiding in the great garden at Hampton Court? I took your little hand as we passed under the frightening statues of the gods, our feet and hosen turning red from the brick paths, walking the passages your father had laid out for your mother.

You did not learn to love from Henry, Bess. Is it truth to say that I taught you love?

Was it there up the stairs in the little columned temple where we swore never to part?

Do not shed tears for me, my Bess. I welcome death now to end all my pains. I never sought to outlive you. Better the world be emptied of me than of you while I yet lived. . . . I could not bear such loneliness. But you will bear my death until so many suns set and rise, as God wills. I pray He sends you many untroubled years, for I cannot write more. Do not grieve for what is lost, but remember that we loved so many years. I have lived and so will die only yours.

Ever your ÔÔ,
Robin

Elizabeth heard guards outside her doors and they began to pound on the wood, which eventually splintered. She held

Robin's secret letter to the candle's flame and watched the words blacken and the paper burn and curl until only the last line remained . . . as it would always remain written upon her heart. Finally, even those precious words disappeared and she dropped the last corner of burning vellum into the cold ashes of her fireplace.

Burghley was suddenly kneeling at her feet. "Majesty, I pray you listen and hear me; England needs you!"

She heard her uneven voice croak from her dry throat. "Ah, my Spirit, you know the only words that will call me to myself."

"Madam," he said, his head bowed. He could not look at her ravaged face. "I do know that you ever have good care for your people, above all."

"Rise, old man," she said, giving him her hand, needing his strength more than he needed hers, in spite of his troubling gout.

Anne brought her some lamb broth and spooned it into her mouth, whispering that she had fasted three days, though Elizabeth did not remember them. As strength flowed into her, she ordered: "I command my palace of Whitehall return to normalcy."

She would hold no official mourning for Robin. The She-Wolf would deal with that. Elizabeth's mourning would be hidden in her heart forever.

Almost at once, Walsingham appeared with a sheaf of orders for a day of national thanksgiving to God for England's victory over Spain, and she signed and commanded as ever. She was bathed and dressed in fresh linen and a gown of black and white. Her face was covered with white paste of crushed alum and white lead, her cheeks reddened as if Elizabeth, queen of this realm, had not changed, though she had for all time.

Yet, through all, her heart echoed with his letter until all the words were a part of her, and his last line gave her the courage to lift herself to her duty for another day, for all her days: *I have lived and so will die only yours.*

AUTHOR'S HISTORICAL NOTE

*T*his is a work of fiction, although with good, historical reasons for both story and passion. We can say with assurance only, "This is what happened." In most instances, we cannot say, "This is how Queen Elizabeth and Robert, the Earl of Leicester, felt about it." They did not leave a full written record of their nearly five decades of close association, but their contemporaries observed and wrote about what they saw and heard.

Do we have absolute proof that they were lovers? Certainly, their lifelong behavior tells us that there was deep feeling between them. During the heat of their youth, especially in the early days after Elizabeth was crowned and free from the control of others, they were seldom apart, and there was no need of letters when there were ears to whisper into. If letters or notes were written, they were destroyed. The surviving letters they wrote in later life were full of health concerns for each other, matters of governance and protests of caring. If there were other letters of a more intimate nature from Elizabeth to her Robin, they were destroyed during the English Civil War, 1649–1660, when Kenilworth was stormed and looted by Parliamentarian forces. Oliver Cromwell later drained the great mere so that there is little left of the Kenilworth Elizabeth visited that glorious July of 1575. A local group has attempted to revive the garden to its original splendor. You can see their results at my Web site, www.jeane westin.com.

There was a last letter of a single page. But was there a second page to the surviving letter from Robert to the queen? He knew he was dying. I could not imagine that he would have gone from her after a lifetime of intimacy without expressing his deepest feelings and memories . . . more than, "I kiss your feet." If there were a second page to his last letter, Elizabeth could not have allowed it to survive, though she saved the page she could and kept it beside her bed in her treasure box until she died.

The intensity of Elizabeth's grief expressed when she locked herself into her privy chamber for three days (some sources say four days), refusing drink and food, tells us that she was shaken profoundly. What she felt during those long days and nights, I have imagined.

What happened to Douglass Sheffield after she was sent from court? She eventually remarried and spent years in Paris. She always claimed that the Earl of Leicester had married her, but there were no witnesses, no priest and no documentation. A few years after Elizabeth died, Douglass petitioned an English court to recognize the marriage and name her son Robert as the earl's heir. The court denied each petition, after which Douglass's son, the younger Robert Dudley, took himself to Italy, leaving his wife and children, remarried and became wealthy and titled on his own.

Lettice, Robert's second wife, was hastily remarried to her son Essex's young friend Sir Christopher Blount, only to lose both son and husband to the headman's ax when Essex rebelled against Elizabeth's rule a decade later. Lettice did not marry a fourth time, but lived on well into the next century, dying at the exceptional age, for that or any other time, of ninety-one years.

Learning that Lettice and Blount were with Robin at Rycote when he died, Elizabeth ordered an autopsy to rule out rumors that the Earl of Leicester had been poisoned. Not satisfied with a negative finding, she hounded Lettice to pay back all that Leicester owed the Crown, which took most of what he had left his wife. With matters of money, Elizabeth did not forgive.

Although Essex at the height of his influence with the queen managed to gain an audience for his mother, Elizabeth hedged again and, according to most historians, did not meet with her.

Did Lettice come to Leicester's bed dressed as Elizabeth? The story is apocryphal, but possible. Her resemblance to the queen was well-known and discussed by many and could not have escaped the Earl of Leicester's notice.

The resemblance between Leicester in his youth and his stepson, the Earl of Essex, Lettice's son, was also noted by several contemporaries and was hinted at in the 2006 movie starring Helen Mirren as Elizabeth. We'll never know for certain if Essex was Leicester's son, but the dates match. If I have further maligned Lettice's already blemished legacy, I apologize.

In the first years of Elizabeth's reign, many in her court, including foreign ambassadors, thought she and Robert would marry, and rumors circulated throughout England and the Continent that they were married and that Elizabeth was pregnant. It was everywhere observed that they behaved with intimacy, touching, whispering and having furious arguments, with Robert stalking off and Elizabeth calling him back as they both cried. William Cecil, Lord Burghley, Elizabeth's Lord Treasurer and the councilor closest to her for nearly forty years, thought the queen and the Earl of Leicester were lovers as late as 1572. We will never know for a certainty, which leaves the door wide-open for a writer's imagination and novels like this one.

As always, I thank Shirley Parenteau, my first gentle reader; "Lady" Ashley Lucas, my beck-and-call IT savior; and any number of booksellers in the U.S. and the U.K. who found requested books by long-out-of-print and almost forgotten scholars, especially the wonderful biographer Frederick Chamberlin, who deserves not to be forgotten.

Finally, and as always, I acknowledge the genius of my editor, Ellen Edwards, and the encouragement and support of my agent, Danielle Egan-Miller. Recognition also should go to my patient, supportive husband, Gene, and my wonderful daughter, Cara.

Copy of His Last Letter
in Modern English

I most humbly beseech your Majesty to pardon your poor old servant to be thus bold in sending to know how my gracious lady doth, and what ease of her late pain she finds, being the chiefest thing in the world I do pray for, for her to have good health and long life. For my own poor case, I continue still your medicine and find that (it) amends much better than any other thing that hath been given me. Thus hoping to find perfect cure at the bath, with the continuance of my wonted prayer for your Majesty's most happy pres- ervation, I humbly kiss your foot. From your old lodging at Rycote, this Thursday morning, ready to take on my Journey, by Your Majesty's most faithful and obedient servant,

R. Leicester

Even as I had writ thus much, I received Your Majesty's token by Young Tracey.

I most humbly besech god to gyue yo[u] poore
old Eynne to Q[ueen] the best in sending to know how my
gracious La[dy] dothe, and what ease of her late payne she
fyndeth, beyng the chefest thing in this worlde I do
pray for & for hir to haue good helthe and long lyfe
for my none poore care, I entend to god that nothing
and fynde yt amend much better then at my cumyng
hyther yf euer hys good wo . . . . That long to
fynde perfect cure at y[e] bath, with the continuance
of my wonted prayer for yt. . . I humbly kysse . . . .
yor old lodging at hyrott the thursday morning
ready to take on my Iorney

by yor most faythfull and
obedient Eynne

R. Leycester

About the Author

Jeane Westin began her writing life as a freelance journalist, then wrote a number of nonfiction books and finally came to her first and true love, historical novels. She published two novels, with Simon & Schuster and Scribner, in the late 1980s and after a long hiatus is once again indulging her passion for history. She lives in California with her husband, Gene, near their daughter, Cara, and has been rehabilitating a two-story Tudor cottage complete with dovecote for over a decade. You can reach her at www.jeanewestin.com.

HIS LAST LETTER

ELIZABETH I AND THE EARL OF LEICESTER

JEANE WESTIN

A CONVERSATION WITH JEANE WESTIN

Q. Much has been written about Elizabeth I. What inspired you to write His Last Letter *and how does it differ from other novels about the Virgin Queen?*

A. So much of my research into Elizabeth I's reign from 1559 until 1588, the year of the Spanish Armada's defeat, involved her relationship with Robert Dudley, Earl of Leicester. They seldom parted without great pain on each side, and his almost immediate illnesses brought her running to him. I wanted to explore just what this relationship had meant in their private times, the parts of their lives they kept hidden forever. Elizabeth, although severe at times in her desire to be a supreme ruler, was a conflicted woman. I wondered what that conflict meant to Elizabeth and to her Robin in terms of everyday denial; the changing but constant hope and rejection Robert suffered; and the queen's overarching fear of losing him, which made her reluctant to allow him out of her sight.

Also, I wondered how their love affected the important events of her reign and, especially, why such a charismatic man clung to the dream of marrying her for so long. . . . What reason could he have had other than the tantalizing promise of marriage and his own deeply felt emotion?

Including Leicester, Elizabeth had thirty-four suitors during her lifetime. She used foreign marriage negotiations as a way to forge alliances or to delay attacks by France and Spain on her half-island, as Pope Sixtus termed it, and succeeded brilliantly. The constant threat of a foreign marriage, which would have meant Robert's inevitable dismissal from court, or even death, must have taken a toll on him. I wondered how he coped with that fear and his gradually fading hopes.

Q. How does His Last Letter *differ from other Tudor novels?*

A. I've read many, but I don't claim to have read them all. I believe that there are as many possible "portraits" of this great but ultimately unknowable queen as there are authors and historians. We all bring different perspectives to bear because we've lived different lives and our experiences influence how we view her. This makes the possibility of novels about Elizabeth Tudor limitless. I, for one, am not bothered by this conundrum. It is difficult to say what author has been more right. . . . Elizabeth is the only one who really knows, and she took her secret to the grave.

Q. Tell us about the real letter from Robert Dudley to Elizabeth I around which this novel is conceived.

A. The surviving letter, inscribed *His Last Letter* in Elizabeth's hand, rests in the United Kingdom's National Archives, London, England. I could not believe this was all Leicester would have written, though I knew anything that questioned her virginity could not have been allowed to survive. Even in her later years the Virgin Queen was as determined as ever to protect her reputation for all time. How could she possibly have known that society's concepts of behavior for women would change so much in succeeding centuries?

Q. Did Elizabeth really lock herself in a room for three days upon hearing of Robert Dudley's death?

A. Yes, although accounts vary as to whether it was for three or four days and nights. The court must have been alarmed. There would have been consensus among the queen's council that the door be forced. It was splintered and broken on the order of William Cecil, Baron Burghley. No one knows what happened behind those doors while they were locked. I imagined the scene as I thought Elizabeth would have lived it, given her temper, her penchant for drama and her sense that with Robert gone she was without a living soul who truly knew and loved her.

Q. You strongly suggest in the novel that Elizabeth was not technically a virgin, that she did consummate her love for Dudley on at least one occasion. Is there a historical basis for this perspective?

A. There is no hard evidence, but many in the court of that time thought they were lovers, including

Burghley, who seldom left court. There was also talk about the queen having other lovers: Sir Thomas Heneage, Sir Christopher Hatton, Sir Walter Raleigh and even de Simier, the French stand-in for the Duc d'Alençon. At that time, it was beyond belief that a woman could exist without a man. (That attitude has only recently changed, if it really has.) Considering Elizabeth's flirtatious nature and her constant need for adoration, it seems logical that she would have returned Robert's devotion, especially after he had stood by her during troubled times.

Q. When did Elizabeth first come to be known as the Virgin Queen, and how much of a hand did she have in promoting this identification?

A. I don't believe it happened quite as deliberately as portrayed by Cate Blanchett in her first Elizabeth movie (1998), although it's possible that the queen calculatedly imitated the Virgin Mary to replace the banned icon worship of the English people. It's certainly an intriguing and dramatic idea. I believe it was more gradual, because the people, the Parliament and Elizabeth's council repeatedly urged and expected her to marry and produce an heir until she was in her midforties. It appears to have been almost impossible for the people of that time to imagine an attractive woman of power and wealth not to be in need of a husband, to turn Jane Austen's famous line upside down.

As for advancing the idea of her own "divinity," Elizabeth was a consummate public relations practitioner. Because she had produced no heir and had no intention of doing so, she set about to make herself immortal to quiet fears or possible unrest since she would die without issue. In countless portraits, she had her face portrayed as youthful long after it had begun to age. (The lead in her cosmetics would have pitted and aged her skin.) Until the very end of her reign, she maintained her athletic ability, hunting and walking, as a sign to others and perhaps to herself that she retained her youthful vigor.

Q. Discuss attitudes toward sex during the Tudor period. How knowledgeable were people? Did men know how to please women, or were most of them clumsy lovers? Did women expect to experience orgasms? Did couples know how children were conceived? Did the Elizabethans know there were ways to enjoy one another that were much less likely to result in pregnancy? Did Elizabeth and Leicester take advantage of that?

A. Most of these questions are impossible to answer with any surety, although pornography is as ancient as sexual attraction. Sexual pictographs had their uses in very ancient times as a stimulant to the sex act, for visual gratification, or for the record . . . Cro-Magnon bragging rights, if you will. Michel Houellebecq in *The Possibility of an Island* writes: "An animal is prepared to sacrifice its happiness, its physical well-being and even its life in the hope of sexual intercourse alone." As animals, humans cannot be so different. For a more detailed account of practice and beliefs, read *Sex in Elizabethan England* by Alan Haynes.

If you read Shakespeare's sonnets, it is impossible not to acknowledge the sexual tension. It's even more evident in Philip Sidney's "Astrophel and Stella."

When young Sidney was in love with Lettice's daughter Penelope Devereux, he wrote:

> *O think I then, what paradise of joy*
> *It is, so fair a Vertue to enjoy.*

He may have been talking about hearing her read his poetry out loud, but I don't think so. As it turned out, Penelope had very little virtue, but Sidney's sexual desire was, and still is, very plain.

We must remember that for a great many centuries, including the Elizabethan era and beyond, the Church, whether Catholic or Protestant, frowned on sex for pleasure and only reluctantly agreed that it might be necessary for procreation. Some people then, as now, probably went their own way in bed. In the London of that time, sex of every description was on sale in streets and alleys. For women flocking to London from the country (which happened more and more, especially after the enclosure laws turned cottager plots into sheep pastures and forced people off the land), the only possible occupations were as wives, servants or prostitutes.

Well into the seventeenth century it was thought that if a woman experienced an orgasm during sex, she would become pregnant. Naturally, since couples often wished to avoid pregnancy, they also wished to avoid a woman's orgasm. Nevertheless, despite whatever efforts they made, families were large, and children tended to arrive at regular intervals.

It was known that to prevent pregnancy the man needed to use a sheath, but these were primitive devices, made from sheeps' intestines and tied on with ribbon. You can guess at how eagerly or effectively they were used.

Elizabeth and Leicester lived in a sensual time and the court's atmosphere was superheated. To think that they abstained from intimate contact, or at least experimentation, for all their lives together taxes my imagination. Whatever they did away from other eyes, we can only guess at and never know.

We do know that Elizabeth had menstrual problems during most of her life, which gave rise to questions about her being fully female. In *His Last Letter* I've dramatized Elizabeth and Leicester's physical relationship as I thought it could have been.

Q. Compared to the Tudor period, our culture is so sexually free, it might be hard for some readers to understand why Elizabeth was so obsessed with retaining her identity as a virgin. Can you explain the consequences if people could prove she'd had sex with Dudley?

A. Her worth on the marriage market would have been lost, or greatly diminished. It was important for a queen's heirs to be "certified," because they were in line for the throne. If there was the slightest doubt, other claimants could be expected to rebel against a bastard heir. Single women were considered suspect in that society; it was deemed almost impossible for them to be virginal. Elizabeth's insistence on her virginity made her into a lasting icon.

Q. Do you think Elizabeth decided early on that she would never marry? If so, why? What problems did that create for her? What problems did it solve?

A. She told her childhood playmate, Robert Dudley, when she was only eight years old that she would never marry. Her father's marriages and her disappearing "mothers" most certainly played a role in her decision; the question of a husband's dominance over a wife must have also influenced her choice. I think we see the problems it created for her. She toyed with the idea of marriage, most of the time facetiously, but occasionally, I believe she was truly conflicted, especially when the time left in which to have children was almost gone.

Q. Just how ambitious was Robert Dudley? From a historical perspective, which was stronger—his love for Elizabeth or his desire for power?

A. Robert Dudley was very ambitious. It was in his blood. Both his father and grandfather had risen high in their Tudor king's favor and then fallen so far as to suffer the ax. But whether his lust for power was stronger than his lust for Elizabeth is unknowable. I do know that long after Robert's marriage to Lettice Knollys, Elizabeth could still hurt him and he could hurt her. What does that indicate to you? When all passion and caring are gone, so is the ability to be touched by deep emotion.

Q. What do we really know of Lettice Knollys, and was she actually the jealous, spiteful woman you portray in this book?

A. We know a great deal, although perhaps not deep into her heart. We know that she found her way to Leicester's bed more than once and over a decade or more. Whether, at first, he was persuaded that she was Elizabeth is unknown, but I couldn't resist the idea. Also, there is no evidence that she killed her first husband or Leicester's young son. Historically, Leicester was accused of poisoning both. No one could die without suspicion falling on Leicester. He had risen too far, too fast and stayed there for too long to be widely loved. Although in later life he became a devout Protestant, almost a Puritan, it did not serve to rehabilitate him with the public.

Q. It's intriguing to contemplate Dudley's reasons for marrying Lettice. Does history suggest he was sincerely drawn to her because she looked like Elizabeth? Or, knowing that Elizabeth hated her cousin, in marrying Lettice was Dudley getting back at Elizabeth, as only he could, for refusing to marry him?

A. These are both possibilities that history has not proved or disproved, to my knowledge. We do know that Elizabeth hated Lettice even before Leicester married her, although as a Boleyn cousin she had her as a lady-of-the-bedchamber and, early on, allowed her at court. The queen was often angry at her because Lettice dressed too well and looked too good in the queen's eyes. As Edith Sitwell noted in *The Queens and the Hive*, there cannot be two queens in one hive. Elizabeth knew that. Lettice was a slow learner.

Q. You suggest that the young Earl of Essex was Dudley's son by Lettice. Is there a historical basis for this idea? Do we have any reason to suspect that Elizabeth knew, and that her knowledge influenced her indulgent behavior toward Essex?

A. Unfortunately, as with so many historical might-have-beens, there is no proof, but there was a resemblance noted by some in the court who had known Robert Dudley. I thought the possibility created another explanation for Elizabeth's need for Essex beyond the somewhat sad motive of a much older woman loving a young man who uses her affection. It would be an intriguing path to explore.

Q. Elizabeth remains a towering historical figure. Has she always been so, or has public opinion about her risen and fallen over the centuries since her death? Aside from the cult of her personality, what lasting legacy did she leave as a monarch?

A. Imagine that one of our presidents was in office for forty-five years. Wouldn't people tire of him/her? The same thing happened with Elizabeth, helped along by a series of droughts and bad harvests during the last decade of her reign. Although she was still beloved, it was an exhausted, old love and people looked forward to their new king, James I. Fast-forward twenty or thirty years after a quick tiring of the Stuart kings, and Elizabeth's reign was remembered as a Golden Age. Her lasting legacy was an England emerging into the Renaissance, and her own self . . . Gloriana.

Q. Since the publication of The Virgin's Daughters, *has anything about readers' responses particularly surprised or delighted you?*

A. The hunger of readers to know more and guess more about Elizabeth I has surprised me. We know so much about her reign, thanks to her diligent councilors, but we still don't know much about her psychology. Our guessing game about why she did what she did and said what she said, at the same time so wise and so puzzling, is fascinating to us. Check out www. elizabethfiles.com if you want to see the range and depth of readers' interest. Her life has been a subject in almost every artistic medium, and few other historical figures can command as wide an audience. If we were ever fully satisfied, we wouldn't see her every three or four years in another TV series or movie, with the finest actresses playing her. I have seen most of the screen portrayals, although not the early silents, nor the operas or plays. My favorite for historical accuracy is *Elizabeth R*, the six-part BBC miniseries of 1971 with Glenda Jackson as the queen. For lavish production values and fabulous cheekbones, I love both Cate Blanchett movies, *Elizabeth*, 1998, and *Elizabeth: The Golden Age*, 2007.

Q. What other books about Elizabeth, Leicester and the Tudor period do you particularly recommend?

A. There are too many to list, but here are a few of my favorites, both novels and nonfiction: *I, Elizabeth*, by Rosalind Miles; *Elizabeth I*, by Anne Somerset; *Her Majesty's Spymaster*, by Stephen Budiansky; *Sweet Robin*, by Derek Wilson; *Elizabeth and Leycester*, by Frederick Chamberlin; *Elizabeth and Leicester*, by Milton Waldman. The last two books are long out of print but available with a search.

Q. What have you been reading lately? What do you hope to read soon?

A. I'm reading *Wolf Hall* by Hilary Mantel, which won the U.K.'s Man Booker Prize, and *The Sun Over Breda* by Arturo Pérez-Reverte. I love his charismatic hero, Captain Alatriste. I also listen to books on CD at night, when I want to interrupt my own story. Currently I'm listening to *The Last Wife of Henry VIII* by Carolly Erickson. I just finished Jeannette Walls's two memoirs, *The Glass Castle* and *Half Broke Horses*, both remarkable books. My to-be-read pile is much too big to list here, but at the top of the stack is *The Queen's Governess* by Karen Harper.

QUESTIONS FOR DISCUSSION

1. Elizabeth I has been portrayed countless times in novels, biographies, movies, and plays. Discuss the different versions of her, and which ones you especially like or don't like. How does Elizabeth in *His Last Letter* measure up to the others?

2. If a movie were made of *His Last Letter*, who should play Elizabeth? Who should play Dudley and the other major characters?

3. It's been suggested that Elizabeth loved Dudley but was so afraid of sex and childbirth that she vowed early in life that she would never marry. Discuss the emotional and political reasons why she might have made that decision. What were the advantages? The disadvantages?

4. Discuss the mental process Eizabeth might have undergone to both consummate her love for Dudley and convince herself that she was a virgin queen.

5. In your mind, should Elizabeth and Dudley's love be called one of the great love affairs of all time? Must all great loves remain unfulfilled, or is that just an idea fostered by male writers and mythmakers?

6. Discuss the dynamics of the relationship between Elizabeth and Dudley in *His Last Letter*. Were they obsessed and emotionally unstable, or do you think their love matured over the years?

7. What particularly interests you about the Tudor period? Why do you think it's so popular now?

8. Discuss the role of Lettice Knollys in the Elizabeth/Dudley relationship.